The bank raiders had just stuffed all the hastily gathered banknotes into a Gladstone bag and were backing away from the counter, revolver still aimed, when Freddy Brown walked in. He'd come to pay in his wedding present cheque and wasn't best pleased when he was hit on the side of the head with the revolver. In fact it was sheer fury that drove him out into the street in time to see the blue van making a getaway, and then he was after them, pounding along the Walworth Road. When the police car caught up with him, Freddy leapt in and they raced in pursuit. But then, well up Denmark Hill, the van vanished and they could find no trace of the raiders' whereabouts

It was Vi and Tommy Adams, who lived on Denmark Hill, who were to find themselves dangerously involved with Ginger Carstairs and Dusty Miller, the Camberwell raiders.

# THE CAMBERWELL RAID

## Mary Jane Staples

## CORGI BOOKS

**THE CAMBERWELL RAID**
**A CORGI BOOK : 0 552 14469 X**

First publication in Great Britain

**PRINTING HISTORY**
Corgi edition published 1996

Set in 10/12pt Linotype New Baskerville by
Phoenix Typesetting, Ilkley, West Yorkshire

Corgi Books are published by Transworld Publishers Ltd,
61–63 Uxbridge Road, London W5 5SA,
in Australia by Transworld Publishers (Australia) Pty Ltd,
15–25 Helles Avenue, Moorebank, NSW 2170,
and in New Zealand by Transworld Publishers (NZ) Ltd,
3 William Pickering Drive, Albany, Auckland.

Reproduced, printed and bound in Great Britain by
Cox & Wyman Ltd, Reading, Berks.

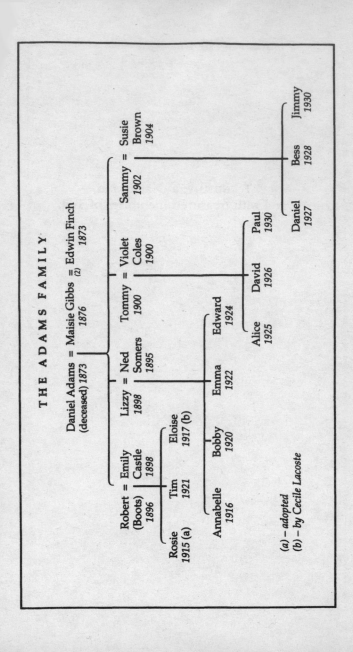

# THE ADAMS FAMILY

Daniel Adams = Maisie Gibbs =(2) Edwin Finch
(deceased) 1873    1876         1873

Robert = Emily    Lizzy = Ned    Tommy = Violet    Sammy = Susie
(Boots)  Castle    1898   Somers   1900   Coles    1902    Brown
1896     1898             1895            1900             1904

Rosie    Tim    Eloise
1915 (a) 1921   1917 (b)

Annabelle  Bobby   Emma          Alice   David   Paul      Daniel   Bess    Jimmy
1916       1920    1922          1925    1926    1930      1927     1928    1930
                          Edward
                          1924

(a) – adopted
(b) – by Cecile Lacoste

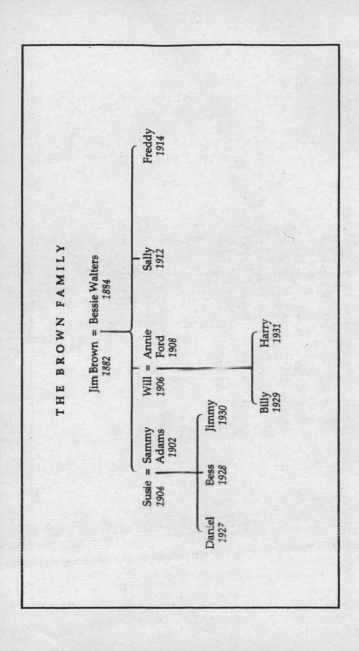

THE BROWN FAMILY

Jim Brown = Bessie Walters
1882              1884

Susie = Sammy          Will = Annie          Sally          Freddy
1904    Adams          1906    Ford          1912            1914
        1902                   1908

Daniel    Bess    Jimmy              Billy    Harry
1927      1928    1930               1929     1931

# Prologue

During the first two months of 1935, up to the time when blustery March blew in, the Press and the wireless of Britain had supplied the people with the usual mixture of national and international news.

Among other items of interest, it was noted that the aged Field-Marshal Hindenburg, in dying the previous year, had given Adolf Hitler the opportunity to make himself virtual dictator of Germany. Hitler, accordingly, was flexing his muscles and threatening not only his neighbours but also fellow Germans who didn't agree with him and his Nazis. He kept talking about Germany's need for 'living room', and the necessity of dealing ruthlessly with all political opponents. And he was also making it clear he didn't feel Germany's Jewish people were an asset to the country. Mrs Susie Adams of Denmark Hill, Camberwell, asked her husband, Mr Sammy Adams, what he thought about Hitler. Off his German chump, said Sammy, or he wouldn't wear a Charlie Chaplin moustache.

There was also news of an incredibly fascinating addition to the media, called television. It was so far advanced that in February pictures had been broadcast from Crystal Palace to a selected audience. The selected audience was so spellbound that it might have been lost for words had it not been made up of the kind of people who never were.

Then the BBC banned radio artistes from making jokes about fat people, cross-eyed people, coloured people, marital infidelity and men who were effeminate. Twelve-year-old Emma Somers asked her mother, Mrs Lizzy Somers, what the latter meant. It means, well, that they're a bit delicate, said Lizzy. Emma, who thought that meant they caught colds easily, said oh, poor things, what a shame.

The Hon. Unity Mitford, who had a crush on Adolf Hitler, had also been in the news. She'd written to a Nazi newspaper to boldly declare that along with her beloved Fuhrer she hated Jews. Shocks went through the British people that one of their own could make such a spectacle of herself. A fifth form pupil of West Square Girls School asked teacher Miss Polly Simms what she thought of that. Miss Simms said every country had its quota of idiots, but it was frightfully bad luck for Britain to have one as ghastly as the Hon. Unity.

There had been speculation in some newspapers about whether or not debutantes would be allowed to wear muffs when presented at Court. That was a question that made hard-up people spit, especially those short of boots and shoes, but it was reported all the same.

The BMA announced that its recommended minimum weekly intake of food for one person, including a Sunday roast, costed out at five shillings and tenpence ha'penny. The Government thought anything over four shillings and sixpence was lashing out a bit, and accordingly unpatriotic in view of the economic need to tighten one's belt.

Something that hadn't been mentioned either by the Press or the wireless was the fact that there was going to be a double wedding at St John's Church, Walworth, on Easter Saturday. The vicar was keeping calm about it, the brides-to-be, Miss Sally Brown and Miss Cassie Ford, were beginning to feel slightly fluttery, and the would-be bridegrooms, Horace Cooper and Freddy Brown respectively, were doing what they could to think up witty speeches that wouldn't fall apart.

Meanwhile, a couple of downright unpleasant characters, Dusty Miller and Ginger Carstairs, were planning a bank robbery which, if successful, would take them off to the fleshpots of South America via France.

# Chapter One

'Blimey, snow!' cried gleeful kids of Walworth on a morning in late March, noses pressed to cold window panes.

'Bother that,' said a great many Walworth mums.

'I ain't rapturous, either,' said a dad or two.

Some indignant people with a few coppers to spare used two to ring up the wireless people from public phone boxes and complain that the wireless weathermen hadn't said anything about snow last night. The wireless people said so sorry, it was a sudden and unexpected chilly front after a spell of unseasonal warmth that did it. A likely story, said several people, and just when some of us had started to leave off our winter vests and all.

Nineteen-year-old Cassie Ford spoke to her widower dad when he came down for breakfast.

'Dad, have you seen outside?'

'That I 'ave, Cassie,' said Mr Ford, known as the Gaffer. 'Looks like Christmas.'

'Blow that,' said Cassie, ladling out steaming hot porridge, 'it's my weddin' next month. Suppose it's snowing then? I'll freeze. Freddy won't think much of a frozen bride.'

'Don't you worry yerself, pet,' said the Gaffer, sprinkling sugar over his porridge, 'I daresay you'll still be a nice blushin' bride when you get to the altar.'

'Not if I'm frozen stiff I won't,' said Cassie.

'Well, that's what Freddy'll expect, yer know, Cassie, a blushin' bride,' said the Gaffer, a twinkle in his eye.

'Dad, you daft ha'porth,' said Cassie, 'blushin' brides only happen in books.'

'Well, do yer best,' said the Gaffer. 'Freddy'll be a mite disappointed if you ain't blushin' a fair bit.'

'If the weather's like this,' said Cassie, 'I'll just have a pink nose. I'll die if I 'ave to say me vows with a pink nose.'

'Yer pink nose won't notice if you can manage a few nice blushes, pet,' said the Gaffer.

'Dad, I'll hit you in a minute,' said Cassie.

'Serve me right for pullin' yer leg, eh, Cassie?' said the Gaffer, and Cassie smiled. She loved her affectionate old dad and all his bluff ways. She served him two thick slices of toast when he'd finished his porridge, and was pleased when he helped himself liberally to the marmalade, because she'd made it herself with Seville oranges bought cheaply from the East Street market. He was going to lodge with her and Freddy in the house they'd contracted to rent in Wansey Street. Mind, Freddy's brother-in-law, Sammy Adams, had advised them not to get permanently attached to renting. It might keep a roof over your heads, he said, but that roof's never going to be yours, it'll always be your landlord's. Buying even a little two-up, two-down place would be a better bet, he said. Cassie said she didn't think they'd be able to afford the mortgage. Well, said Sammy, don't let that stop you looking, and as soon as you spot a suitable place, come and see me, and I just might finance you. Oh, said Cassie, would you really loan s, Mister Sammy? At affordable repayments, said Sammy. Freddy's as good as part of the family, he said, and so will you be, Cassie, when you're Mrs Freddy. Cassie was so touched she gave him a kiss.

Sammy charged her tuppence for it.

'Well now,' said the Gaffer, when he'd finished his breakfast, 'I'd best get off to the railway, Cassie. There'll be a few frozen points this mornin', I shouldn't wonder. Glad I wasn't on early shift.'

'Dad, you got all your winter woollies on?' asked Cassie.

'You bet I 'ave,' said the Gaffer, taking his overcoat off the peg on the kitchen door.

'All of them, Dad?'

'The lot, startin' with me winter combinations,' said the Gaffer. 'I wasn't born yesterday, yer know.'

'Where's your woollen scarf?' asked Cassie.

'In me coat pocket,' said the Gaffer. He fished it out and wrapped it around his neck. 'So long, love, see yer this evening.'

'Dad, would you like a nice hot meat stew for supper, with suet dumplings?' asked Cassie.

'Be a treat and a half, that would, me pet,' said the Gaffer, who knew suet put body and flavour into dumplings. He kissed her and left.

Cassie washed up the breakfast things, closed off the kitchen fire with the damper so that it would burn slowly all day, put on her winter coat and hat, and went off to her own job, to a florist's shop in Kennington, her feet and legs snug in Russian boots. Such footwear was popular in winter, and had not yet come to be called Wellingtons.

Just a few more weeks, she thought, as she walked through the snow to the Walworth Road. Just a few, that was all, before she gladly gave up her poorly paid job in a cold shop to become a housewife. The prospect was an exciting one. Well, it was Freddy to whom she was going to be a housewife, and she'd have her dad to care for as well. Sewing, darning, cooking, baking and housework would be all of a full-time job, and she'd make sure the kitchen would always be warm and cosy. And on Saturday evenings, she and Freddy would go to the pictures. And then there'd be their marital relationship, which Freddy said he was looking forward to as he hadn't had one so far – oh, help, his grin had got wicked lately.

Her face tingled in the cold snowy air.

A neighbour's young son made himself heard as he approached.

'Watcher, Cassie, what yer blushin' for?'

'I'm not, you saucebox,' said Cassie, passing him by.

'Well, yer hooter is,' he said.

Which made Cassie think again of arriving for her wedding with a pink nose. Oh, blow that. She wanted sunshine, colour, and a ride to the reception in Mr Eli Greenberg's pony and cart. Lovely old Mr Greenberg had come to the house, knocked on the door, raised his old round hat, smiled at her and then said that as Freddy was as good as related to the Adams family, and seeing that Lizzy, Boots, Tommy and Sammy Adams had all ridden to their wedding receptions with their spouses in his pony and cart, might he have the pleasure of carting her and Freddy likewise?

Well, since Cassie had always dreamed of riding as a bride in a carriage and pair, Mr Greenberg's pony and cart represented a dream come true, good as. So she told him it would be a blissful pleasure for her.

'Vell, vell, Cassie, and vhat a pleasure for me too, ain't it?' said the beaming Mr Greenberg.

'But it's a double weddin', did you know?' said Cassie.

'Vhat don't I know, eh?' said Mr Greenberg. 'Ain't it Freddy's sister Sally and her young man, Orrice Cooper? All velcome, Cassie.'

'Oh, bless your warm heart, Mr Greenberg,' said Cassie, 'come in and 'ave a cup of tea.'

'Cassie, ain't I stepped over a thousand Valvorth doorsteps for a cup of tea? Vhat kindness there is here.' And Mr Greenberg thought how fortunate his family had been in electing to come to the United Kingdom when they left Russia many years ago. They had thought of Germany, because it was so much nearer, but his father, very knowledgeable and well-read, had said no, that he was going to pay good money for papers that would admit them to the United Kingdom, because there they would always have the protection of laws laid down centuries ago by the Tudor and Plantagenet kings.

There was no protection these days for the Jews of Germany. Hitler's laws had made them non-persons.

The snow was a thick carpet, and although it turned to dirty brown slush beneath the wheels of traffic on main roads, in many places it remained untrodden and virgin white. In the Denmark Hill area it covered gardens on which only robins, blackbirds and sparrows left their footprints in search of breadcrumbs scattered by kind residents.

Robert Adams, known as Boots, came home from the office on a bus. Alighting at a stop in Red Post Hill, he crossed the churned-up road and entered the gravelled drive of the family house. The thick snow covering the drive bore the depressed imprints of feet. He was ambushed then, by his son, his daughters and his wife. Snowballs came flying at him from both sides, followed by yells of laughter.

'Got you, Daddy!' That was Rosie, just down from university for her Easter vacation. She and other students had been released a little early because of an outbreak of measles affecting three young ladies.

'Got you, Pa!' That was Tim, as lively as his mother.

''Ello, Papa!' That was Eloise, just eighteen and Boots's daughter by a Frenchwoman.

'Give in, lovey?' That was his wife Emily, still energetic at thirty-six.

'Not yet,' said Boots, the snowballs still coming, his overcoat patterned with white. But he made a dash for the front door, all the same. Rosie, in a warm coat and woollen hat, appeared in front of him, glowing and laughing.

'Hello, Daddy, old love,' she said. She'd arrived from Oxford during the afternoon.

A snowball from Tim struck Boots in his back.

'How do I come to be an Aunt Sally?' he asked.

'Luck of the game,' said Rosie. The snowballing stopped, and Boots kissed her on her cheek. She gave him an impulsive hug, and snow transferred itself from his coat to hers.

'Papa, I'm 'ere too.' Eloise claimed his attention. She had come over from France for Christmas, when, shy and nervous, she had met all the families related to her paternal grandmother, Mrs Finch, whom she was astonished to find was often referred to as Chinese Lady by her daughter and sons. That apart, the affection, kindness and whole-hearted welcome

17

given by everyone touched Eloise deeply. She was drawn into every kind of seasonal festivity, including hilarious party games on the evening of Christmas Day, by which time all shyness and nervousness had disappeared, so much so that Postman's Knock was a delight to her. She had never played it in France, never, but the Adams and Somers families played it for all it was worth, and Eloise had never received so many kisses from so many extrovert males. Her father's brothers were exciting, Uncle Tommy the handsomest of men, Uncle Sammy charged with electricity, while the brother-in-law, Uncle Ned, was most engaging. And one cousin, fourteen-year-old Bobby, was as bold as you like.

'Alors! Is it right for you to kiss me like that?'

'No idea,' said Bobby, 'I've only just started.'

'Excuse me?'

'Yes, you're the first girl I've kissed,' said Bobby. 'Can I have another one?'

'No, no, we are cousins,' said Eloise, but she giggled and Bobby had another one.

The Christmas with her new-found family and the close relationship she established with Boots, her father, decided Eloise once and for all to make her home with them. So two weeks after she returned to France, Boots went over with Emily to collect her and bring her to England for good. Since when she had established herself. In Emily, she found an outgoing and friendly stepmother, and in Chinese Lady she discovered an understanding, if old-fashioned, grandmother. In Rosie, she found an affectionate and supportive sister, and in thirteen-year-old Tim, she found a good-natured half-brother. He let her know he was willing to put up with

18

another sister as long as she didn't get bossy or interfere with his cricket and football. In Mr Finch, Chinese Lady's second husband, she found a calm and reassuring grandfather. As for Boots, she quickly became devoted to him. He was so easy to talk to, with a fascinating sense of humour and the kind of little undercurrents that made some men much more exciting than others. She felt exceptionally pleased with herself for being his daughter. One thing had puzzled her, however. She knew he had married Emily late in 1916, and therefore his other daughter Rosie could not have been born earlier than 1917, and some months later than herself. Yet Tim had mentioned that Rosie would be twenty in May. So Eloise asked Boots about Rosie, and Boots who, like the rest of the family, simply regarded his elder daughter as an Adams, nevertheless had to acknowledge Rosie was adopted.

'Oh, I am your only real daughter, Papa?' said Eloise.

'You're both my daughters, both very real to me,' said Boots.

'But—'

'There are no buts, Eloise, and no differences in what you both mean to me,' said Boots. 'Do you understand?'

'Yes,' said Eloise, 'yes, I understand.' The conversation, like many she had with him, was in French. She had, however, taken lessons in English during the three months prior to Christmas and could speak it passably well. Boots encouraged her to use it, and the family, particularly Mr Finch, helped her to enlarge her vocabulary. Like her late mother, however, she could not pronounce aspirates, which was why, after

Boots had been ambushed, she dropped an aitch in saying, 'Papa, I'm 'ere too.'

'So I see,' smiled Boots. 'Was it your idea to have everyone chuck snowballs at me?'

'No, mine,' said Emily.

'Was there a good reason?' asked Boots, as they all entered the house.

'Yes, I wanted to feel sixteen again,' said Emily.

'Well, that's a fairly good reason,' said Boots.

Chinese Lady, appearing in the hall, asked, 'What's been goin' on out there?'

'Just a few snowballs whizzing about, Grandma,' said Tim.

'I might of guessed your father would forget his age as soon as he got home,' said Chinese Lady.

'No, that was Mum,' said Tim, 'she wanted to be sixteen again.'

'Em'ly, you been throwin' snowballs?' said Chinese Lady.

'Only a few, Mum, and only at Boots,' said Emily.

'Yes, we all did,' said Eloise, and as Boots unbuttoned his coat she moved and helped him off with it. Rosie smiled. Eloise had become the first to do things for Boots. 'Papa, 'ow wet your coat is. We must dry it at the fire.'

'No need,' said Boots, 'it'll dry on the hallstand.'

'No, no,' said Eloise, 'it will feel cold and damp when you put it on in the morning. I will 'ang it on the fireguard.' And off she went with the coat to the kitchen. Chinese Lady and Emily followed. Tim looked at Boots and Rosie, a grin on his face.

'I like her all right,' he said, 'but she'll get us a bad name.'

'How?' asked Boots.

'Calling you Papa,' said Tim.

Rosie laughed. Boots regarded her with affection.

'Nice you're home, poppet,' he said.

'Love it,' said Rosie, 'so come on. Nana's making a pot of tea. One day we'll all drown in tea.'

'Not a bad way to go,' said Boots, as they moved towards the kitchen, 'and more respectable than drowning in beer as far as your grandmother's concerned.'

'What a sober thought, Dad,' said Tim with a flash of wit, and Rosie thought that despite the stimulating atmosphere of Somerville, home was where she belonged. Home was family. A family of fun.

'Well,' said Mrs Bessie Brown of Caulfield Place, Walworth, that evening, 'I still can't properly take it in, our Sally and Freddy both gettin' married on the same day, Easter Saturday.'

'Well, keep tryin', me old Dutch,' said lean and wiry Mr Brown, 'and when you've took it in, you'll get used to it. There's still a bit of time to go.'

'Orrice's mother has been ever so kind and helpful,' said placid Mrs Brown, 'she's a real lady.'

'So are you, Bessie,' said Mr Brown, 'and I ain't reluctant to say so.'

'I never knew our Sally more up in the clouds,' said Mrs Brown.

'It's love, I reckon,' said Mr Brown.

'I think it's love,' mused Mrs Brown.

'I already said that,' pointed out Mr Brown, toasting his feet at the kitchen fire and pulling on his pipe.

'Sally's never been in love serious before,' said Mrs Brown.

'Well, she is now,' said Mr Brown.

'Our Sally, head over heels like she was only seventeen, would you believe,' said Mrs Brown.

'Picked the right bloke, though,' said Mr Brown.

'And then our Freddy and all,' said Mrs Brown, conjuring up imaginative pictures of Freddy and Sally at the altar together, along with their respective marriage partners. 'I always thought he'd marry Cassie one day.'

'I reckon Cassie always thought so too,' said Mr Brown. 'Mind, Freddy put up a good fight.'

'Oh, you saying something, love?' said Mrs Brown.

'I've spoke one or two words,' said Mr Brown, 'but I don't think you've been listenin'. I'd say you're up in the clouds with Sally.'

'Wasn't it 'andsome of Sammy to give Freddy a rise of ten shillings?' said Mrs Brown. 'He told Freddy to put it into his savings so that he and Cassie could buy their own house later on.'

'That's what I call practical,' said Mr Brown.

'Don't you think that's sensible?' said Mrs Brown.

'Well, Bessie, I did just say—'

'Then there's Sally come home from work today with a promise from Sammy that after the honeymoon, he's promotin' her to the Oxford Street shop as assistant manageress,' said Mrs Brown. 'I can't hardly take it all in.'

'Well, like I already mentioned, Bessie, keep tryin' and—'

'You saying something else, love?' said Mrs Brown.

'Only a word or two, Bessie,' said Mr Brown.

'Sally's gone round to see Orrice and give him the news,' said Mrs Brown. 'Of course, her job will only last until she starts havin' a family. Still, she could hardly wait to go and tell Orrice.'

'Taken one of 'er clouds with 'er, I shouldn't wonder,' said Mr Brown.

'What's that?' asked Mrs Brown.

'Nothing much, Bessie,' said Mr Brown.

'You're not startin' to talk to yourself in your old age, are you, love?' said Mrs Brown.

'Might as well,' said Mr Brown.

Jim Cooper, returning to the kitchen after answering a knock on the front door, said, 'That was Sally. She's now in the parlour with Horace.'

'Oh, much more suitable than the shop,' smiled Mrs Rebecca Cooper, a handsome woman of immaculate appearance.

'Horace deserves a medal for his perseverance,' said Jim. Their adopted son had conducted his courtship of Sally at her place of work, the Adams dress shop in Kennington. He'd survived a number of discouraging confrontations with her until Sally suddenly realized she was enjoying the most exhilarating and challenging moments of her life. That led to compatibility, to many outings together and, inevitably, to their first ecstatic kiss. Sally immediately followed this by saying, 'Yes.'

'Beg pardon?' said Horace, a promising professional cricketer with the right amount of good looks. 'I mean, yes what?'

'Well, you've been saying for ages you're savin' up to get married to someone, so it might as well be me,' declared Sally.

'You're not someone,' said Horace, 'you're a lot more than that.'

'Oh, yes?' said Sally.

'Yes, my idea exactly,' said Horace.

'So?' said Sally.

'Let's have another one,' said Horace.

'Another kiss? Wait a bit,' said Sally, 'is it me you're savin' up for or not?'

'Well, seeing that I don't know how I could live without you, would you do me the honour, Miss Brown?' asked Horace.

'Oh, mutual, I'm sure, Mr Cooper,' said Sally, 'so how could I refuse?'

'Well, then?' said Horace.

'Yes, let's have another one,' said Sally, entirely pleased with herself for having had the intuitive good sense to wait for a young man as refreshing as Horace to come courting. She smiled. 'Two, if you like, Horace.'

So Horace had helped himself to a double encore, and that led to arranging a double wedding with Cassie and Freddy on Easter Saturday.

This evening Sally had called to tell Horace that after their honeymoon she was transferring to the Adams dress shop in Oxford Street as assistant manageress. And Sammy Adams, she said, was going to pay her thirty-five shillings a week.

'Thirty-five shillings, Horace.'

Horace whistled.

'Handsome, very handsome,' he said. 'We could think about buyin' the house we're goin' to rent in Kennington Park Place. Who's goin' to take charge of our earnings?'

'I am,' said Sally, 'and I'll give you some of yours back each week for pocket money.'

'Hold on—'

'I'm sure your dad gives your mum his earnings,' said Sally, 'and I know my dad gives his to my mum. It's traditional.'

'Sounds crafty to me,' said Horace. 'Let's toss for it.'

'Not likely,' said Sally, 'I might lose. Anyway, the job'll only last until – well, until.'

'Until what?' said Horace.

'Oh, I'll leave that to you, lovey,' said Sally.

'I get it,' said Horace, 'you mean until – well, until.'

'Yes, that's it,' said Sally.

'Who's blushing?' asked Horace.

'Not me,' said Sally.

'Must be me, then,' said Horace.


'This is it,' said Dusty Miller, a few minutes after Ginger Carstairs had arrived in his lodgings in Stead Street, Walworth. He produced a plank of stout timber, ten inches wide, two inches thick and a yard long. Six inches from the end of the plank a semi-circle, three inches deep, had been cut out of it. 'That drops over the handle, Ginger, and the plank then bars the door on the outside. Which means?'

'The door can't be pulled open from the inside,' said Ginger Carstairs.

'You're right first time,' said Miller.

'Well, of course I bloody well am,' said Carstairs, as much of a cold-eyed character as Miller was, 'it was my idea, wasn't it?'

'Now don't get shirty,' said Miller.

'Listen, the whole thing's my baby, and that puts me in charge,' said Carstairs. 'So I'll point out you'll need to drill a hole at the other end of the plank to take a long nail. One blow from a hammer has got to drive the nail into the door to hold the plank in place, or it'll swing downwards and drop away from the handle. And there won't be time for more than one blow. Have you got that?'

'The hole's already drilled,' said Miller. 'I'm a professional, and the next time I'm way behind an amateur will be the first.'

'Some professional, considering you've slipped up and done time,' said Carstairs.

Miller growled.

'Just a few months for handling stolen goods,' he said.

'I haven't done any,' said Carstairs.

'Well, you wouldn't have, would you?' said Miller. 'This is your first job. What was it you said made you join the free-booters?'

'I'm a rebel in search of quick riches, that's what I said.'

'So you did,' said Miller. 'When d'you get the shooter?'

'In good time,' said Carstairs.

'Hope you realize that if we're copped, it'll be a long stretch for both of us,' said Miller. 'At the Old Bailey, no-one likes shooters.'

'You can't rob a bank with a bow and arrow,' said Carstairs.

'I'm still not sure we can do without a driver and a running engine,' said Miller.

'I'm not in favour of a three-way split,' said Carstairs. 'I'll do the driving, as agreed. Now, let's go through the plan again.'

# Chapter Two

A couple of days later, Tim confided to Rosie that he thought Eloise was getting to be a bit sugary with their dad, that she behaved as if she owned him.

'Never mind, Tim old thing,' said Rosie, 'it won't last, and the reason why it's happening is because for years Eloise hasn't had a father or even known there was one around. Think how lucky you and I have been, we've had Boots to ourselves for years and years. We can put up with Eloise making claims on him now, can't we?'

'Yes, but it's "let's go to the park" or "let's go out" all the time,' said Tim, 'and it's just said to Dad and it only ever means her and Dad.'

'And what does Dad do?' asked Rosie.

'Oh, he says, "Good idea, let's all go."' Tim grinned at what that meant. It meant his dad played fair and square.

'Yes,' said Rosie. 'You see, Tim, no-one's ever going to own all of Boots. Well, no-one should ever completely own any of us. But there are weak men and women who let it happen, who become dominated by one particular person. Heavens, Tim, that must be like being dead. A sense of belonging is much the best thing, old lad, not possessiveness or being possessed. That's very special, a sense of belonging to the ones we most want to belong to.

27

For us, for you and me, it's belonging to Boots and Emily, and the rest of our family.'

'I suppose you know you've got into the habit of saying Boots and Emily instead of Mum and Dad, do you?' said Tim.

'Have I?' Rosie smiled. 'Oh, well, I'm probably allowing university to make me precocious. Nana will have something to say to me when she realizes it.'

'Funny she never minds anyone in the family calling her Chinese Lady,' said Tim.

'Oh, that goes back years and years, Tim, to when your dad, your uncles and your Aunt Lizzy were all precocious themselves. Precocious kids.' Rosie laughed. 'Can you see your dad as a kid?'

'Can you?' asked Tim.

'No, only as the lovely kind man I first knew as a child,' said Rosie, 'when I first wanted to belong to him. So we must be nice to Eloise because she spent seventeen whole years without knowing she belonged to him at all.'

'Rosie, you're the best girl ever,' said Tim, 'and no feller could have a nicer sister.'

'Well, you're not so bad yourself, are you, old lad?' said Rosie, and lightly ruffled his hair. 'Shout if you ever need help. I'll hear you, because I'll always be somewhere around.'

'Good on you, Rosie,' said Tim.

The following morning, Saturday, saw sunshine and the disappearance of all traces of snow. But some people who'd put their winter woollies back on weren't sure about leaving them off again. This problem didn't bother a certain Lilian Hyams, for she never wore such things. A fashion designer in the exclusive employ of Adams fashions, Lilian was now living in her own little house, two up, two down, in King and Queen Street, Walworth. By reason of Sammy Adams's generous monetary appreciation of her talents, Lilian had become almost affluent. Well, affluent enough to buy the house, which Sammy had found for her. It was close to East Street market, and she liked the markets of London, as most of her kind did. A war widow, her husband having been killed on the Somme, Lilian at thirty-nine had left her years of mourning and privation far behind to bloom into a lush-looking, healthy brunette with velvety brown eyes that sometimes reminded Sammy of Rachel Goodman's lustrous orbs. Lilian had recently attracted the admiration and attention of Abel Morrison, owner of a shop in the market. Since Mr Morrison was decidedly portly and accordingly a strain on his waistcoats, Lilian did her best to keep her distance. The bloke was kind enough, but Lilian, while owning a fulsome figure herself, had no real liking for surplus flesh on men. If she could have had anybody, it would have been Sammy Adams who, in her eyes, was the most electrifying man in the rag trade. Unfortunately, Sammy was the doting husband of his wife Susie. Otherwise, for the pleasure of being his wife herself, Lilian would have willingly converted to the Christian faith. Ah, well, from around some corner somewhere, someday, there might appear a lovely bloke akin to Sammy. Mind, at her age, she didn't want to wait too long.

Coming out of her house to begin her journey to the Adams factory in Shoreditch, she bumped into the milkman. Well, there he was, right on her doorstep, in his white working-coat and peaked cap.

'Hello, hello,' he said, retreating from her private person, 'what's all the hurry, then, missus?'

'Are you a policeman?' asked Lilian.

'No, your new milkman,' said Bill Chambers.

'Then what d'you mean by addressing me like a bobby?' asked Lilian, looking him over. He was an improvement, physically, on the previous milkman, Ernie, who was something of an old codger.

'I'm Bill, not Bobby, missus, and I've been deliverin' your milk all this week. Old Ernie's gone to his rest.'

'My life, he's dead?' said Lilian.

'Old Ernie?' said Bill. 'Not him. Last for ever, he will. No, he's retired.'

'I should be bamboozled by having you tell me he's gone to his rest as if he'd passed away?' said Lilian.

'No, he's gone to live with his widowed sister in her country cottage by Chislehurst,' said Bill, healthy-looking and muscular. 'She'll see to his feet.'

'His feet?' said Lilian.

'Well, you could say it's his feet that have gone to their rest,' said Bill informatively. 'After treading these here pavements for forty year and more, they've earned it, and his sister'll see they get it, and find him a cosy pair of slippers into the bargain, I shouldn't wonder. I've taken over his round. I've been fortuitously promoted.'

'You've been what?' said Lilian.

'It's a fact, missus, seeing my previous round was near the Elephant and Castle. Any round near there puts a bloke in danger of being run over six times a day.'

'Six?' said Lilian. 'But wouldn't once be enough?'

'Beg yer pardon?' said Bill.

'Run over once, wouldn't that be enough for any-body?' asked Lilian.

A grin appeared on the new milkman's face and he took a more interested look at his customer. Lilian allowed the survey. He then referred to his customers' book.

'You're Mrs Hyams?' he said.

'I am,' said Lilian.

'Might I say I'm pleased to meet you, Mrs Hyams?'

'Might I ask why it's pleasing?'

'Search me,' said Bill, 'except it's just a sudden feeling that's taken up residence.'

'Are you always like this?' asked Lilian, who hadn't met many milkmen quite as vocal as he was.

'Like what, lady?'

'Talkative,' said Lilian.

'Only since I was born,' said Bill. 'Well, accordin' to my old lady, I came into the world with my mouth open and asking where Paddington railway station was. Well, some do, some don't, y'know. Might I ask if you're goin' out, seeing you've got your coat and titfer on?'

'Yes, I'm going to my job,' said Lilian.

'I'm holdin' you up,' said Bill. 'Well, there's your milk, on your step. Any eggs?'

'Eggs?' said Lilian.

'New-laid, fresh from the dairy's country farm in Hampstead, and now available to all our customers,' said Bill.

'Not today, thank you,' said Lilian.

'Well, just leave a note in one of the empties any time you're thinking of makin' an egg custard,' said Bill. 'I'll be round again this afternoon to collect what's owing on your bill, seeing it's a Saturday. Won't keep you now. Good day to you, Mrs Hyams, it's been promising to have had the pleasure of meetin' you personally.'

'Promising?' said Lilian, hiding a smile. 'Why promising?'

'I don't know how that slipped out,' said Bill, 'I'm a reserved bloke normally.'

'My life, are you sure you are?' asked Lilian.

'You noticed, I daresay,' said Bill.

'Not so far,' said Lilian, and laughed.

'So long, lady,' said Bill, and returned to his float. Although milk churns and cans had been superseded by bottled milk, the Walworth dairy's floats were still horse-drawn, and Bill gave his nag a pat that set it into motion. Lilian took the bottle of milk through to her kitchen larder, and then left the house. She passed the milkman and his float on her way to Browning Street and the bus stop. He watched her. Her coat was stylish and her hat, of light brown chamois, was fur-trimmed. She looked expensively kitted out, and Bill wondered if her husband had a job as well. You didn't see a lot of expensive clothes in Walworth. Nor too many women as handsome as she was. Lucky old Hyams, whoever he was.

At the Shoreditch factory, Lilian spent part of the morning supervising the delicate finishing touches to two bridal gowns, one for a young lady called Cassie Ford, the other for Susie's sister Sally. Sally was Sammy's sister-in-law, Cassie well-known to Sammy and the rest of the Adamses. To strengthen the relationship, Cassie was marrying Sally's younger brother Freddy. The brides-to-be had had their first fitting of the gowns, both of white silk and designed to float. Lilian's main problem had been to ensure that one gown did not outshine the other, for it was to be a double wedding in St John's Church, and Lilian herself would be there.

Finishing at twelve noon with the rest of the factory staff, she was back home before one. She treated herself to a light lunch, then changed into a costume for her Saturday shopping expedition. The sunshine had brought warmth and she did not need a coat. But she put on a light hat.

Opening her front door she almost repeated the process of bumping into the new milkman.

'I should believe this?' she said with a smile.

Bill Chambers, customers' book in his hand, said, 'Have I had the pleasure, missus?'

'What pleasure?' asked Lilian.

'Of meetin' you personally?'

'Only for about ten minutes at twenty-to-eight this morning,' said Lilian. The factory began work at eight, and Lilian usually got there at about eight-fifteen. 'You informed me that old Ernie's feet had gone to their rest at his sister's.'

'Well, so I did,' said Bill. 'I'm complimented that you remembered. Might I say I'm admirin' of your togs?'

Lilian looked extremely well-dressed in her brown costume and pristine white blouse. She liked the feel of good clothes.

'Does your dairy encourage you to comment on your customers' togs?' she asked, smiling.

'Not precisely,' said Bill, 'nor exactly, either. Polite's the word for our relationship with one and all, missus. No familiarities. Still, I know a nicely attired lady when I see one. Now let's see, one pint of milk Mondays, Wednesdays, Fridays and Saturdays. That's one-and-fourpence for this week. Wait a tick – any eggs?'

'You asked me that this morning,' said Lilian.

'Did I?' said Bill, and pushed his peaked cap back a bit, and scratched his hair with his pencil. 'Well, it's new, y'know, egg availability, and I'm givin' the good news to all my customers. Would you like some?'

'Not today, thank you,' said Lilian. 'I'll slip a note into an empty when I'm in need.'

'Good idea,' said Bill, 'very good.'

'You suggested it yourself, this morning,' said Lilian.

'All the same, I'm admirin' of you catchin' on, Mrs Hyams.' Bill smiled. 'Now, one-and-fourpence, did I say?'

'That and other things,' said Lilian, then paid up. Bill thanked her like a gent and went off whistling on his float. Lilian went up the street to the market, which was alive with Saturday afternoon crowds, from darting and diving young kids up to sharp-eyed grannies of any old age. In such crowds, it was bustling women who won most scrimmages. Bustling women were born market shoppers, and knew the worth of a plump and experienced elbow. Lilian was not a bustler herself. She'd been educated, in fact, at a Jewish establishment that was prone to sternly correct any tendency in a girl to be forward, aggressive or unfeminine. All-knowing motherhood was the ultimate goal to which they were pointed. Lilian, however, had had no children by her late husband. He'd been sent to France with his unit not long after they were married, and the day he finished his embarkation leave was the last time she saw him. From then on until Sammy took her on as a designer in 1925, Lilian had existed on close terms with poverty.

She didn't at all mind the market crowds. She was a Londoner and accordingly part of London's crowded scenes. She eluded elbows and bodies with ease. She bought fruit and vegetables from her favourite stalls, and her shopping bag would have begun to bulge if it hadn't been for the fact that she only ever had to shop for herself. A voice eventually accosted her ear.

'Well, well, what a pleasure, Mrs Hyams.'

She turned. Mr Abel Morrison, proprietor of a leather goods shop, was beside her, his kind smile broadening his double chin. It was a shame that he was stout and also two inches shorter than Lilian, because he really was a very kind man. He was also of an age, forty-three, when he was willing to be a comfort to a good woman like Lilian. He'd been a bachelor married to his shop long enough.

'Hello, Mr Morrison, out of your shop on a Saturday afternoon and all?' said Lilian.

Mr Morrison, a large green baize apron covering most of his shirt, waistcoat and trousers, lifted his bowler hat to her.

'Young Amos Stein is presently keeping an eye on things,' he said, 'but I should leave him in charge for longer than five minutes? Not without heart failure. I saw you from my shop doorway and said to myself, "Abel, let Mrs Hyams know you've seen her or she'll reproach you." For five minutes, then, I've left Amos in charge. My word, Mrs Hyams, a splendid woman you look, don't you? Tomorrow, yes, I shall call for you at two thirty in the afternoon and take you for

35

a bus ride to Hyde Park, providing the weather is fine.'

'No, really, Mr Morrison—'

'I insist,' said Mr Morrison with an even kinder smile. A bustling woman buffeted his back, impelling him forward, and Lilian avoided a clash with his rotundity only by an elusive sideways movement. 'I'm begging someone's pardon?' he said, turning.

'Move over, Charlie,' said the woman, 'you're in me way.'

'I'm not Charlie, madam,' said Mr Morrison.

'Course you are,' said the woman, heaving herself into a vacant space, 'everyone in trousers is a bleedin' Charlie, ain't 'e? And me old man's Charlie number one. Useless, poor bloke.' Off she went, bustling, and Mr Morrison turned back to Lilian. Alas, Lilian was no longer there. She was elsewhere, amid a sea of faces.

'So sorry, Mr Morrison,' she called, 'but I got carried away.'

She vanished then, and Mr Morrison went back to his shop. However, he'd call for her tomorrow, as he'd promised. She was a lonely widow, poor woman.

Lilian, of course, didn't see herself like that.

Boots and Emily took Eloise up to the West End shops in the family car that afternoon. Rosie went too. Tim, hearing that there was a shopping expedition in the offing, made himself scarce in case he had a weak moment and allowed his mum to wheedle him into the car.

'Where's Tim?' asked Emily as Rosie opened the car door for her.

'Hiding,' said Rosie.

'Hidin'?' said Emily.

'Oh, he'll pop out once we've gone,' said Rosie.

'But what's he hidin' from?' asked Emily.

'West End shops,' said Rosie.

'But everyone likes the West End shops,' said Emily.

'Not Tim,' said Rosie.

'That boy is funny, isn't he?' said Eloise, due to attend Pitman's College in the City after Easter in order to perfect her written English and to learn touch typing.

'Like his father,' said Emily, with all four of them now in the car.

'For which we're grateful,' said Rosie.

'Oh, yes, funny is better than long faces,' said Eloise, and Emily smiled as Boots motored out of the drive and down Denmark Hill towards Camberwell Green and the West End.

Rosie was also smiling. Eloise had managed to put herself in the front passenger seat beside Boots. Rosie found such antics amusing.

As for Tim, he went to Brockwell Park to watch a football match between Browning Street Rovers and their deadliest rivals, Manor Place Rangers. The Rovers were captained by Nick Harrison, the fiancé of Tim's cousin, Annabelle Somers, daughter of his Aunt Lizzy and Uncle Ned. Annabelle was there along with other girl supporters, and so were two of Nick's sisters, Alice and young Fanny, as well as Cassie Ford. Freddy Brown, Cassie's own fiancé and right halfback for the Rovers, was playing alongside Nick.

The game had just kicked off when Tim arrived. He was a footballer himself, playing for his school team on Saturday mornings. He received a warm greeting from Annabelle, a gorgeous-looking girl of eighteen with glossy chestnut hair and large brown eyes.

'Tim, lovely to see you,' she said.

'Don't mention it,' said thirteen-year-old Tim, 'just give us a kiss.'

Tim being her favourite male cousin, Annabelle gave him a smacker on his cheek.

'I saw that,' said Cassie.

''Ere, yes, what's goin' on?' asked Chrissie Thompson, known as Dumpling on account of her cuddlesome plumpness. Married to the Rovers' right back, Danny Thompson, Dumpling was in aggravated expectancy of their first child. Well, nothing had aggravated her more than finding out exactly what Danny had done to her on their honeymoon last August. Dumpling was so keen on football, playing as well as watching, that she'd thumped Danny for putting her in the family way. Still, as he said, it did mean she'd be having their first little footballer in May or thereabouts. 'Annabelle, what's all that kissin'? Oh, it's you, Tim.' All the girl supporters knew Tim, for he often came to watch the Rovers in action. 'My, ain't you growin' a good-lookin' boy?'

'Pardon his blushes,' said Annabelle.

'I don't see any,' said Alice, whose young man, Johnny Richards, was also doing his stuff for the Rovers. Her young sister Fanny, noted for her sauciness, darted a glance at Tim. Tim, a typical Adams, and accordingly gregarious, gave her a friendly smile. Fanny actually blushed. Her family, knowing her well, would have said it was her first ever blush. But then her family didn't know she was experiencing her first crush. Tim, a slim lad, was tall for his age and had his dad's dark brown hair and grey eyes. Fanny thought him thrilling. He thought her an engaging young pussycat, with her girlish little nose and her straw-coloured pigtail that was tied with black ribbon.

'Sorry about me embarrassing looks,' he said with a grin, and put himself between her and Alice. Fanny went sort of quivery as elbows touched, and she even blushed again. 'How's yourselves?' he asked.

'Oh, we're in the pink, Tim, thanks,' said Alice, a trim and nice-looking young lady of nineteen.

'Is Nick still cheerful about getting married to my cousin Annabelle?' asked Tim.

'I think he's walkin' on air,' said Alice, as the footballers surged up and down.

'I'll tell Annabelle, she'll like that,' said Tim, and turned his attention on the game. 'Any score yet, Fanny?' he asked.

'Beg pardon?' gulped Fanny, not at all her usual self. Well, a girl of thirteen suffering her first crush was bound to have the kind of problems that played havoc with her teenage aplomb, if she had any, and Fanny had her fair share and a bit more – usually.

'No score yet,' said Alice, 'the game's only been goin' for ten minutes.'

'Oh, lawks, there goes me poor old Danny,' said Dumpling. Danny had been floored by the hefty Manor Place centre half, Bonzo Willis, sometimes known as Bonzo the Elephant. 'That won't do me better 'alf much good, not in 'is delicate condition.'

'He doesn't look delicate from where we're standing,' said Tim, 'does he, Fanny?'

Oh, crikey, he's talking to me, thought Fanny.

'Beg pardon?' she gulped again.

'It's 'is state of 'ealth,' said Dumpling, face rosy beneath her knitted blue and white supporters' hat. 'We're expectin', yer know, Tim, so we're both delicate. Mind you, it's more 'is fault than mine.'

'I think I've heard about it,' said Tim.

'We all have,' said Alice.

'Yes, and it's mucked up me football career,' said Dumpling.

'Oh, what a shame, you poor woman,' said Cassie.

'Still, think of the patter of tiny feet,' said Annabelle.

'In football boots,' said Cassie.

'Crikey, Nick's down now,' said Dumpling.

Nick had crashed following a hefty tackle.

'That's broken his leg, I shouldn't wonder,' said Cassie, 'and him gettin' married to you in June, Annabelle, you poor woman.'

'Cassie, stop calling all of us poor women,' said Annabelle.

Nick, upright again and uninjured, scored the first goal for the Rovers a minute later, planting an elbow in Bonzo's ribs on the way, which the ref didn't notice. The girls danced about in triumph, Dumpling making light of her extra weight. In any case, she'd been told exercise was good for expectant mothers. Fanny, forgetting her nervous condition at being elbow to elbow with Tim, almost took off in her delight.

'You're going up and down a bit, Fanny,' said Tim.

'Oh, help,' breathed Fanny, 'did it notice?'

'Not half,' said Tim. 'D'you do athletics at your school?'

'Me?' Fanny was all over goosepimples. 'Me do athletics?'

'Running and jumping?' said Tim.

'Oh, help,' said Fanny faintly.

'What d'you want help for?' smiled Tim.

'Yes, what's up with you, Fanny?' asked Alice.

'Me, Alice?' said Fanny.

'You sound as if your tongue's 'aving an off-day,' said Alice.

'Fanny's all right,' said Tim, 'she's just been jumping up and down a bit.'

'Well, Nick scored a goal,' said Fanny.

'That's as good an excuse as any for jumping up and down,' said Tim. 'D'you like films, Fanny?'

'Beg pardon?' gasped Fanny, all over more quivers.

'Going to the pictures,' said Tim.

'Me?' said Fanny helplessly. Having a crush on a boy was awful weakening when he was standing so close to her and being so friendly.

On the field, Bonzo Willis, miffed about his team conceding a goal, took his umbrage out on Freddy and sent him flying.

'Oh, me beloved Freddy,' breathed Cassie. She'd taken to calling him that on suitable occasions. It made other girls shriek. 'That hurt me all over,' she said.

'Oh, poor woman,' said Annabelle, and Cassie giggled.

The ref had a few words with Bonzo.

'Me?' said Bonzo. 'I ask yer fair and square, ref, is it my fault Browning Rovers are all bleedin' legless?'

'Language, language,' remonstrated the ref.

'Someone said something, then?' asked Bonzo, sorry to see Freddy was up on his feet and relatively uninjured.

'That Bonzo Willis is a shockin' hooligan,' said Cassie.

The game went on, the Rovers hanging on to their

lead. At half-time, they came and mingled with the girls. Nick said hello to Tim, and took a slice of lemon from Fanny.

'It's a good game,' said Tim.

'Hello, hero,' said Annabelle, arriving at Nick's side.

'Don't mention it,' said Nick.

'Leg muscles bearing up, are they, lovey?' smiled Annabelle.

'Funny you should ask,' said Nick, 'I think I'd better stay in bed tomorrow and give 'em a rest.'

'You'll be lucky,' said Annabelle, 'you're coming up in the morning to take me to church, and in the afternoon you're playing the piano with me in our front room.'

'I'm off the piano,' said Nick, 'I'll think of something else we can do.'

'Don't say things like that in front of Tim, you shocker,' said Annabelle.

Tim smiled. He stayed until the end of the game, talking to Alice and Fanny from time to time, and Fanny gradually got hold of herself. But she went to pot again when, just before he left, Tim told her he'd take her to the pictures himself one day, if she liked. She could only gulp that she would like.

When Tim got off the bus at the stop in Red Post Hill, a small motorized baker's van approached. It passed the standing bus at a steady speed. Tim noted the name, 'Joseph Roberts, Family Baker'. Not our local baker, he thought casually. He little knew it, but the van was on a nefarious practice run from a certain bank in Camberwell to North Dulwich railway station. Ginger Carstairs was driving, Dusty Miller in the passenger seat. From North Dulwich they would take a train which, with a change, would get them to Tonbridge and from there to Dover and a ferry to France.

But not today, of course.

# Chapter Three

'Time I left,' said Major Charles Armitage.

'If you must,' said Cecily Bennett, an old friend. They'd had a long lunch at the Criterion, and then spent the afternoon at her Maida Vale house. A divorcee, Cecily was a well-known London socialite, noted for her avant-garde parties, especially during the war. It was happenings at some of those mad wartime parties that had led to her divorce. As for Charles Armitage, a young lieutenant in 1914, he'd been among the Army men who'd enjoyed themselves at her house on several occasions just after the outbreak of war. Then they'd gone off to France. 'Pauline will be waiting for you, old thing?'

'If she's not drunk,' said Major Armitage, now on the reserve list. He had an estate in Surrey to look after.

'Divorce her, you idiot,' said Cecily.

Major Armitage, a handsome man of forty-three with a well-trimmed military moustache, looked her in the eye.

'And marry you?' he said.

'You could do a lot worse, ducky,' said Cecily, forty-two.

'I daresay,' said Major Armitage, 'but I can't dump Pauline, you know that.'

'Pity,' said Cecily.

'I've an estate, an alcoholic wife and what else? Very

little. No children, and a dissolute younger brother who's waiting for me to kick the bucket so that he can inherit. But I still can't divorce Pauline. She'd end up as a down-and-out. God, if only she'd given me a child before she took to the bottle, I'd have something worthwhile to live for.'

'You've said that before,' murmured Cecily.

'Well, it's true, damn it,' said Major Armitage.

'Cheer up, ducky, at least you came out of the war all in one piece,' said Cecily.

'Oh, I'm thankful for that, believe me,' he said, 'but my life at the moment is damned empty.'

Something reached the tip of Cecily's tongue, but it stayed there, unspoken. She was unsure whether or not it would do any good. She had kept it from him for years. Wisely, she thought.

He left then, kissing her warmly for old times sake, and although she was a woman disinclined to take anything too seriously, she let her thoughts linger on a certain event for quite a while after he had gone.

Two hours later, when she knew he'd be home, she telephoned him and asked him to come up and see her tomorrow afternoon, Sunday. He asked why.

'I've something of interest to tell you,' she said.

'Tell me now,' he said.

'Not over the phone. Here, tomorrow afternoon. It really is something of interest to you, very personal interest.'

'Not about divorcing Pauline, for God's sake.'

'Far from it,' said Cecily. 'How is she?'

'Drunk,' said Major Armitage.

'Rotten bad luck, old thing. You'll come tomorrow?'

'Very well,' he said.

'Gird yourself,' she said.

She had made up her mind to tell him, particularly as she had found an old slip of paper among some ancient miscellanea in a bureau drawer.

That evening Freddy called for Cassie to take her to a cinema up West. Cassie said it was a bit expensive, a West End cinema, and Freddy said well, yes, it was, but she deserved a bit of expensiveness now and again, seeing she was engaged to marry him. Cassie said she was overjoyed to know he appreciated how lucky he was. Freddy said luck like that was easy to live with.

At the Walworth Road bus stop they met Lilian Hyams. Cassie introduced the stylish woman to Freddy, letting him know she was Sammy Adams's fashion designer, and the lady who was making the wedding gowns for herself and Sally.

'Pleasure,' said Freddy, shaking hands with Lilian.

'Pleasure for me too, meeting Cassie's fiancé,' said Lilian, and eyed him in approval. Freddy, now in his twenty-first year, was a decidedly manly-looking bloke, with an air of typical Walworth cheerfulness. 'Oh, the little alterations to both gowns have been done, Cassie. When would you like me to give you the final fitting?'

'Can you come round tomorrow afternoon?' asked Cassie.

'I'm giving Sally her final fitting tomorrow morning, so should I say no to tomorrow afternoon for you when I can say yes?' smiled Lilian.

'Then you can stay to tea,' said Cassie.

'Well, that's nice of you, Cassie,' said Lilian.

'You goin' up West now?' asked Cassie.

'Yes, treating myself to a seat at the Alhambra,' said Lilian. 'Gracie Fields is the star turn tonight.'

'We're goin' to the Empire cinema to see a film,' said Cassie, thinking what a shame it was that such a fine-looking woman as Mrs Hyams didn't have an escort. The bus for the West End pulled up then, and she and Freddy parted company with Lilian, who preferred the lower deck while they went upstairs. When they were seated, Cassie said, 'Freddy, d'you know a nice bloke that would suit Mrs Hyams?'

'Well, there's me,' said Freddy.

'Don't go off your rocker,' said Cassie.

'All right, how about Mr Richards, the widower bloke that lodges next door to me?' suggested Freddy.

'Him? But he must be nearly seventy,' said Cassie. 'Freddy, you're barmy.'

'We're all a bit that way, y'know, Cassie,' said Freddy.

'Yes, Boots always says everyone is,' said Cassie, 'so I suppose whoever I married would be fairly dotty. Still, I think I'll be able to manage.'

'You don't have to worry about that,' said Freddy, 'I'll be doin' the managing.'

'Wishful thinking more like,' said Cassie.

They enjoyed a lovely evening at the cinema, and she was thoughtful on the bus going home.

'What're you thinking about?' asked Freddy.

'Us,' said Cassie.

'What for?' asked Freddy.

'I like thinking about us more than about things like dustbins or fish markets, don't I?' said Cassie reasonably. 'Freddy, it's not long to the weddin' now, so I want you to make sure you take care where you're walkin' and what you're doin'. You're not to fall off

47

a kerb or walk under ladders, and you're not to catch something like tonsilitis or flu. I don't want you not turning up at the church because you've been careless.'

'Well, Cassie, if I didn't 'ave to go to me daily work I could stay careful in bed from now to the weddin',' said Freddy.

'Freddy, I don't think much of that as a sensible answer,' said Cassie.

'Don't you worry, Cassie,' said Freddy, 'I'll get to the church, even if I break both me legs fallin' off a kerb.'

'Oh, yes, I'd like that, wouldn't I, you turning up with two broken legs,' said Cassie. 'I want you there all in one piece.'

'That's me own lifelong wish, Cassie, to be all in one piece on me weddin' day,' said Freddy. Lowering his voice, he added, 'I mean, what's goin' to 'appen in private later if I'm not?'

'I can't hardly wait to find out, can I?' said Cassie, and a little giggle escaped.

Alighting eventually from the bus, they began their walk to Cassie's home via East Street. A middle-aged couple approached, bawling at each other.

'I just dunno why I ever married you, Joe Turner, you been dozy all yer life,' yelled the woman.

'Could I 'elp it that me belt broke?' hollered the man.

'You could've 'eld yer trousers up, couldn't yer, instead of lettin' 'em fall down in front of people right outside the fried fish shop. Disgracin' me like that, wait till I get you 'ome.'

'I pulled 'em up, didn't I? And I'm 'olding them up now, ain't I?' The man nearly collided with Freddy.

48

Freddy did a quick shuffle, the man did a lurching one, the clash was avoided, and Freddy went on with Cassie. A female bellow followed them.

'Now look what you've done, the pair of yer, made 'is bleedin' trousers fall down again!'

'Oh, I'll fall over,' gasped Cassie, having hysterics.

'Not now, wait till after the wedding,' said Freddy.

'All right,' said Cassie, 'but ain't life a dream, Freddy?'

'So are you,' said Freddy.

Over breakfast the following morning, Mrs Susie Adams regarded her three children, Daniel, Bess and Jimmy, thoughtfully. She was expecting her fourth. Sammy noted her look.

'Penny for 'em, Susie,' he said.

'A hundred and sixty, that's what I'm thinking about,' she said.

'I'm hearin' things,' said Sammy.

'What things, Dad?' asked Daniel, eight.

'Things I don't believe,' said Sammy.

'What things is them, Daddy?' asked Bess, six.

'Search me,' said Sammy.

'I'm speakin', Sammy Adams, of a hundred and sixty guests at the double weddin',' said Susie.

'Is that a fact, Susie,' said Sammy. 'Well, I've never been more relieved in all me life.'

'And everyone sittin' down,' said Susie. 'Have they got a hundred and sixty chairs at St John's Institute?'

'I'll phone the vicar and ask,' said Sammy.

'I don't ever remember there being as many as that,' said Susie. 'Bess, stop makin' a sandcastle of your porridge. Sammy, have you thought about wearin' a top-hat?'

'I can truthfully say no,' said Sammy.

'Sammy, you'd look ever so distinguished in a top-hat,' said Susie.

'Wasser top-hat?' asked four-year-old Jimmy.

'Something I'm not goin' to wear,' said Sammy.

'It's what the King puts on his head sometimes,' said Bess.

'Fortunately, I'm not the King,' said Sammy, 'just a simple bloke born and bred in Walworth, where they chuck things at top-hats.'

'What things, Dad?' asked Daniel.

'Bricks,' said Sammy.

'Bricks is nasty,' said Bess. 'Well, I fink they are.'

'Don't you worry, plum pudding,' said Sammy, 'no one's goin' to chuck bricks at any top-hat I won't be wearin'.'

'There's a nice man's shop in Regent Street,' said Susie, 'we can buy one there.'

'I didn't hear that,' said Sammy.

'Dad,' said Daniel helpfully, 'Mum said there's a nice man's shop in Regent Street where you can buy one.'

'I didn't hear that, either,' said Sammy. 'Anyway, sunshine, let your mum know you have to wear tails with a topper, and I don't have tails.'

'We can buy those as well,' said Susie.

'Any more funny stories?' said Sammy.

'You'll look lovely in tails and topper, Sammy,' said Susie, with her family tucking into their usual Sunday breakfast of fried eggs and bacon.

'I've gone deaf again,' said Sammy. 'D'you get me, Susie?'

'Yes, I get you, Sammy love,' said Susie, 'you've gone deaf again.'

'Good,' said Sammy, 'subject closed, then.'
Susie smiled.

Boots drove his family to church. He dropped Emily,
Tim and Rosie off a little early at the Denmark Hill
church, and then took Eloise to the Roman Catholic
shrine for Mass. Eloise offered her cheek to him for
a kiss before she got out of the car. Boots obliged.

'Papa, I like you very much,' she said.

'And you're really happy living with us?' smiled
Boots.

'Oh, yes. But more with you. You are such a nice
man.'

'I'll tell your stepmother that,' said Boots, 'it may
have escaped her.'

'Of course not, Papa, 'ow could it?' said Eloise,
and laughed as she alighted. She really was happy
with her new-found family, liking Tim, Emily and
the grandparents, while just a little in awe of Rosie
because of her striking looks and her very English
air of composure, which she thought aristocratic. She
was also just a little jealous, because not only was it
obvious the whole family had a particular affection
for Rosie, there was also something special between
her and her father. How can that be, Eloise often
asked herself, when she is only his adopted daughter?

Kind Mr Abel Morrison, willing to be a comforting
figure in the lonely life of Mrs Lilian Hyams, was at
her house at two-thirty precisely. The widow, alas, was
not at home.

'Dear, dear,' he murmured, when there was no
reply to any of his knocks, 'she's forgotten I promised
to call.'

Not at all. Lilian, taking heed of his intentions, had departed for Cassie's home with the boxed wedding gown at two-twenty, and thus escaped him.

Major Armitage arrived at the Maida Vale house at three-fifteen, having travelled up in his car. He was admitted into Cecily's drawing-room by her house-keeper, and as soon as they were alone he said, 'Now, what's your game, old girl?'

'It's no game, old boy, it's something I've decided you should know,' said Cecily, and proceeded to acquaint him with details. She referred to one of the early wartime parties she had given during August, 1914, just after the outbreak of hostilities. He had arrived in company with other officers and some excited girls they had picked up in the West End. He was a lieutenant then, and waiting for orders.

'I remember,' he said, 'but I can't think you can tell me anything about one more pre-embarkation party that could be called important now.'

'You disappeared with one of the girls,' said Cecily.

Major Armitage furrowed his broad brow.

'Did I?' he said. The furrow smoothed itself out and a little smile arrived. 'What was she like?'

'Pretty but brainless, and slightly drunk,' said Cecily.

'I don't suppose that at that particular time I was interested in whether a girl was intellectual or not, or how much drink any of us had had.'

'I'm sure you weren't,' said Cecily, 'but I have to tell you she came back to the house in October. Agitated. And pregnant.'

'What?' said Major Armitage.

'She swore she had never been to bed with

52

any man except you. Not that she remembered your name. I made the mistake of saying I remembered her disappearing with one of the lieutenants, and she said yes, it was one of them all right, and that he was the first and only man she'd made love with. She told him so at the time, even if she was a bit squiffy, she said. Now she was going to have his baby, she complained, so what was he going to do about it?'

'Good God,' said Major Armitage.

'She asked if I could get in touch with him and let him know, because he ought to do right by her as an officer and gentleman. I think she actually said officer and gent. I said I didn't know your name, that a lot of officers were coming and going casually at the time, treating my place as open house. Well, I decided I had to protect you, Charles old thing. She simply wasn't your type, believe me. Of course, I said I'd make enquiries, so she wrote her name and address on a slip of paper and gave it to me. I put it somewhere and let it go at that.'

'Cecily, that was all you did for her?' asked Major Armitage.

'You think I should have done more?' said Cecily. 'What, exactly? Given her your name and the name of your regiment? What would you have done if she'd written to tell you she was expecting your baby? Married her? Of course you wouldn't. She came from Deptford, but tried to sound as if she was some kind of superior shop assistant. She made a terrible mess of it.'

'I'd have at least tried to find some way of helping her,' said Major Armitage.

'Oh, I think she'd have accepted money, if you'd offered enough,' said Cecily. 'The point is, Charles, you're in need of a son or daughter, and out there somewhere you have one. God knows how he or she has been raised, but what you could offer as the father would be irresistible.'

'Ye gods,' said Major Armitage, 'are you serious, Cecily?'

'I thought you were, about having a son or daughter to make your life less empty,' said Cecily. 'I thought hard as to whether or not I should tell you, and since you were so down in the dumps yesterday, I decided I would. Either you've a son and heir or a daughter, and if there are some rough edges to one or the other, I don't doubt you could arrange for them to be smoothed out, to turn a son into a gentleman or a daughter into a lady. Never mind the mother's background, it's your blood that counts.'

'Damn it,' said Major Armitage, 'there's the mother to consider, and a stepfather, probably.'

'My dear man,' said Cecily, 'we're dealing, aren't we, with someone who'd be nineteen years old now, not a child needing a mother, or a stepfather.'

'Did the girl ever come back again?' asked Major Armitage.

'No, never,' said Cecily. 'Perhaps she found some man willing to take her on, and the child. If so, why not accept they'll have their price and let you take over?'

'That child, now a young man or a young woman, might refuse to be taken over,' said Major Armitage. 'At nineteen, how would you feel about some man turning up to make a father's claim on you?'

'Well, ducky, if my life until then had been in Deptford, and I were offered what you could offer, I'd feel delighted,' said Cecily.

'Would you? You'd be happy about being separated from your mother?'

'At nineteen, would that seriously worry me?' Cecily smiled. 'I don't think so, not if it meant going from rags to riches. Oh, I daresay the takeover would appeal more to you if the child were a tender six or seven, but all the same, it's making you think, isn't it?'

'Can I be sure the child is mine?'

'I had a quite certain feeling at the time that although the girl wasn't exactly a lady, she was telling the truth about losing her virginity to you,' said Cecily. 'This is her name and address.' She handed over a slip of paper, slightly brown with age. Major Armitage examined it. It gave a name and address, Millicent Tooley, 4 Warwick Street, Deptford.

'I wonder, does she still live there?' he said.

'If you're going to make enquiries, my dear, you'll at least have to start from there, won't you?' said Cecily.

'It's absurd, Cecily.'

'Is it?' said Cecily. 'The existence of a son or daughter? I think you'd give your right arm to have him or her home with you, wouldn't you? It might even make Pauline chuck her bottles away and turn into a mother. So what d'you propose to do?'

'Think about it,' said Major Armitage.

'Well, you can think about it over tea,' said Cecily. 'I'll order a tray.'

She rang for her housekeeper.

In her bedroom the following morning, Lilian, up and dressed, was just about to go down when she heard the clink of milk bottles accompanied by a tuneful whistle. She looked through the window and saw the milk float outside the house next door. Down she went, and when she opened her front door there was the milkman himself on her step.

'What, again?' she said.

'Hello and good morning, missus,' said Bill Chambers. 'Well met, I'd say.'

'If it keeps happening, we'll get talked about,' said Lilian.

'No cause for that,' said Bill, 'politeness is the watchword between me and all my customers. It's laid down by the dairy.'

'So you've already said,' smiled Lilian, at the beginning of maturity and looking fulsomely fetching in an attractive dress of ivy green.

'Well, Mrs Hyams, the fact is I do my best to treat my lady customers respectfully, which keeps me from being thumped by one of my own milk bottles.'

'And from being thumped by your wife,' said Lilian.

'It might, yes, I daresay it might, Mrs Hyams, except I'm not married, having spent ten years courtin' my landlady's daughter Dorothy. Well, just as we were finally about to get officially engaged, she upped and married a bloke from round the corner, and her mother went with her. I don't know about her dad, I think he ran off with a lady tram conductor during the war. Anyway, when Dorothy and her mum hopped it, I was left in charge of a whole house and a piano they didn't want in Rockingham Street, by the Elephant and Castle. Now what would a bloke like me want a piano and a whole house for? I ask you, what?'

'I don't know what you're grumbling about,' said Lilian, 'not now you're free to go out and find a wife and put her in charge.'

Blue eyes twinkled at her.

'Well, I'll be bottled,' said Bill, 'I never thought of that. I'd say you've just given me a prize piece of advice, right out of a wise loaf of bread. I'm regarding you, Mrs Hyams, with complimentary admiration. But with polite respect, of course.'

I've got another Sammy here, thought Lilian. Give him a soapbox and he could make a name for himself.

'What did you say your name was?' she asked, King and Queen Street visibly stirring now.

'Bill Chambers.'

'Well, Bill, start looking,' said Lilian.

'For a woman who wouldn't mind takin' charge of a piano and a whole house?' said Bill.

'And you and your laundry,' said Lilian.

'What a thought,' said Bill. 'Might I present you with a pint of fresh?' He placed a bottle of milk in her hand. 'With my personal compliments. Any eggs?'

'Are you getting commission on the eggs you sell?' asked Lilian.

'Penny on every half-dozen,' said Bill.

'Well, I'll think of buying some later this week,' said Lilian.

'Mrs Hyams, it's my personal pleasure to have become acquainted,' said Bill, and off he went with his nag and his float, whistling.

That leaves me needing to hurry to work, thought Lilian, closing the door. But one couldn't deny oneself a doorstep chat with an outgoing milkman who had a gift of the gab.

A certain house in Wansey Street having been vacated, Cassie and Freddy were there first thing after supper,

57

finishing a job they'd begun yesterday evening, stripping the kitchen of its ancient wallpaper. This was the house in which they were going to live when they were married, and they were already renting it. The first thing they'd wanted to do was repaper the kitchen. Freddy was a natural at this sort of job, Cassie a willing learner. She was on a stepladder, stripping from the ceiling downwards. Freddy was on his knees, cleaning up the lower half of the wall.

'By the way, Cassie,' he said.

'Yes, Freddy dear?' said Cassie lovingly.

'Sammy's goin' to see we get a good start to our married lives by givin' us a cheque,' said Freddy.

'A cheque?' said Cassie.

'For fifty pounds,' said Freddy.

Cassie nearly fell off the stepladder.

'How much?' she gasped.

'Fifty quid,' said Freddy.

'Lord, as much as that?' said Cassie in gasping delight.

'He popped into the brewery this afternoon to tell me,' said Freddy.

'It's all of fifty pounds?' said Cassie, breathless.

'It's because I'm 'is brother-in-law and work for him, and because you're goin' to be fortunate enough to be related to me by marriage,' said Freddy.

'He didn't say that, I bet,' said Cassie.

'More or less,' said Freddy.

'Me fortunate?' said Cassie. 'Crikey, what a laugh. I'll fall off this ladder in a minute. It's you that's goin' to be fortunate. Freddy, you do realize how lucky you are, I suppose?'

'Well, Cassie, you've said so before—'

'I could 'ave been asked by the Lord Chamberlain if I'd met him,' said Cassie.

'He's nearly ninety,' said Freddy.

'Still, never mind,' said Cassie, 'isn't Sammy a lovely man? I mean, fifty pounds, Freddy. It's more than I earn in a year.'

'I've got to start a bank account,' said Freddy, 'it's Sammy's suggestion. He wants us to buy this house as soon as we can. He said us payin' rent 'urts him. So me dad's goin' to give me time off to pop into the bank when I've got the cheque from Sammy. Like the idea, Cassie?'

'Oh, I could kiss Sammy,' said Cassie blissfully.

'He'll charge you for it,' said Freddy. 'He always says that if 'e didn't charge, females would be kissin' him all the time and interferin' with his work. Incident'lly, Cassie, we'd better change places.'

'What for?' asked Cassie. 'I like it up here.'

'Yes, but the point is, Cassie, with you up there and me down here, it's takin' me mind off me work,' said Freddy.

'What d'you mean?' asked Cassie, an old apron over her dress.

'Well, from down here, Cassie, your frock looks a bit short,' said Freddy. 'If you get my meaning.'

'Freddy Brown, you're blessed-well lookin', you libertine,' said Cassie.

'Libber what?' said Freddy, scraping away.

'Yes, I read it in a book,' said Cassie, 'and it means sort of licentious.'

'I don't like the sound of that,' said Freddy.

'Well, you shouldn't be lookin',' declared Cassie.

'Bless me, I ain't been, not on purpose, just accidental now and again,' said Freddy, 'but I'm

59

still nearly blind. I'll say this much, Cassie, you've got a lovely pair of tent pegs from down here.'

Cassie descended the stepladder, rolled up an old newspaper and walloped him with it.

'Take that,' she said.

Freddy, straightening up, said, 'Was it my fault you were up there and I was down here?'

'I like it up there, not on my knees,' said Cassie. 'Freddy, stop looking, it's not nice.'

'Can I help it if I like your legs?' said Freddy. 'Funny about that, really, likin' girls' legs.'

'Excuse me,' said Cassie, 'but if I catch you likin' someone else's, I'll ask me dad to chop yours off.'

'Ruin me football, that will,' said Freddy.

Cassie laughed.

'Freddy, I like you likin' mine,' she said.

'All right, get up that ladder again, Cassie.'

'Not likely, not till you've got your head down,' said Cassie. 'Freddy, fifty pounds all at once and a bank account, just think of it,' she said.

'It makes me feel rich,' said Freddy, and dug into his pocket. He came up with a silver threepenny-bit and put it into her hand. 'There, all yours, Cassie, I don't mind splashin' out just now.'

'Wait a bit,' said Cassie, 'what's it for?'

'For showin' me your legs,' said Freddy.

Cassie shrieked, then hugged him.

'Oh, I do like you, Freddy,' she said.

'Don't mention it, Cassie, just get up that ladder again,' said Freddy.

At suppertime, Rosie remembered something.

'Tim, I saw Pam Willis this afternoon,' she said.

'Who?' asked Tim.

'Pam Willis, from down the road,' said Rosie. 'She asked after you, and if you'd like to meet her in her doorway when you weren't busy.'

'Ah,' said Mr Finch.

'H'm,' said Boots.

'What's that h'm for?' asked Chinese Lady.

'Oh, it's just one of Daddy's usual h'ms,' said Rosie. 'Tim, should you have girls asking after you when you're not yet fourteen?'

Tim eyed his elder sister with a grin.

'I'm on to you, Rosie, don't think I'm not,' he said.

'Ah, perhaps Tim is starting quick,' said Eloise, 'like French boys do.'

'Startin' what quick?' asked Emily.

'Kissing,' said Eloise.

'Not with young girls, I hope,' said Chinese Lady. 'I never minded any of my sons socializing early, it helps young people to mix proper, but I never encouraged any kissin' of young girls not old enough for it.'

'Who's looking at me?' asked Tim. 'I've not been socializing with Pam Willis. Crikey, she's only twelve.'

'But she sent you her love, Tim,' said Rosie.

'She did what?' asked Chinese Lady.

'Well, more or less,' said Rosie.

'More or less sounds about right at her age,' said Boots.

'Boots, kindly don't say things like that,' said Chinese Lady.

'Why not, Nana?' asked Rosie.

'I don't trust him when he says things that don't make sense,' said Chinese Lady.

'Perhaps he does not mind Tim starting quick,' said Eloise.

'Well, he should,' said Chinese Lady, who had come to feel, gratefully, that Eloise wasn't as Frenchified as she might have been. To Chinese Lady, anything specifically French was suspect on account of her belief that the natives of France were a lot too improper in their talk and behaviour.

'Oh, French boys do it in the dark, yes, and before the girl can say no,' smiled Eloise.

'Don't look at me,' said Tim. 'Listen, Eloise, did you get kissed in the dark when you were young?'

'I am old now?' said Eloise.

'All right,' said Tim, 'when you were younger?'

'Oh, many times, yes,' said Eloise.

'And all before you could say no?' smiled Boots.

'Perhaps not every time,' said Eloise, 'and not until I was sixteen.'

'Well, perhaps I don't mind when a girl is sixteen, except it shouldn't be in the dark,' said Chinese Lady.

'Oh, I think a kiss in the dark is sometimes rather nice, Nana, isn't it?' said Rosie.

'Sounds as if you've had some of that, Rosie,' said Tim, and she laughed.

'I hope, Em'ly, you won't encourage Tim to do it with Pam Willis,' said Chinese Lady.

'I should say not,' declared Emily.

'I wouldn't know how to start,' said Tim.

Rosie smiled. Tim was like Boots, he had the same kind of easy-going nature, and it had its appeal even at his age. Girls were going to like him later on. She gave him a wink.

'Pam will help you,' she said, 'when you're both older.'

Eloise laughed.

'Rosie, you are so entertaining,' she said.

'Oh, you're not far behind, Eloise,' smiled Emily.

'I think that means we've now got two of a kind in this house,' said Boots.

'We're a fortunate family,' said Mr Finch.

'Yes, let's hang on to both,' said Boots.

# Chapter Four

Rosie's natural grandfather, Mr Albert Tooley, was a
widower of fifty-nine and a little like Cassie's dad in
his bluff ways, rugged looks, and the soft heart that
beat beneath his sturdy front. He was giving his best
bowler hat a buff this evening. Well, it was just after
seven and at eight he was due to go out and meet
Ada Franklin, a laundress, at the Deptford Arms,
where he'd enjoy a pint of old and mild and have
the pleasure of treating her to a milk stout. The
lady, fifty-two, was a cheerful body and nicely plump.
Further, she'd never been wed, but was always joking
that she'd had more than one chance to be churched,
only each time the bloke had seen her coming. Well,
there was a lot of her, she said. Far from being against
that, Mr Tooley had thoughts of a second marriage.
He had only a few more years at his job with the
Deptford Council in front of him, and reckoned he
and Ada would make a good old Darby and Joan together. His savings and a bit of a pension would look
after his and her years of retirement. He had a happy
idea that Ada's thoughts were coinciding with his, so
this evening, when she was halfway through her milk
stout and accordingly mellow, he meant to pop the
question. His nephew's wife, Nellie Nicholls, who was
fond of him, was encouraging him to take the plunge.

His thoughts were interrupted by a knock on his
front door. He occupied only the ground floor

himself. A young couple with a small child lodged upstairs. Opening the door, he found a tall distinguished-looking man in a trench coat and bowler hat on his step. He had a military look, emphasized by his handsome moustache.

'Hello,' said Mr Tooley, 'don't think I've 'ad the pleasure, have I?'

'Sorry to disturb you,' said the caller, 'but I'm looking for a lady who I believe used to live here.'

Blimey, thought Mr Tooley, a toff looking for a Deptford lady?

'Here? You sure?' he said.

'I was given this address,' said Major Armitage, 'but am prepared to believe she doesn't live here now. I'm wondering if you know of her.'

'What's the lady's name?' asked Mr Tooley.

'Millicent Tooley.'

'Come again?' Mr Tooley blinked.

'Millicent Tooley,' repeated Major Armitage. 'Would you know of her?'

'I ought to,' said Mr Tooley, 'she's me daughter.'

Each regarded the other in extreme curiosity then, Major Armitage seeing a rugged but honest-looking man in a blue serge suit with iron-grey hair. A working man, and the grandfather of the child. It was something to know he was not coarse or bruising.

Mr Tooley wondered if the caller was from the plainclothes police. Milly had left a few debts behind in her time. No sense of responsibility, and she never had had. The last he'd heard of her, she and that smooth-talking husband of hers had been running an entertainments troupe which performed at seasides in the summer and got a few bookings in northern music halls during the winter. Milly had always been mad about the theatre, but had never got anywhere that put her in the money. Nor had her husband, some sort of a magician, whose hands had let him down when too much drink gave them the shakes at the wrong moments.

'You are Mr Tooley?' said Major Armitage.

'I am. Mind, me daughter has always been known as Milly. Might I ask why you're enquirin' after her?'

'Mr Tooley, have you a few minutes to spare?' asked Major Armitage.

'I've got time to spare until ten-to-eight, when I'll be on me way to keep an appointment,' said Mr Tooley. 'You're welcome to step into me parlour.'

'Thank you.'

'Mind you, the kitchen's warmer, the fire's going,' said Mr Tooley, standing aside.

'The matter's confidential, Mr Tooley,' said Major Armitage.

'I'm a widower, I live on me own, with just a young couple and their infant, lodging upstairs,' said Mr Tooley, wondering what 'confidential' meant exactly.

'The kitchen, then,' said Major Armitage, appreciating the straightforwardness of Milly Tooley's father. 'My name, by the way, is Armitage.'

'This way, Mr Armitage,' said Mr Tooley, intrigued now. Well, the bloke was undoubtedly a toff in his appearance, manner and speech. He took him through the passage of the old Victorian terraced house and into the kitchen, where the range fire radiated warmth. The room was tidy, its table covered by a blue and grey check oilcloth, easy to wipe down and keep clean. On it stood a silver-plated cruet. A bowler hat and a stiff brush sat next to it. 'Help yourself to a chair.'

66

'Thank you,' said Major Armitage. He placed his own bowler on another chair. Mr Tooley sat down opposite him.

'You've got me curious, Mr Armitage.'

'Yes, that's understandable,' said Major Armitage, 'and I'll come straight to the point of my visit. Mr Tooley, I should like to frankly ask you if your daughter Milly had a child sometime during the first half of 1915, a child fathered by an Army officer.'

'Eh?'

'Did she?'

'So help me, that's winded me,' said Mr Tooley, and thought then of his granddaughter Rosie. If Rosie had forgotten her mother, she had never forgotten him. Twice a year she called, always with Boots Adams, her adoptive father, a man Mr Tooley greatly admired. During her years as a growing girl, a man could see how attached she was to Boots, much as if he was the sunshine of her life. And what a lovely girl she was, in looks and nature. Mr Tooley thought about how she always sent him birthday and Christmas cards, and with each card there was always a little affectionate note. Rosie was pure gold, with none of Milly's selfishness or shallowness. Her adoption by Boots and his wife Emily had to be the best thing that had ever happened to her. But what was this toff's interest in Milly all about? 'It beats me, Mr Armitage, you asking a question like that.'

'I'd be obliged, Mr Tooley, if you'd answer it,' said Major Armitage.

'Well, I can tell you yes, she did 'ave a child,' said Mr Tooley. 'Out of wedlock on account of fallin' from grace, as they say, which considerably upset me and her mother.'

'Was the child a boy or a girl, Mr Tooley?' Major Armitage was asking his questions in a quiet, civilized fashion.

'A girl.'

'A girl. I see.'

'And grown up lovely, believe me,' said Mr Tooley, 'but would you mind telling me what business it is of yours?'

'I'm her father,' said Major Armitage.

'God save the perishing Navy, you're what?' said Mr Tooley.

Major Armitage unbuttoned his coat, slipped a hand into his jacket pocket and drew out a silver cigarette case. He opened it.

'A cigarette, Mr Tooley?' he said. Mr Tooley was more in need of a large brandy than a cigarette, but he took one. A match was struck, and its flame served to light the cigarettes for both men, when Major Armitage then said, 'Yes, I'm the father of the girl, Mr Tooley. It happened, I'm afraid, at a time when London was full of people intoxicated by the fact that the country was at war with Germany. It was, of course, the intoxication of the self-deluded, and a large number of us lost our heads, including your daughter and me.'

'Bloody hell, I know Milly lost hers,' said Mr Tooley.

'However,' said Major Armitage, 'you must believe me when I tell you I hadn't the remotest idea I'd left your daughter pregnant. I was posted to France with my regiment before August was over, and have to admit I gave no thought to my brief time with her, which was just a matter of a few hours at an early

68

wartime party. I'm sorry, of course, at the way things turned out for her.'

'Hold on, mister, if you didn't know you'd left Milly expecting, what's brought you 'ere now?' asked Mr Tooley.

'A friend of mine, a lady who was giving parties daily in her house during the first days of the war, has only just acquainted me with details of the consequences. It was in her house, I'm afraid, that I—'

'Seduced Milly,' said Mr Tooley.

'I'm not here to deny it,' said Major Armitage.

'What galled me as much as anything was that Milly didn't even know your name,' said Mr Tooley. 'Or if she did, she couldn't remember it. Not a nice thing, that, Mr Armitage, a father being told by 'is daughter that she was going to 'ave a baby by a man whose name had passed her by. But it's over and done with now, so what's brought you here? An idea you ought to say sorry to Milly?'

'I imagine too many years have gone by for that idea to be much good,' said Major Armitage. 'Can you tell me what the girl is like?'

'Rosie?'

'That's her name, Rosie?'

'Baptised Rose, but always called Rosie,' said Mr Tooley, 'and I can tell you she's a fine young lady. More, she's clever too, she's at Oxford.'

'Oxford?' Major Armitage looked astonished. 'Oxford University?'

'Sure as I'm sitting here in me own kitchen,' said Mr Tooley. 'Mr Armitage, it's a regretful thing, y'know, a man by reason of being casual missing out the years he could've spent with a daughter like Rosie. Still, if you can be blamed for what you did with Milly, you can't be blamed for what you didn't know about.'

'Mr Tooley, this is actually true, my daughter Rosie is an undergraduate at Oxford University?'

'Some place there called Somerville,' said Mr Tooley. 'And if you don't mind me saying so, I don't see you as 'er father, just as a gent that played a casual part in the making of her as a babe. Nor would she see you as her father. She's got a fam'ly, Mr Armitage, one that's given 'er everything she's ever wanted, mostly a special kind of affection.'

'A family? Do you mean her mother and a man we could say was her stepfather?' said Major Armitage.

'Milly and 'er husband, you mean?' said Mr Tooley. 'Milly never wanted 'er. Understandable in a way, but no credit to her. No, Rosie was adopted years ago. Best thing of her life, that was.' Mr Tooley looked at his kitchen clock. Twenty minutes to eight. 'I suppose it was natural, you coming here out of interest, but you can take it from me you don't 'ave to worry about Rosie. She's a young lady that's always been happy right from the day she was given a new home at the age of five.'

'I appreciate all you've said, Mr Tooley, but the fact remains I am her father, and I'd like to see her.'

'Mr Armitage, you're years too late. You fathered 'er, yes, I grant that, but to Rosie there's only one man she'll ever want as her father, and that's the man who took 'er in when her mother deserted her, and then adopted 'er.'

'Who is he and what does he do?' asked Major Armitage.

'He's a natural-born gent name of Adams, with a business,' said Mr Tooley, 'and that's about as far as you and me can go about all this. I appreciate 'ow you feel now you've found out you fathered Rosie, but it's best to leave it as it stands, Mr Armitage. Now I've got to get ready to go out.'

'Do you have a photograph of Rosie, Mr Tooley?'

'I've got snaps by the dozen, being 'er grandfather, but they're private. Like I said, best if you stay out of 'er life after all these years. I'll see you to me street door.'

Major Armitage did not argue, nor did he show the extent of his feelings. He allowed Mr Tooley to show him out. He thanked him for his time, shook hands with him and said goodbye.

However, when Mr Tooley left the house a few minutes later, Major Armitage was still in the vicinity, and once Rosie's grandfather had disappeared into the darkness of the March night, he returned to the front door. He had taken note of its latchcord. He pulled it, the door opened, and he went in. He was very quiet in his closing of the door. He was a man with a fine war record, and he owned reasonable principles, but such was his interest and his excitement, he had few qualms about stretching them. Using the light of struck matches, it did not take him long to locate a drawer in the parlour cabinet that contained a photograph album. He took the album into the kitchen, where the gas mantle was turned low. He turned it up, all his movements quiet. He could hear a few sounds from upstairs. In the album were pasted snapshots of a girl from her very young years to what was obviously the present.

Absorbed, he turned the pages, noting that as a girl child, fair of hair, she looked sweet. As a growing girl, delicious. As a young lady, no less than quite lovely. In some of the snaps, there were other people, children and adults. Which of the men and women were her adoptive parents, he did not know, but he did observe that the women had style, the men an air of self-assurance. In one of two of the later snaps, Rosie looked positively striking, her clothes faultless.

'Ye gods,' he murmured, 'she's an Armitage to the life.' He was ready to swear she resembled his younger sister to a startling degree.

When he was ready to leave, he had with him one snapshot that had come adrift from its page, and which he thought showed her to be about seventeen. She would be nineteen now, and twenty sometime this year. And she was at Somerville, the women's college in Oxford. And the name of her adoptive father was Adams. She would have taken that name.

Oxford had to be his next step. At Somerville College, he would make discreet enquiries. No wait, the students would be on Easter vacation now.

He returned to the parlour, struck matches, and examined a particular drawer again, moving the album aside. He found a letter, written and signed by Rosie. It gave her home address. He memorized it and put the letter back.

He left the house as quietly as he had entered it.

Mr Tooley, who had walked to the pub in a slightly perturbed state, put the man Armitage out of his mind once he was in cosy company with Ada. They chatted like friends who had known each other for years. Ada's milk stout did its work, increasing her habitual jolly approach to a sociable atmosphere. Mr Tooley suggested a woman like she was shouldn't live alone, she was made for being good company to a bloke.

'Which bloke?' said Ada.

Mr Tooley said there were blokes and blokes. Too right, said Ada. Mr Tooley then asked if she'd recently thought about getting married.

'Me at my age?' said Ada, laughing into her milk stout.

Mr Tooley assured her she was the right age for some men.

'Some? 'Ow many?' asked Ada. 'More than one's not legal, I'll 'ave you know, Albert.'

'There's one bloke I've got in mind,' said Mr Tooley, 'and he'd make it legal.'

'Which one's that?' asked Ada.

'Yours truly,' said Mr Tooley.

'Bless me soul, you ain't proposin', are yer, Albert?'

'Well, yes, I am, Ada, to tell you the truth.'

'Lord Above!' said Ada, 'And 'ere's me been thinking for months that you'd never ask.'

'Ada, 'ave another milk stout,' said Mr Tooley.

'Don't mind if I do, seein' you're goin' to church me, Albert,' said Ada, her buxom self mellow all over.

That's one thing the Armitage toff didn't do, said Mr Tooley to himself, he didn't church Milly. Well, now that I come to think, I'm ruddy glad he didn't. Boots, who's always been a friend to me, deserves Rosie more than her natural father does.

Ongoing March, acknowledging the approach of April, gradually became bright with sunshine, and several daffodils raised their heads in Browning Street Gardens and Kennington Park to look around in suspicion of frost or snow. There was none of either, so they burst into golden yellow.

Miss Polly Simms, taking advantage of the academic lull following end-of-term exams, negotiated a day off from her teaching post at West Square Girls School to join Rosie and Eloise in a carefree trip to London Town. Eloise had been to the West End before, in company with Boots and Emily, but was still delighted to have Rosie and Polly show her the facades of famous theatres and their billboards, and take her in and out of shops. Polly's pleasure came mainly from her strongly established friendship with Rosie, her favourite person after Boots. They gave themselves a leisurely hour or so for lunch, choosing that well-patronized and handsome restaurant, the Edwardian Trocadero, in the pulsing heart of the West End. Before the menus were brought to them, Eloise excused herself to powder her nose, which gave Polly the chance to ask Rosie for the latest news on developments at home.

'Developments?' said Rosie.

'Regarding Eloise's attitude now that she's been with you for three months,' said Polly.

'You could say the attachment is strengthening day by day,' smiled Rosie.

'Her attachment to all of you generally?' said Polly.

'To all of us generally, and to her new-found father in particular,' said Rosie.

The menus arrived, and one was left for Eloise.

'Inevitable, I suppose, that she favours Boots,' said Polly.

'Oh, she's really quite sweet,' said Rosie, 'although she'd monopolize him, if she could. But he's too sensible to allow that.'

'Well, Rosie my sweet, I really wouldn't want anything to break up the special relationship you and Boots enjoy,' said Polly. 'You two go together like mustard and cress, like Adam and – let's see, ducky, who was Adam's first and most cherished daughter?'

'God knows, but I don't,' said Rosie, which brought forth Polly's quick brittle laugh. 'And isn't it Adam and his wife Eve who go together like mustard and cress?'

'If you say so,' murmured Polly, hoping Rosie didn't mean Boots and Emily.

'Special relationships are sacred, of course,' said Rosie. And she smiled at Polly, well aware that this vivacious and endearing woman considered her own relationship with Boots to be distinctly special and closely guarded.

Mr Tooley thought about calling Boots from a public phone box to let him know Rosie's natural father had turned up out of the blue. But he decided against. After all, the bloke had departed in as civilized a way as you'd expect of a gent, accepting the advice that the best thing was to go back to being anonymous. Yes, that was the word, anonymous. Mr Tooley couldn't ever remember Rosie asking who her father was, and he didn't think she'd ever asked Boots any inquisitive questions about him. Not that Boots could have answered them. Mr Tooley knew he had told her how she came about, and he'd done that when she was of an age to understand and not to brood about it. And the fact was, Rosie never showed the slightest interest in either her natural mother or the man who had fathered her. She lived for her adoptive family, and always had from the time they took her in. Even at five, when she first came to know Boots, he was the one she saw as a coveted father figure.

No point really in phoning Boots, no point in mentioning something that might stir things up, not when the natural father had accepted the situation. Anyway, perhaps Boots and Emily would come with Rosie to his wedding with Ada in due course. He might just have a quiet word with Boots then.

'We'll have to do three or four practice runs,' said Ginger Carstairs that afternoon.

'Tell me something I don't know,' said Dusty Miller.

'We need to arrive at the station just before the train's due,' said Carstairs, 'it's not going to be too clever if we have to hang about on the platform getting noticed, and it'll make me cross if we get there too late and miss it.'

'Point is, we can't advance the time that we do the bank,' said Miller.

'No, we can't,' agreed Ginger Carstairs, 'it's got to be just before the bank shuts to avoid inconvenient interruptions. I've decided we've got to give the main road a miss, and come out on Denmark Hill by way of back streets. Too much traffic on the main road. Buses, trams, lorries, carts and God knows what else. That's what made us five minutes late on our first practice run. We'd have missed the train. We'll begin the new practice run not later than six minutes after three-thirty tomorrow, since we don't plan to hang about in the bank. I've got the new route worked out, and just to make sure how long it takes us on average, we'll do a couple of other runs before our collecting day. Who's that?'

The street door had resounded to a double knock.

'Well, a double knock's for upstairs,' said Miller. 'That's me.'

'Leave it,' said Carstairs.

'No, my landlady's in, and if I don't answer it, she will,' said Miller. 'She knows I'm up here.' Down he went and found the milkman on the doorstep.

'Caught you,' said Bill Chambers amiably. He was on his afternoon round. 'You were out Saturday, so mind if I collect the owings now?'

'How much, mate?'

'A bob, Mr Barnes,' said Bill.

'Here we are,' said Miller, who was calling himself Barnes for the time being. He paid up. Bill recorded the payment in his book.

'Any eggs?' he said.

'Do I look like a chicken?' said Miller, and closed the door. Not in the least upset, Bill returned to his float. Then something struck him.

The bloke Barnes was another customer who didn't have milk every day. Well, he wouldn't, would he, being single. So what about that comely Mrs Hyams? All she had for herself and Mr Hyams was four pints a week, which wasn't usual for a married couple. A pint a day was what most couples ordered, and more, of course, if there were kids, and there were plenty of kids in Walworth. Very prolific, many Walworth married couples were, as if a lot of kids made up for a lack of other possessions. Well, no-one could say the lively kids of Walworth were a liability. Not that they were always dear to their mums and dads. Bill had heard angry mums and bawling dads threatening to drown their offspring. Still, when they grew up and got jobs they contributed their whack to the housekeeping, which was a mellowing thing to most mums and dads. I might have had some kids myself if Dorothy hadn't taken all of ten years to hold me off. I think she was keeping me in reserve.

Anyway, on account of Mrs Hyams only using four pints of milk a week, she couldn't have any of her children living at home. Four pints, in fact, would hardly be enough for herself and Mr Hyams, and she certainly couldn't make much custard or rice puddings. Perhaps they used some condensed milk here and there. I'll have to sell her off that stuff, thought Bill, and persuade her to order extra pints of our fresh cows' milk. Not that she doesn't look a healthy woman. Never saw a healthier. Wonder if she's synagogue? Well, I don't think Hyams is a good old Anglo-Saxon monicker. Makes no difference, though, she's still the best-looker on my round.

Bill led his horse and float around a standing blue van painted with the sign 'Joseph Roberts, Family Baker', and went whistling on his way.

Miller, meanwhile, having rejoined Carstairs, suggested it hadn't been a very good idea to have left the van outside. Carstairs said it wouldn't be there above a minute more, and in any case people didn't notice bakers' vans. People were just lumps of dough who could walk and talk. All the same, said Miller, a pro wouldn't have left the van there. Carstairs gave him a stony look.

'Well, Charles?' said Cecily over the phone.

'What are you ringing about?' asked Major Armitage from his country pile.

'I'm simply curious to know if you've been making enquiries,' said Cecily.

'In short, yes.'

78

'Well, then?'

'It's a girl,' said Major Armitage.

'You have a daughter, old thing?'

'Yes, and an astonishing one. She's a student at Somerville College, Oxford.'

'Heavens,' said Cecily, 'not a Deptford cockney?'

'Far from it, I fancy,' said Major Armitage, and recounted the more relevant details of his conversation with the girl's grandfather, a Mr Tooley. Cecily ventured to say that adoption meant the claim of the natural father had no standing in law. Major Armitage said he'd contest that, for he'd signed no papers himself. Cecily suggested that before he began any legal contest, he should first find out how the girl would react.

'I mean, is she going to jump for joy at the prospect of leaving her adoptive parents for a new life with you?'

'I intend to visit the family and to meet her, and to take it from there,' said Major Armitage.

'And if the family and she herself oppose your wishes?'

'I mean to fight,' said Major Armitage. 'The adoptive parents have had their time with her. Now I need to have mine.'

'She's of a marriageable age, Charles, and you may not have her for longer than a year.'

'I don't see it like that. She's an Armitage, certainly in looks and probably in character. Frankly, I've very little idea of what her mother looked like, but I take your word for it that she was pretty. However, having seen so many snapshots of Rosie herself, I'd say she was positively an Armitage. She belongs far more to me than to her mother or her adoptive parents. I've consulted my solicitor, but he's a glum old pessimist, and thinks, in fact, that counsel will advise me I've no case.'

'You'll wait for that opinion before making any further move?' said Cecily.

'Not at all. I shall call on the adoptive parents, since I obviously need to sound them out. And candidly, I can't wait to meet my daughter.'

'Then I wish you luck, my dear,' said Cecily. 'Judging by much of what you say the grandfather told you, you may find yourself regarded as an unwanted intruder.'

'I'm prepared for initial reactions to be hostile,' said Major Armitage, 'yet I feel the girl won't be totally unresponsive. However deep her attachment is to her adoptive parents, I believe some rapport will develop between us.'

'You believe, of course, that one Armitage will recognize another,' said Cecily.

'A blood link can't be set aside, Cecily.'

'You mean she may elect to take up life as an Armitage and live under your roof because of the blood link?'

'It's a reasonable possibility,' said Major Armitage.

'Then again I wish you luck, dear man,' said Cecily.

## Chapter Five

Nick was having a meeting with Freddy, Horace and Horace's old school friend, Percy Ricketts, in Ma's parlour. Under discussion were the duties of a best man, which meant, as Nick had said, that it had got to be serious stuff. We all know, he said, that both brides aren't the kind of young ladies to put up with sloppy performances. Nick himself was Freddy's best man, and Percy was taking on the same role for Horace.

'Nothing to it,' said Percy, once he'd been put fully into the picture by Nick and Freddy, who had attended other weddings. This was Percy's first as an adult guest, and certainly as a best man.

'Just remember not to misplace the ring,' said Horace, 'and to make your speech short.'

'And clean,' said Freddy. 'There's two brides, remember, and I'm on knowledgeable terms with both, Sally bein' my sister and Cassie havin' been me best mate for years. I can inform you, Percy, any dubious stuff like did you 'ear the one about the bride that called for a policeman, and they'll both ask to 'ave you removed.'

'So might my mother,' said Horace. 'She's a Christian lady, as you all know—'

'Granted,' said Nick.

'But she's not fond of anything dubious,' said Horace.

'Fortunately, my mum can never get the drift of what's saucy about weddin' jokes,' said Freddy, 'but Cassie won't go for knickers bein' mentioned.'

'Nor Sally,' said Horace.

'Well, I'll admit I've never made a best man's speech before,' said Percy, 'but I've heard there's always some funny stories.'

'Funny's all right,' said Nick, 'but nothing you couldn't tell your grandma.'

'Well, what about this one?' said Percy. 'The bridal couple were at their honeymoon hotel, the bride Myrtle was in bed and the bridegroom Claud was in the bathroom along the corridor. He was all ready to join his blushing young bride, bein' in his pyjamas, but he was takin' his time to clean his teeth and so on. Well, he was girding himself up for his weddin' night, naturally, so he was takin' a long time. Eventually, however, he made his way back to the room, but on account of his nerves and bein' a bit dithery as well, he went into the wrong one.'

'What a chump,' said Horace.

'There was a woman in the bed,' continued Percy, 'and she sat up a bit smart when Claud entered. He saw she was about forty, so he went a bit pale and said, "Ruddy hell, Myrtle, have I been as long as that?"'

'That'll pass,' said Freddy.

'Minus ruddy hell,' said Horace.

'Yes, I like it,' said Nick, 'I'll polish it up a bit and use it.'

'You what?' said Percy.

'Yes, thanks, Percy,' said Nick.

'Hold on,' said Percy, 'it's my story.'

'Yes, and it's a good one,' said Nick, 'so I'll use

it. Luckily, I'll be making my speech first, Cassie and Freddy being the younger couple.'

'I'm bein' robbed,' said Percy, 'and I thought we were all mates.'

'Yes, but Nick's captain of the football team,' said Freddy.

'Bugger that,' said Percy, 'no-one's marrying the football team.'

'Tell you what,' said Nick, 'I'll give you a poem you can include in your own speech.'

'What poem?' asked Percy, and Nick quoted.

' "There was once a girl called Sally
Who floated up the aisle on a Saturday,
But in front of her bloke
Her elastic broke,
And down dropped her knickers, unhappily." '

'That'll do nicely,' said Freddy. 'Unless Orrice minds.'

'Here, hold on,' protested Percy, 'I thought you said knickers weren't to be mentioned?'

'Chance it,' said Freddy.

'I might if the poem was any good,' said Percy, 'but it's ruddy pathetic, and besides, it's takin' the mickey out of Sally, and Orrice as well.'

'Orrice 'asn't said so,' pointed out Freddy.

'Well, I'll say it now, that joke's out, Percy,' declared Horace.

'Here, don't look at me,' said Percy, 'it came from Nick.'

'Don't use it,' said Horace. 'If you do, Sally will break legs. Ours. She'll know it's a put-up job.'

'All right, I'll have my story back,' said Percy, 'and you can keep your poem, Nick.'

'Sorry, Percy,' said Nick.

83

'Yes, 'ard luck, mate,' said Freddy, 'good try.'

'Whose side you on?' asked Percy.

'Nick's,' said Freddy, 'he's my best man. And I daresay you can find another story.'

'Yes,' said Horace, 'how about the one where a bloke married a twin sister? On their weddin' night, when they were undressing, she said jokingly, "How d'you know I'm not my sister Shirley?" "Easy," he said, "you don't wear French knickers."'

'I like that,' said Freddy.

'Yes, you can use that, Percy,' said Nick.

'Here, what's the idea?' said Percy. 'It's knickers again, and accordin' to the way you lot are goin' on about it, Sally and Cassie won't stand for it.'

'Chance it,' said Freddy, 'it's short and sweet.'

'Well, it's better than Nick's third-rate poem,' said Percy. 'But what about your mum, Horace?'

'Good point,' said Horace, 'I almost forgot about Mum. No, she won't favour it. Use Nick's poem instead.'

'But you put a downer on it,' said Percy.

'We're stuck,' said Horace. 'At least, you are, Percy.'

'Can't we be serious?' said Percy.

'Give over,' said Freddy, 'we're all dead serious. We've got to be, like Nick said, when it's Cassie and Sally's big day. I don't want Cassie takin' me aside and kickin' me knees to bits on account of your speech bein' dubious, Percy. It'll ruin me 'oneymoon. And Orrice won't want Sally ruining his, either. So pull yerself together, chum, and cut out all this saucy stuff.'

'Yes, use your loaf, Percy,' said Nick.

'Yes, make your speech a bit decent, Percy,' said Horace. 'You were normal at school. Well, fairly.'

'Do I look as if I'm peculiar?' asked Percy.

'Not from where I'm sitting,' said Nick. His Ma put her head in at that point.

'You boys all gettin' together satisfact'ry?' she said.

'What boys?' asked Nick.

'All of you,' said Ma. 'Are you 'aving a proper talk about the weddings?'

'Serious, Mrs Harrison, serious,' said Horace.

'Tell her another,' muttered Percy.

'What was that?' asked Ma.

'Nothing much, Ma,' said Nick.

'Well, don't do a lot of nothing much,' said Ma, 'and I'll bring you all in a nice cup of tea and some 'ome-made cake in a few minutes. My, I do like to see young men preparin' serious for weddings.'

'Percy's larkin' about a bit,' said Freddy.

'Well, one or two little jokes won't hurt,' said Ma, and returned to her kitchen, where she informed the rest of her family that the young men were preparing serious for the double wedding.

'You sure, Ma?' asked fifteen-year-old Amy.

'She can't be sure if she said serious,' commented Alice.

'In my time as a young man,' said Pa, a con artiste now going straight by reason of Ma's egg saucepan always being ready to hand, 'I can't remember treating anything seriously.'

'Well, Nick's different,' said Ma.

'Some hopes,' said young Fanny.

'If that lot in trousers are in the parlour being serious,' said Alice, 'I'm a spotted duck. I'm goin' out now, to meet Johnny. He's another one.'

'What, another spotted duck?' said Amy.

'No, another clown,' said Alice.

'Why'd you go out with 'im, then?' asked young Fanny.

'I like clowns,' said Alice, departing with a smile.

Ma put the kettle on.

In the parlour, poor old Percy, a decent but slightly naive bloke, was still a bit unsure about exactly what was expected of a best man. He was, of course, up against three serious jokers. He'd just been told by Freddy that one of his duties on behalf of Horace was to inspect Sally's wedding garter before she floated up the aisle.

'You sure?' he said.

'It's tradition,' said Freddy.

'Well, I don't mind a bit of tradition,' said Percy, 'I'll have to make arrangements.'

'Good idea,' said Nick.

'Well, I'm glad we got somewhere at last,' said Percy.

Ginger Carstairs and Dusty Miller, a determined, ruthless and ambitious pair of crooks, began their new practice run from Cadiz Street, off the Walworth Road, at six minutes after three-thirty the following day, under a cloudy sky. Ginger, at the wheel of the baker's van, drove left into the Walworth Road and its busy traffic, proceeding only a short distance before turning right into John Ruskin Street. Dusty Miller pointed out that although kids weren't out of school yet, those under school age were bound to be about in the back streets. Carstairs, going at a steady speed, said street kids were being allowed for, but wouldn't hold them up as the main road traffic did. Sure enough, young boys and girls were in evidence, playing their street games, but they ran onto the pavements as the van approached.

Carstairs, keeping to the steady speed, drove on, turned left into Camberwell New Road, hit a little traffic, and then freed the van from what there was by turning right into Flodden Road. More young street kids were seen, but no traffic to speak of, and on the van went into Denmark Road. Miller said watch the kids. Carstairs said shut up, and drove to the end of Denmark Road to cross Coldharbour Lane into Cutcombe Road. No hold-ups of any real kind had been encountered so far.

'You've got it all worked out, I'll give you that much,' said Miller.

'It's necessary planning,' said Carstairs, and turned left into Bessemer Road, then right into Denmark Hill, where traffic, unburdened by any trams, was always light. 'Here we are, Denmark Hill, how about that for an easy ride?'

'Sweet,' said Miller.

The speed of the van was now about twenty-five miles an hour. Carstairs slowed at the approach to Red Post Hill, turned left into its leafy suburban atmosphere, and drove without haste all the way to North Dulwich railway station, then past it to reach a short row of lock-ups. The van turned and came to a stop outside the first one. Miller alighted, unlocked the doors, opened them, and Carstairs drove the van in

The time taken for the drive from Cadiz Street had been nine minutes, which left them seven minutes to catch the required train. They'd need a couple of minutes to do a quick change of clothes and to see the van was left out of sight in the lock-up.

'It could be tight, all the same, if we do hit a snag,' said Carstairs, 'but there's less chance of that if we keep to this route.'

'If we miss the train, the only alternative is to sit here in the van out of the way and catch the next one,' said Miller.

'Listen, cloth ears,' said Carstairs, 'I've told you, if we catch the next train we'll miss the connection for the Dover line, and the bloody ferry as well. The important thing is to get out of this area as fast as we can, and then out of the country double-quick.'

'Agreed,' said Miller.

'But we'll do two more practice runs before the day of the job,' said Carstairs.

'Several,' said Miller.

'Two,' said Carstairs. 'Any more than that, and we'll begin to be noticed.'

'I'll grant that,' said Miller.

'Hoo-bloody-ray,' said Ginger Carstairs sourly.

They returned to Walworth by bus.

'Try it on, Sammy,' said Susie that evening.

Sammy looked at the shining black top-hat she was offering. The kids, all three, were agog.

'What's that?' he asked.

'A top-hat,' said Susie.

'Nothing to do with me,' said Sammy.

'Daddy, go on, put it on,' said Bess.

'Not me,' said Sammy, 'I might get stuck with it.'

'No good arguin', Dad,' said Daniel. 'If Mum says you've got to try it on, you've got to.'

'And I've got to be firm and say no,' declared Sammy, 'and you all know me when I'm firm. No surrender, that's me.'

'Sammy, stop showing off and try this hat on,' said Susie.

'Excuse me, kids,' said Sammy, 'but I've got to wash me hands before supper. If Queen Mary phones, I'll be upstairs, but only for five minutes.' He made for the living-room door. A hand caught hold of the tail of his jacket and stopped him in his tracks.

'Try the hat on first,' said Susie.

'Told you, Dad,' said Daniel, 'told you you'd got to.'

'Well, I'll unfirm myself just for once, and just to let your mum know I'm reasonable,' said Sammy, and took the topper. He placed it on his head. It slid down and came to rest on his ears. The kids shrieked. So did Susie, come to that. 'What's happened?' asked Sammy. 'Everything's gone dark.'

'Dad's 'ead's gone and disappeared,' said Jimmy.

'And nearly all his face,' said Bess, and indulged in a surfeit of giggles.

Sammy removed the topper and looked at Susie. Susie straightened her face.

'Might I be permitted to ask where you bought this large so-called headgear, Mrs Susie Adams?' enquired Sammy.

'Oh, I didn't buy it, Sammy, I borrowed it from Mr Greenberg to see if a top-hat suited you,' said Susie.

'Well, this one doesn't,' said Sammy.

'Oh, I don't know,' said Susie, 'it did something for you, and if we stuffed it with newspaper, it could do even more.'

'Am I hearing you right, Mrs Adams?' said Sammy. 'This piece of head furniture that hides me face does something for me? Might I remind you I've been frequently complimented on the look of me kisser?'

'Who by?' asked Susie.

'I'm not saying I'm Ronald Colman, but—'

'Who by?' asked Susie.

'Well, Susie—'

'Mrs Rachel Goodman, I suppose,' said Susie.

'Daddy's got a nice face,' said Bess.

'Well, we'll see it's not covered up for the weddin', pet,' said Susie. 'We'll make sure there's enough newspaper in the topper.'

Sammy put the topper on a chair and sat on it. It cracked and crumpled beneath him. He stood up and everyone looked at the ruined headpiece.

'Crikey, you've done it now, Dad,' said Daniel.

'It's gone flat,' said Jimmy.

'Saves a lot more argument, though,' said Sammy.

Susie burst into laughter. There was only one Sammy, and the whole family knew it. But it had been fun, putting the wind up him about a top-hat.


At ten minutes to eight, Tim answered a ring of the doorbell. He recognized at once that a gent had come calling, not someone from Billingsgate.

'Hello,' he said.

'Good evening,' said Major Armitage, 'does Mr Adams live here?'

'Well, yes, he does,' said Tim, 'he's my dad.'

'Would you be kind enough to give him my card and ask if he could spare me some time?'

Tim took the card and looked at it under the hall light. It told him the caller was Major Charles Armitage of Headleigh Hall, Godalming, Surrey. Tim, curious, looked up at him.

'D'you know my dad?' he asked. 'I mean, did you meet him in the war somewhere?'

'No, I don't know him,' said Major Armitage, 'and I don't imagine I ran into him during the war. Was he an officer?'

'No, a sergeant,' said Tim.

'I see,' said Major Armitage. Sergeants came in all kinds. Tough but unimaginative, loud but competent, courageous but bullheaded, highly disciplined but wooden, brief of words but full of initiative. 'I hope he can spare me a little time.'

'Come in,' said Tim. The caller stepped into the hall, and Tim closed the door. 'I won't be a minute, I'll tell my dad,' he said, and went through to the living-room used by Boots and his family. Chinese Lady and Mr Finch had the use of another, but on most evenings gatherings were communal, as on this occasion. 'Dad, there's a gent,' said Tim, 'he wants to see you.'

'A gent?' said Boots.

'An extra posh one,' said Tim. 'Here's his card.'

Boots took it.

'Who is it?' asked Chinese Lady.

'A Major Armitage,' said Boots.

'In uniform, Tim?' asked Mr Finch, thinking that perhaps the call was to do with Boots being on the Officers' Reserve list.

'No, he's not in uniform, Grandpa,' said Tim.

'You must go and see 'im, Papa,' said Eloise.

'Well, I will, of course,' said Boots, getting up.

'Shall I come with you?' asked Rosie, who had slipped so easily into the atmosphere of home.

'If I need help,' smiled Boots, 'I'll call for all of you.' Out into the hall he went to come face to face with the visitor, a man as tall as himself, with strong handsome features, intelligent eyes and a distinguished appearance. And Major Armitage, hat in his hand, saw a man of obvious self-assurance with an expression that seemed as whimsical as it was enquiring.

'Mr Adams?'

'I'm Adams, yes,' said Boots, and shook hands. 'What can I do for you?'

'I'd be obliged if I could talk to you for five minutes or so,' said Major Armitage.

'Come into the study,' said Boots.

A study, thought Major Armitage, and the large house itself with its handsome hall. Some sergeants do rise in the world, but not many.

'Thanks, Mr Adams,' he said, and they entered Mr Finch's study, often used by Boots.

'Take a seat, Major.'

'I'm on reserve, Mr Adams.'

So am I, as a lieutenant, thought Boots, but he didn't say so. They both sat down, and he said, 'Fire away, Major Armitage.'

'Difficult,' said Major Armitage with a faint smile.

'Why?' asked Boots.

'To begin with, it concerns a certain occasion in August, 1914,' said Major Armitage.

'This can't concern me, surely,' said Boots.

'It did, subsequently, Mr Adams,' said Major Armitage, and recounted details of his brief time with a girl called Milly Tooley and its consequences. The recounting had the effect of making Boots tighten his jaw. So here he was at last, the man who had fathered Rosie, the man he had often suspected to be very different from her graceless mother. Rosie had a natural air of definite grace, and all the charm and composure of the well-born. She was undoubtedly her father's daughter and had never related to her mother in any way. Boots listened in silence to further details, those concerning a visit to Rosie's grandfather, Mr Tooley of Deptford, which were followed by Major Armitage saying, 'You'll understand, Mr Adams, that having discovered I had a daughter, and that you and your wife had adopted her, my immediate wish was to meet you and have you introduce her to me.'

'Yes, that's understandable,' said Boots.

'Is it true she's an undergraduate at Somerville, Mr Adams?'

'Yes, it's true,' said Boots.

'Remarkable,' said Major Armitage.

'Why remarkable?' asked Boots, thinking deeply.

'The circumstances of her birth.'

'And the background of her mother? But I daresay not all mothers of undergraduates come out of a top drawer.'

'And I daresay you're right, Mr Adams. Your son informed me you served in the war. What regiment, may I ask?'

'7th West Kents,' said Boots.

'Present at the first battle of the Somme,' said Major Armitage, 'and distinguished itself in the fierce fight for Trones Wood. May I meet my daughter?'

'And after you've met her?' enquired Boots.

'I'll be frank, Mr Adams. My hope is that she'll accept a new life with my wife and me.' Mrs Armitage, in an unusually sober moment, had promised to quarrel with her bottles of brandy if Rosie came to live with them. Major Armitage did not know if she'd keep that promise, but yes or no, it would make no difference to his own feelings concerning Rosie. 'Can you understand that too?'

'Easily,' said Boots, 'and I suppose you'll understand the idea won't have this family's blessing.'

'I wouldn't suppose otherwise, Mr Adams, but I hope you'll allow me to put the proposition to my daughter.'

Damn the man and his constant references to his daughter, thought Boots. He did not dislike him, he was civilized, and although distinctively military in his looks and bearing, there was no suggestion of arrogance or upper-class superiority. There was, however, the quiet confidence of a man who felt the blood relationship would win the day. He had nothing with which to reproach himself, for he simply hadn't known about Rosie until now. And the discovery had made him act immediately.

How would Rosie herself react when introduced to her natural father? What kind of feelings would she have for him? She had never disguised her feelings for her adoptive family, she had always shown uninhibited affection. She cared for all of them. But her natural father, what would meeting him do to her?

'You're entitled to meet her, Major Armitage, and as for talking to her in the way you want to, I wouldn't dream of trying to prevent you.'

'Thank you, Mr Adams.' Major Armitage smiled. 'You're not quite my idea of—' He checked himself.

'Of a sergeant?' said Boots. 'Well, I began life very plainly, but grammar school and the war changed me a little. Now excuse me a moment while I fetch Rosie.'

'Mr Adams, as I'm happy to wait, may I suggest you first tell her who I am and why I'm here.'

'Well, I wouldn't want her to be unprepared,' said Boots, and left the study, closing the door behind him. Tim appeared.

'You'll do, Tim. Would you tell Rosie to come and see me?'

'You're asking just in time, Dad,' said Tim. 'Rosie's been sitting on the edge of her chair for ages.'

'Why?' asked Boots, serious of expression for once. Rarely did shocks or surprises do a destructive job on his facade of good-humoured self-assurance, but the arrival of Rosie's natural father had created a crack or two. 'Why, Tim?'

'Why?' said Tim. 'But you know what Rosie is, Dad. If you've got problems, they're hers as much as yours.'

'Who said I've got problems?' asked Boots.

'Rosie said she's got a feeling you have. Of course, girls are like that, they've got feelings I've never heard of. I'll tell her you want to see her.'

Rosie came out into the hall a few moments later. Boots was sitting on the stairs.

'Look here, old thing, why are you sitting there, and what's happening?' she asked.

'Well might you ask,' said Boots. 'Come and join me for a minute or so.' Rosie, seating herself next to him, saw a strangely rueful look on his face. It immediately worried her. Deeply attached to her adoptive father, and quite sure no-one would ever mean as much to her as he did, she had come to know him as well as she knew herself. She knew that something was disturbing him as much as his expression was disturbing her. Not that he looked stricken or shocked, just strangely rueful, but that was enough for her.

'Daddy?' These days, because she felt so adult, so grown up, and so close to him, she always wanted to call him Boots, but the old familial word slipped out

95

on a warm and vibrant note. 'Tell me, what happened between you and your visitor?'

He gave her a smile. That had its rueful edge too.

'Rosie, brace yourself for a dramatic surprise,' he said.

'Oh, as long as it's dramatic and not dreadful, I'm sure I'll survive,' she said, and slipped her arm through his.

'Rosie,' he said gently, 'the visitor, Major Armitage, is your natural father.'

'Oh, my God,' said Rosie, stiffening.

'Too much for you all at once, poppet?' said Boots.

It took her a little while to answer. Then she said, 'Give me another moment to recover.'

'It's knocked you for six?' said Boots. 'Yes, I daresay it has, Rosie, but let me point out the staggering coincidence. Only a short time ago I discovered a daughter I fathered during the war, and a few days ago Major Armitage made the same discovery about you. Life, Rosie, always has something up its sleeve just in case we take the status quo too much for granted.'

Rosie took a deep breath and then said quite calmly, 'How does Major Armitage know he fathered me?'

Boots told her the facts of the matter, the facts as detailed by Major Armitage, and finished by saying, 'I don't think we can dispute it, Rosie love.'

'So, Grandfather Tooley confirmed it?' said Rosie.

'It seems he confirmed your mother had a child, and it seems he gave Major Armitage your name and address. He felt, I suppose, that Major Armitage was entitled to know something about you.'

'I'm surprised he didn't phone us,' said Rosie.

'Yes, I'd have expected him to,' said Boots, 'but you're taking it all very calmly, Rosie.'

'I'm a little dizzy, but otherwise recovered, thank you, ducky,' said Rosie. 'Is Major Armitage still here?'

'Yes, in the study, waiting patiently to meet you.'

'Then I must let him, of course,' said Rosie. 'But first, you still care for me as your own, don't you?'

'That's something you never need to ask,' said Boots. He could never help his feelings, nor forget the long-ago effect she had had on him when, his blindness cured, he saw for the first time the little girl who had sat on his doorstep with him and been such a shyly eager companion to him during the last months of his disability. Rosie had an unbreakable hold on his affections. 'But Major Armitage is your natural father.'

'Daddy old love, no-one will ever take your place with me, don't you know that?' said Rosie. 'No-one would ever mean the same to me as you do. Tell me, what is Major Armitage like, and what's your opinion of him?'

'He's a very civilized man, Rosie, and I found nothing to dislike about him.'

'Spoken like a diplomat,' said Rosie. 'Or a gent, shall we say?' she added, smiling. 'What matters most is the simple fact that I was born, that I'm glad I was, and that I came to belong to you and your family. That's all that's important, isn't it? You understand, don't you, what all these years have meant to me?'

'They've meant a great deal, Rosie, to all of us.'

'Well, now I'll go and meet Major Armitage, this civilized man with nothing to dislike about him.'

'I'll wait out here,' said Boots.

'You won't,' said Rosie, 'you'll come with me. We must stand together. We always have, and we always will. So come on.'

They walked to the study and entered. Major Armitage might have been pacing about, but wasn't. He was still seated, but came to his feet at once. He brushed his moustache, his first indication that he wasn't as calm as he had appeared to be, and then he and Rosie were face to face. Momentarily, he was mesmerized. Rosie was hardly less than a striking young woman in a royal blue dress of simple cut. Frills and flounces had no appeal for her. She dressed in a way that was faultless. He noted that, and the fact that she was quite lovely. God, yes, she was like his sister Beatrice, the beauty of the family.

Rosie saw a man of handsome and distinguished appearance, with a thick moustache and a military air. She judged him to be over forty, some years older than Boots, who was thirty-eight. She felt no great surge of emotion. He had fathered her, yes, but it was Boots who had given her a home, a family and years of treasured happiness.

'Major Armitage,' said Boots, 'this is Rosie, the young lady you wish to meet.'

'Thank you, Mr Adams, I'm delighted to have the opportunity to say hello to her,' said Major Armitage, thinking her superb, and thinking too that she had the same kind of self-assurance as her adoptive father, a man who might have been awkward or hostile, but had been neither. 'Shall we shake hands, Rosie?'

'Yes, I think we should,' said Rosie, entirely composed, and he took her hand and lightly pressed it. 'So you are the gentleman in question,' she said, smiling.

'Well, I'm the man who was deprived by circumstances of knowing you existed,' said Major Armitage.

'Oh, it's happened to other men,' said Rosie, thinking of Boots and his brief time with a young French war widow.

'I don't, of course, excuse myself for my conduct,' said Major Armitage.

'You mean for making love to my mother?' said Rosie, and it occurred to Boots then that it had been many years since she had mentioned her mother. She had always seemed to regard her as non-existent.

'Yes, I don't excuse myself for that, or for my irresponsibility,' said Major Armitage, 'but you must believe me when I tell you I had no idea of the consequences. I regret very much that I've not known about you until now.'

'Please don't reproach yourself, Major Armitage,' said Rosie, 'I've no regrets myself, not a single one, about how life developed for me. I've been remarkably happy.'

'And you've also done remarkably well, Rosie, to have arrived at university,' said Major Armitage. 'That gives me great pleasure. You're very much like my sister Beatrice in looks, do you know that?'

'How could I know?' said Rosie. 'I've never met her.'

'I should like you to, and I should like to get to know you. Would you care to spend a week at my home while you're on Easter vacation?'

'How kind,' said Rosie, 'but all my time is taken up with my family.'

'Your adoptive family,' said Major Armitage.

'My family,' said Rosie.

'Well, do think about sparing some time for me,' he said. 'You're an Armitage, you know.'

Rosie's smile was polite.

'I'm an Adams,' she said.

'By adoption, yes, but—'

'By feelings,' said Rosie.

'But not by blood, Rosie.' Major Armitage was still as civilized as a man could be under the circumstances.

'Is one more conscious of blood than feelings?' asked Boots.

'The blood line can't be set aside, Mr Adams.'

'Neither can feelings,' said Rosie, 'nor the sense of knowing where one belongs. I was born to belong to the Adams family, and to me nothing could have been more natural.'

'Well, at least give me the chance to get to know you a little better than I do now,' said Major Armitage. 'Come down to Godalming, to my home, even if only for a day to begin with.'

'But what purpose would it serve for you to get to know me a little better?' asked Rosie, feeling that Boots was right, that there was nothing one could dislike about this man.

'I have a hope that you'll come to accept you have two families,' said Major Armitage, 'your Adams family and mine.'

'Is that feasible?' asked Boots.

'Do you have sons and daughters of your own, Mr Adams?'

'I've a son and another daughter,' said Boots.

'Another daughter?' said Major Armitage, with a slight lift of an eyebrow.

'Yes, I've Eloise as well as Rosie,' said Boots.

Major Armitage smiled.

'Yes, I see how you feel,' he said. 'However, I've no children myself, and you'll understand how much I'd like to have Rosie under my roof for some of the time during her vacations. Can you spare me a day, Rosie, to begin with? I'll collect you and also drive you back.'

'What is your home like?' asked Rosie.

'A large house and a large estate near Godalming.'

'Estate?' said Rosie. 'My word, that does sound grand. Is there a farm?'

'Indeed there is.'

'Cows, chickens, horses and so on?' smiled Rosie.

'Yes.'

'Well, that's famous,' said Rosie, 'so yes, I'll come for a day, as long as I'm allowed to bring my brother and sister with me.'

'Your brother and sister, yes, I see,' said Major Armitage. 'It's a condition that they come with you?'

'It's an acceptable one, isn't it?' said Rosie, and he thought he could not have asked for any child of his to be more impressive of manner, speech and composure.

'Very well,' he said. 'Mr Adams has my card. Perhaps you'll phone me to let me know which day suits you.'

'Oh, I'll give you reasonable notice,' said Rosie, then spoke to Boots. 'Shall we offer Major Armitage some refreshments now?'

'Thank you, but I won't stay longer,' said Major Armitage, 'I've a drive to Godalming in front of me. Let me just say again how delighted I am to have met you, Rosie. Mr Adams?' He offered his hand. Boots shook it. 'You've been very civilized.'

Rosie smiled at that, and let Major Armitage shake

her own hand, his grip warm and friendly. He made
no attempt to kiss her. He said goodbye, and Rosie
and Boots both saw him to the front door. Outside in
the darkness was a parked car. He put himself into it,
switched on the lights, started the engine and drove
away.

Rosie closed the door.

# Chapter Six

'Well?' said Rosie.

'All very civilized, would you say?' said Boots with a smile.

'Well, that seems to be the word of the moment, doesn't it?' said Rosie.

'How d'you feel now?' asked Boots.

'Like a whisky and soda?' said Rosie.

'Pardon?' said Boots.

'May I?' asked Rosie.

'Has Somerville taught you to drink?'

'Not yet,' said Rosie, 'you can start me off.'

'With a whisky and soda?' said Boots.

'Good idea, sweetie,' said Rosie. 'I know your company commander, Major Harris, started you off on whisky when you were nineteen and in the trenches. You've said so. I'm nineteen myself, nearly twenty. I promise not to get addicted, I'd simply like a pick-up after all that civilized stuff. Come on, old sport, there's some in the study – Grandpa's – and we know he won't mind.'

Boots led the way back to the study, saying, 'I'm not sure you'll like it.'

'Oh, well, I'll hold my nose while I drink it,' said Rosie. She watched while he took a bottle of whisky and two glasses from the study cabinet, then a soda syphon. He seemed quiet and introspective. He chose to have neat whisky himself, but added a good splash of soda to hers. He handed her the glass. 'Bless you, old sport,' she said, and took her first ever mouthful of whisky and soda. Her nose wrinkled. 'Blimey,' she said, taking off her Uncle Tommy, 'what's it made of, any old iron?'

Boots laughed, and that made her smile.

'Told you,' he said.

'Oh, I'll fight it to a finish,' she said, and drank more. 'If it's good for you, and it always is, it must be good for me. Listen, Boots lovey—'

'Pardon?' said Boots again.

'Oh, sorry about the familiarity, it must be the whisky,' said Rosie. 'No, but listen, you aren't worried, are you?'

'About what might develop?'

'Nothing will,' said Rosie. 'I've met him, I don't dislike him, and I'll spend a day with him, in company with Tim and Eloise when the weather's warmer. Then that will be that.'

'I don't think it will stop there,' said Boots, 'I don't think he'll allow it to. He'll want you under his roof part of the time. He said so.'

'Well, dear old thing, he can say it again a dozen times, but it won't happen.'

'Sometimes,' said Boots, 'you sound like Polly.'

'Oh, something of Polly rubs off on all of us, doesn't it?' said Rosie.

'Finish your drink,' said Boots. 'We need to speak to the rest of the family.'

Rosie drank the rest of her whisky and soda without flinching. It picked her up, but she said, 'I think that's my first and last.'

'It is as far as I'm concerned,' said Boots.

'Nana's going to have a fit about Major Armitage,'

said Rosie. 'So are my uncles and my Aunt Lizzy.'

'I've had my own fit,' said Boots, and Rosie laughed again, which made him think that the arrival in her life of her natural father hadn't disturbed her to any great extent. She'd gone through her meeting with him as easily and unaffectedly as if he'd merely been a new neighbour. Had she been hiding her real feelings? Was it due to her real feelings that she'd promised to spend a day with him? Reading his thoughts, Rosie slipped her arm through his to let him know she was an Adams until the cows came home. Then they went off to tell the rest of the family what the visit of Major Charles Armitage had meant.

The news that Rosie's natural father had appeared and declared himself took quite a time to recount because of constant interruptions born of astonishment and disbelief. In the end, Chinese Lady of all people was left dumbstruck. Mr Finch took the revelation philosophically. Tim was gaping. Emily was hardly happy. Eloise, however, was fascinated.

'Rosie, 'ow wonderful, isn't it? Your own Papa, like I now 'ave.'

'Eloise,' said Rosie, the calmest person present, 'your own Papa is also mine.'

'You bet,' said Tim, 'I'm against that Army gent butting in.'

'I can't believe it,' breathed Emily, 'I just can't believe it's happened, not after Boots findin' out about Eloise.'

'Finding out about Eloise was the happiest thing,' said Rosie.

'For me, yes,' said Eloise.

'For all of us,' said Rosie.

'That is so nice to say so, Rosie,' said Eloise. 'But you are not 'appy about this gentleman finding you?'

'In your case, Eloise,' said Rosie, 'I think you needed to be found. I didn't.'

'I'm blessed if I know what to say,' said Emily.

'Oh, you'll think of something, Mum,' said Tim.

'I'll think of something myself when I get my breath back,' said Chinese Lady, sitting as straight and upright as befitted any matriarch of extreme self-respect, even if she was temporarily dumbstruck.

'Take your time, old lady,' said Boots.

'I've never been more flabbergasted,' said Chinese Lady, 'first Eloise and now Rosie.'

'Yes, it's like unexpected dads popping up all over the place,' said Tim.

'Tim, it's not funny,' said Emily.

'Well, Rosie's not crying,' said Tim, 'and nor is Eloise.'

'That boy's gettin' flippant,' said Chinese Lady, 'and I know where he gets it from. Rosie, you sure all this wasn't upsettin' for you?'

'A surprise, Nana, not an upset,' smiled Rosie.

'Life has a multitude of messenger boys,' said Mr Finch, 'messenger boys who lie in wait to thrust telegrams at us, telegrams either welcome or unwelcome.'

'Have you got anything to say, Boots?' asked Chinese Lady.

'Beware of messenger boys bearing unwelcome telegrams,' said Boots.

'I don't know I can make sense of that,' said Chinese Lady, 'nor why this has anything to do with telegrams. Rosie didn't get one. I hope you've let her know you're not goin' to allow Major Armitage to interfere in her life.'

'We're standing shoulder to shoulder,' said Rosie. 'The only thing that's going to happen is a visit to Major Armitage's home. I'd like Eloise and Tim to come with me, and it'll be one day during Tim's Easter holiday.'

'Rosie, you're goin' to spend a day with Major Armitage?' said Emily.

'He's really quite nice, and that was all he asked of me, to visit his home for a day,' said Rosie.

'Oh, I will come, Rosie, and Tim, yes, won't you, Tim?' said Eloise.

'If Rosie would like me to,' said Tim.

'Were we invited, Boots, you and me?' asked Emily.

'The point of the exercise, Em, is for Major Armitage to get to know Rosie a little better,' said Boots.

'Why?' asked Emily, who felt, unhappily, that Rosie's ties with her adoptive family were being threatened.

'Good question,' said Boots.

'No-one needs to worry,' said Rosie.

'I might not be able to help worryin',' said Emily.

'It's odd he didn't ask to meet Em'ly while he was here,' said Chinese Lady. 'If I'd been Rosie's father, I'd of wanted to meet whoever had been a mother to her all these years.'

'I think,' said Boots, 'he was so taken with Rosie and her intellectual look—'

'My what?' said Rosie.

'Intellectual look,' said Boots.

'I never heard such unsensible talk,' said Chinese Lady, 'Rosie's got lovely looks.'

'Yes, she is beautiful, isn't she?' said Eloise, utterly intrigued by everything.

'We're a privileged circle in the looks of our ladies,' said Mr Finch, who thought the undercurrent of agitation in Emily and Chinese Lady natural if unnecessary. He thought, in fact, that Rosie would deal calmly with any problems.

'If I could finish,' said Boots, 'I think Major Armitage was so impressed by finding Rosie a young lady brilliant enough to be at university, that something like asking to meet Emily never entered his mind.'

'Well, it should of,' said Chinese Lady.

'An oversight, I daresay,' said Mr Finch.

'Well, no oversight is goin' to come between this fam'ly and Rosie,' declared Emily.

'Bless you, Mum,' said Rosie, 'and trust me to make sure it doesn't.'

'Lord above,' said Chinese Lady, 'I can't believe what's come about after all these years. Edwin, I think I'd like a little drop of port.'

'And I'll have a whisky,' smiled Mr Finch. 'Join me, Boots?'

'A finger,' said Boots.

'Perhaps Rosie would like something herself, something a little stronger than usual,' said Mr Finch.

'No, I don't think so, Grandpa,' said Rosie, and glanced at Boots. He winked.

'Edwin, did I hear you suggestin' someone should pour strong drink into Rosie?' asked Chinese Lady.

'Someone can .pour some into me,' said Emily, 'I feel I've been hit over the head.'

'Em'ly,' said Chinese Lady, 'I hope some of us can stand up to shocks without takin' to strong drink.'

'No, all right, Mum,' said Emily, 'I'll just make do with a little brandy.'

'I'll have a beer,' said Tim.

'Not at your age,' said Chinese Lady.

'Can you make do with ginger beer, Tim?' asked Boots.

'I think I'll have to,' said Tim.

'What would you like, Eloise?' asked Emily.

'Oh, I will help Papa pour the drinks and then choose what I would like, if you please,' said Eloise, and went to the sideboard with Boots and Mr Finch. She put herself between them. She likes men, thought Rosie.

'Rosie?' enquired Mr Finch.

'Oh, some tonic with a little vermouth, Grandpa, thanks,' said Rosie.

Over the drinks, the family returned to the discussion concerning what Chinese Lady called a chronic shock. Mr Finch eventually suggested they leave Rosie to look after all developments.

'Good idea,' said Tim, 'Rosie's got sense.'

'Mind you,' said Chinese Lady, 'I suppose Lizzy and Tommy and Sammy and the others will have to be told. I don't know what Lizzy will say, when it's come so quickly on top of Boots findin' out about Eloise.'

'Oh, I think they'll all survive, Nana,' said Rosie.

'Yes, none of us have dropped dead,' said Tim.

'Em'ly, stop that boy bein' flippant,' said Chinese Lady.

'But I wasn't being flippant,' said Tim. 'I mean, we're all still alive.'

Chinese Lady showed a very faint smile.

'An extra pint, milkman, if you'd be so obligin',' said Mrs Herbert of King and Queen Street. It was Saturday, and Bill Chambers was on his afternoon round, which included persuading his customers to settle their bills for the week.

'Extra pint? Pleasure, missus,' said Bill, which it was. He augmented his small wage with commission on every pint sold. He fetched a bottle from his float. Mrs Herbert fished about in her purse for the required amount of money to cover her owings. 'You're a valuable customer with all the extras you have,' said Bill. 'You and your family like milk puddings, do they?'

'You can say that again,' said Mrs Herbert, taking the bottle and handing over coins. 'It's me kids, and me old man as well. Next thing you know, they'll all turn into milk puddings themselves.'

'Some customers don't have as much milk as I'd like,' said Bill. 'Your neighbour, Mrs Hyams, for instance.'

'Well, she's a nice woman and only orders what she needs, I suppose,' said Mrs Herbert. 'Bein' a widow and out at work, she wouldn't want a lot.'

'A widow, is she?' said Bill. 'Well, as I'm fairly new on this round, I don't know everything about every customer.'

'Good thing too,' said Mrs Herbert, smiling, 'we don't want our milkman knowin' everything, do we?'

'See your point, Mrs Herbert,' said Bill. 'So long now.' On he went, cajoling his horse to follow, and he knocked on Lilian's door. Not long home from her morning's work, she answered it. 'Well, good afternoon to you, missus,' said Bill, 'nice weather we're havin'.'

'Are we?' said Lilian, fulsome figure nicely wrapped up in light blue blouse and a navy blue skirt. 'It's been raining, hasn't it?'

'Not much,' said Bill. 'Could I have the pleasure of extracting one-and-fourpence from your handsome self?'

He's got saucy eyes, this one, thought Lilian, plus a turn of speech that could flatter some women.

'Any eggs?' she said.

'Well, blow me,' said Bill, 'you're askin'?'

'You're usually offering,' said Lilian.

'Sell you a dozen, if you like, Mrs Hyams.'

'What a kind man,' said Lilian, 'but could you make it half a dozen?'

'I could and I will, and won't charge you any more than a bob,' said Bill.

'What's your normal charge, then?' asked Lilian.

'One and tenpence for a dozen, a bob for half a dozen and not a penny more. That's a promise. By the way, seeing you're a widow woman, might I have the pleasure of callin' for you tomorrow afternoon and doing a saunter round Regent's Park with you?'

'Might you what?' asked Lilian.

'Thought I'd ask, y'know,' said Bill.

Someone coming from the direction of the market thought it appropriate to stop then. It was none other than kind Mr Morrison.

'Good afternoon to you, Mrs Hyams,' he said.

'Out of your shop again, Mr Morrison?' said Lilian.

'It's in the hands of the lad for five minutes,' said Mr Morrison. 'Well, didn't I tell myself to come along and let you know I'll knock on your door tomorrow to make up for the disappointment last week? I should let a disappointment spoil things? No, no. I—'

'Well, never mind, Mr Morrison, it's very thoughtful of you, my life, yes,' said Lilian, 'but I shall be at

Regent's Park with my gentleman friend tomorrow.'

'I am hearing this, Mrs Hyams my dear?' said Mr Morrison.

'Yes, and I won't keep you,' said Lilian, 'especially as I'm busy trying to get my milkman to sell me some eggs. Goodbye, Mr Morrison.'

Mr Morrison blinked, sighed in defeat and took his portly self back to the market and his shop.

'Mrs Hyams, the gentleman friend you mentioned sounded like me,' said Bill.

'What makes you think that?' asked Lilian.

'You mentioned Regent's Park as well,' said Bill.

'Oh, it was all said to discourage Mr Morrison from calling,' smiled Lilian. 'He's a kind enough bloke, so I didn't have the heart to simply tell him to push off.'

'All right, I won't say a word,' promised Bill. 'I'll just pick you up tomorrow about half-two.'

'You'll what?' said Lilian.

'Trust me,' said Bill, 'I know the gent's shop, but I'll pass it by, I won't blow the gaff. I don't like embarrassin' a lady.'

Lilian laughed.

'My life, I should be blackmailed on my doorstep?' she said.

'I'll get your eggs,' said Bill. 'My word, you're a handsome woman, Mrs Hyams.'

Tommy Adams, arriving home from his half-day stint as manager of Adams Fashions' Shoreditch factory, was greeted in the hall by his wife Vi.

'Tommy, have you heard about Rosie and an Army man who says he's her father?' she asked.

'Come again?' said Tommy.

'Yes, Em'ly's been on the phone,' said Vi, and Tommy listened as she gave him the details.

'Don't like the sound of it,' said Tommy.

'Em'ly said that Rosie says it's not goin' to make any difference.'

'But she's goin' to spend a day with him, you said. Listen, Vi, if he's an Army major and went out of his way to call on Boots, it wasn't just to meet Rosie. If it had been, he wouldn't 'ave bothered, he'd 'ave let sleepin' dogs lie. Stands to reason. No, you mark my words, Vi, after findin' out about Rosie from Mr Tooley, I'll lay fifty to one this major decided to go to work on her with the idea of gettin' her to part company with Boots and Em'ly.'

'Don't be silly, Tommy, Rosie adores Boots and Em'ly. She'd never leave them. Well, not unless she got married.'

'Rosie's not twenty-one yet, and there's no bloke in her life,' said Tommy darkly.

'Oh, lor',' said Vi.

'We're not partin' with Rosie,' said Tommy, 'not after all she's been to the fam'ly.'

'Still, we can't interfere,' said Vi.

'I'm goin' to fall ill if any more things like this keep happening,' said Lizzy Somers to her husband Ned.

'We'll all fall ill if Major Armitage manages to establish a claim on Rosie,' said Ned.

'What d'you mean?' demanded Lizzy. 'What claim could he have when Boots and Em'ly adopted her official?'

'He'll look for one if he wants to make her part of his own family,' said Ned.

113

'Boots and Em'ly will fight that till they drop,' said Lizzy. 'Honestly, though, wouldn't you think from the way Boots behaved with Eloise's mother, he could have found time to go to bed with the woman Milly Tooley as well?'

'It's not like you, Eliza, to be in favour of improper stuff,' said Ned.

'I'm not,' said Lizzy, 'I'm just saying that if Boots had had an affair with Milly Tooley as well, then both Eloise and Rosie could've become his natural daughters. It's just like him to have been airy-fairy and casual.'

'Can you support that piece of logic?' asked Ned. 'It all sounds a bit weird and wonderful to me. It seems you're saying that Boots, before doing his wartime bit with his French bird—'

'Don't be vulgar,' said Lizzy.

'Eliza, you're saying Boots should have asked his company commander if he could have time off to put a bun in Milly Tooley's oven.'

'Ned Somers, don't be so common,' said Lizzy.

'Considering Boots hadn't any idea at the time of who Milly Tooley was, you're flying a bit high, aren't you, Eliza?'

'Well, you know what I mean,' said Lizzy. 'And Rosie would've loved to have been Boots's natural daughter.'

'Perhaps,' said Ned. 'But I've always thought she's enjoyed a special kind of happiness in knowing Boots and Emily wanted her and couldn't wait to make her their own. I think however Major Armitage might go about establishing a claim and a father's relationship with Rosie, he'll never get the affection from her that she gives to Emily and Boots. In fact, if he makes things difficult for them, Rosie will quite likely blow his house up and him with it.'

'Oh, Lord, she wouldn't do anything like that, would she?' breathed Lizzy.

'Well, you know what I mean,' said Ned, smiling.

'It's a peculiar thing,' said Sammy, frowning, 'but me whole life has been one fight after another. I'm still fightin' to wear the trousers in this fam'ly, Susie, as a self-respectin' husband and father should, and where've I got with that?'

'Nowhere,' said Susie, in private conversation with him.

'It's not for want of tryin',' said Sammy.

'I never knew anyone more tryin', Sammy,' said Susie.

'I'm serious,' said Sammy.

'So am I,' said Susie.

'I'm dead serious about not likin' this bloke callin' himself Rosie's father.'

'It seems he is her father,' said Susie.

'That means another fight,' said Sammy.

'Not yours,' said Susie.

'It's everybody's,' said Sammy. 'As a start, how much d'you think Armitage would take for disappearin' into the fog again?'

'I don't think that will work, Sammy, I think he's a landowner or something like that, isn't he?'

'You know, Susie,' mused Sammy, 'it often occurred to me Rosie didn't come from ordin'ry stock, if you leave out that mother of hers.'

'I don't know if her mother was ordinary, Sammy, but from all I've heard about her, I'm sure her first love was for herself.'

'There'll have to be a fam'ly conference,' said Sammy.

'No, there won't, not this time,' said Susie.

'There's always—'

'Not this time, Sammy.'

'Susie, did your parents ever teach you not to interrupt your better half?'

'No, Mum never mentioned it, nor Dad,' said Susie.

'Disgraceful,' said Sammy. Susie smiled. He gave her a frowning look, and made a subconscious note of the fact that she and Rosie both had blue eyes like Wedgwood saucers. 'Now look, Susie—'

'No fam'ly conference, Sammy. I've spoken to Lizzy and Vi, and we've all agreed not to interfere.'

'Interfere? Interfere?' Sammy went slightly hoarse with shock. 'Listen, Susie, when there's a cry for help from any Adams—'

'There's no cry for help, Sammy love, not from Rosie or Boots or Em'ly, and your mum hasn't asked any of us to come round, either. It was different with Eloise, when your mum wanted to make sure we all accepted her. This time we can mind our own business, and let Boots and Em'ly and Rosie sort out any problems.'

'Susie, I've got an uncomfortable feeling you're beginning to talk like the Prime Minister,' said Sammy.

'Oh, d'you really think so, Sammy love?' said Susie. 'Aren't you sweet?'

'Susie, you're not the Prime Minister, and it's me you're talkin' to,' said Sammy. 'I'm statin' it's my firm intention to rally round Rosie and make sure this so-called dad of hers doesn't drag her off to his castle or whatever.'

'Rosie's nearly twenty,' said Susie, 'and won't be dragged off anywhere by anybody,' said Susie. 'Still, to please you, Sammy, we'll all rally round.'

'Well, bless you, Susie.'

'As soon as Rosie asks us to,' said Susie.

'Sometimes, Susie, as I've mentioned before, I get a feeling you don't always listen to me,' said Sammy.

'I always listen to you,' said Susie, 'I like listening to you. You're my lover. I'm carrying more proof of it.'

Sammy grinned.

'Well, all I can say, Susie, is that if there'd been two like you, I'd have married both,' he said.

'Oh, I'd have drowned the other one,' said Susie, 'and you can believe that.'

Rosie and Tim, meeting Annabelle by arrangement, travelled on a bus with her to Brockwell Park to watch Browning Street Rovers playing another of their vigorous and highly diverting football matches. Not until they were off the bus and walking through the park gates did Annabelle speak about Major Armitage, when she said she simply couldn't believe how he'd arrived out of nowhere. Rosie said she hadn't been able to believe it herself at first. Annabelle pointed out what other members of the family had, that what was most unbelievable was the coincidence of Boots and Major Armitage both finding out they were unknown fathers.

Tim cut in to say it was a coincidence that nearly knocked him out. Rosie said they weren't unknown fathers now, but that Major Armitage wasn't necessary to the family as Eloise was. So Annabelle asked why Rosie was going to spend a day with the major. To impress on him that he wasn't necessary to her, said Rosie.

'But couldn't you have told him that when he was with you and Uncle Boots?' asked Annabelle.

'I could have,' said Rosie, 'but he'd have thought that very unfair, my making that kind of decision when we'd only just met. So when I do see him again, I'll be able to tell him I've had time to think and that we can only be pen-friends.'

'Pen-friends?' said the astonished Annabelle, a glowing brunette in a cherry-red coat and a little round black fur hat. 'Did you actually say pen-friends, Rosie?'

'Yes, I'll write him the occasional letter and send a card each Christmas,' said Rosie.

'I hope I'll be present when you tell him he's only going to be a pen-friend,' said Tim.

'Well, something like that, Tim, but you won't be there, you'll be somewhere else with Eloise,' said Rosie. 'You're both coming with me for the day to let him see we're all part of a happy family, but I'll spend a few minutes alone with him.'

Annabelle smiled. Although pen-friends sounded absurd, she knew it meant that Rosie, so attached to her adoptive family, was not going to take up a relationship with her natural father that would affect her relationship with Uncle Boots and Aunt Emily.

'What's Major Armitage really like?' asked Annabelle, the football pitch in sight.

'Quite distinguished, and quite the gentleman,' said Rosie.

'How does he compare with Uncle Boots?' asked Annabelle.

'Oh, very favourably,' said Rosie.

'If that's bad news for Uncle Boots, I don't think much of it,' said Annabelle.

'I only mean they're both very civilized,' said Rosie.

'Anyway, Rosie's against anything that's bad news for Dad,' said Tim.

'Well, bless her,' said Annabelle, 'so am I.'

'Bless us all,' said Tim.

They arrived on the touchline, where they were greeted with exuberance by Dumpling, Cassie and all the other girl supporters, although Dumpling complained that because of her condition she was never going to get a game with the Rovers this season. It wasn't, she said, as if she was in agreement with her condition, it had sort of come about when she had her eyes shut.

Girl supporters shrieked.

The teams ran onto the field.

At this moment, Major Armitage was in conference again with his solicitor, who was still discouragingly negative. Counsel had suggested an equable arrangement could only come about through the attitude of the adoptive parents and the young lady herself. Well, damn it, Major Armitage said, as far as I could judge her attitude is all in favour of the Adams family. Counsel informs us, said Mr Harvey Arnold, the solicitor, that the most you can hope for is confirmation by the natural mother that you're the father, this to be further confirmed by a paternity test. But he's adamant that you've no hope of setting the adoption aside, no hope at all, and we're in debt to him for this opinion. You mean *I* am, said Major Armitage. However, he added, I'll see what comes of my next meeting with my daughter.

## Chapter Seven

Sammy arrived on the doorstep of the house in Red Post Hill on Sunday morning. Rosie, opening the door, smiled at him.

'Hello, Uncle Sammy.'

'Hello yourself, Rosie. I thought I'd drop in as I was passin'.'

'Passing to where?' asked Rosie.

'Pardon?' said Sammy.

'I mean, on a Sunday morning, where can you pass to except to church, and it's not time yet,' said Rosie.

'Blow me,' said Sammy, 'it was only yesterday that your Aunt Susie was talkin' to me like the Prime Minister, and now you're doing it. What's happening to Adams females?'

'Uncle Sammy, if you've dropped in to talk to me or to Daddy, come this way.' Rosie, elegant in a Sunday dress of turquoise-green, took him into the sitting-room on the ground floor. 'Well, Uncle Sammy?'

'Well, Rosie, the fact is there's a bit of a fam'ly crisis, I suppose,' said Sammy.

'Is there?' asked Rosie.

'Concernin' some well-off Army gent presumin' to be your natural dad,' said Sammy.

'If anyone's a natural dad to me, Uncle Sammy, it's your brother Boots,' said Rosie.

'Well, I'm glad to hear it, Rosie.'

'Oh, don't mention it, Uncle Sammy.'

Sammy regarded her searchingly. She smiled.

'Strike me pink, you're a cool one, Rosie, which I might say makes you a bit like your Aunt Susie.'

'My, that's very flattering,' said Rosie, 'I'm a great admirer of Aunt Susie.'

'So am I,' said Sammy, 'except I can't get any change out of her, which puts me off-balance sometimes. However, in regard to the crisis that's come about, I want to offer me heartfelt support.'

'Aren't you a love, Uncle Sammy?'

Sammy coughed.

'Um, all for one and one for all, y'know, Rosie,' he said.

'Well, that's famous, Uncle Sammy, the Adams musketeers riding to the rescue,' said Rosie.

'Something like that,' said Sammy.

'But there's no crisis,' said Rosie, 'just a little hiccup. I can see to it.'

'Rosie, you sure?'

'Quite sure, Uncle Sammy.'

'What makes you quite sure?' asked Sammy.

'I'm an Adams,' said Rosie.

'Well, so you are, Rosie, and always have been, and we know who made you one, don't we?' said Sammy.

'Yes,' smiled Rosie, 'the Lord-I-Am.'

'Now, Rosie, you don't want to take too much notice of what your Uncle Tommy and me sometimes say about Boots. We're only pullin' his leg.'

'Oh, but it suits him,' said Rosie, who was in favour of her adoptive father's easy command of life. 'He wears the title with a natural air. Haven't you said he was a natural Lord Muck when he was at school?'

'Bounced off him it did, Rosie, every time the street kids called him that. He took the fam'ly over by the time he was sixteen. Chinese Lady didn't notice it, but it happened. Well, you know your dad, he does everything sort of unnoticeably. But his best acquisition was you, Rosie, which is why we don't want to lose you.'

'Uncle Sammy, you're very sweet,' said Rosie.

'You're a one and only, university and all,' said Sammy with honest admiration. 'Mother O'Grady, Rosie, you're goin' to outshine all of us in the end.'

'I don't want to outshine any of you,' said Rosie, 'only to be one of you.'

'You've been one for years, Rosie.'

'I'm happy to think so, Uncle Sammy, because I mean to remain one,' said Rosie. 'Does that satisfy you?'

'Comin' from you, it does, Rosie. Still, now I'm here, I'd better show my kisser to your grandmother or she'll want to know if I've gone off her as me everlastin' Ma.'

'Come this way, Uncle Sammy,' said Rosie.

When Sammy got back home, Susie waylaid him and wanted to know where he'd sneaked off to. Sammy said he'd always been incapable of sneaking off, that he'd just gone out sort of absent-mindedly. A likely story, said Susie. It so happened, said Sammy, that he found himself passing Boots's house, so he popped in, as it wouldn't have been family-minded to pass by.

'Oh, dear, I think you're comin' it, Sammy Adams,' said Susie.

122

Sammy assured her it was nothing of the kind, but that he did happen to see Rosie.

'Sammy, didn't I tell you not to interfere?' said Susie.

'Crikey, Dad,' said Daniel, he and Bess having put in an appearance, 'you don't half dig holes for yerself.'

'Daddy, you're only supposed to dig holes for flowers in the garden,' said Bess. 'Well, I fink you are.'

'Anyway, what did Rosie say?' asked Susie.

'That she's an Adams,' said Sammy.

'Well, of course she is, you silly,' said Susie. 'I could have told you that's exactly what she would say. Now you can get ready to take us to church.'

'Listen, Daniel, and you too, Bess me pudding,' said Sammy, 'when you grow up and you're old enough to vote, vote for your mum to be Prime Minister.'

'But, Dad, shouldn't you be Prime Minister?' asked Daniel.

'Don't make jokes like that in front of your mother,' said Sammy.

'Oh, all right, Daddy, when we've growed up we'll vote for Mummy,' said Bess.

'If you're sure, Dad,' said Daniel.

'Yes, let's see how your mum looks in a Prime Minister's top-hat,' said Sammy.

Susie laughed.


In the afternoon, Lilian Hyams allowed her milkman, Bill Chambers, to take her for a saunter around Regent's Park. Because of his entertaining tongue, which gave forth frequent allusions to her well-dressed personability and the benefits of egg custard, she wore a smile most of the time.

The following morning, when she was back at work, Tommy entered her office. She was at her drawing-board and looking thoughtful.

'Got you beat, the new designs?' said Tommy.

'Hope not,' said Lilian, 'or Sammy will give me notice. Should I suffer that kind of broken heart? Not likely. Tommy, tell me, can you see me as a milkman's lady friend?'

'It's got possibilities,' said Tommy, 'you might get your milk free. On the other hand, I've always thought someone like a rich sheik of Araby might fancy you. You'd get free jewels then, and a couple of camels.'

'What for, spending time in his tent?' said Lilian.

'I ain't supposin' it would be out of wedlock,' said Tommy, grinning. 'Anyway, what milkman d'you 'ave in mind?'

'My Walworth milkman,' said Lilian. 'My life, Tommy, I should fall in love with a dairy roundsman?'

'Up to you,' said Tommy.

'I let him take me to Regent's Park yesterday, and we fed the ducks,' said Lilian.

'You mean he's actually started courtin' you?' said Tommy.

'I've got odd feelings about that,' said Lilian.

'I felt a bit lively when I was courtin' Vi,' said Tommy.

'How lively?' asked Lilian.

'I'll keep the details to meself,' said Tommy.

'Tommy, a milkman, would you believe,' said Lilian.

'Does he belong to a synagogue?' asked Tommy.

'Not much,' said Lilian, 'he's a Gentile gent. Should I worry about that?'

'Well, you're lookin' great, Lilian, like you're ready to be courted,' said Tommy. 'By the way, how do Sally and Cassie look in their weddin' gowns now you've finished 'em?'

'Beautiful,' said Lilian, 'even if I do say so myself.'

'Take a bow, then,' said Tommy, 'and before I forget, I came in to tell you Miss de Vere wants you to ring 'er about the new designs after two-thirty this afternoon.'

'That's a change from her wanting to ring Sammy or Boots,' said Lilian. 'Why couldn't she talk to me now?'

'She was rushin' off somewhere,' said Tommy.

'Hoping to waylay Boots on the way, I shouldn't wonder,' said Lilian.

'Well, I'll leave it to you to remember to ring 'er,' said Tommy. 'That's if you can take your mind off your milkman.'

'Hoppit,' said Lilian, and Tommy departed grinning.

Later that day, when Lilian phoned Harriet de Vere, the buyer referred to one of her designs, a white dress with blue stripes.

'You don't like it?' said Lilian.

'Love the style,' said Harriet, 'but we'd like the blue to be navy. Could you do a new sketch?'

'That's no problem,' said Lilian.

'Thanks,' said Harriet.

Lilian did a quick sketch. The result looked like a milkman wearing a blue and white striped apron.

Something's closing in on me, thought Lilian, and the chink of milk bottles is ringing in my ears.

**Meeting frequently in Kennington Park, Dusty Miller**

and Ginger Carstairs were still busy finalizing and polishing up their plans.

March went out with a bit of a noisy rush, and April came in to offer a hint of spring, which was very welcome to the people of Walworth and elsewhere because March had acted up something chronic at times. March in a paddy could make South London's old Victorian houses feel cold and draughty, which never did a lot of good to old people's chilblains.

Cassie and Freddy were gradually furnishing their house in Wansey Street with the aid of Freddy's savings and what Mr Eli Greenberg, the well-known rag and bone merchant, could offer in respect of valuable bargains good as new. They were also putting in some highly necessary decorative work. Concerning that, Cassie said she realized now what a labour of love was. Freddy said yes, the house was a bit of all right, and he was already holding it in kind regard on account of it being their first marriage abode. Cassie said yes, wasn't it blissful labour, decorating it together? Freddy said he couldn't agree more, but could she stop waving her paint brush about?

'Yes, all right, Freddy beloved,' she said. 'Oh, Dad's goin' to help us again at the weekend when we start rubbin' down the upstairs doors.'

'Well, good old Gaffer,' said Freddy. They were painting the door to the scullery, Cassie on one side, he the other, the open door wedged. He was having to keep alert, because whenever Cassie put her head round the door to say something, her paint brush came round too. 'Will that be another labour of love?' he asked.

'Yes, I expect so,' said Cassie. 'Dad's always loved me, and I know he's learned to love you.'

'Was it hard goin', arrivin' at that state?' asked Freddy.

'No, not very,' said Cassie, stroking on magnolia paint. 'Well, when you consider that a lot of Germans 'ave actually learned to love Hitler, it must've been easy for Dad to learn to love you. "Cassie," he said to me once, "Freddy could get to be quite likeable in a crowd." Wasn't that a promisin' remark, Freddy beloved?'

'Cassie, would yer mind not callin' me beloved at football matches?'

'Why not?' asked Cassie.

'It makes some of the Rovers fall about legless, that's why not,' said Freddy.

'Oh, poor dears, I am sorry, they must be gettin' feeble in their old age,' said Cassie. 'Freddy, has Sammy given you the cheque for fifty pounds yet?'

'Not yet,' said Freddy, 'but he will.'

'Don't forget to put it in the bank,' said Cassie.

'All right, Cassie love, I won't forget,' said Freddy. 'He's recommended his own bank. It's got a 'elpful bank manager, he said.'

As for the other forthcoming bride, Miss Sally Brown, she had a bone to pick with Horace and did so in her mum's parlour. She advised him, with her shop assistant's polished plum in her mouth, that she wasn't the kind of young lady to behave in a common way. Horace said he seconded that. He said what had first taken his fancy about her was the fact that she was a very uncommon and superior young lady as well as an eyeful. That knocked him right out, he said, as he'd always had rosy dreams about superior young ladies who were also an eyeful. Of course, he was fairly common himself, he said, but with any luck he might improve. Well, he hoped he would, he said, because he naturally wanted to live up to her, as if he didn't, their neighbours-to-be might talk about him. He'd buy a book about how to become uncommon in six easy lessons, he said. There were books which taught you how to play the piano in six easy lessons, he said, so there were probably similar books about behaviour.

Sally managed to get a word in at that point.

'D'you mind puttin' a sock in it?' she said. They were sitting on the old parlour sofa, a very comfy piece of furniture because it sagged a bit in the middle, and the sag sort of drew them cosily together. Sally never complained about being cosy with Horace, and Horace, of course, was all for it.

'D'you want to say something?' asked Horace.

'If I can,' said Sally. 'Did I ask for you to go on and on like a gramophone, Horace Cooper? I don't remember I did, I just remember tellin' you I wasn't brought up to behave common. That wasn't askin' you to turn yourself into a gramophone, was it?'

'No wonder my mother likes you, Sally, you've got a lovely way of talkin',' said Horace. 'Anyway, what brought common behaviour up?'

'Never mind that,' said Sally. 'I want – Horace, does your mum really like me? Only I think she's a lovely woman.'

'She says I couldn't have picked a nicer young lady,' smiled Horace.

'Well, then,' said Sally, 'I want to know why you told Percy Ricketts, your best man, that he'd got a duty to inspect my weddin' garter with me wearin' it.'

'Well, silly old Percy,' said Horace, 'what a daft haddock, considering he's well past twenty-one.'

'Wait a minute, you haven't said if you told him or not.'

'Let's see,' said Horace, 'we were all talkin' to him, Nick, Freddy and yours truly, but I don't suppose any of us thought he'd take everything seriously.'

'Well, he took my wedding garter seriously,' said Sally. 'D'you know he came round last night to say he desired to make arrangements to inspect it at a convenient time?'

'Did he say that, Sally?' asked Horace. 'What a saucy bloke. Still, it was nicely put, I'll give him that. Then what happened? You plonked him one, I suppose?'

'No, I didn't,' said Sally. 'I first asked him if he thought I was common, and he said far from it. So I invited 'im into the parlour, then went upstairs, put my garter on, came down again and showed it to him.'

'Pardon?' said Horace.

'He liked it,' said Sally, 'and made very nice remarks about my legs.'

'Well, knock me down, I never thought that would happen,' said Horace.

'He's goin' to mention my garter in his speech,' said Sally. 'Oh, and he asked me if a joke about knickers would be all right, and I said all the guests would be disappointed if he didn't. He said he and Nick had made up a little poem that he'd like to use.'

'It'll kill you,' said Horace. 'And listen, what's the

idea of showing your garter to my best man when I haven't seen it myself?'

'You'd like to see me wearin' it?' said Sally.

'I'm not goin' to say no, am I?' said Horace.

'Well, I'll show you,' said Sally.

'I'll be very appreciative,' said Horace.

'But not till we're married,' said Sally.

Horace took that blow like a sport, and kissed her.

'Well, I'm blessed,' she breathed a few seconds later. 'I don't mind a kiss, but what's 'appening to my dress?'

'Don't ask me,' said Horace, and kissed her again.

A large sepia photographic portrait of Sally's whiskery maternal grandfather on the parlour wall closed its eyes. Victorians considered ladies' legs should be covered up.

As for Annabelle and Nick, who were to be married in June, they spent one evening looking at a house in Ferndene Road, off Denmark Hill, not far from her parents' house. Nor, for that matter, was it all that far from the homes of her uncles, Boots, Tommy and Sammy. Chinese Lady, informed of Annabelle's interest in the Ferndene Road property, informed Annabelle in turn that she had her best wishes. A place in Ferndene Road would be very suitable as it would keep her and Nick close to the other families, and she didn't believe in any of her close relatives living in foreign neighbourhoods like Norwood or Streatham. Suppose they got struck down by a serious complaint, she said, they'd get ill at not having their relations close by. Annabelle said it would be awful to be struck down by a serious complaint, and then get ill because her uncles and aunts couldn't pop in to put the kettle on and do some kind nursing. Chinese Lady said yes, you don't want to have to suffer like that, Annabelle. All right, Granny love, said Annabelle, I promise Nick and me won't go and live in a foreign neighbourhood. There, that's a sensible girl, said Chinese Lady, I'll always be close by myself. Granny, you're the best there is, said Annabelle, and meant it. Chinese Lady had her cherished place in the lives of everyone.

The house was lovely, owned at the moment by a well-off couple in their late forties whose son and daughter were both married. They wanted a smaller house now, so had put this one on the market at six hundred and fifty pounds, which might have given Chinese Lady a grievous turn if she'd known. She would have considered such a sum a shocking amount for a young couple to pay. Nick knew a fifteen-year mortgage would mean an average outlay for the first five years of at least two pounds a week. He was presently earning four pounds a week, but having already looked over the house with Annabelle, he knew she'd fallen for it. This second visit was to help them decide. The house with its central door, was double-fronted, with large handsome ground floor windows. Downstairs, there were four rooms and a very spacious and bright kitchen which Annabelle loved. Upstairs, there were three large-sized bedrooms, a smaller one, a play room, an attractive tiled bathroom with its own loo, and a separate loo. Mr and Mrs Lawson, the owners, were more than happy to show Annabelle and Nick over the house again, since they'd taken to this engaging couple. When they reached the smaller bedroom, Mrs Lawson smilingly said it had been used as a nursery bedroom for their children when they were infants, and she pointed out the cot was still there and as good as it had ever been.

'We'll leave it, if you like,' she said, 'as we shan't want it any more.'

'Not unless lightning strikes,' said Mr Lawson, and laughed.

'Oh, we're in the market for being struck,' said Nick, and received a little dig in the ribs from a slightly pink Annabelle. At the end of the guided tour, he said he and Annabelle would like another day or two to consider, would that be all right?

'Of course,' said Mr Lawson.

'We do have another couple coming to look tomorrow,' said Mrs Lawson.

'All right, we'll let you know before then,' said Nick.

When they were out of the house, Annabelle said she really did like it. It was easily better than other properties they'd looked at. Nick said he concurred, but pointed out that the mortgage repayments, especially for the first few years, could mean that with all the other outgoings, he might not be able to keep her in the manner to which she'd become accustomed. Annabelle, a girl with as much sense as her dad, was aware that all her life she had never lacked for anything, that she'd never had to suffer the kind of poverty her mum had known during her years in Walworth. Lizzy indeed, with Ned's willing financial help, had seen to it that none of her children ever went short of essentials, especially good clothes. Lizzy had never forgotten her days of patched and shabby garments, or the time when she first met Ned and there were holes in her stockings. Ned always assured her he hadn't noticed anything except her big brown eyes. Just like village ponds in the sunshine, he said once during the sixth year of their marriage, which so overcame Lizzy that she went all loving and Emma was born nine months later. Ned thought the arrival of Emma was an exceptional reward for a natural compliment. Actually, his admiration for Lizzy's sterling qualities, reflective of her mother's, was constant. She had never failed him or their children.

Annabelle knew a lot about her mum's earlier life and background, and she knew too that Nick and his family had known the same kind of hardships as her mum and her uncles. Nick, like them, had overcome similar disadvantages to turn himself into a lovely young man, just as she thought Uncle Boots had done, even if he had been called Lord Muck. If Nick decided to take out the mortgage on the Ferndene Road house, they would start their married life in a property even better than that of her parents.

'Nick darling?' she said, walking arm in arm with him through the dusk of the April evening.

'I'm here,' said Nick, deep in thought.

'Yes, isn't that nice?' she said. 'I'm fond of togetherness. Nick, if we really can't afford it, I shan't mind. And, anyway, perhaps it would be more sensible to start off in a smaller house, like Mum and Dad have.'

'On the other hand, if we went for a twenty-year mortgage, that would help a lot,' said Nick.

'Oh, could we do that, could we manage more easily then?' asked Annabelle. 'Only it's such a lovely family house. I could keep on working for a while and we could put all my earnings into the bank.'

'You're not going to keep on working,' said Nick. 'Your Great-Uncle John would have me executed if I let you. No, you can't go out to work, Annabelle, not with a house like that to look after. And there's the garden too.'

'Me?' said Annabelle. 'Me look after the garden as well? That's your job.'

'Is it?' said Nick. 'You sure?'

'You bet I'm sure,' said Annabelle.

'All right, I'll look after the garden,' said Nick. 'Mind you, I'll be a novice at it.'

'You'll learn,' said Annabelle. 'Nick, are you really going to say yes, to go for a twenty-year mortgage?'

'I'm going to see that we start off in a house you're already in love with,' said Nick.

'Oh, rapture,' said Annabelle, and hugged his arm. 'Nick, you're lovely to me. I don't know if I'm as deserving as that.'

'Well, I'd like to have enough spare earnings to be able to keep you in decent style,' said Nick. 'You deserve that and more.'

'Nick, I really won't mind if we have to make do a bit,' said Annabelle earnestly.

'You still deserve the kind of clothes you like, and so on,' said Nick. 'The kind I like to see you in.'

'What's so on?' asked Annabelle.

'Woolly vests?' said Nick.

'Oh, yes, I wear those two at a time, I don't think,' said Annabelle. 'Listen, when we get home, can we phone the Lawsons and tell them we've decided?'

'Would you like us to?' asked Nick.

'Nick, I really would,' said Annabelle.

'And we'll also tell them, shall we, that they can leave us the cot?'

'Not likely,' said Annabelle, 'they might think I've already been struck by lightning, and we're not married yet.'

'All right, I'll just say it might come in handy sometime,' said Nick.

Annabelle laughed. As they turned into Denmark Hill, she asked, 'Nick, have you ever had a girl?'

'What, one I carried about with me and put in a cupboard at night?' said Nick.

'No, you daft thing,' said Annabelle, 'you know what I mean.'

'Are you asking me if I've ever made love to a girl?'

'Well, some young men get the urge, don't they, and some girls say yes, don't they?'

'And some of 'em get into trouble,' said Nick, 'and ruin their lives. Ma brought me up not to go in for ruining any girl's life. So I channelled all my urges into football. I expect even Jesus had urges, and what did He do with them? He channelled them into performing miracles.'

'Oh, don't you get urges now you play so much football?' asked Annabelle.

'What's going on?' enquired Nick.

'I'm only asking,' said Annabelle.

'It's a funny conversation,' said Nick.

'No, it isn't, not between you and me,' said Annabelle. 'Anyway, urges are natural, aren't they, when you're in love?'

'Hello, d'you get urges too?' asked Nick.

'Yes, of course I do,' said Annabelle. 'I mean, if we didn't have them, something would be wrong with us, wouldn't it?'

'I suppose we'd both have to have an operation,'

said Nick. 'But I don't feel I need one at the moment.'

'Oh, good, because I don't either,' said Annabelle. 'You don't mind us talking like this, do you, Nick?'

'It's making me feel June's a long way off,' said Nick.

'Crikey,' said Annabelle, 'd'you mean you've got an urge now?'

'I'm giving up talking like this,' said Nick.

'Nick, you're shy,' said Annabelle, and laughed.

When they reached her home she asked him if he'd phone the Lawsons now. Nick said yes.

So he did, and he offered six hundred pounds as a first-time buyer. After some discussion, he and Mr Lawson settled for six hundred and ten, providing Nick would deposit fifty pounds with the agents within two days. Nick said he would, and Mr Lawson said he would advise the other couple that a firm offer had been made and accepted.

When Nick came off the phone, and had received good luck wishes from Lizzy and Ned, Annabelle whisked him into the parlour and kissed him.

'Do that again,' said Nick.

'I'm going to be very nice to you,' said Annabelle, 'and tell you the best thing that ever happened to my dad was my mum, and the best thing that could have ever happened to me was you. Do you remember how we first met, in that lift at the insurance company's offices?'

'That was my luckiest day,' said Nick, so Annabelle kissed him again and told him how improved he was, so different from the grumpy bloke he'd been when bossing the football team's committee about many months ago.

Nick said he begged to differ, he'd never been

grumpy, he'd been patted on the head all his life for being cheerful in the face of all disasters.

'What disasters?' asked Annabelle.

'I'll think of some,' said Nick.

'It's Cassie's and Sally's double wedding soon,' said Annabelle.

'I hope I'll survive the racket,' said Nick. 'I'm set on attending our own wedding.'

'Oh, I do hope you'll be there,' said Annabelle. 'It won't be the same if you're not.'

'I'll make it,' said Nick. 'What a house that is.'

'And it's going to be all ours,' said Annabelle.

'They're leaving the carpets and the fittings,' said Nick, 'and I told them we'd like the cot as well.'

'Nick, we'll never get into the cot together,' said Annabelle. 'Can't we afford a double bed?'


Meanwhile, the atmosphere among Boots and his family was one that had an uneasy lurking aspect. Despite Rosie's calm demeanour, there was an under-current of worry that Major Armitage might attempt to make a claim on her. The family intended to fight that all the way.

Eloise put herself closer to Boots in her wish to be a reassurance to him. She knew all too well by now that he regarded Rosie as his very own, just as much as she herself was as his natural daughter. He was a man of very warm and generous affections.

'We shall keep Rosie, Papa,' she said more than once, 'she is ours, yes, and I am being very nice to her.'

'Well, you're very nice to all of us,' he always said.

*　　*　　*

137

Lilian was finding ways and means to avoid bumping into her conversational and admiring milkman.

Well, a milkman, for goodness sake. Her late husband Jacob, fatally wounded during the second battle of the Somme, had been in textiles and set for a promising career before he volunteered. There was nothing promising about a milkman's career. But he'd unsettled her, and at a time when the thought of marrying again, of having a man in her bed and around the house, had been a recurring one. Her still healthy body had actually begun to feel starved. Oh, holy Moses, she thought, I'm blessed if that milkman doesn't make a woman in my condition look twice. He's got blue eyes like Sammy. The next thing I know I'll be inviting him round one evening. I should worry about that? Yes, I should. He might start thinking about bedtime. So might I.

So she kept avoiding any possibility of bumping into him. And into Mr Abel Morrison too, for that matter.

A lady my age has got to be sensible, she told herself. I don't want a portly bloke or one whose wage means I'll still have to buy my own clothes. A wife has to be a giving woman, so she's entitled to some rewards, like an open invitation to her husband's wallet. Also, would I want to change my religion for a Church of England milkman with a thin wallet, even if he does remind me of Sammy?

My life, why have I suddenly got problems?

Lilian was by no means a grasping woman. She was as warm-hearted as any of her kind, but she was sold on the principle that it was a husband's privilege to keep his wife, not the other way about.

The milkman, Bill Chambers, went whistling on his

round and bided his time. He had taken a healthy fancy to his best-looking customer, a handsome and desirable widow, as the saying was about such women, and as long as the chief Walworth rabbi didn't queer his pitch, he meant to court her. Some men did get to marry Jewish ladies.

# Chapter Eight

The schools would soon be breaking up for the Easter holidays. Miss Polly Simms stopped Emma Somers as Lizzy's younger daughter made for the gate after classes had finished one afternoon. Emma had followed her sister Annabelle to West Square, just as Annabelle had followed Rosie.

'Emma?'

'Oh, hello, Miss Simms,' said Emma, chestnut hair of an even deeper hue than Annabelle's, and eyes just as brown. She was two months short of thirteen, very bright and very self-confident. Out of school, Miss Simms was Aunt Polly to her and all the younger generation of the Somers and Adams families.

'How is everyone at home?' asked Polly.

'Oh, jolly well in the pink,' said Emma, school hat on the back of her head, gymslip reaching to her knees, satchel slung.

'Will you and your family be going away for Easter?' asked Polly.

'Well, if we are, Miss Simms, no-one's told me,' said Emma. 'Sometimes I feel ever so unimportant.'

'Well, you're not,' smiled Polly, 'and you don't look it, or believe it either.'

'Oh, I try to show a brave front,' said Emma. 'Of course, all it does is to make Daddy ask me why I'm sticking my chest out. He says things like that, you know, just like Uncle Boots does.'

'Oh, they're a couple of old soldiers together,' said Polly, eighteen months short of forty and wishing she wasn't.

'Oh, did you know about Uncle Boots and Rosie?' asked Emma.

'What about them?'

'Well, Rosie's dad has turned up,' said Emma.

'Rosie's dad?' said Polly.

'Yes, her real father,' said Emma. 'He called on them one evening, just like that, sort of out of nowhere.'

Polly, always a trim and elegant figure, even in the practical blouse and skirt she usually wore as a teacher, visibly stiffened.

'Emma, for heaven's sake, are you telling me that the man who fathered Rosie has made an appearance in her life?' she asked in disbelief.

'Well, yes, Miss Simms,' said Emma, as pupils flowed or dashed by them.

'Oh, my God,' breathed Polly, thinking of Boots and how he would have taken the blow. It would have been a blow. He and Rosie were a collective symbol of inseparability.

'Aunt Polly?' said Emma, wondering why this long-standing friend of the families looked so shocked.

'What happened between this man and Rosie?' asked Polly.

'Oh, nothing very much,' said Emma, 'except that Rosie's going to spend a day with him at his country home.'

'I see.' Polly pulled herself together. 'Well, stranger things have happened, I suppose. Off you go, Emma, thanks for telling me.'

Off Emma went, joining friends. Only five minutes

141

later, Polly, having excused herself from attending a pre-Easter teachers' meeting, was away herself, in her little sports car, parked as usual by the railed green quadrangle of West Square. She motored fast to Camberwell Green, whipping around traffic.

Boots had just finished a business phone call when his office door opened and Polly slipped silently in.

'Polly?' he said.

She looked at him. Oh, ye gods and little fishes, she thought, he's insufferable in the way he never shows his real feelings. Rosie's natural father has materialized, but he still looks as if he's just heard Max Miller's latest joke.

'No-one thought to tell me,' she said.

'Tell you what?' he asked.

'That the man who fathered Rosie has turned up,' said Polly. 'If Emma hadn't let it slip out fifteen minutes ago, I still wouldn't know.'

'So you've heard,' said Boots.

'Just,' said Polly, 'but no thanks to you.'

'I thought Rosie would have phoned you,' said Boots, getting up.

'Well, she didn't. And you didn't bother, either.' Polly was seething. 'What am I, something the cat brought in?'

'I think you're cross,' said Boots.

'Yes, I bloody well am,' said Polly. 'I count myself a close and faithful lover, and I claim the right to be told of something like this.'

'Well,' said Boots, 'the fact is—'

'Damn the fact, whatever it is,' said Polly. 'You love me, don't you? Yes, you do, I know you do, so what the hell d'you mean by treating me like a dog's dinner?'

'So sorry, Polly,' said Boots, 'phoning you slipped my mind.'

'Like hell it did,' breathed Polly, 'you simply didn't bother.'

Boots looked at his watch. Just after four-thirty.

'Come and have a cup of tea at Lyons, Polly,' he said.

'Sod Lyons,' said Polly, whose vocabulary had been enriched during the war. 'You're unbelievable. Some man, some ghastly character, probably, is actually having the gall to claim he's Rosie's father and to perhaps devastate your family, and all you can do is invite me to have a cup of tea at Lyons?'

'It might calm you down,' said Boots, 'and we can talk. Let's try it, shall we?'

'Well, don't complain if I pour my cup all over your waistcoat,' said Polly.

Boots reached for his hat, took her by the arm and brought her out of his office. In the corridor, they encountered Annabelle.

'Hello, Aunt Polly, haven't come after my job, have you?' she said. 'I'll be leaving in June – oh, that reminds me, Mum's delighted you can come to the wedding. So's Dad. Well, Dad's an admirer.'

'I'll be there, Annabelle,' said Polly, and found a smile.

'Let the switchboard know I'll be out for a short while, will you, Annabelle?' said Boots. 'I've a tea dance date with Miss Simms.'

'A what?' said Annabelle.

'Just a joke,' smiled Boots.

I don't suppose Aunt Emily would call it that, thought Annabelle as she watched them leave. By no means simple, Annabelle had once asked Rosie if

143

she thought Polly Simms was in love with Uncle Boots. No, of course not, said Rosie, despite being certain Polly was. But that certainty was something Rosie kept to herself. Well, said Annabelle, I sometimes think she might be. I mean, there has to be some reason why she's never married. Oh, Polly's married to her wartime memories, said Rosie.

In the Lyons teashop at Camberwell Green, Boots did his best to calm the lady down. Polly really did feel furious that she hadn't been told about Major Armitage. If anyone had suggested it was purely a family matter, she'd have thought they needed their heads examined. However, Boots put her fully in the picture, and finished by saying that as everything fitted, there was no way to dispute the man's claim.

'I'm still peeved you didn't think to phone me, you stinker,' said Polly. 'A fat lot of good it's done me, giving you the best part of my devotion all these years.'

'Well, you know what men are like, Polly,' said Boots, 'we don't always get things right in respect of our best friends.'

'Don't be feeble,' said Polly. 'I'm not a best friend, best friends are ten a penny. I'm your lover, still waiting for you to take me to bed. You'll regret all you passed up when I eventually go off you. Which I will one day.' She made a face. 'When I'm ninety,' she said.

'That's a long way off,' said Boots.

Polly drank her tea.

'Have you spoken to Rosie's mother?' she asked.

'Milly Tooley?' said Boots. 'She called herself Mrs Pearce when I first knew her. No, I haven't spoken to her, nor seen her, since the adoption. She was married then to a stage magician called Rainbould. Where she is now, God knows.'

'Her father, Mr Tooley, might know,' said Polly.

'Is there something on your mind, Polly?' asked Boots.

'Only the fact that Milly Rainbould might know if Major Armitage is definitely the man who fathered Rosie,' said Polly.

'Would she know after all these years?' asked Boots. 'Would she be able to say with certainty he was the man who seduced her? According to what Mr Tooley told me when Rosie was five, Milly couldn't even remember the man's name, only that he was an officer.'

'Wake up, you idiot,' said Polly.

'Have I missed something?' asked Boots.

'Only the obvious, that if Milly Rainbould couldn't recognize Major Armitage as the man in question, any attempt he might make to be legally declared Rosie's father would start off on very shaky ground,' said Polly.

'Frankly,' said Boots, 'I've no doubts myself.'

'But you'd fight, wouldn't you, if Major Armitage tried to have the adoption set aside?'

'All the way,' said Boots.

'Then create some doubts,' said Polly.

'Have you got a slice of chicanery in mind?' asked Boots.

'You could get arrested for using a word like that in a Lyons teashop,' said Polly.

'I'm not too much in favour of something that would deny the man his right to be accepted as Rosie's natural father,' said Boots.

'But you're against the adoption being set aside,

145

you've just said so. Any doubts would make the law reluctant to go along with him. Listen, old sport, didn't you once tell me you had to pay Rosie's mother as much as five hundred pounds in order to agree to the adoption?'

'The amount meant a lot more to her than Rosie did,' said Boots.

'So she likes money,' said Polly. 'I don't know why I'm on your side after being treated like a casual passer-by, but I am. So let's talk, but come closer first.'

Boots smiled, moved to the chair that was at right angles to hers, and they talked, at the end of which Boots said nothing doing to Polly's suggestion that she'd take a hand in the matter and do Major Armitage in the eye by hook or crook. Polly asked why not. It's trickery, said Boots. Don't make me laugh, said Polly. Leave it, said Boots. Polly said she'd talk to Rosie sometime. Rosie will surprise you, said Boots.

'Exactly who's goin' to Cassie's and Sally's weddings?' asked Vi over supper that evening. Their three children were making hungry inroads into sweet lamb chops, creamy mashed potatoes and tender cauliflower covered with a sauce.

'All the grown-ups,' said Tommy.

'Is that us?' asked David, eight.

'No, of course not, soppy,' said Alice, nine, 'we're not grown-ups.'

'Nor's me,' said Paul, four.

'Let's see,' said Tommy, 'it's Grandma Finch and Grandpa Finch, Aunt Em'ly, Uncle Boots, cousins Rosie and Eloise—'

'She ain't grown-up, is she?' said David.

'Who, Eloise?' said Vi, still soft-eyed and soft-spoken in her thirty-fifth year.

'Yes, and she's French,' said Alice.

'She's eighteen,' said Tommy, 'and your Aunt Sally said that was old enough. Then there's Aunt Susie and Uncle Sammy, Aunt Lizzy, Uncle Ned and Annabelle.'

'Crikey, all that lot and not us?' said David.

'We're children,' said Alice.

'There's just not room for everyone, David lovey,' said Vi.

'I don't mind,' said David. 'Well, there's kissin' at weddings.'

'Hello, hello, 'ave we got another Uncle Sammy here?' asked Tommy.

'Yes, your Uncle Sammy always complained about kissin' when he was your age, David,' smiled Vi.

'I ain't surprised,' said David, 'kissing's all wet.'

'I never been to a weddin',' said Paul.

'You're lucky,' said David, 'it's saved you a lot of wet kissin'.'

'Daddy doesn't do wet kissing,' said Alice, 'does he, Mum?'

'Well, I've never had a wet one from him yet,' said Vi.

'Billy Martin 'ad six from Dolly Harris last week,' said David.

'He had what?' said Tommy. Billy Martin and Dolly Harris, both eleven, were at the same school as Alice and David.

'Well, she ain't half big for her age, Dad,' said David.

'Yes, and all Billy's struggles were in vain,' said Alice. 'Poor boy,' she added solemnly.

'I'd 'ave helped him,' said David, 'but I'm not tall enough yet. Crikey, I never seen such wet kisses, they nearly drowned him.'

'Nearly a fate worse than death, was it?' grinned Tommy.

'Dad, can you cut the bits of meat off me chop?' asked Paul.

'Well,' said Tommy, 'you can—'

'No, he can't,' said Vi.

'Grandma always let us gnaw our chop bones,' said Tommy.

'Manners, Tommy, if you don't mind,' said Vi. Since moving to this quite grand house on Denmark Hill and acquiring a daily help and a gardener, Vi had thought everyone's manners ought to be in keeping. Well, it really was a grand house compared to their previous one, the front approach so wide that a lorry could have been driven through the entrance gate and past the side of the house to the back garden itself. Tommy didn't see why they should change their way of living, but men, of course, weren't as particular about some things as women. The funny thing was that although Tommy didn't know it and wouldn't have believed it if she'd told him, he'd gradually taken on the style of a prosperous gent of leafy Denmark Hill. Well, for instance, he now had a Donegal tweed suit with a matching hat for weekends, which, in her eyes, made him look like a handsome country squire. Also, he made a proud dad's remarks about what a little lady Alice was, and he wouldn't let young Paul tread in puddles like an old-time street kid, such as he'd been himself in his Walworth years. Further, every time the gardener addressed him as 'guv'nor' he gave him a sort of gracious nod. 'We've got to take notice we've come up in the world, Tommy,' she said.

'We've done that all right, Vi,' said Tommy, 'but chop bones are just the same, and no-one's lookin'.'

'I am,' said Vi, and her children glanced at her, all of them wishful to gnaw at what was left of their tasty chops. She smiled placidly. 'Oh, all right, then, just this once,' she said. The kids set to with their fingers and teeth.

'Tell you what, Alice,' said Tommy, 'as you're missin' the Easter Saturday double weddin', I'll take you all to Brighton in the car on Easter Sunday, and your mum can come as well.'

'My, aren't you gracious?' said Vi, and smiled again.

'Well, Dad's our gracious Lord of the Manor,' said Alice. Their house was called 'The Manor'.

'Oh, I come from a fam'ly of lords,' said Tommy. 'Your Uncle Sammy's what you call a business lord, and your Uncle Boots 'as been Lord-I-Am since I don't know when.'

'Granny Victoria always says Uncle Boots is a born gentleman,' declared Alice. Granny Victoria was Vi's mother and a woman who, originally, had disapproved of Tommy as a prospective husband for her daughter on the grounds that unlike his brother Boots, he was a bit common. Well, said Vi eventually, if Tommy's common, so am I, and we're going to be common together. That gave her mum a fit and also a bit of heartburn, but when Tommy made good in the firm's business there were no more fits or heartburn, only a mother-in-law proud to inform her neighbours that her daughter had made a respectable and prosperous marriage.

'What's a born gentleman, Daddy?' asked Alice.

'One that looks like your dad when he's wearin' his tweed suit,' said Vi.

'Crikey,' said David, 'he just looks like our dad to me.'

'Well, I don't aspire to bein' like your Uncle Boots,' said Tommy, 'but what I can aspire to is me belief that our Alice is a born lady.'

'What, her?' said David. 'But she's just me sister.'

'Yes, she's mine as well,' said Paul, and his young brow furrowed as if even at his age there were family problems he had to face up to. 'She's both our sister.'

'Oh, don't mention it, I'm sure,' said Alice, wearing her nine years in the happy knowledge that she'd soon be ten and accordingly entitled to a lovely new frock. A new frock as a present was always second to none as far as Alice was concerned.

'Anyway, you're a sport, Dad, if you're goin' to take us to Brighton,' said David.

'It's a promise,' said Tommy.

Vi gave him a fond look. Tommy always counted his blessings, and his three children were high on his list. Tommy, Boots and Sammy, locked into business though they were, were all family men. Vi put that down to Chinese Lady's influence.

'What's for afters?' asked Alice, and that put a stop to any more talk about weddings that were only for grown-ups.


'Well, hello, and how's yourself, Mrs Hyams?' said Bill Chambers the following morning.

Bless the man, he's diddled me, thought Lilian. She'd heard him and his milk bottles, and she'd waited for him to continue on before leaving her house. But he'd come back, leaving his float a fair way up the street towards the market. There was a bottle of milk in his hand.

'Is it safe, leaving your horse and cart up there?' she asked, looking, in a spring costume and brimmed hat, a fair old treat to Bill's discerning optics.

'Safe as houses,' he said. 'Black Bess won't move an inch until I tell her to. I forgot Mrs Worboys ordered an extra pint. That's the third time I've been forgetful lately. Something's come over me. Might I presume to say I admire your titfer, Mrs Hyams?'

'How kind,' said Lilian. 'But I must get on or I'll be late for work.' It wouldn't have mattered. Sammy let her enjoy flexible hours. All he was concerned with were her imaginative designs. 'Nice to have seen you, Mr Chambers.'

'Might I have the pleasure of takin' you to the Leicester Square cinema this evening?' asked Bill. 'Call for you about seven, shall I?'

'My life, this is so sudden,' said Lilian.

'Would you say so?' asked Bill, very admiring of her well-dressed look. 'I mean, following our afternoon in Regent's Park, where if I might presume to mention it, you looked as good as Fay Compton, is an invitation to the West End flicks sort of unexpected?'

'Well, perhaps not,' said Lilian.

'Natural consequence,' said Bill, 'so I'll knock about seven this evening. Won't keep you any longer now. Best wishes to you, Mrs Hyams.'

He's surrounding me, thought Lilian.

'Have I told you about my milkman?' she asked Tommy later at the factory.

'The one who fancies you?' said Tommy.

'He says he doesn't know what's come over him.'

'Sounds like he fancies you for real,' said Tommy.

'Do me a favour,' said Lilian. 'Look, I know I'm not the Duchess of York, but a milkman, I ask you.'

'You mentioned that before,' said Tommy. 'What's wrong with a milkman?'

'All right for a dairymaid, I suppose,' said Lilian. 'This one's coming round tonight to take me to the Leicester Square cinema.'

'Well, treatin' you to a cinema seat won't mean you'll 'ave to marry him, will it?' said Tommy.

'Not unless he overpowers me while the big film's on,' said Lilian.

'Take a bit of doin' on a back seat, that would,' grinned Tommy. 'Unless he's an acrobat.'

'Here, d'you mind?' said Lilian. 'Stop making me feel weak-minded.'

'Hello, he's got you thinking, 'as he?' asked Tommy.

'What about?' asked Lilian.

'Acrobatics,' said Tommy.

'Call that funny, do you?' said Lilian, and chucked her paint rag at him.

However, nothing happened in the cinema about which Lilian could complain to the manager. Bill was a perfect gentleman. On the way home on a bus, she asked him if he realized they didn't speak the same religious language. Bill said he'd never been bothered by that sort of thing. Lilian said she was Jewish.

'Fanatical, like?' said Bill.

'Not all that much,' said Lilian, 'but Rabbi Solomon keeps an eye on me occasionally.'

'Oh, is that the tall bloke in a bowler hat and a black beard?' asked Bill.

'That's him,' said Lilian.

'Friend of mine,' said Bill, 'I deliver his milk and eggs. A kind bloke. I can't see him comin' round to boil me in oil just for takin' you to the flicks once or twice a week. By the way, have I had the pleasure of bein' told your first name?'

'Not yet,' said Lilian.

'Would it be Esther?'

'Not to my knowledge,' said Lilian.

'Salome, say?'

'Here, leave off,' said Lilian.

'Fanny, then?' said Bill.

Lilian burst into laughter, and passengers turned their heads to look.

'It's Lilian,' she said.

'Well, I don't know why you were shy about it,' said Bill, 'nothing wrong with Lilian, y'know. I like it.'

'Thanks,' said Lilian, 'you can leave me an extra pint tomorrow morning.'

'Pleasure,' said Bill. 'Does that mean you're expectin' company.'

'No, just that I'm going to make a milk pudding,' said Lilian. 'On the other hand, I will have company, I suppose, if you happen to drop in tomorrow evening.'

'Well, that's a welcome invite, that is,' said Bill, 'and I'll be pleasured to keep you company.'

What made me invite him, thought Lilian. I'm daft.

And that wasn't all. She didn't need an extra pint; or a milk pudding.


Ginger Carstairs and Dusty Miller had checked more than once on the closing time of the bank. Each time it had shut its door to customers promptly at three-thirty.

At home, young Fanny Harrison wondered if Tim Adams would actually ever take her to the pictures.

# Chapter Nine

Rosie telephoned Major Armitage at his Godalming home on Friday morning. He at once said he was delighted to hear from her.

'How kind. Thank you, Major Armitage.'

'I'm your father, Rosie.'

'Oh, yes, we both understand how that came about,' said Rosie. 'Anyway, will it be convenient to visit you tomorrow with my brother and sister? It's Saturday and convenient for all of us.'

'I'll come and fetch the three of you,' said Major Armitage. 'I'll leave early and be there by not later than nine-thirty. And I'll drive you back, of course. Believe me, I can't wait to show you around. I'm hoping it will persuade you to spend the Easter weekend here.'

'That's next week,' said Rosie, 'when I'll be attending a double wedding with most of my family.'

'That's a pity,' said Major Armitage.

'Not for us,' said Rosie.

'No, I did mean for me, of course. However, tomorrow, then.'

'Yes, tomorrow, thanks so much,' said Rosie. 'Good-bye for now.'

She informed Chinese Lady of the arrangement, and Chinese Lady looked a bit dubious.

'You sure it's wise, Rosie?' she said.

'Oh, but it's right for 'er to go, isn't it?' said Eloise.

'If your Aunt Victoria happened to drop in,' mused Chinese Lady, 'I could get her to read Rosie's teacup. Your Aunt Victoria's got the gift. It's always been sorrowful to me that I've never been able to read tealeaves meself. If I could, they might tell us what Major Armitage might be up to.'

'It won't make any difference, Nana,' smiled Rosie.

The breezy milkman dropped in on Lilian that evening, as promised. Lilian was determined to put up a fight, although she'd made it difficult for herself by donning a velveteen dress of a delicate peach shade that did splendid justice to her healthy figure. Bill said she was a pleasure to behold, and Lilian said she supposed he talked like that to all his lady customers. Bill said he looked after their dairy requirements, as he was obliged to, but regulations didn't allow him to talk familiar to them. Lilian said he talked very familiar to her. Bill said that was different, they'd been out together and were coming to be intimate friends.

'Intimate my foot,' said Lilian.

Bill, looking around her plushly-furnished living-room, said, 'You've made a nice home for yourself, Mrs Hyams. You wouldn't like a piano, I suppose, the one I got lumbered with when Dorothy and her mum moved out? I don't play meself.'

'I don't have room for a piano,' said Lilian.

'I wouldn't say that,' mused Bill, 'and I'd like comin' round regular to listen to you playing. I'm fond of piano music. Did you make yourself a milk pudding with that extra pint?'

'I haven't had time,' said Lilian.

'Well, as I'm here, I'll make one for you,' said Bill, 'I've done a lot of good cookin' in my time. Where's the kitchen?'

'You're not getting into my kitchen,' said Lilian. 'You can sit down and I'll bring in a pot of tea.'

'If you need any help, just call,' said Bill.

It was like that all evening, Bill a bloke with his mind made up, and Lilian a woman fighting a rearguard action. It was all quite lively in its way. When she told him she was a fashion designer, he said that was a lot different from being a dairy roundsman, and that if she'd designed the dress she was wearing she must be very talented. Lilian said yes, she was, that her name was well-known in the fashion world. You could probably make a good marriage with a prosperous somebody from Paris, said Bill. Yes, I probably could, said Lilian. Somebody from Paris could be an advantageous French husband to you, said Bill. Yes, he could, said Lilian. Still, as he hasn't turned up yet, said Bill, you won't mind me comin' round now and again? I won't mind at all, said Lilian, providing you're invited. Very right and proper, said Bill.

When he finally left, Lilian didn't feel defeated, but she did feel she ought to put barbed wire around her defences. Or perhaps when she next saw him, she'd tell him Rabbi Solomon wasn't too pleased at her allowing a Gentile bloke to cross her doorstep.

Still, what a lively evening.

\* \* \*

Boots and Mr Finch had departed for their respective offices by the time Major Armitage arrived the next morning. Emily had elected to stay home so that she could run an eye over the man claiming to be Rosie's father. She and Chinese Lady were determined to meet him, and they came out of the kitchen into the hall with Eloise when Rosie answered the ringing doorbell. And there he was, mature, distinguished and moustached, dressed in country tweeds, his motoring cap in his hand.

'Good morning, Rosie,' he said.

'Good morning, Major Armitage,' said Rosie, composed of manner and delightful of appearance. Her tailored spring costume of royal blue looked perfect. He regarded her in fascination, still finding it difficult to believe how striking she was, and how excessively different from what he had envisaged when Mr Tooley first told him the child had been a girl.

'I'm delighted again,' he said.

'Thank you,' said Rosie. 'Oh, before we go, would you like to say hello to my mother, my grandmother and my sister?'

Major Armitage received this polite, smiling reference to her family with a smile of his own. He had no intention of making any kind of wrong move.

'Yes, I should like to, indeed I would,' he said, and Rosie introduced him, first to her mother, Mrs Adams, then to her grandmother, Mrs Finch, and finally to her sister Eloise. Major Armitage shook hands with each of them in turn, declaring it a great pleasure to meet the people who had cared for Rosie all these years. He might have said his daughter Rosie, but didn't. He was pleasant, courteous and friendly, and neither Emily nor Chinese Lady could find any outward fault in him. As for Eloise, she thought him very distinguished and soldierly, a typical English country gentleman, even if he hadn't been very gentlemanly in the way he had fathered Rosie.

Tim appeared, holding his cap.

'Oh, hello,' he said.

'You and I have met before,' smiled Major Armitage.

'Yes, so we have,' said Tim, 'how'd you do, sir?'

'I'm fine,' said Major Armitage, and looked at Rosie. 'Are we ready to leave?' he asked.

'All ready,' said Rosie, and she and Tim and Eloise left a couple of minutes later, after the Major had said goodbye to Emily and Chinese Lady, and assured them he would return with the three young people in the evening. No reference to the fact that he was Rosie's natural father had been made by anyone.

'Well, I don't know, I'm sure, Em'ly,' said Chinese Lady, when they were alone. 'I never met a more civil gentleman, and it flummoxed me a bit.'

'Mum, he was civil all right,' said Emily, 'but a real gentleman wouldn't interfere in Rosie's life, not when she's been one of us all these years. I wish Boots had been here instead of goin' to work. Well, for once in me life I just didn't know what to say, I'd have been willing to leave it to him.'

'Boots wouldn't of said anything, Em'ly, he'd have just been polite,' remarked Chinese Lady. 'He's goin' along with Rosie, he's letting her make up her own mind about things. Mind, he won't just stand about if Major Armitage tries to get the adoption set aside as unlegal. Boots will fight that all right.'

'I like Rosie for takin' Tim and Eloise with her,' said Emily. 'Well, it's to show Major Armitage she feels closer to them than him. Oh, 'elp, did you see his car? It's posh all over.'

159

'I still like horses and carts meself,' said Chinese Lady. 'No good will ever come of motorcars. They're not natural.'

The motorcar was a Bentley. Tim was almost awestruck. Rosie had made him sit in the front, next to Major Armitage, while she sat in the back with Eloise. Eloise was a very intrigued young lady, with an intuitive feeling that Rosie was more taken with her natural father and his background than she cared to admit. It was right for her to be loyal to her adoptive parents, of course, but not wrong for her to have feelings for Major Armitage, who was obviously very rich. Not that Rosie's adoptive parents were poor, oh, no, the business had made them prosperous, but Major Armitage was a landowner and looked an aristocrat as well. Why, he could probably make a debutante of Rosie, and have her presented at Court. Could Rosie resist that? Eloise had promised she would help to ensure that Rosie's life remained unchanged, but one couldn't work miracles, of course. If Rosie did decide to live with her natural father, well, thought Eloise, I will make it up to my own father and be as good as two daughters to him. Yes, it would be up to her to see that he didn't miss Rosie.

With the car heading towards Purley and Reigate, the day fresh but fine, Rosie murmured, 'What are you thinking about, Eloise?'

'Oh, I am thinking about everything,' said Eloise, 'and that I 'ave never been in a car like this.'

'It's a Bentley,' smiled Rosie.

'I know of Rolls-Royce cars,' said Eloise, and Major Armitage, despite his preoccupation with the traffic and his ambitious interest in Rosie, picked up the accent in Eloise's English.

'A Bentley is on a par with a Rolls-Royce, but has more dash to it,' he said.

'Dash? What is dash, please?' asked Eloise.

'More go,' said Tim.

'More go?' said Eloise.

'Quite so,' said Major Armitage.

'Ah, I think I know,' said Eloise.

Rosie, smiling, said, 'Eloise's late mother was French, Major Armitage.'

'I see,' he said. 'The present Mrs Adams is the second wife of Mr Adams?'

'Mr Adams met Eloise's mother in France during the war,' said Rosie.

'I see,' said Major Armitage again, the Bentley gliding effortlessly past cars and buses by making use of clear tram tracks.

'Yes,' said Tim, 'but—'

'No buts, Tim, it was love at first sight,' said Rosie. 'Eloise will tell you so.'

Tim caught on.

'Yes, I've heard her say that,' he said, and Eloise smiled and squeezed Rosie's arm gratefully for the words that had let Major Armitage infer a certain marriage had once taken place.

On the Bentley went, passing through Croydon and Purley to head for Dorking and the road to Guildford and Godalming, the engine purring, Eloise examining the passing countryside and remarking on the fresh green colours of spring. Major Armitage participated without effort in the many moments of general conversation which kept the atmosphere from becoming strained, although at no time did Rosie appear other than completely at ease.

Just before they reached Godalming, Major

Armitage took a left turn into a road of green verges. He passed over a little crossroads in half a mile, and Tim noticed a signpost marked 'Headleigh Hall'.

'Well, I'm blessed, you're signposted, sir,' he said.

'So we are, Tim, so we are,' smiled Major Armitage.

Tim, who'd been brought up by parents who had no fixed prejudices, had none himself. So, while he was against any attempt by Major Armitage to change Rosie's life in any way that would affect her relationship with her adoptive family, he could not help liking him. Nor could Eloise, and for that matter, nor could Rosie herself.

Half a mile from the crossroads, Major Armitage turned right between two open iron gates and entered a long drive bordered by lime trees. The way broadened out after two hundred yards, and Headleigh Hall appeared then, a manor house built of warm rose-red brick faced with stone, its double front doors imposingly huge. The car continued on, passing the tall side of the mansion and executing a slow sweeping turn that brought it round to offer a view of the rear facade. It was magnificent, with its array of many windows, its two outer gables and a smaller central gable. These gables formed the letter 'E', indicative of an Elizabethan manor house.

Major Armitage had slowed down to no more than five miles an hour. Perhaps this was to allow his passengers time to take in the full splendour of his country home, and to let Rosie in particular reflect on what life there could hold for her. At any rate, the eyes of all three passengers were open wide.

'Crikey,' breathed Tim.

'Oh, 'ow beautiful,' said Eloise.

'Lovely,' said Rosie, and the Bentley came to a

gentle stop close to a great sward of green grass. From there she and Tim and Eloise were offered a captivating view of the house and a breathtaking view of the estate. The bright day sharpened the colours of every vista and touched the rose-red brick with sunshine.

'It's like a castle,' said Tim.

'Not quite, Tim old chap,' said Major Armitage, and eased himself out of the car. He opened the passenger door, and Eloise alighted, followed by Rosie. Tim emerged, and they all stood together to gaze in fascination at the view of parkland, farm and copses.

'Wonderful, isn't it?' enthused Eloise.

'Armitages have lived here for close on a hundred and forty years,' said Major Armitage. 'You can imagine what kind of a family home this was for us. I've two brothers and three sisters, all married with their own families now. I've no children myself.' He smiled. 'Except for Rosie,' he added. 'My wife, unfortunately, is a semi-invalid. Ah, here she is.'

The doors in the central gable opened to the movements of a manservant, and a woman stepped out to slowly descend the terrace steps. She was tall and thin, with a mass of dark hair. Over her brown dress she wore a light brown cardigan, which Rosie thought very odd. It destroyed elegance. The woman advanced, and Major Armitage went to meet her.

'The girl is here, Charles?' she said in a deep throaty voice.

'With her brother and sister,' he said. 'Come and meet them.' She walked with him, her movements delicate and deliberate. Her face was thin, though her lips were full, her skin slightly mottled, and her hazel eyes a little glassy. Major Armitage introduced the young people to her. Her smile for Eloise was one that appeared, flickered briefly and was gone. That which she bestowed on Tim, a personable boy, fixed itself in such a way that Rosie thought her parted lips could not relax. However, they did. Then, as Rosie herself was introduced, the slightly glassy eyes took her in, and she spoke, huskily.

'So this is our daughter, Charles.'

The surprised eyes of the young people made Major Armitage say quickly, 'My daughter, your stepdaughter.'

'How lovely she is,' said Mrs Armitage. 'Bring her in, Charles. The others may go.'

'Pardon?' said Tim.

'Is there a misunderstanding?' asked Rosie.

'No, you may stay, my dear,' said Mrs Armitage, 'but we have no need of the others, whoever they are. Carter will drive them to the station. Come, my husband and I will show you Headleigh Hall, and where we shall accommodate you.' She was throatier, huskier. 'A beautiful suite of rooms.'

'Slow down, Pauline,' said Major Armitage, a little edge to his voice, 'you're running ahead of events. Order some coffee for our guests, some refreshments. It's been a long drive.'

'Refreshments?' Mrs Armitage ran the tip of her tongue over her bottom lip. 'Yes, of course.' She turned, took two paces and stumbled. It was Rosie who darted and prevented her from falling. Major Armitage, looking more put out than concerned, nevertheless reached his wife's side and put an arm around her.

'I shouldn't have let her leave her bed,' he said

to Rosie. 'Her condition varies, you know, but today she insisted she was well enough to get up and meet you. She was keen to do so. If you'll excuse me for a few minutes, I'll see to her.'

'I'm quite all right,' said Mrs Armitage, pushing at him. But her face looked distorted, as if she was fighting pain. It wasn't so much pain, however, it was a need for brandy, the tipple to which she was incurably addicted. She'd made her effort, because of Rosie, but she had no staying power.

Major Armitage took her up the terrace steps and into the house, Rosie following along with Eloise and Tim, Eloise thinking she knew what was wrong with Mrs Armitage, the same thing that had been wrong with the brother of her Uncle Jacques. Alcohol.

The manservant reappeared and, at a nod from Major Armitage, took the guests into a drawing-room, where colour, framed paintings and exquisite furniture leapt to dazzle the eye. The floor was almost fully covered by a hunting carpet, and above the marble fireplace was a gilt Chippendale overmantle whose several mirrors flashed light.

'Please be seated,' said the manservant, 'and I'll bring refreshments.' He was a very dignified character, and made his exit in almost lordly fashion.

'Bet you a bob he's the butler, Rosie,' said Tim.

'Ah, an English butler,' said Eloise, ''ow grand. But poor Madame Armitage, so ill, isn't she?'

'She seemed very weak,' said Rosie.

'She flopped,' said Tim. 'Lucky you caught her, Rosie. But did you hear her telling me and Eloise to push off? What a queer old bird.'

'She cannot 'elp it,' said Eloise, 'but I was amazed. Such a strange-looking wife for such a handsome man, yes? Oh, but see this room, isn't it *enchante*? They are aristocrats, yes. Imagine, your father an aristocrat, Rosie. Ah, you are one also because of your birth.'

'My birth doesn't make me feel I belong to this place,' said Rosie quietly. 'Once and for all, Eloise, I am an Adams, and you must understand that, sister dear, or we shall fall out.'

'Oh, but—'

'You are an Adams too,' said Rosie, 'and usually no Adams falls out with another. Our grandma doesn't allow it, and will speak her mind if it happens.'

'I'll be the one to get it in the neck if you two quarrel,' said Tim. 'Grandma always blames the one that's wearing trousers. Crikey, though, is there anything grander than this place except Buckingham Palace?'

'I am astonished,' said Eloise, 'but I did not mean to upset you, Rosie.'

'Oh, all over,' smiled Rosie, and Major Armitage entered the room then.

'My apologies,' he said. 'So sorry my wife had one of her turns.' He had put her to bed with a weak brandy and soda, brandy being the only refreshment her mind had been on. He had, however, taken the bottle away, although he knew it was quite possible she had another cunningly hidden somewhere. He was angry with himself for having taken the risk of letting her meet Rosie, but she had insisted she must, that she would be quite capable. He might have known she wouldn't be. 'What, no refreshments yet?'

'They're here, sir,' said the manservant, re-appearing again. He advanced carrying a large silver tray on which there were biscuits, coffee, sherry and lemonade, together with cups, saucers, small plates, jugs and glasses. He placed the tray on a low rosewood table that stood in front of the fireplace.

'Now,' said Major Armitage, 'who'd like coffee, who'd like sherry and who'd like the cook's first-class lemonade?'

'Coffee, if you please,' said Eloise, her tiny hat, a Juliet cap, sitting neatly on her brown hair. Rosie, crowned with a round navy blue hat, smiled at their host.

'Yes, coffee for me too, please,' she said.

'I think I'll have a sherry,' said Tim.

'You mean a glass of the cook's lemonade,' smiled Rosie.

'Oh, one or the other, I don't mind,' said Tim airily.

'I'll see to them, Martin,' said Major Armitage.

'Very good, sir,' said the manservant, and left.

Major Armitage poured the coffee. Eloise asked for hers to be black. Rosie asked for a dash of milk with hers.

'Or cream?' smiled Major Armitage.

'Well, cream, well, I'm blessed,' said Tim, 'there's a new song out, "You're The Cream In My Coffee".'

'Oh, then let's go along with the song,' said Rosie.

Rosie and Eloise received their coffee, and Tim was given a glass of lemonade. Major Armitage poured himself coffee with just a little milk, and sat down with his guests around the table. He offered the biscuits, which weren't refused. He took one himself, since they were the cook's own shortbread recipe.

'A little something to keep us all going until

lunch at one,' he said, then spoke about his estate and what there was to see, the gardens, the parkland, a wood in which pheasants might be spotted, the stables and a dairy farm. Tim asked questions about everything in the manner of a naturally interested boy, and Eloise asked questions in the manner of a very intrigued young lady. Rosie asked no questions at all. She was taking in Major Armitage's attitude and making a gradual assessment of the very pleasant gentleman. She felt there was far more to him than civilities, there had to be when one realized he had this magnificent manor house and its large estate to run. But just for himself and his wife, a place like this? No sons or daughters, except herself? It was understandable, his wish to have her under his roof. She did ask one question eventually.

'Are you your father's heir, Major Armitage?'

A little sigh escaped him at her formal use of his name and rank, but his pleasant smile followed. He was prepared to exercise a great deal of patience with his striking daughter.

'Yes, as my father's eldest son, I shall inherit,' he said.

'And you'll be Sir Charles Armitage then?' said Rosie.

'Yes, the title's hereditary,' said Major Armitage, at which Eloise looked more intrigued and Tim blinked.

'How very nice for you,' smiled Rosie.

Ah, thought Eloise, she is impressed.

Crikey, thought Tim, that's something to tell the family.

'Would you all like to be shown around the house?' asked Major Armitage. 'There'll be time

168

before lunch, and this afternoon I'll take you over the estate.'

'Eloise and Tim would love to see the house,' said Rosie. 'Myself, I should like to talk to you.'

Major Armitage felt then that whatever was in her mind it was in his favour.

'I'd be very happy about a talk, Rosie,' he said, 'and I'll get Martin to take Tim and Eloise on a tour of the house.'

'Excuse me, sir,' said Tim, 'is Mr Martin your butler?'

'Yes,' said Major Armitage.

'First time I've met a butler,' said Tim.

'Butlers are an invaluable species, Tim. At least, good ones are.' Major Armitage got up and rang for Martin. The dignified manservant, middle-aged, was not long in presenting himself.

'You rang, sir?' he said, and Major Armitage asked if he would be good enough to show Tim and Eloise around the house. 'A pleasure, sir,' said Martin, and stood at the open door waiting for the boy and the young lady in question to join him there.

'You'll be all right, Rosie?' said Tim, coming to his feet along with Eloise.

'Yes, of course, Tim,' said Rosie.

'I assure you, I won't eat her,' smiled Major Armitage, and Tim and Eloise left in company with the stately butler. The door closed behind them. 'May I now tell you what an exceptional pleasure it is to have you here, Rosie?' said Major Armitage.

'All three of us?' said Rosie.

'I meant you particularly.'

'I do understand how you feel,' said Rosie, 'and

I'm sorry, of course, that your wife has been unable to give you children. Major Armitage, do—'

'Must you call me that, Rosie?'

'I really don't feel I can call you father,' said Rosie. 'Never mind, worse things happen, don't they? Anyway, do you have a solicitor?'

'A solicitor?' Major Armitage looked hard at her. Rosie smiled. 'Rosie, are you going to suggest I should do something about establishing a father's claim on you?'

'Heavens, no, nothing of the kind,' said Rosie. 'You have a solicitor, yes, of course you have, a family solicitor, I daresay. Have you spoken to him about me?'

'Frankly, yes,' said Major Armitage.

'You've asked him, perhaps, if you have a chance of setting my adoption aside?'

'I asked him for counsel's opinion.'

'Someone who would make a case for you in a civil court?' enquired Rosie.

'Having met you, I don't think I can be blamed for wanting you under my roof,' said Major Armitage.

'That's a little absurd, though, isn't it?' said Rosie. 'You've managed without me for nineteen years.'

'Only because I knew nothing of your existence,' said Major Armitage, keeping quiet about counsel's opinion.

'I didn't mean that unkindly,' said Rosie, 'but the fact is, if you hadn't found out about me it wouldn't have seriously mattered, would it? What one has never had or never known, one can't miss, isn't that true?'

By God, thought Major Armitage, does any young woman have as much composure as this one?

'True, yes,' he said, 'but I did find out.'

'So you've been consulting your solicitor in the hope of establishing a legal claim on me, and in the further hope that that would persuade me to live here, at Headleigh Hall?' said Rosie.

'I won't deny it.'

'Well, I'm going to ask you not to proceed,' said Rosie. 'You see, if you take any steps, any steps at all, that will mean my adoptive parents having to go to court to fight you, you will never see me again. I don't wish them to have those kind of worries. I think perhaps you feel you could have the adoption set aside, and then be able to make me leave my family and live here. But I don't think the adoption could be set aside.'

'Rosie, no, I haven't thought of making you do that,' said Major Armitage, 'I've only thought I'd like the chance to have you living here some part of each year.'

'In the hope of turning me into an Armitage?' said Rosie.

'You are an Armitage, I swear it.'

'All my happiness has come from being an Adams,' said Rosie. 'It really would be useless to fight my adoption in court, for I'm sure it would never work, and in any case, there is no way you could compel me to live here for even a week if I didn't want to. I have to tell you a second time, you would never see me again. As it is, if you'll leave things as they are, I will promise to visit you four times a year.'

'That would be the sum total of our relationship, four daily visits from you a year?' said Major Armitage.

'The sum total before was nothing,' said Rosie.

171

'By God, Rosie, you argue your case like the very devil,' said Major Armitage. He knew, of course, he had no case himself.

'I simply don't wish to have you fight my adoptive parents,' said Rosie. 'They've given me too much for me not to fight for them, to ensure they have no worries.'

'Are you so very attached to them?' asked Major Armitage.

'More than you perhaps will ever realize, much more,' said Rosie.

'Well, the last thing I want is to be left completely out in the cold,' said Major Armitage, 'and must settle for seeing you four times a year. Would you agree, however, to us writing to each other?'

'I always answer any letters I receive,' said Rosie. 'You're very likeable, you know, and I'm pleased about that.'

'I shall follow your career with great interest,' said Major Armitage, 'and will always offer any help you may need.'

'It's agreed, then, you'll instruct your solicitor to take no further action?' said Rosie.

Major Armitage smiled wryly.

'It's agreed,' he said. 'By heaven, what a splendid young woman you are, Rosie. I shall always regret not knowing of your birth.'

'Would you, then, have married my mother?' asked Rosie.

'I'm not sure I can answer that,' said Major Armitage.

'Well, I shan't press you to,' said Rosie, certain he would have thought twice about marrying the shallow woman who had been her mother. In any case, if she had been given the power to change things, she would have changed nothing that had happened to her since the days when, as a little girl, she had first come to know Boots. 'We can call ourselves friends now, can't we?'

'I won't quarrel with that,' said Major Armitage, 'it's a beginning.'

Rosie smiled. She had secured what she most wanted, freedom from worry for Boots and Emily. She didn't really think the law would have quashed the adoption on the grounds that the natural father had had no say in the matter, but she'd hated the thought of Boots and Emily being dragged into court. Actions in civil courts could be prolonged, and were meat and drink to barristers.

'I shall keep my promise to visit you,' she said.

'It's the kind of beginning I must accept,' said Major Armitage.

'Well, a friendly beginning is much more acceptable than an unfriendly finish, isn't it?' smiled Rosie.

# Chapter Ten

The rest of the day was very pleasant for Rosie, Tim and Eloise. They enjoyed a superb lunch in a beautiful dining-room, with Major Armitage a friendly and attentive host. His wife was not present.

After lunch, he took them around the gardens, where a profusion of daffodil and tulip beds blazed with spring colour, and rhododendrons and azaleas were bursting into flower. Eloise exclaimed in excited admiration, hiding the fact that her curiosity was close to boiling point. She was sure that Rosie's private conversation with Major Armitage had resulted in something to Rosie's advantage. Ah, yes, as his only child, Rosie must mean much to him, and because of all he had, this magnificent house and estate, he must mean something to her, despite her love for the Adams family.

Eloise whispered a question.

'Rosie, what 'appened, if you please?'

'I'll tell you later.'

'No, now. I'm your sister.'

'Later,' said Rosie.

From the gardens they went to the stables and saw the string of horses kept by Major Armitage. There were carriages too, but kept only for show and not for use. The tour became extensive, and everything reflected the affluence of Major Armitage as a landowner, or rather, as the heir to it all. His three guests engaged him throughout in animated conversation, and because of the vitality and unspoiled nature of all three, he experienced new regrets that his wife had given him no children, children who might have grown to become very much like these had, Rosie especially.

They returned to the house for tea, Tim very voluble about all they had seen and very taken with the hospitality and friendliness of their host, while Eloise was still fascinated by everything, and more particularly, of course, by what had taken place between Rosie and her father.

After tea, at Rosie's request, Major Armitage drove them back home. He said nothing about what had been agreed, and Rosie said nothing, either. Eloise had the fidgets about being kept in the dark, but Tim had none. He knew Rosie better than Eloise did, and was sure she'd have played Major Armitage with a straight bat. A bloke could always rely on Rosie.

The journey from Godalming was quite lively, the passengers finding plenty to say to each other and to Major Armitage, who had shown himself to be charming as well as civilized. When they reached the house in Red Post Hill, Rosie asked him if he would like to come in, and he said if Mr Adams could possibly spare him ten minutes, he'd like to talk to him.

Boots, of course, was willing, and they met again in the study, while Rosie at last eased the frustrations and curiosity of Eloise by recounting how she had dealt with Major Armitage. Emily, Tim, Chinese Lady and Mr Finch also listened.

In the study, Major Armitage spoke to Boots of his conversation with Rosie, and how an agreement had been reached. He was frank in admitting he'd hoped Rosie would spend several weeks a year at Headleigh Hall. However, she was a young lady with her own ideas about what was fair to all concerned.

Boots smiled.

'She actually said, did she, that she'd never see you again if you went against her wishes, Major Armitage?'

'She was quite uncompromising in her ultimatum, Mr Adams, and I was left defeated. I must congratulate you and Mrs Adams for bringing her up so well, for obviously allowing her to develop in her own way. Although I'm her father, it's you and Mrs Adams who command her affections and loyalties, and I only ask for you to go along with her promise to visit me four times a year. If that's all I can have, I must accept it, and I hope you'll put nothing in the way of it.'

'I wouldn't dream of trying to persuade Rosie to break a promise,' said Boots.

Major Armitage regarded him sombrely.

'You say you were a sergeant with the Royal West Kents during the war, Mr Adams?'

'That's true,' said Boots.

'Why not an officer?'

'My background was wrong,' said Boots, 'I'm one of the ordinary people.'

'Rubbish, man,' said Major Armitage, 'if you're ordinary, I'm a pink elephant. Do you see yourself as ordinary?'

'Not all the time,' said Boots, looking whimsical.

'Mr Adams, there's going to be another war.'

'I know,' said Boots.

'Well, watch out for it. Nothing is going to stop that

madman Hitler. Now, if you'll excuse me, I must get back. Give my regards to Mrs Adams, whom I met when I arrived this morning, and thank you for your time and understanding. Perhaps on one of Rosie's visits to Headleigh Hall, you and Mrs Adams can be my guests too. You'll be very welcome.'

'Thanks,' said Boots. 'I'll see you out.'

Meanwhile, Emily, Eloise and Chinese Lady had spent time blinking and staring at Rosie while she told them all they needed to hear, doing so with the calmness of a young lady who did not seem to realize that, aside from Tim and Mr Finch, her audience was quivering. Tim only ever quivered when he went in to bat for his school cricket team in moments of crisis, and Mr Finch was a man who was always as calm as Rosie herself. What Rosie came up with in her exposition amounted in the end to a triumph, but at no time did she sound smug about it. Her sense of humour danced about a little, and all her references to Major Armitage suggested she found him a very reasonable and likeable man. Well, bless my soul, thought Chinese Lady, our Rosie, what education's doing for her is a lot more than mine did for me except reading, writing and arithmetic. She takes after Boots, that's what, he was always good at learning and at not turning a hair about anything. Our Rosie's modelled herself on him, she's always looked up to him, and even liked his airy-fairy ways. And now she's been and gone and cooked Major Armitage's goose for him, and done it in a nice fashion, I'd say, like a lady.

'Rosie, there's not goin' to be a fight, no-one's havin' to go to court?' said Emily.

'No-one,' said Rosie.

'Congratulations, Rosie,' smiled Mr Finch who, truth to tell, had anticipated this kind of outcome.

'I am amazed,' said Eloise, not for the first time that day. 'Mama, you should have seen the gentleman—'

'I did see him, when he came this mornin',' said Emily.

'No, no, I mean in 'is grand house with all 'is land,' said Eloise. 'Such an aristocrat. I should not 'ave been able to argue with 'im myself, no, my feet would 'ave been shaking in my shoes. Imagine, Mama, Rosie saying no to all of it. Amazing, yes, isn't it?'

'Here, leave off, Eloise,' said Tim, 'Rosie was never going to say yes to living there.'

'But it was so magnificent,' said Eloise.

'This is Rosie's home, Eloise,' said Chinese Lady.

'Yes,' said Tim. 'I bet even if Rosie was invited to Buckingham Palace for a week, she'd still come back home to us.'

'With honours, Tim,' said Mr Finch.

'Rosie, I'm so relieved,' said Emily, 'and I'm sure me and your dad won't mind a bit about you visitin' Major Armitage four times a year. I think it's right you should. I mean, he did father you and he's been very agreeable about not makin' any trouble.'

'Well, he and Daddy have something in common,' said Rosie, 'they're both gentlemen. Mind you, Daddy's funnier.'

'You can say that again,' smiled Emily, 'except I'm not always sure I laugh in the right places.'

'It's a blessing that some of you don't mind Boots talkin' out of the back of his head at times,' said Chinese Lady, 'and like I've said before, he didn't get it from me or his late dad. Still, I will say your Aunt Victoria always remarked on him bein' a born gentleman. And now what's 'appened, Em'ly? Our Rosie's handled Major Armitage like a born lady.'

'Yes, you see, Grandmama, she was born of the English nobleman,' said Eloise, 'so she was a lady at birth, wasn't she?'

'I didn't mean that,' said Chinese Lady, 'I meant the way she's been brought up at home. She might easily have been like her—' Chinese Lady checked herself before mention of Rosie's mother fell tactlessly from her lips. 'Well, never mind that, I'm sure we're fortunate in all our young people. I've spent a worrying day thinkin' about Rosie, but Boots was right in saying we had to leave it to her to sort things out, which was sensible of him and a change from bein' a bit casual. Yes, our Rosie's turned out a very capable young lady.'

'Agreed, Maisie,' said Mr Finch.

'There you are, one up to you, Rosie,' said Tim, 'you're a lady. And what's more, you don't half play with a straight bat. Of course, I knew you would.'

'Oh, don't mention it, Tim lovey,' smiled Rosie.

'What is playing with a straight bat, please?' asked Eloise.

'I think it means not getting bowled out,' said Mr Finch. German-born, he had come to know cricket. One couldn't fully relate to Boots and his family without having a love of cricket.

'What is "bowled out"?' asked Eloise.

'Summer's coming,' said Tim, 'so you'll soon learn.'

Boots came in then. He looked at Rosie, a smile on his face.

'Well done, poppet,' he said, and Rosie warmed to his expression, one of frank and grateful affection.

'Boots, has Major Armitage gone now?' asked Emily.

'Yes, and without leaving any complaints behind,' said Boots. 'He'd like to have Rosie under his roof, of course he would, but accepts things have to be the way she wants.'

'Well, perhaps he's a nice man, after all,' said Emily.

'Yes, he's nice,' said Rosie.

'But you still knocked him for six, Rosie,' said Tim.

'Bowled him over,' said Emily, and laughed. She was up in the clouds about not losing Rosie.

'What is "knocked for six" and "bowled over", please?' asked Eloise.

'That's more cricket,' said Tim.

'I don't understand,' said Eloise.

'Oh, you will once we start to teach you the game,' said Tim.

'If it's fine on Easter Sunday, Eloise,' said Boots, 'we'll let you open the batting.'

'No, no,' begged Eloise, 'it will frighten me to death.'

'Can't be helped,' said Tim.

'All in the game,' said Boots.

'Some game,' said Rosie, and laughed.

Chinese Lady smiled. Her family was still intact.

Later, when everyone was retiring to bed, Rosie intercepted Boots on his way to switch off the outside lamp.

'I told you not to worry, didn't I?' she said.

'Did you have it all worked out from the start?' he asked.

'No, not from the start,' said Rosie, 'only after some due thought processes. Pleased with me, are you, old thing?'

'Love you,' smiled Boots.

Which was all Rosie needed to hear as a reward. She might be a composed young lady and a promising undergraduate, but her adoptive father meant more to her than even he realized.

## Chapter Eleven

An open car pulled up outside the florist's shop in Kennington Park Road. Cassie, raven hair worn long and tied with a bright ribbon as always, glanced up from just inside the doorway, where she was rearranging a huge display of daffodils in a large stone pot. Recognizing the driver, she called to Mrs Dewhurst, wife of the owner of the shop.

'Oh, won't be a tick, I'm just goin' to have a word with someone I know.'

'That Freddy of yours, I suppose,' smiled Mrs Dewhurst, who was making up a bouquet.

'Bless him,' said Cassie, and out of the shop she went to speak to the driver. It wasn't Freddy, it was Boots, and Cassie's smile sparkled in the morning light.

'Hello, Cassie.'

'What're you doin' here?' asked Cassie.

'Hoping to see you,' said Boots.

'Oh, that's nice,' said Cassie, 'and I won't tell Em'ly, or Freddy. Only I can't go riding with you, Boots. Well, I can't leave the shop, I've got to work conscientiously this week, which is my last. I'm leaving Thursday, the day before Good Friday, and gettin' married Saturday. Oh, lor', I think I've already got butterflies. Imagine that. I mean, it's only Freddy, not the Prince of Wales. Mind, I don't mind it's only Freddy, because he's always been devoted, and I'm really quite fond of him.'

'Yes, I believe the latest gossip is that he's your beloved,' said Boots.

'Oh, that Annabelle,' said Cassie, 'I suppose she's the one who makes gossip stretch all the way from Walworth to Denmark Hill. Oh, what did you mean about hoping to see me?'

'I've something for you,' said Boots. 'I understand Sammy's giving Freddy a wedding cheque for fifty pounds.'

'Yes, would you believe?' said Cassie happily. 'A cheque for all of fifty pounds to put into a bank.'

'Well, here's one for you, Cassie,' said Boots, extracting an envelope from the inside pocket of his jacket. He handed it to her.

'What d'you mean, one for me?' said Cassie.

'A cheque for fifty pounds, Cassie,' said Boots, 'from Emily and self to you, with our very best wishes. You'll make a go of it with Freddy, I'm certain you will, and along with Sammy and Susie, Emily and I want to give the pair of you a good start.'

Cassie stared at the envelope.

'Fifty pounds for me?' she breathed, eyes a little misty.

'You'll find the cheque inside,' said Boots.

'Oh, crikey, I'm overcome,' said Cassie, 'I never knew anyone nicer. I could easily marry you if I wasn't marrying Freddy and you weren't already married to Em'ly.'

'Well, as I don't think it would be a good idea to get rid of either of them,' said Boots, 'we'll have to leave things as they are. Good luck, Cassie, see you at St John's on Saturday.'

'Boots, I'll never know how to thank you,' said Cassie, 'but I can kiss you, can't I?'

'Frankly,' said Boots, 'I'm all for it, and if anyone catches us we'll talk our way out of it.'

'Oh, you've always been so nice to me,' said Cassie, and leaned over the car and kissed him warmly and fondly. When he drove away, her eyes were a little misty again. Well, who wouldn't feel overcome by such kindness? It was no wonder that many Walworth people had such fond memories of the Adams family.

Crikey, fifty pounds. When Freddy received a similar cheque from Sammy, they'd have a hundred pounds between them. They'd put it all into the bank and save it until they were in a position to think of buying a little house. It was what Sammy and Boots wanted them to do.

From Kennington, Boots went on to Blackfriars to look in on Mr Eli Greenberg, whose large covered yard contained mountains of second-hand goods of every description. Boots, who was on his way to the Shoreditch factory, broke his journey at the yard. He needed to speak to the genial rag-and-bone man, a character so ubiquitous in the practice of his trade that there was scarcely anyone in the whole of South London who did not know him.

Mr Greenberg was at home in a manner of speaking, although invisible until he materialized out of adjoining stacks of kitchen chairs.

'Ah, Boots my friend, to vhat do I owe the pleasure of seeing you?'

'How's life, Eli?' asked Boots.

Mr Greenberg raised mittened hands and sighed.

'You ask that of a man vith a spending vife and

three stepsons?' he said. Not long ago he had married a widow with three growing lads. 'Boots, the expense, it vill mean no shirt to my back and an early grave.'

'But your bed's warmer, I daresay,' said Boots.

'Boots, Boots, I should ruin myself for the compensation of a varmer bed?' said Mr Greenberg, but there was a twinkle in his eye. He may have been over fifty, but no-one could have said he was a fading physical specimen. 'Vhat can I do for you?'

'Listen,' said Boots, and spoke to him about a matter touching on the double wedding, a matter he'd first broached a few days ago. Mr Greenberg smiled, and the smile became a beam. He assured Boots that all was in hand, the necessary hire had been arranged and the deposit paid. Boots said good, that he and Sammy would settle all expenses, and that it was time Eli had a telephone installed. Mr Greenberg turned pale.

'Boots, I should have more expenses? Vhy, ain't I got enough? And vhat vould a telephone do for me that I can't do on my rounds? And is talkin' on a telephone the same pleasure as talkin' as I am to you now?'

'You've got a point,' smiled Boots. 'Anyway, thanks for arranging everything. I've spoken to Freddy and Horace, but not a word to the brides, of course.'

'Nor from me, Boots, not vun, until the day,' said Mr Greenberg, tapping his nose. 'Mind, a joy for them, von't it be?'

'Especially for Cassie,' said Boots.

'Ah, Cassie, such a joy alvays, ain't she?' said Mr Greenberg.

'Granted, Eli,' said Boots. Cassie, he knew, was a hard-up girl, earning a mere pittance at her job, and it was her affectionate old dad who kept her in good clothes. But Cassie had never been known to be other than as happy as a sprite of spring. 'So long, Eli, see you at the church, old lad.'

'Business is necessary, Boots. Vun has to live. But friendship is precious, ain't it so?'

'I think you've got something there,' said Boots, and left.

Cassie rushed round to see Freddy that evening. Using the latchcord, into the house she went like one of the family, and through to the kitchen, where Freddy was talking to his mum and dad. Sally was upstairs, doing things relating to her wedding. Freddy was talking about his own wedding, ominously close for a bloke who was going to have a struggle to assert himself as Cassie's better half.

'Oh, hello, everyone,' said Cassie, sparkling with life and rapture.

''Ello, Cassie love,' said Mr Brown.

'My, you do look lovely tonight,' said Mrs Brown.

'Yes, don't I?' said Cassie. 'Isn't Freddy lucky?'

'Oh, he's grateful as well for what the Lord's providing him with,' said Mrs Brown. 'You're goin' to be a lovely bride, Cassie.'

'Yes, aren't I?' said Cassie. Freddy grinned. In many ways, Cassie was never going to grow up. He liked that.

'Well,' he said, 'what I'm specially lookin' forward to is—'

'Freddy, not now, not in front of your mum and dad,' said Cassie. 'Oh, d'you know why I've come round?'

186

'No, I don't exactly know right now,' said Freddy, 'but I expect I will in a minute.'

'Yes, all right, Freddy beloved,' said Cassie, and thereupon put him and his parents in the picture about the wedding gift from Boots and Emily. In proof thereof, she produced the cheque from her handbag. 'I nearly cried all over him when Boots gave it to me.'

'Goodness me,' said Mrs Brown breathlessly, 'I'd have cried buckets gettin' a lovely weddin' gift like that.'

'Yes, and on top of the canteen of cutlery they've already given us,' said Cassie. 'I was overcome.'

Freddy, examining the cheque, said, 'I'm overcome meself, Cassie, I'm goin' to have to phone Boots and thank him personally.'

'Freddy, you can bank the cheque with your own when Sammy gives it to you, can't you?' said Cassie.

'Well, it's made out to you,' said Freddy.

'No problem, son,' said Mr Brown. 'Just get Cassie to endorse it on the back.'

'What's endorsin'?' asked Freddy, a stranger to banking procedures.

'Just her signature,' said Mr Brown. 'That sort of makes it over to you as far as the bank's concerned, and I think Sammy's goin' to let you 'ave your own cheque tomorrer. He's callin' in in the mornin'. You've been in touch with the Walworth Road bank, ain't you?'

'Yes,' said Freddy, 'and the manager's goin' to have everything ready for me. I'll only 'ave to do some signing.'

'Freddy, you'll be seeing the bank manager himself?' said Cassie.

'It's the regular thing with a new customer,' said Freddy.

'Freddy, I could get proud of you seeing the bank manager himself,' said Cassie.

'Yes, it does sound compliment'ry,' said Mrs Brown.

'It's Freddy's cheque the manager wants to shake hands with,' said Mr Brown.

'Freddy, take mine as well,' said Cassie, 'then we'll start the account with a hundred pounds. Oh, I'm nearly faintin'. I mean, a hundred pounds that's all ours.'

'What a lovely start to your marriage, Cassie,' said Mrs Brown.

'Lucrative, Bessie,' said Mr Brown, 'and 'andsome as well.'

'All right, Cassie love,' said Freddy, 'sign your cheque, then.'

A pen and ink were brought from the mantelpiece by Mrs Brown, and Cassie endorsed the cheque. After which, she said, 'Oh, don't you think it's nice havin' friends like Boots and Sammy, Freddy?'

Freddy looked at her. She seemed a bit misty-eyed.

'Well, yes, I do, Cassie,' he said, 'and it's even nicer for me havin' a friend like you.'

'Freddy, you silly, I'm not your friend.'

'Yes, you are, Cassie,' said Freddy, 'you're my friend for life.'

Lilian, on arriving home from work that evening, found a note on her mat from her milkman. She read it with a smile.

*Dear Mrs Hyams,*

*I thought I'd just drop you a line to say the eggs are specially good this week, all brown ones of a large size, so if you need six of the best, just put a note in your empty tomorrow morning. Also, I'm doing myself the pleasure of calling on you tomorrow evening in the hope we can spend a few hours together as I haven't had that pleasure for a few days and it's made me feel gloomy, which isn't my style. Yours truly, Bill.*

After digesting the missive, Lilian asked herself why she was smiling. After all, he was still only a milkman, and while she wasn't toffee-nosed she did think herself good enough for a more affluent bloke. And Rabbi Solomon had dropped in yesterday evening to ask if a rumoured friendship with a Gentile person was true. Lilian said rumours concerning any of her friendships ought to be treated as nobody's business but her own. Rabbi Solomon shook his head at her, and suggested there was promise in the fact that Mr Abel Morrison had an affectionate regard for her. Lilian said Mr Morrison was a kind man, but not her type.

She thought now that her milkman was more her type because he amused her and didn't own any surplus flesh. And because he kept reminding her of Sammy. She smiled again.

There were callers at the Red Post Hill house that evening. Lizzy and Ned, Annabelle and Bobby, Vi and Tommy, and Susie and Sammy, all dropped in to congratulate Boots and Emily on having such a remarkable daughter as Rosie. They were a demonstrative tribe, the Somers and Adams families. Rosie was hugged and kissed on account of her kind but firm approach to her natural father, which had shown just how permanently attached she was to her adoptive family. Chinese Lady thought the occasion called for a glass of port all round. Amid the celebratory hubbub, Rosie quietly disappeared. Noticing her absence, Emily went in search of her and found her in her room.

'Rosie?'

Rosie turned, a hankie in her hand. It startled Emily to see that her eyes were wet. She couldn't remember when Rosie had last shown tears. As a growing girl, she had rarely cried. As a young woman, never. Except now.

'Sorry, Mum love,' said Rosie, 'I'm not really as cool as everyone thinks.'

'Well, who cares, Rosie?' said Emily. 'We all hide some feelings, don't we, we all try not to let ourselves down. It's been upsettin' for you as well as us, hasn't it, findin' your father was out there in his own world.'

'Mum dearest,' said Rosie, 'that was a shock and a surprise, but not upsetting. What made me suddenly feel weepy was the realization a few minutes ago that—' She stopped to dab her nose.

'That everyone came round to let you see what you mean to all of us,' said Emily. 'Bless you, Rosie darling, we all love you, and it's nice you're like the rest of us, that there's times when you just can't 'elp showin' your feelings. You're ours, Rosie, and none of us could stand losin' you. You're an Adams, never mind who you were born of. Boots meant to make you an Adams from the very start, and what Boots wants he always goes quietly about gettin'. He's not as much of an earthquake as your Uncle Sammy, but his results are just as good. You're one of his very special results, Rosie love.'

'Oh, help,' said Rosie, 'now I need my hankie again.'

*     *     *

Sammy was at his Southwark brewery the following day. He exchanged some profit-making business chat with the manager, had a few cheerful words with Mr Brown, the foreman, and then called Freddy. He took him outside into the temperamental April sunshine. Well, it was the kind of sunshine typical of April, all present and correct one moment, and going absent without leave the next.

'Well, Freddy me sport, are you lookin' forward to doing the honours with Cassie, or have you got twitches?' Sammy asked.

'No good havin' twitches anywhere near Cassie,' said Freddy, 'she'd spot 'em a mile off and take advantage.'

'What sort of advantage?' asked Sammy, as electric with vitality as ever. He had an automatic self-rechargeable battery. His one problem was that Susie seemed to be able to unplug him, and he didn't know anyone else who could do that, not even his redoubtable mother.

'What sort?' said Freddy. 'The kind where I give in and flop. I won't say it ain't enjoyable after a fashion, but it always puts her one up. There's something about females like Cassie that makes a bloke feel he's got no legs, let alone a will of 'is own.'

'Take my advice, Freddy, and as soon as Cassie has spoken her vows, make sure she understands you're goin' to wear the trousers,' said Sammy. 'Marital trousers look after your legs and keep 'em firm and standin' up.'

'Pardon?' said Freddy, his slightly wavy brown hair ruffled by the breeze.

'Legs, Freddy, trousers,' said Sammy, showing the wisdom of experience. He was nearly thirty three, Freddy, his brother-in-law, not yet twenty-one, although a forthcoming bridegroom for all that. 'Did you have your mind somewhere else?'

'On account of the wedding's so close,' said Freddy, 'I don't know where me mind is most of the time. But I've got to say it's always been me intention to keep Cassie from puttin' the trousers on.'

'I can mention it's never been out of my mind all the time I've been married to Susie,' said Sammy. Not that it's done me any good, he thought, she was standing me on my head well before we got spliced, and I can't remember I've ever regained me correct posture. 'It's only natural, Freddy, for the bloke to be the boss. Otherwise, where does that leave you and me? Fixin' new tap washers and pushin' the pram. As me old friend Eli Greenberg once said, it's a sorrowful thing that female women ain't as respectful to blokes as they used to be. They don't seem to honour their spouses like Queen Victoria and her kind did. Very sorrowful that is, Freddy, and sad as well. Mind, there's compensations. Happy ones, I might say. In any case, you've got yourself a young rose of good old Walworth in Cassie. Pretty as Peggy O'Neill as well. Good luck to you, Freddy, and don't allow for workin' in this brewery all your life. I'm not allowin' for it myself, something'll come up to your advantage one day. Cassie deserves a husband with real prospects, and I can't say fairer, can I? So I'll keep an eye open for the right kind of prospects. Well, you're as good as fam'ly, and here's that weddin' bonus I promised. It's from me and Susie, with our compliments.' He handed Freddy the cheque for fifty pounds.

'Mother O'Grady,' said Freddy, 'what a bonanza.

Thanks a million, and lots more on top of that. Cassie'll do cartwheels twice over. Well, she 'ad a cheque herself yesterday for fifty pounds from Boots and Em'ly.'

'Well, trust Boots to see someone came up trumps for Cassie,' said Sammy. 'Has she banked it?'

'No, I'm goin' to bank it with mine,' said Freddy.

'Get it done rightaway, Freddy.'

'I'll get time off before the bank shuts,' said Freddy.

'And think about what I mentioned ages ago, about buyin' a house and not renting one all your life,' said Sammy. 'Renting's hard-earned money down the drain. And don't forget to arrange yourself in the position of being Cassie's better half.'

'Believe me, I won't forget,' said Freddy, 'but the thing is, Cassie might do some of her own arranging.'

'I sympathize, Freddy, I sympathize,' said Sammy, and left.

# Chapter Twelve

It was twenty-eight minutes past three in the afternoon, and the bank in the Walworth Road was about to close its door to customers. The last one had just left. The last, that is, except for two persons sitting at the table that was provided for depositors to write out a cheque or fill in a pay-in slip. They looked like professional gentlemen in suits of clerical grey and smart bowler hats worn over dark hair. Both also wore glasses and fine kid gloves. The broader gent had a thick black moustache, the other a neat black one. The latter was taking time to write out a cheque. The former had a long flat item wrapped in brown paper beside his chair, and a brown Gladstone bag on his lap.

One of the two cashiers ventured to say the bank was closing any moment. The person with the thick moustache got up and said, 'Oh, we'll close it for you.' Which induced the other person to rise swiftly and to approach the counter with the cheque, while Dusty Miller of the thick moustache walked smartly to the door and put the catch down.

'Excuse me,' protested the cashier, and his colleague frowned.

'Don't say a word or ring any bells,' said Dusty Miller. Both cashiers gaped then, for a revolver with a silencer was suddenly in chilling evidence. Ginger Carstairs was pointing it through the grille at the elder cashier, a slightly balding bank employee. 'See what I mean?' said Dusty, and executed an excellent leap that took him up onto the counter, from where he looked down on the cashiers. He dropped the Gladstone bag in the lap of the balding clerk, now ashen-faced. 'Fill it with all you've both got in your tills,' he said, 'and fill it fast, or you'll get your face blown in. And not a word to mother, eh? Right, get filling.'

Temporary paralysis came to an end, and both cashiers opted for safety first in the face of the steady and wicked-looking revolver. Cold eyes stared at them from behind horn-rimmed spectacles as they emptied their tills of banknotes, wads of them, most neatly banded in units of a hundred pounds.

'Faster, you buggers,' growled Dusty Miller, poised on the counter and looking down on the hasty but fumbling transfer of the banknotes from tills into the Gladstone bag. Ginger Carstairs said not a word, but concentrated on frightening the cashiers to death. The tills were quickly emptied. 'Right, hand it up,' said Miller, and it was lifted to him. Behind partitions and walls was the faint sound of the rest of the bank staff at work. 'Now, keep your mouths shut for five minutes before you yell for mother, or you'll still cop a packet. Understood?'

The shaken cashiers nodded. Miller leapt down with the Gladstone bag, Carstairs backed from the counter, revolver still aimed, and picked up the slat of wood that was wrapped in brown paper. Miller made for the door, released the catch and opened it, at which point Freddy appeared.

'Thanks,' he said, 'thought I'd left it too late.' He slipped past Miller, but Carstairs clubbed him with the revolver. Luckily, haste made it a glancing blow that struck the side of his cap first, but it staggered him and sent him to the floor. Out went Carstairs in the wake of Miller, who turned and pulled the door shut. Carstairs, revolver tucked away, slammed the wrapped slat of wood into position. The door handle broke through the wrapping, and Dusty then pushed a long nail through the slat at a point marked with a blob of ink. Ginger drove it into the door with one solid whack from a hammer. Then, the hammer pocketed, they turned and walked side by side at a brisk pace, the Gladstone bag swinging, their grey suits and bowlers giving them the appearance of City gents who had found a reason to do a bit of financial business in Walworth.

Two CID officers, a detective-inspector and a detective-sergeant, were travelling in a new Austin police car delivered only that morning to their Camberwell station. The supply of cars to facilitate and expedite police work was increasing. The officers, who had been out on a test run, were now heading back to Camberwell along the Walworth Road.

Inside the bank, Freddy climbed shakily to his feet, his painful head of very little account in comparison with his rage. One could have said Freddy was an amiable young man who let the world go by without exhibiting any desire to muck it about. But if anything could make him turn primitive, it was vicious bullies or people who perpetrated grievous bodily harm in pursuit of villainy. He knew he'd have been out cold if the blow had landed squarely. The morale-shattered cashiers were raising the alarm now, and out came the chief clerk, rushing at the door. It couldn't be opened, it was stuck fast.

'Phone the police, phone the police!' he shouted, the bank now alive with outraged staff.

'Where's another way out?' bawled the furious Freddy.

'Here, this way,' called a clerk, and Freddy, not bothering to nurse his bruised head, dashed through the door that had been opened by the chief clerk, who called after him.

'Wait, wait, who the devil are you?'

'They hit him,' called the balding cashier, as shaken as Freddy was bruised, 'and it's upset him. He's after them and he'll recognize them.'

Freddy, shown the way, emerged into Cadiz Street. As he did so, a baker's van, dark blue, passed him, going towards the Walworth Road. With the driving section of the vehicle open on both sides, Freddy gaped. Bloody hell, there they were, as large as life, one at the wheel, the other with the Gladstone bag on the floor behind his legs. Freddy noted the baker's name, 'Joseph Roberts', then shook his aching head, ignored what it did to him, and pounded after the vehicle. It turned left into the Walworth Road, filtering into the traffic. Freddy reached the corner at a moment when it was passing by and a very pretty girl was waiting to cross the road. She might have diverted him, for she was a little like Cassie, but he was too insane in his rage, and he wanted to bawl at the driver of a slow-moving tram, 'Follow that van!'

He saw the vehicle move to the centre of the road, indicating it was going to make a right turn. It slowed. Oncoming traffic was against it. Freddy guessed it was intending to turn into John Ruskin Street, a little way on from Fielding Street. Precisely at that point in the event, the police car reached Cadiz Street, slowing up because of the tram, which had halted and was letting passengers off. The chief clerk arrived then, having gone after Freddy in the knowledge that he was an important witness. He saw the police car, now at a stop, and he rapped urgently on the passenger window. Freddy put himself beside him. The window was wound down, and the plainclothes detective-inspector barked, 'What's the trouble?'

'The bank's been robbed by two men, we're ringing your people, and this young man—'

'They're in that baker's van, the blue one, name of Joseph Roberts,' interrupted Freddy, with the chief clerk listening.

'What van?'

Freddy took a look. The van had made its distant turn and had disappeared. Freddy pulled open the rear door of the police car and threw himself in.

'John Ruskin Street,' he said, 'they've just turned into John Ruskin Street. Would you mind gettin' after them fast? I can point their van out for you. They've hurt my bloody head with a revolver, and I want them caught.'

The inspector, turning in his seat, took a quick shrewd look at Freddy, then said to his sergeant, 'Go, man, go.'

Traffic behind, held up by the stationary police car, was getting impatient. A horn sounded. The police car shot away then, its bell clanging.

Freddy said again that the name on the van was Joseph Roberts, that he'd seen it when it was passing him in Cadiz Street.

'Sod it, street kids,' hissed Miller as Carstairs drove

along John Ruskin Street at a steady speed. The governing tactic was not to burn up the road, not to rush like the clappers and draw attention to themselves. A baker's van, proceeding steadily, would attract no curious glances. It would, probably, hardly be noticed. But there were too many street kids about for Miller's liking, all the same. Some schools had broken up for Easter. While there was no need to scorch along, they couldn't afford to dawdle. Miller growled his current dislike of street kids.

'Calm down,' said Carstairs, 'we're on course.' Nevertheless, the kids had to be watched. They were playing their games and mucking about all over the place. 'Kids don't bother me as much as traffic jams. Walworth Road can be a curse when you're in a hurry. We're right for time, even—'

'Watch out!' breathed Miller, cursing the possibility of an accident that would ruin the day for them.

Carstairs swerved around a saucy boy kid who was yards from the pavement and who put his thumb to his nose as the van went by. Miller, hiding his temper, managed to wink at him through his spectacles.

'I'll get that one when he's older,' said Carstairs, thin lips hardly moving. 'What was I on about? Yes, even though that interfering sod in the cap could have messed up our timetable, we're where we should be right now.'

'You copped him a blinder,' said Miller.

'Serve him bloody right,' said Carstairs, avoiding all possible contact with the more devilish kids. On the van went, and it was only thirty yards from Camberwell New Road when the sound of a clanging bell reached their ears. 'What's that, ambulance, fire-engine or what?'

Leaning, Miller poked out his head and looked back.

'Christ,' he said, 'it's or-bloody-what, it's a police car, it's just turned in from the Walworth Road. Move, Ginger, move!'

Carstairs accelerated, then braked for the left turn into Camberwell New Road.

The police car, clanging, sped in pursuit, Freddy having sighted the van.

'That's the one,' he said, leaning forward on the back seat.

Kids stared at the oncoming car. The van, way ahead, turned into Camberwell New Road. The police car came on fast, kids scattering out of its noisy way. It was when the car was a mere few yards from the turn that two young boys ran from the lefthand pavement into its path. The detective-sergeant braked hard, the tyred wheels screeched and the car skidded, mounting the pavement just at the corner of Camberwell Road. Freddy, thrown about, still managed to glimpse the van as it turned right into Flodden Road, but the incident had given the bank robbers an advantage they weren't aware of.

A minute later, they entered Denmark Hill. Some-where behind, a bell began to clang again.

'Bugger it,' said Carstairs.

'Same here,' said Miller, and swore under his breath.

'Plan cancelled for the time being,' said Carstairs. 'They'll catch us before we reach the lock-up and the station. We need a hideaway before they hit Denmark Hill.'

The police car, having been backed off the pave-ment and turned, had actually only just resumed the chase, and by the time it entered Flodden Road, under Freddy's guidance, the van was well up Denmark Hill, Miller looking back for signs of the pursuit.

'How the hell did it get on our tail so fast?' he growled.

'More to the point, how the hell do we lose it?' said Carstairs.

Traffic was light on the hill, and there was not a single pedestrian about. Carstairs saw an escape route on the other side of the road. Miller almost left his seat as the van took a sharp right-angle turn, Carstairs driving it through the open gate of a wide entrance drive, damaging a low protruding branch of one of a series of young trees forming a hedge from the top of the drive down to the bottom of the back garden. On the van went, passing the side of a large handsome house called 'The Manor'. Carstairs braked and spun the wheel to make a tight left turn before the van launched itself into a flower border of the back garden. It pulled up on the crazy paving of a patio at the rear of the house, shuddering to a stop outside French windows.

What had been speeding up the hill one moment was out of sight the next, hidden behind the large handsome house.

Approaching the hill from Bessemer Road, the clanging police car stopped. There was a woman standing on the corner. The inspector, window down, called to her, asking if she'd seen a blue van, a baker's van. Yes, she called back, she had.

'Which way did it go, left or right?'

'Right. It's gone up the hill.'

'Many thanks.'

The car resumed the chase again, Freddy's bruised temple aching.

Vi was ready to put the kettle on. Alice and David would be home from school soon, and, as always, she'd give them cups of tea and slices of cake. Paul too. He was poring over a picture book at the moment, his lips moving as he did his best to read large-print captions. Vi and Tommy were helping him with his alphabet and with simple words before he began attending school himself. Tomorrow, Alice and David's school was breaking up for Easter. Vi liked Easter, it was always a kind of leap into spring, sometimes showery, sometimes breezy and sometimes lovely. She hoped it would be lovely for the weddings of Cassie and Freddy, and Sally and Horace. The Adams families had only just got to know Horace, but approval was general. He was a bit like Annabelle's Nick, sort of vigorous and cheerful, which was bound to appeal to the Adamses. They didn't go much on young men who were a bit like wet weekends.

A strange noise disturbed her. It seemed to begin at the side of the house and to continue round to the garden, following which silence fell. Vi went through from the kitchen to the spacious sitting-room. She stopped dead. Visible through the closed French windows was a baker's van. A what? I'm dreaming, she thought, or I'm seeing things. A van in the back garden, on our new crazy paving? George the gardener might have had something to say about that. He always considered it was as much his garden as hers and Tommy's, but it was his weekly half-day off.

Well, I'm going to have something to say myself, thought Vi. Her daily help, Mrs Ross, had left at three, her usual time. Vi opened the French windows and stepped out. The April breeze caught her. Her fair hair rippled and the skirt of her dress fluttered.

There was no-one in the van. At least, not in the driving seat. Well, I'm blessed, she thought, who drove it round here, then, the baker's ghost? The intermittent sunshine, becoming momentarily bright, threw sudden shadows. Vi turned to the source of the shadows, and there they were, the people who had brought the van round to the patio. Bowler hats, grey suits, kid gloves, spectacles and moustaches. Expressionless faces and cold eyes, eyes that stared at her through the spectacles. A little shiver ran down her back.

'Who are you, what d'you want, why have you brought this van into our garden?' Vi spoke as firmly as she could, although she hardly recognized her own voice.

'Go inside,' said Dusty Miller.

'D'you mind going away and takin' this van with you?' said Vi, wishing Tommy was home.

'Go inside.'

'I won't, not until you go away.'

A hand fastened on her shoulder, spun her round and pushed her back into the sitting-room.

'Mummy?' Paul was there, staring at the two people following his mother into the room.

'It's all right, Paul lovey,' said Vi, 'you go and meet Alice and David. They'll be on their way home now.'

'He's not going anywhere, Mrs Whoever-you-are,' said Miller, 'and nor are you.' Ginger Carstairs picked Paul up and sat him in an armchair. The spacious room, attractively furnished, was bright with light and colourful chintzes. It was a room Vi loved. From there, one could see so much of the wide garden, the French windows always offering an expansive view.

'Who else is in the house?' asked Miller.

'No-one,' said Vi.

'There's someone,' said Miller.

'No, it's the wireless in the kitchen, it's playing afternoon music, that's all,' said Vi, trying not to communicate her fears to Paul. The boy was dumb and staring as the cold calculating eyes of the intruders looked her up and down.

'Have you got other children?' asked Miller. Carstairs might have been in charge, but was letting Miller do all the talking.

'Yes, two,' said Vi, 'and you just heard me say they'll be on their way home from school now. If you want something, please take it and go.'

'Where's your husband?'

'At work,' said Vi.

'What time will he be home?'

'About six,' said Vi.

'He's got a fine house.'

'He's earned it,' said Vi, fighting her tremors, 'he started at the bottom, and he's worked for everything he's got.'

'You're lippy, lady. Don't be lippy. This old man of yours, has he got a car as well?'

'Yes, he uses it to get to work,' said Vi. She moved closer to the armchair on which Paul had been unceremoniously dumped. He lifted his hand and she took it, pressing it warmly and comfortingly. 'What is it you want?'

'Don't ask questions,' said Miller. 'But I'll answer that one. We want a car. That's all. Your old man's due home about six, you said?'

'He's not often late,' said Vi.

'Listen, when your other kids get here, let them in and say nothing out of place. We'll look after this one and keep him cosy.'

'They'll come in through the kitchen,' said Vi.

'Well, when they do, go and meet them,' said Miller. 'Tell them you've got visitors, and bring them through to meet us, remembering we'll be looking after this one. Right?'

'I'll remember,' said Vi, racked.

'Does your old man let himself in?'

'Yes, by the front door, with his key,' said Vi.

'Well, that'll suit us,' said Miller, 'we don't want a lot of inconvenience. Are you fond of your old man?'

'He's my husband,' said Vi. Always soft-spoken, she answered that particular question very quietly. Like all the other Adams women, Lizzy, Emily, Susie and Chinese Lady, Vi had an old-fashioned respect for the marriage state, never mind that Lizzy, Emily and Susie also had modern women's ideas about how to circumvent any Victorianism in a husband without hardly trying.

'Husbands are made for providing, are they?' said Miller, whose wooden expression hadn't changed one iota. Nor, for that matter, had that of his partner in crime. They were a pitiless pair at this stage of the operation, and not prepared to suffer any more setbacks to their acquisitive venture into the realms of the get-rich-quick fraternity. Carstairs had thrown in a calculation on their way from the bank to Cadiz Street and the parked van, to the effect that there were sixty bundles of banknotes at least. Worth six thousand smackers and more. A bloody fortune, Miller had said. The Gladstone bag was presently resting on an armchair, Carstairs standing guard over it, watching Miller and Vi alternately. 'Answer up,' said Miller to Vi.

'My husband provides for all of us,' she said. Young Paul, gulping, found his piping voice then.

'Mummy, can't these men go away?'

'Oh, they will, lovey, as soon as Daddy gets home,' said Vi, 'so don't worry, they're not going to hurt us.'

'Right,' said Dusty. 'You do as you're told, lady, and I'll guarantee there'll be no accidents, like taking this kid for a nice long walk.'

'You wouldn't—' Vi stopped at the sound of the kitchen door opening and closing, followed by the clatter of David's shod feet on the tiled floor. Miller jerked his thumb, and put a hand on Paul's shoulder. Vi hastened to the kitchen. David was pouring himself a glass of water, and Alice was getting a tin of sherbet powder from the larder. They both liked sherbet water. It fizzed, and it tickled nostrils.

'Oh, hello, Mum,' said David. The wireless was still entertaining housewives with light music.

'Listen,' said Vi, making an effort to sound normal, 'we've got visitors,'

'Oh, special ones?' said Alice, fair hair bright, soft and curling.

Heaven help me, thought Vi, what else can I do except what they've told me to? They've got Paul.

'Yes, they're a bit special,' said Vi, 'and you can come and meet them.'

'Can I have my sherbet drink first?' asked Alice. David gave her his glass, now fizzy with sherbet, and filled another with tap water, at which point the music stopped and the announcer came through with a newsflash. Vi stiffened. A bank robbery had taken place at a branch in the Walworth Road, by Camberwell, South London. Two men were involved, one of them known to be armed with a revolver. They had made their escape in a blue baker's van. The name on the van was Joseph Roberts. Any information concerning its whereabouts would be welcomed by the police, but as the men were dangerous the public was warned to stay clear of them. A very accurate description of the two men, based on detailed information given by bank staff, began to follow.

Vi, spellbound, listened to the description with her heart almost stopping.

'Mummy?' said Alice. It was her turn to stare. Vi wheeled round and saw the man with the thick moustache standing at the open kitchen door. He too was listening to the newsflash. Without a word he walked swiftly in, crossed to the wireless set on the dresser and switched it off. Vi knew why, of course.

'Why's he done that?' asked David.

'Never you mind, kid,' said Miller.

'It's our wireless,' said Alice in girlish protest.

'Well, count yourself lucky,' said Miller, 'not everyone's got a wireless. Or a garden. Or a car. Now come and meet my friend. Bring 'em,' he said to Vi, and he stood aside, watching her in his expressionless way.

'Yes, come on, David, come on, Alice,' she said, 'let's go into our garden room.' They called it that sometimes because of its expansive view of the lawn, the flower beds and the shrubbery.

Alice and David, puzzled rather than alarmed for the moment, let their mother lead them through to the sitting-room, Miller following. There, Alice and David saw the other visitor, who was dressed just like the first one. Ginger Carstairs, standing beside the armchair in which Paul was seated, eyed Vi's elder children without comment.

Paul said, 'Mum, I want to pay respects.'

'What's he mean, that he wants to piddle?' asked Miller.

Vi was a gentle-natured woman, and for all that she'd been born a Camberwell cockney, she disliked earthiness. The word used was of a mild kind, but still not one she wanted spoken in front of her children. True, they did hear all sorts of words at school, where there was a mixture of kids, some well-behaved and others saucier than Max Miller. Sometimes Alice and David came home asking what did this word or that word mean, and Vi always told them they were ugly words that nice people never used. Vi believed children should be allowed their years of innocence, whatever their backgrounds.

'Paul means he wants to go upstairs,' she said.

'Same thing, I suppose,' said Miller. 'A bit finicky in this house, are you?'

'No, not finicky,' said Vi, putting on a valiant front in the knowledge that any visible fear or nervousness would acutely disturb her sons and daughter, who were already very uncomfortable.

'Take the little 'un upstairs, then,' said Miller. 'We'll keep your other two company. Wait, have you got a phone?'

'Yes, course we have,' said David, 'and I don't know why you're talkin' to our mum as if you don't like her.'

'Mum's nice,' said Alice.

'Beg your pardon, I'm sure,' said Miller, his mockery of a deadpan kind. He looked around. 'Where d'you keep the phone?'

'It's in the hall,' said Vi.

'And there's one upstairs as well, is there?' said Miller.

'No, course not,' said David. 'What do we want one upstairs for when we've got one downstairs?'

Paul wriggled. Carstairs, a sudden little touch of irritation showing, put a hand on his arm and pulled him from the chair. Miller nodded.

'My friend'll take the boy,' he said.

'I'd rather you let me,' said Vi, her teeth beginning to clench, but she had to watch helplessly as Paul was taken from the room.

'We 'aven't had our cup of tea and cake yet,' said David accusingly to Miller.

'Well nobody has, have they?' he said. 'We're visiting because we've got some business to do with your dad, and what with one thing and another, your mother hasn't had time to put the kettle on. She can do it now. I like my tea strong and sweet, missus. No cake, just some piping hot brew. The kids can have cake. You can leave them with me while you make the pot.'

'I'll go with Mum and help her,' said Alice.

'So will I,' said David.

'You're set on that, are you?' said Miller.

'Yes,' said Alice, sure now that her mum didn't like these visitors any more than she did, or David did. David was beginning to show his pugnacious look. It was the kind of look he showed if he thought Alice was being ragged at school. Teachers weren't always on hand to give bullies a slap. David could land a

209

punch if he decided he had to. 'Yes, me and David'll both go and help Mum,' she said.

'We'll all go,' said Miller.

'We don't need you,' said David.

'We'll all go,' said Miller again. 'We don't want to lose each other, do we, sonny?'

'I don't mind losin' you,' said David, and Vi gave his arm a little squeeze. He looked up at her. Vi was actually able to smile. It was an effort, but she managed it.

'Come on, lovey,' she said.

When Carstairs brought Paul down, everyone finished up in the kitchen. Carstairs sat at the table with Paul. Miller stood close to the door. Vi had the kettle going, and Alice and David were close about her, as if guarding her.

Miller took his bowler hat off after a while, showing a wealth of wavy black hair. He ran the side of his hand over his forehead, and Vi thought he's nervous, he's perspiring. He's a monster, but his nerves are showing. Is he the one who's got the revolver?

Carstairs looked stonily at Miller, thin lips tight with contempt.

Vi, noticing that too, said to herself, no, that's the one with the gun, the one who hasn't said a single word so far. Oh, dear Lord above, what's Tommy going to do when he gets home to this?

She felt these brutal intruders were capable of anything, and she wasn't far wrong.

Dusty Miller, son of a Kent miner, was a man with an obsessive envy of all who had been born in better circumstances. At school, he thieved in bullying fashion from boys large or small. In his first job, as an engineering apprentice, he thieved all he could lay his hands on. Found out, he was summarily sacked. He took up a career as a thief, and far from having served only one prison sentence, he had been in and out of gaol countless times. His envy of moneyed people grew, and he hated the middle classes. He developed, inevitably, a need for instant riches, and he knew only one way to put real money into his pocket.

He had met Ginger Carstairs by chance, in a pub. His spiteful envy of better-off people was outmatched by his new acquaintance's hatred of everyone, full stop. The parents of this particular specimen of misanthropy were Bohemians of a thriftless, loose-living and wholly selfish kind, with not the faintest idea of parental responsibilities. Ginger Carstairs grew up hating them, hating their debts, their creditors, their associates and the whole bloody world. Escape could only come about by the acquisition of money and a totally new environment.

That money was now literally in the bag, but departure from the country had, for the moment, been nipped in the bud. To restore the balance, Ginger Carstairs was quite prepared to subject Vi and her family to any kind of mental torture.

That included the woman's husband when he arrived home.

Miller was fully one with Carstairs in this, even though by now neither liked the other. That was inevitable, given the extent of their obsessive dislikes.

# Chapter Thirteen

The CID men had searched for the vanished quarry up hill and down dale. When their car entered Denmark Hill, the van could not be seen, but the woman on the corner had been positive in declaring it had turned right and gone up the hill. The policemen, with Freddy still aboard, travelled fast to Herne Hill, stopping there to ask people if they had seen the van. Response was negative, and the inspector surmised it had turned off somewhere along Denmark Hill or Herne Hill. Freddy, head still aching, said what now, then? The sergeant said they needed a little bit of luck, that no-one could find a needle in a haystack without a little bit of luck.

'More like a bucketful, I'd say,' said Freddy.

Back the police car went, to search for clues by way of the roads and avenues off Denmark Hill. Stops were made whenever there was a chance to question a pedestrian, but all such enquiries brought nothing of any consequence. While the sergeant asked questions of people at North Dulwich railway station, the inspector made a quick call to his headquarters from the public phone box there. He was informed that Scotland Yard itself had all the details of the robbery, given by the bank manager and some of his staff. The inspector was able to offer a further detail, that of the baker's name on the van. A young man, Mr Brown, had provided that information and was presently in the police car after being assaulted by the robbers. Headquarters said they knew that, the chief clerk at the bank had advised them of it, and Scotland Yard were arranging for the BBC to issue a newsflash. The public had to be warned, since the wanted men were obviously dangerous.

Subsequently, time was spent going up and down the streets, roads and avenues off Herne Hill, but entirely without success. The van could be anywhere south-east of London by now, but at least police all over the Home Counties had its description. Freddy was eventually driven home, where the inspector thanked him for all his help, informed him a wireless announcement had been made that might bring results, and then advised him to see his doctor about his bruised head.

'I think I'll make do with a Guinness,' said Freddy.

'Have I heard Guinness is good for a sore head?' asked the sergeant.

'I haven't meself,' said Freddy, 'but I'm gettin' married on Saturday, and I've heard it's good for that.'

The sergeant laughed, the inspector smiled.

'Well, the best of luck, Mr Brown,' said the inspector. 'Sorry about your head, but it's a pleasure to have met you. When we've caught the buggers, you'll be wanted as a witness. Fair enough?'

'Fair enough,' said Freddy.

'Freddy!' exclaimed the normally placid Mrs Brown a few minutes later. Her younger son had acquainted her with the afternoon's happenings.

'Nothing to worry about, Mum,' said Freddy, 'except it's me fond 'ope that the geezers don't get

213

away with the loot, nor with givin' me a headache.'

'Oh, Freddy me pet.'

'Steady, Mum, don't make me sound like I've lost me teddy bear. I'm a bit more advanced than that, y'know, I'm nearly a married man.'

'Yes, I do know, Freddy love, and that's what makes it all the more upsettin',' said motherly Mrs Brown, 'you 'aving to say your vows in front of the vicar with a nasty lump on your head.'

'Is it nasty?' asked Freddy. He knew it was tender, but he didn't know how lumpy it looked.

'Oh, never mind, it'll have gone down come Saturday,' said Mrs Brown. 'Sit down and I'll make a nice restoring pot of tea. Fancy me hearin' about the robbery on the wireless and not knowin' you were there and bein' grievously assaulted. It said on the last announcement that a young man tried to stop them escapin', and that they'd committed a very grievous assault on him. Well, it was something like that.' She put the kettle on.

'No, I just happened to get in the way,' said Freddy, 'so one of them clobbered me. I'm still sore about that, and I don't suppose Cassie will like it, either. She said once that I 'ad a noble loaf of bread. I don't know what she'll say about me nobility bein' out of shape for the weddin'.'

'Oh, a loving bride won't worry about the condition of your head, Freddy,' said Mrs Brown, setting out cups and saucers on the kitchen table. 'I mean, as long as everything else is in order, as you might say, there shouldn't be any real worries.'

'Mum, are you bein' saucy?' asked Freddy.

'Why, I've never been saucy all my life,' said Mrs Brown, 'my parents didn't ever believe in bringing up saucy daughters. Freddy, would you like an Aspro with your cup of tea and then a nice lie down?'

'Not much,' said Freddy, thinking about the vanishing trick performed by the robbers and their van. What a couple of peculiar crooks in their City bowlers and grey suits.

'Imagine you chasin' all over Denmark Hill with the police in the car,' said Mrs Brown from the scullery. She poured boiling water into the teapot. 'Your dad and Sally won't 'ardly believe what happened when they get home, which'll be any minute now.'

'What gets me is where that van got to,' said Freddy. 'I mean, nobody seems to 'ave spotted it, and the police must've asked at least thirty people in the area.'

'Now it's not your worry, love,' said Mrs Brown, placing the teapot on the table. 'Nor don't you want to worry, it'll only make your headache turn chronic.'

'Well, I'll tell you this, Mum,' said Freddy, 'I don't want to turn up for the weddin' in a chronic condition.'

'That's it,' said Mrs Brown comfortingly, 'let the police do the worrying.'

Vi wanted to scream. The atmosphere was chilling, with scarcely a word being spoken. Everyone was waiting for the arrival home of Tommy. The cold-eyed pair were standing, one by the door, one by the French windows. The light was dull, the April evening having turned grey with heavy clouds. Alice, David and Paul were sitting together on the settee, Alice with her arm around young Paul. All three of them kept glancing at the man with the thick moustache, the one who had done all the talking at first but now

215

hadn't opened his mouth for twenty minutes. That Gladstone bag was at the feet of the other unlikeable character, the one with a small moustache who had said nothing throughout. Yet somehow Vi felt this was the more dangerous of the two. She hated it whenever those cold eyes turned on her children. She sensed boyish truculence in David. Perhaps it was because he saw himself as an aggressive protector of his sister. Young though he and Alice were, they couldn't have failed to realize these intruders were a threat of a very unpleasant kind.

Vi, her throat dry, said, 'Alice, would you and David like another sherbet drink? And would you like one too, Paul?'

'Stay where you are, lady,' said Miller. 'No drinks. You've all had tea.'

'I don't like you, mister,' said David.

'Mutual, my lad, mutual,' said Miller. He looked at the clock on the mantelpiece. Twenty-five to six. 'Settle down,' he said. The room became compulsively quiet again.

The phone rang six minutes later. Vi jumped.

'The phone, Mum,' said Alice.

'Answer it,' said Miller.

Vi came to her feet, Carstairs, at the door, opened it for her and followed her out. Vi lifted the receiver.

'Hello?' she said, her dry throat making her voice sound husky.

'Vi?' It was Tommy. 'I'm a bit late leavin', I've had a fabric supplier here. Thought I'd let you know I'll be a little late 'ome.'

'How – how much late?' asked Vi.

'Should be with you by six-twenty,' said Tommy. 'Vi, you all right?'

Vi, feeling the cold eyes on her back, said, 'Yes, I'm fine, Tommy. Thanks for lettin' me know. See you when you get here, then.'

'By the way, there's been a bank robbery in Camberwell, did you know?' said Tommy.

'Oh, you can tell me about it when you get home,' said Vi, her nerves on the brink of shattering.

'I'm on my way,' said Tommy, and rang off.

Vi put the receiver back and turned. They were both there, looking at her, eyes boring into her.

'Well?' said Miller.

Vi swallowed and said, 'That was my husband. He'll be a little late, about twenty minutes.'

'Won't be here, then, until twenty after six?' said Miller.

'He's only just leavin',' said Vi, 'and he has to drive from Shoreditch. There's a lot of traffic this time of an evening.'

'Pity,' said Miller, 'but as long as he gets here, there'll be no trouble. Go back to your kids, the youngest one's snivelling.'

Vi hastened back, and they followed her in. Paul was letting go the occasional sob. Alice and David were trying to comfort him. The young boy, seeing the return of his mother, quietened.

'He thought you weren't coming back, Mum,' said Alice.

For the first time, Carstairs spoke.

'Little fool.' It was a gruff, irritable comment.

'He's not a fool,' said David, 'he's frightened, that's all. You're ugly, you are, and so's the other bloke.'

'Keep him quiet, missus, or I'll clip his ear,' said Miller, and looked at the clock again. Fourteen minutes to six. Carstairs nodded at him, and gestured

217

at the French windows. He turned and noted a key on the inside. He locked the windowed doors and put the key in his pocket. He walked over to Carstairs, and they left the sitting-room, closing the door behind them. Miller had the Gladstone bag under his arm.

'Listen,' whispered Carstairs, 'the coppers are bound to be out and about all evening. They have to suspect we're somewhere in the area, and I wouldn't put it past the interfering sods to stop all vehicles for miles around, on the grounds that we wouldn't be stupid enough to be using the van. We can pass on our appearance, but not with the bag or the loot. So we'll leave it until midnight before we make a move. The coppers will be thin on the ground by then. Right?'

'You're the boss,' said Miller, 'but I don't fancy keeping company with this prissy lot until bloody midnight.'

'Getting on your nerves, are they, Miller?'

'And yours,' said Miller.

'What's the answer, then?' asked Carstairs.

'Tie them up, and lock them up,' said Miller.

'Bloody brilliant,' said Carstairs. 'We were going to have to do that, anyway, before we left. All right, so we'll get them out of our way earlier. If the husband gives trouble, put him in the land of Nod. We'll catch a ferry tomorrow. Now let's get back to these fairies.'

'First,' said Miller, 'how'd you like having had to keep your mouth shut since we went into the bank?'

'It's no strain.'

'A bit hard on you, though, eh, Ginger?'

'I'll manage,' said Ginger Carstairs.

When they re-entered the sitting-room, David was on his feet and trying to open the French windows with a key that had been lying on the mantelpiece. Carstairs swooped and dragged him away by the collar of his jacket. David twisted round and aimed a kick. Carstairs slapped his face.

'Stop it,' said Vi, 'stop it. You're disgustin', you're both disgustin'. David, come here.'

The boy obeyed, his face flushed and angry.

'I thought I told you not to make accidents happen?' said Miller to Vi. 'They will happen if you let that kid try to open any more doors.'

'It won't be repeated,' said Vi quietly.

Miller drew the curtains to, covering the French windows. This shut out the view of the van and dimmed the light in the room, which didn't improve the situation for Vi and her children. They felt locked in.

The time came up to six o'clock and Vi thought, Tommy will be on his way now

She felt a great need for his presence.


'Rosie?' said Polly over the phone.

'Oh, hello, Polly,' said Rosie, 'how's your famous self?'

'Famous,' said Polly. 'May I come and see you this evening?'

'Love you to,' said Rosie, 'but is there a special reason?'

'Yes, I want to talk to you about a certain gentleman,' said Polly.

'Do you mean Major Armitage?' said Rosie.

'Yes, I believe that's his name,' said Polly.

'Polly, I think you've already talked to Boots my dad about him,' said Rosie. 'In Lyons.'

'Oh, he told you, did he?' said Polly.

'Well, we do communicate,' said Rosie.

'I know you do,' said Polly.

'Didn't you talk to him again last night?' asked Rosie.

'Yes, he had the grace this time to let me know you'd settled things satisfactorily with Major Armitage,' said Polly, 'but can the gentleman be trusted?'

'Yes, I think so,' said Rosie.

'Trusted to be content with seeing you only four times a year?' said Polly.

'I think so,' said Rosie.

'Well, in case trust is shattered, and I'm a cynic myself, I've an idea to offer,' said Polly.

'Yes, I know,' said Rosie, 'but didn't Boots say no to it in Lyons?'

'He's developing fusspot principles,' said Polly. 'I'm coming over this evening to talk to you. I don't have any fusspot principles myself.'

'Oh, come over and have a chat, anyway,' said Rosie.

'I will,' said Polly. 'By the way, how has your French sister taken all this?'

'As if crazy goings-on are peculiar to English people,' said Rosie. 'She's amazed that I don't show any enthusiasm for being the daughter of what she calls an English nobleman. She's sweet, but impressionable.'

'Major Armitage impressed her, did he?' said Polly. 'Sounds dangerous. Yes, I'll come and talk to you, ducky.'

'Count yourself one of the family, Polly,' said Rosie.

I would be, thought Polly, if I'd got to Boots before Emily did.

'See you, sweetie,' she said, and rang off.

*      *      *

The tension was at a peak, Vi's nerves tightly
strung. That these two unpleasant people simply
had to be the ones who had carried out the
armed bank robbery was obvious, and she could
only hope that Tommy would let them have what
they wanted – his car – and that they would
then disappear with it. Tommy was a good-natured
man, but not a simple one. He might not be as
disarming or as subtle as Boots, or as quick-thinking
as Sammy, but he was no fool. He would see at
once that there was no point in putting his family
in danger. That was the last thing he would do,
unless his immediate reaction was to hit the roof.
Tommy, tall, broad and muscular, could give a
very good account of himself, and the sight of
his family at the mercy of these men might just
make him furious enough to go hammer and
tongs at the intruders. He wouldn't know, as she
did, that they were the bank robbers, that they'd
shown themselves to be as hard as nails, and that
one of them was armed, according to the wireless
newsflash.

Time seemed to hang in demoralizing fashion, the
while the children sat together in silence and the ugly
eyes watched them. The minutes crept like crippled
snails towards six-twenty, and when that time finally
arrived, Vi was rigid in every limb.

Miller and Carstairs waited. Tommy's family waited.
The minute hand crept slowly on.

When it came, the sound of the front door opening,
Alice and David both visibly quivered, and Alice's
teeth took a tight hold of her bottom lip. It was only
David who spoke.

'That's our dad,' he said.

'Call him,' hissed Miller to Vi.

Vi got up. Carstairs opened the door. Vi, swallowing again to prevent her voice from cracking, called.

'We're in here, Tommy.'

Tommy, hanging his hat on the hallstand, walked through the hall into the sitting-room and found himself looking at a silencer fixed to a steely-blue revolver. Above it, icy grey eyes stared at him through spectacles. The children gasped at the sight of the revolver, and Vi's blood ran cold.

'Glad you got here at last, mister,' said Miller.

'What the hell are you two doin' here, what're you up to?' asked Tommy. 'And take that thing away,' he said to Carstairs. 'You crazy, or what? Vi, what's been 'appening?'

'Tommy, they—'

'Shut up,' said Miller.

Tommy's jaw tightened. He had never looked into the vicious threat of a revolver before, but that did not disturb him as much as the fear and fright now undisguised on the faces of his wife and children. A cold but controlled fury took hold of him.

'I wouldn't be in your shoes if you've done anything to hurt my wife and kids,' he said.

'Don't be a squirt, mister,' said Miller, 'your wife knows there's been no trouble, nor will there be unless you get an idea you can be a hero. Heroes make me throw up. Is your car outside?'

Tommy gave him a ferocious look. Vi sensed the extent of his fury and the effort he was making to keep it under control. She prayed for him, for all of them. He glanced at Ginger Carstairs, a plain-faced character with thin lips, a jutting nose and a small moustache.

'What's it to you where my car is?' said Tommy to Miller. 'And what's Charlie Chaplin's cousin wavin' a gun about for? What is he, a cowboy comic?'

A flicker of rage momentarily distorted the hitherto expressionless countenance of Ginger Carstairs.

'He's not waving it, mister, he's holding it nice and steady, and it's aimed right between your eyes,' said Miller. 'You just make sure it doesn't go off bang, if you see what I mean. For a start, he won't like you saying he looks like Charlie Chaplin.'

'Well, let him speak for 'imself,' said Tommy, brain working rapidly as he played for the time he needed to make up his mind about what to do. 'Or has he got a gummed-up north-and-south?'

Carstairs' thin lips tightened, and Miller scowled. What a pair of odd-looking misfits, thought Tommy, but I don't need to be told they're bloody dangerous.

Miller said, 'Did I ask you, mister, if your car was outside? Yes, I did. So answer up.'

'You leave my dad alone,' burst out David.

'Shut your mouth, kid,' said Miller, and Tommy gave David a reassuring look.

'The car's outside in the drive,' he said.

'That's better,' said Miller. 'Well, it's like this. See my friend there? Yes, that's him. The two of us need the car. Don't mind if we borrow it, do you? Makes no difference, of course, if you're going to raise an objection, we need it and we'll be taking it. Keys?'

'Well, I'm a reasonable bloke,' said Tommy, ignoring the threat of the revolver, 'but as I've got a feelin' I might not get the car back, I'd like to know what you want it for. I mean, is it for an emergency, like drivin' your mothers to hospital for operations? Only you could get an ambulance for that, and use me phone to call one up.'

Miller's stony look took on an extra ugliness. Oh, my God, thought Vi, they'll kill Tommy in a minute if he keeps talking like that.

'Mister, we don't appreciate jokes,' said Miller, 'we're after serious chat. Any more funny stuff, and you'll get clouted by my friend. It'll hurt. I asked for your car keys, so divvy up.'

'You can tell me what you want the car for, can't you?' said Tommy. Carstairs gave him a vicious dig in his chest with the revolver. Alice uttered a little cry of distress, David clenched his fists, and young Paul gazed dumbly. Tommy, chest bruised, said, 'That's bein' serious, is it? See what you mean.' He fished the car keys from his pocket and handed them to Miller.

'Now why didn't you do that when I first asked?' said Miller.

'Well, it takes a bloke time to think straight in this kind of set-up,' said Tommy. 'I'm not used to seeing my fam'ly 'aving to entertain people like you.'

'That's it, make me cry my eyes out,' said Miller. 'Now see here, we can all be reasonable. And you can afford to be, can't you? It seems to me you've got money in the bank. Well, look at this place. Very handsome. Suppose you don't get the car back, suppose it ends up in a Scottish bog? You can buy yourself another, I'd say.'

'That's where you're takin' it, are you, to Scotland?' said Tommy.

'Slip of the tongue,' said Miller. It wasn't, of course. A mention of Scotland by this family to the police would cast a very convenient red herring. 'You be

224

reasonable and we won't take goody-two-shoes with us.' He nodded at Alice. 'Any hard stuff in the house?'

Tommy wished Boots, Sammy and Ned were at hand. He knew he could do little by himself. In any case, he had to avoid the kind of action that would provoke these buggers into taking it out on Vi and the kids. His brain began to work, to make him think straight.

'You mean whisky?' he said.

'Thanks for the offer,' said Miller, 'we can do with a snifter. It's been a bit tiring, looking after your wife and your brats, and we won't be motoring off just yet. Your wife can bring the bottle and two glasses. You sit down with your kids.'

The gun gestured. Tommy sat down between Alice and Paul, putting an arm around the boy. He was thinking very straight now. Lilian Hyams had a wireless set in her design office. She liked to listen to the music programmes while she was working. Tommy, passing by after a short visit to the shop floor, heard the newsflash. Lilian's door was open. He went in and they listened together to the account of the Camberwell bank robbery. He remembered now the description given of the crooks. Bloody hell, they were here, in his house, in their bowlers, spectacles and grey suits, and there was a Gladstone bag on the floor by the door. One man was tall and thickset, the other thin, but there was no difference in their stony looks. Bowler hats, grey suits and glasses, thought Tommy. City gents. Some hopes.

Vi went to fetch the whisky and the glasses from the cabinet in the living-room. Miller went with her. Tommy gritted his teeth.

'Listen,' he said to the thin dour character with the gun, 'if you're here to clean us out of what valuables we've got and then scarper, why don't you get on with it? We'll stay quiet, me and me fam'ly.'

'Shut up,' said Ginger Carstairs in a low-pitched, irritable growl.

Vi returned with the bottle of whisky and three glasses not two. Miller followed her, closing the door behind him, and the family felt locked in again.

'I brought an extra glass,' said Vi, and Tommy marvelled at her courage and her lack of hysterics. Could she possibly know these were bank robbers? Had she heard the news on the wireless? The set had been silent when he came in. 'You'd like some whisky too, wouldn't you, Tommy?'

'You bet I would,' said Tommy.

Miller glanced at Carstairs. Carstairs nodded.

'All right,' said Miller to Vi. 'You pour.'

Vi put the glasses down on a table, then drew the cork from the whisky bottle.

Paul, gulping, said, 'Could I have something, Mummy?'

'I'll get all of you some sherbet drinks,' said Vi.

'The kids can 'ave that, can't they?' said Tommy to Miller, and Miller glanced at Carstairs again. He received another nod.

'Okay,' he said, 'but the whisky first.'

Vi poured a good measure into each of two glasses, and Tommy noted the slight tremble of her hand. Miller took up the two glasses and put one into Carstairs' left hand. Vi poured a smaller measure for Tommy. Unlike Boots, he hadn't yet acquired a taste for whisky, and Vi knew just a few mouthfuls would be as much as he wanted. If she was suffering, she felt he was suffering even more, simply because he was the man of the family and was responsible for all of them. The fact that he was as helpless as she was would be crucifying him.

'There you are, love,' she said, and handed him the glass. Tommy looked up into her eyes.

'That's my girl,' he said. They'd had years of marriage, and Vi, because she was undemanding, had never had tantrums or complaints. In Tommy's eyes, she was the best of the Adams wives. 'Bless you, Vi,' he said, and took a mouthful of the whisky. It fired his blood.

'Bless you too, Tommy,' said Vi. It was their favourite exchange.

'Bless us all,' said Alice bravely.

'Give it a rest,' said Miller sourly.

'Can I get the sherbet drinks now?' asked Vi.

'I'll get them,' said Tommy.

'You won't,' said Miller, 'she will.'

He again accompanied Vi out of the room, and again Tommy gritted his teeth.

David muttered, 'They're ugly, that's what they are, ugly.'

Vi came back with the glasses of sherbet water on a tray. And she'd been allowed to pour a glass of cold water for herself, her body stiff because the thickset man had stayed close to her all the time, hard eyes taking in the undulating lines of her figure.

# Chapter Fourteen

After supper that evening, Sally dropped in on Cassie before going round to see Horace. Cassie and her dad knew about the bank robbery, but not about the incident involving Freddy, which Sally related to her. She listened with her eyes wide open, then put aside the pillow cases she was embroidering, and fled to see Freddy, leaving Sally with her dad.

Reaching the Caulfield Place house in the dusk, she let herself in by the latchcord as usual. Well, Freddy's home had been her second since first meeting him and becoming his best girl mate. Into the kitchen she swooped.

'Freddy!' It was a cry from the heart, delivered in dramatic fashion, one hand pressed to her bosom in the manner of Ellen Terry doing Lady Macbeth.

'What's up, lost your titfer?' said Freddy. Cassie was bareheaded.

'Oh, Freddy, your poor head,' breathed Cassie, 'Sally's just told me how you suffered from being 'eroic.' Mr Brown strangled a cough. Mrs Brown murmured placidly. Freddy grinned. 'Freddy, you're not still hurtin', are you?'

'Only me loaf, and only a bit,' said Freddy. 'The rest of me is in order, Cassie, which Mum says is a relief to all concerned.'

'Oh, it's a relief to me too, Freddy love,' said Cassie. 'I nearly died while I was listening to Sally. Oh, your poor head, Freddy, you shouldn't have put it where those criminal hooligans could hit it. Sally said you've got an awful lump. Let me see.'

She leaned over the seated Freddy and searched his thick hair with gentle fingers. Mr Brown looked on in some amusement, Mrs Brown with a smile. Those two, Cassie and Freddy, she thought, they'd been the soul of togetherness for years, and Freddy's lasting complaint that they'd been years of being sent barmy had died a death these last few months. They'd make a good marriage, Freddy and Cassie. Their kind did make good marriages, a lot better than the upper classes with their dubious goings-on and their divorces.

'You're there, Cassie,' said Freddy.

'Crikey,' breathed Cassie, 'what a lump. Oh, 'elp.'

'Put me head out of shape, has it?' said Freddy.

'Oh, your hair hides it, Freddy, you've got nice hair,' said Cassie. 'The hurt won't stop you comin' to the weddin', will it? I'd drown meself in the Serpentine if we 'ad to put it off.'

'Oh, I'll be able to walk, Cassie, don't you fret,' said Freddy. 'I'm all right everywhere else. Did I mention that?'

'Yes, you did say. Oh, thank goodness. Freddy, tell me everything about what 'appened.'

'Let's talk in the parlour,' said Freddy.

'Yes, you do that, Freddy,' said Mr Brown, accepting that a family parlour should be exclusive to courting couples whenever it was only right and natural. Over the years their own parlour had been exclusive in turn to Susie and Sammy, then to Will and Annie, and now to Freddy and Cassie along with Sally and Horace, although at different times, of course. Mr

Brown remembered moments in the parlour of Mrs Brown's parents. Very nice moments, those had been, even if Bessie had blushed a bit.

'Yes, you can use the parlour, love,' said Mrs Brown.

'Come on, Freddy beloved,' said Cassie, not a girl whose shyness had ever come between her and what was acceptable among courting couples. Freddy had been totally admiring of her natural demonstrations of affection, even if they had made him dizzy.

In the parlour he recounted exactly what had happened when he arrived at the bank with the two wedding cheques, and when he went with the police in an attempt to catch up with the van. Cassie said even if the crooks hadn't been caught, Freddy was still a hero. Not many girls marry heroes, she said.

'You're not marryin' one yourself,' said Freddy. 'I just got hit on me loaf of bread, that's all.'

'Freddy, I do hope you're not goin' to do a lot of arguing when we're married,' said Cassie.

'Well, all right, Cassie, just a bit now and again to keep me end up,' said Freddy. He frowned. 'I'm still bloody puzzled about that van, y'know.'

'Language, please, Freddy,' said Cassie, sitting comfortingly close to him, and letting the gas mantle cast saucy light over her imitation silk stockings.

'Can't 'elp me language, Cassie, I still can't make out where that van got to.'

'Well, it turned off somewhere, didn't it?' said Cassie.

'Obviously, as Sherlock Holmes would say—'

'No, he says elementary.'

'Does he? You sure, Cassie? Only I've read some of his cases, and I don't know I ever—'

'Freddy, everyone knows he says elementary.'

'Well, leave me out,' said Freddy, 'I'm not everyone. Anyway, the police know the van must've turned off somewhere. It's obvious, but exactly where?' Freddy frowned with frustration. 'We asked people all over the side streets and roads if they'd noticed it, and nobody 'ad. I've just told you that.'

'No, I don't mean streets or roads,' said Cassie, 'I mean some sort of hiding-place, like a – well, like a barn, say.'

'A barn?' said Freddy. 'A barn? Don't go off your chump, Cassie. A barn somewhere around Denmark Hill or Herne Hill? You only find barns on farms.'

'Excuse me, Freddy Brown,' said Cassie, 'but kindly don't address me as if I'm an ignorant young lady, or I'll bite your lump. I meant something like a barn, and I said so.'

'Oh, beg yer pardon, Cassie, so you did,' said Freddy. 'Good point. In fact, I think you might've put a clever finger on that vanishin' trick. Cassie, you're not always just a pretty face.'

'I know that,' said Cassie.

'Mind you, I always notice your looks first,' said Freddy. 'I mean, who wouldn't? Your intellect catches up later.'

'Oh, you dear, what a nice compliment'ry word,' said Cassie, and kissed him lovingly.

Freddy came out of that in search of air.

'Don't get me legless, Cassie, not just now,' he said. 'Only you've set me thinkin' that some of the bigger and older houses around the area might still 'ave stables. Or, wait a bit, suppose a house had one of those new car garages and it 'ad been left open, suppose the owners were out?'

'But, Freddy, wouldn't someone have seen the van if it went in?' asked Cassie.

'Well, the police never came across anyone who did,' said Freddy. 'There's a lot of big houses on Denmark Hill that were built years ago, but I don't know I noticed which of them had had garages built. I think I'll take a bike ride.'

'What, now?' said Cassie.

'You're a clever girl, you are, Cassie, you've hit on a way the van could've disappeared, because they'd 'ave closed the doors as soon as it was in. We lost the chance of bein' right behind them up Denmark Hill when the police car mounted the pavement and skidded round in John Ruskin Street.' Freddy went on to explain why he'd got the incident on his mind, that he was dead against crooked geezers robbing banks, that if he'd paid the cheques in earlier, for instance, they'd have got away with his and Cassie's hundred quid on top of other people's savings, including Sammy's. He was also dead against any crook using a gun. Innocent people could end up dead, he said. In addition, he was still bloody vexed about being clobbered. Cassie told him again to mind his language. Freddy pointed out that being bashed by a revolver could have injured his loaf of bread so badly that he'd have missed getting married to her, which would have made any bloke use language. So he had a thing about seeing those crooks nicked, because it would have upset her if the wedding had been injured as well, and he didn't like her being upset. He reckoned that if the crooks had gone into hiding they wouldn't be showing themselves yet, not while the police still had a big search going on. 'So you see, Cassie, I think I will take a bike ride and look around some of the bigger houses on Denmark Hill and Herne Hill.'

'Not without me you won't,' said Cassie. 'Suppose you get knocked on the head again? It really could stop you gettin' married to me.'

'I don't think—'

'You're not goin' without me, d'you hear, Freddy Brown?'

'Now look, Cassie—'

'I don't mind you bein' a hero once,' said Cassie, 'but twice is once too much.'

'All right,' said Freddy, 'you can borrow Sally's bike and ride with me.'

'Yes, I'll do that,' said Cassie, 'because you're not goin' without me.'

'We'll just tell Mum and Dad we're goin' for our last bike ride as an unmarried couple,' said Freddy. Cassie made a face. 'What's up?' he asked.

'I didn't like you saying our last bike ride.'

'Only as single people,' said Freddy.

'I still didn't like it,' said Cassie.

Freddy put a hand under her chin and kissed her.

'If there's one thing you can be sure of, Cassie,' he said, 'it's that we're not goin' to lose each other. I'll see to that. You've sent me off me chump at times, and I can't say you 'aven't, but girls like you don't come ten a penny, Cassie.'

'Freddy, you do say quite nice things sometimes,' said Cassie.

'There's no charge,' said Freddy, headache getting better.

For the time being, Carstairs was in sole charge of the family, and the revolver had become an ever-present

233

menace. To add further to Vi's intense worries and Tommy's agonizing, Alice wasn't with them. For some reason, the other ratface was exploring the house and had taken Alice with him. As insurance, Tommy suspected, against a successful attempt to turn the tables on his partner. Tommy, rage close to the surface, might have considered taking on the challenge, for compared to himself, the slim sod with the gun was a runt. To create an opportunity would only need a distraction. That this blank-faced crook could keep that revolver in sight in the presence of children was sheer evil-mindedness, and Tommy would have taken great pleasure in laying the bloke out cold. Unfortunately, there were too many ifs and buts, including the possibility that the gun might go off in front of Vi, Paul and David.

David was stiff-bodied because of the absence of his sister. Paul was sitting on Vi's lap, cuddling close. Tommy kept meeting Vi's eyes. Hers looked cloudy. His tried to be reassuring.

The large handsome house seemed unnaturally quiet, as if ugly silence was smothering it.

Carstairs was in a cold temper because of the disrupted plan, the plan that should have put them aboard a cross-Channel ferry by now. Miller had been silently swearing under his breath ever since they realized that somehow the police had got on their tail.

He returned at last from his exploration of the house, bringing Alice into the room with him. Alice was pale, her mouth quivering. But she refused to cry. The man had said nothing to her during his tour of the family home, but had kept his hand on her shoulder throughout. On his way round the place, he found a large ball of strong cord in a cupboard.

He picked it up and when they came down the stairs eventually, he placed it on the hallstand. Now he gave her a little push that sent her on her way back to the settee, where she sat down next to her father. Tommy put an arm around her.

'That's my treasure,' he said.

Carstairs glanced at Miller, and Miller nodded to indicate he had found a room suitable for incarcerating the family. Carstairs returned the nod. Miller picked up the bottle of whisky and his empty glass from the table. Carstairs glared at him and mouthed an imprecation.

'Okay, later,' said Miller, and put the glass and bottle back on the table. 'Right,' he said to Tommy, 'we're all going upstairs. On your feet, you and your wife and kids.'

'If you don't mind,' said Tommy, 'we'll stay here. You've got the car keys, the car's in the drive, and you can both shove off as quietly as you like. We obviously can't stop you.'

'Are you simple?' said Miller. 'Or d'you think we are?'

'I don't know what I think,' said Tommy. 'In fact, I don't still know if I can think at all. It's the circumstances, if you take my meanin'. They're new to us. How'd you get here, by the way, and what made you pick this house for whatever it is you're up to?' He knew from what he had heard on the wireless that they'd been using a baker's van, but he couldn't recall seeing it in the drive when he arrived home.

'Dad, there's a van outside the French windows,' blurted David.

Carstairs showed a spasm of irritation, and Miller said, 'Kid, why don't you shut up?'

Jesus, thought Tommy, so that's what they did, drove the van round to the back of the house, where it couldn't be seen from the road.

'What's my son mean, a van?' he asked. 'Is it yours? If it is, what d'you want my car for?'

'You're a dab hand at trying to start up conversations,' said Miller. 'Cut it out, and forget about informing on us as soon as we leave. I told you to get on your feet, all of you, so move. Any tricks, and we'll do what we said, take the girl with us.' Tommy and his family rose. 'That's better,' said Miller, 'and it didn't hurt, did it?'

'Everything hurts,' said Vi, Paul beside her and his hand in hers.

'Well, bloody hard luck,' said Miller, and opened the door. 'This way, single file, and follow me.' He led them out of the room and along to the staircase. Carstairs, falling in behind them, noticed the large ball of cord on the hallstand and picked it up.

What the hell are they up to, thought Tommy, why the hell can't they just push off and stop frightening my kids? God knows what it's doing to Vi. Why the hell are they torturing her? But he knew he needn't have asked himself those kind of questions, because every answer was all too obvious. They intended to make sure, once they did leave, that neither he nor any of his family could inform on them. Not for a while, at least. So he guessed they were going to lock him and Vi and the children in one of the bedrooms. One of the back bedrooms on the second floor, probably. It would be too high for anyone to think of opening the window and climbing down, and too far from the road for any shout for help to be heard. Sod it, thought Tommy, we may have to wait all night for our daily help to arrive in the morning. Fortunately, she'd got her own key. They'd be able to arouse her attention.

'Come on, come on,' growled Miller from the first floor landing.

Why was it, thought Vi, that that one alone did the talking? The other hadn't said a word as far as she knew. She thought about that, and turned her head as she and Paul began to ascend the second flight of stairs. She met Tommy's eyes.

'Good on yer, Vi, we're all here,' he said quietly.

The phone rang then.

The unexpected sound brought everyone to a dead stop. Miller called down to Tommy.

'Answer it, but don't start a long conversation, and mind what you say.'

Tommy went down to the hall, Carstairs following him. He picked up the phone and steeled himself.

'Hello.'

'Boots here, Tommy.'

'How'd you do,' said Tommy, and something hard dug into his back, something that told him to cut out the wet stuff.

'Listen,' said Boots, 'I'm driving Emily, Chinese Lady and our stepdad to the weddings. Our stepdad's car is out of action with front axle trouble. You're driving Vi, of course. Could you take Rosie and Eloise as well?'

'Pleasure,' said Tommy, 'I'll pick them up.'

'Thanks,' said Boots. 'Love to Vi and the kids.'

'You're comin' over now?' said Tommy.

'I'm doing what?' said Boots.

'It's a bit inconvenient,' said Tommy.

The gun jammed into his back.

237

'I'm not with you,' said Boots.

'No, sorry, I'm not thinking straight,' said Tommy. 'See you some other time, Boots.' A hand wrenched the receiver from him and replaced it. Miller came down the stairs, leaving Vi and her children on the landing. He rushed at Tommy.

'Who's coming over, you bugger?' he asked.

'That was my elder brother,' said Tommy. 'I put 'im off by telling him it was too inconvenient.'

'Did it put him off?' said Miller. 'How do we know it did? Well, if he does arrive, he'll wish he'd stayed at home, and you'll wish you'd made him. Get back to your family.'

Vi gave his hand a squeeze when he rejoined them. She knew, as he knew, that what he had said over the phone would set Boots thinking. Boots had done a fair amount of thinking for the Adams families in his time. Vi felt she wouldn't be surprised if he rang back in a little while.

Under compulsion, the family went all the way up to the top floor, and the next move fitted everything else that had happened. They were forced into the attic, which had no windows, only a skylight.

The phone rang again.

'Bloody hell,' hissed Miller, and grabbed Tommy's arm. 'Get down there and answer it, you bleeder.'

Tommy experienced a lunatic desire to smash the man's face in, but down he went, Miller following. Carstairs pulled the attic door shut and locked it. The key had been hanging from a hook just inside the door.

In the hall, Tommy answered the phone, with Miller at his elbow.

'Hello?'

'Tommy,' said Boots from the other end of the line,

'why did you say I was coming over this evening and then tell me it was too inconvenient?'

'I wasn't thinking straight,' said Tommy.

'Why?' asked Boots.

'Anyway, don't come over this evening,' said Tommy. 'Can't stop to talk now, we've got visitors. So long, Boots.' He replaced the phone.

'Your brother again?' said Miller.

'Yes,' said Tommy.

'So he's not coming over?'

'Not now I've definitely put 'im off,' said Tommy.

'Just as well, for him and for you,' said Miller. 'Listen, what's a half-baked cockney like you doing in a house like this?'

'It's a long story,' said Tommy.

'You're a pain in my backside, d'you know that?' said Miller.

'I could say a few things about you,' said Tommy.

'Don't,' said Miller, 'I'm sensitive. Get back upstairs, or are you thinking of taking me on?'

'I'm not a bleedin' idiot,' said Tommy, 'I'm not takin' either of you on while you've got my wife and kids under lock and key.'

'That's the first time you've talked sense,' said Miller, and Tommy made his ascent of the handsome mahogany staircase. Miller followed, thinking here was a middle-class cockney, for Christ's sake. Bloody disgusting. How had the ponce managed it? By being lucky, you bet. But he was no idiot, and the bugger probably knew that he and Carstairs were in disguise even if the prissy woman didn't. Not that it mattered. None of them would get to see himself or Carstairs as they normally were.

A sour smile touched Miller's lips.

# Chapter Fifteen

Lilian answered the door to her visitor.

'Good evening, Mrs Hyams,' said milkman Bill Chambers, looking a stalwart in a double-breasted chalk-striped grey suit and a trilby hat. 'Consequent on the note I left, I'm here by arrangement.'

'Not my arrangement,' said Lilian, looking a lush armful in a cosy cream machine-knitted jumper and a pleated chocolate-brown skirt.

'Still, I'll come in if you'll let me get my feet over your doorstep,' said Bill. 'Might I mention you dress well, Lilian?'

'Come in,' said Lilian, 'but let's be formal in case Rabbi Solomon is listening.'

'Formal? Never 'eard of it, not in Walworth,' said Bill, and stepped in. It put him immediately into her living-room. There was not enough space for a passage or a hall in these little flat-fronted houses in King and Queen Street. Lilian closed the door, and Bill, taking his hat off, looked around. 'Cosy,' he said, nodding at inviting armchairs.

'Yes, you mentioned that before,' said Lilian. 'Perhaps you'd like to stay long enough for a cup of tea?'

'Well, I do have something on my mind that might take me off double-quick,' said Bill.

'Oh, don't mind me,' said Lilian, slightly piqued.

'You've 'eard about the bank robbery?' said Bill.

'Yes, I heard it over the wireless at work,' said Lilian.

'Well, I had a mental flash of lightning just as I was on my way to you,' said Bill.

'A flash of lightning?' said Lilian. 'About what?'

'The van the crooks were usin',' said Bill. 'Some crooks. Ruddy dangerous heathens more like, with their flamin' shooters. Robbery ought to be a kind of risky pastime, not a declaration of war.'

'Yes, but what about the van?' asked Lilian.

'I saw it once,' said Bill, 'outside a house in Stead Street. I've got an idea it belonged to the lodger, bloke name of Barnes. Not my idea of a friendly geezer, he's got eyes that look right through you. So I went out of my way a bit on my walk here, and knocked on the door. There was no van outside, of course, and no lodger at home, either. The landlady, Mrs Wetherby, said he'd given up his room this morning, but hadn't left any forwarding address. It strikes me, Mrs Hyams, if you don't mind our sociable evening bein' postponed, that I ought to inform the police.'

'You should have gone to the police station immediately,' said Lilian.

'Well, there was a bit of etiquette to consider,' said Bill.

'A bit of what?' said Lilian.

'It wouldn't have been good manners to have gone to the police station without lettin' you know,' said Bill, 'not when you happened to be expecting me. I didn't want you to be a disappointed victim of me bad manners.'

'My life, a disappointed victim?' Lilian laughed. 'You're a bit of a card, aren't you, Mister Milkman?'

'Call me Bill. Well, I'd better shoot off to the police station now, Mrs Hyams, and save our sociable meetin' for tomorrow evening.'

'D'you mind if I come with you?' said Lilian. 'I've never been in a police station, and what you've got to tell the police sounds exciting.'

'Be a pleasure to have your company, Mrs Hyams,' said Bill. 'I suppose you could say that what I've got to tell 'em amounts to a short piece of required information. If they want to lock me up for not passing it on earlier, I hope I can get a character reference from you as one of me more imposing customers.'

'Well, if it does come to that,' said Lilian, putting her hat and coat on, 'I'll do my imposing best for you.'

Their bicycle lamps shining, Cassie and Freddy were pedalling slowly up Denmark Hill. Houses showed lights behind drawn curtains, and some of the larger residences had lamps above their doors.

'I'll start lookin',' said Freddy, dismounting. 'You take care of the bikes, Cassie.'

'D'you mean stand about holding them?' asked Cassie, peering suspiciously at him. The April evening was now dark.

'Just while I pop in and out of drives,' said Freddy. 'It's too dark to see from the road.'

'Excuse me, Freddy Brown,' said Cassie, 'but if you think I'm goin' to stand here holdin' two bikes while you wander off in the dark, you can think again.' A lumbering bus with a load of passengers passed them. 'It's dangerous, and besides, I'm not goin' to. You don't mind I've got my own ideas about what I do?'

'No, I don't mind, Cassie, you can stand on the pavement,' said Freddy. 'Buses don't come after you on pavements, not unless the driver don't know where the road is. All right, then, that's settled, you wait here on the pavement with the bikes, and I'll start lookin' for houses with garages.'

'Freddy love, you don't want me to kick your legs to bits when you've already got a sore head, do you?' said Cassie.

'Well, no, I don't,' said Freddy, 'but we don't want to be here all night talkin', and I can't see what's wrong with you waitin' 'ere on the pavement.'

'I didn't come with you to do waitin',' said Cassie. 'I came to make sure you don't do anything silly. And when I said dangerous, I meant dangerous for you. So we'll do the lookin' together. I like you bein' protective, but not if it means me standin' here holdin' two bikes. You wheel yours and I'll wheel mine.'

If there was one thing Freddy had learned in thorough and sometimes suffering fashion over the years, it was that Cassie had a mind and a will of her own.

'All right, me pet, come on,' he said.

They began a survey of the houses on this side of the hill. A bright half-moon came out of clearing clouds, and that lightened the darkness. Freddy felt this side of the hill offered the best prospects, because the van could have turned in in a split second. He wasn't quite sure what he expected to see, he had a vague picture of an open gate, a drive and a garage. Supposing a garage showed up? Its doors would be closed, so what could that tell him? Nothing. Unless it had a side window and the moon didn't mess him about. Still, Denmark Hill was the area immediately beyond Camberwell, the area where people had begun to own cars and where some garages had been built.

243

He and Cassie kept going, wheeling their bikes and taking a look at the frontages and the drives of the larger houses. There was one with a garage, built against the side of the property. Freddy opened the gate and ventured in, Cassie behind him. The garage's double doors were open, the garage itself empty.

'They're out,' said Cassie. 'Gone to Buckingham Palace, probably.'

'Could be the flicks,' said Freddy, and back they went to the pavement, continuing their hopeful search. Cassie whispered that if they did pick up clues, Freddy wasn't to do anything except go at once to the police. Freddy said he'd like a crack first at the unfriendly bleeder who clobbered him.

'Freddy, your language lately, I don't know what's come over you,' said Cassie, as they took a look down one more drive. 'You've never been brought up to be a common blasphemer like Ron Bargett down our street. What's that?'

'It's a car,' said Freddy, stopping outside another house, 'it's just parked in the drive.'

'I can't make out if there's a garage,' said Cassie.

'No, there's not,' said Freddy.

'Freddy, wait a bit,' said Cassie, 'this is takin' an awful long time, and I just remembered we didn't tell my dad we were goin' out. I mean, if we 'ave to do this all the way up Denmark Hill, then all the way down again on the other side, then do Herne Hill, we'll be here till Christmas. Freddy, we can't be here till Christmas.'

'Nor even all night,' said Freddy, 'or your dad might ask what they call impertinent questions.'

'It's pertinent, Freddy, it's in books.'

'Well, look,' said Freddy, 'let's just cover Denmark Hill, both sides. I've got a feelin' the van disappeared before it reached Herne Hill because there were people by the Herne Hill shops. The police stopped to ask, but none of them 'ad seen the van.'

'I suppose we're not on some wild goose chase, are we?' said Cassie, beginning to have doubts. 'It sounded a good idea at first, but do we both still think the van could've turned off into someone's open garage? Only if it did, what about the people who own the house? If they were out at the time in their car, and they'd found their garage shut when they got back, they'd have opened it and seen the van, wouldn't they?'

'And then got clobbered,' said Freddy. 'But you might be right, Cassie, we might be lookin' for what we won't find, but while we're still 'ere, let's cover Denmark Hill.'

'Well, all right,' said Cassie.

Accordingly, they finished a search of possible places on this side of the hill without finding anything that offered a credible pointer. They crossed the road and began a not very hopeful look at properties on that side of the hill. Eventually they reached a house of very handsome proportions, set well back in a wide frontage. There was a car standing in the drive, and beyond it was space full of shadows thrown by the house. No garage. They were about to go on when Freddy noticed something in the light of the bright half-moon. There was a line of young trees bordering the righthand side of the drive, and one of them showed a cracked lower branch hanging limply. The parked car was well clear of the border. Freddy leaned his bike against a gatepost and said he wondered how the branch got broken. Cassie said the car must have been driven in too close to the trees. Freddy said he might as well take a look. The house was silent, but there were some lights on. Freddy examined the higher bodywork of the car, but couldn't see any signs of a dent in it. Funny, he thought. If something else had hit the branch, the owner would either have done a repair job or cut the branch off, not left it looking a mess. Well, that's what I would have done, thought Freddy.

He noted what a wide space there was at the side of the house, where the black shadows were cast.

'Cassie, I'll just take a look down there,' he whispered.

'It's too dark,' whispered Cassie.

'But something hit that branch, Cassie, and I don't think it was the car. Suppose there's a large shed down there that could take the van? I might as well have a quick look. Won't be a tick.'

'I'll ring my bicycle bell if I see anything happening,' said Cassie, and kept watch as Freddy went past the car and into the darkness. He disappeared. Cassie surveyed the house and its front door, feeling sure someone would come out. No-one did, and in any case Freddy was back within a minute.

'Oh, me gawd, Cassie,' he whispered, 'we've found it.'

'Oh, my Sunday elastic,' breathed Cassie, 'you sure?'

'Sure,' said Freddy. 'But there's no-one in it.'

'Shall I take a look?'

'No, I don't think so, Cassie, just in case,' said Freddy, looking at the house with acute interest.

'Whose place is it?' asked Cassie.

'No idea,' said Freddy, 'but I noticed it was called "The Manor". Let's get fast to the Camberwell police station.'

'Wait, did you say "The Manor"?' asked Cassie in horror.

'Yes, the name's on the gate,' said Freddy. The gate was open at right angles to its post. Cassie went close and peered. Yes, there it was, the name plate. 'The Manor'.

'Oh, Lord,' she breathed.

'What's the name matter?' asked Freddy. 'It's the van that's important. It's parked at the back of the house.'

'Freddy, "The Manor" is where Tommy and Vi Adams live, with their fam'ly,' breathed Cassie.

'What?' said Freddy.

'Yes, you know Tommy and Vi Adams, we've both met them at Boots's house, and you must've met them at Sammy's weddin' to Susie,' said Cassie. 'I know their address, because I send Christmas cards. Freddy, you're positive those men aren't in the van?'

'It's empty, Cassie, believe me,' said Freddy, mind working fast.

'Freddy?' It was a shocked enquiring whisper from Cassie.

'Yes, I'm thinkin' the same as you, that if they're not in the van they could be in the house,' breathed Freddy. 'In which case, what's 'appening to Tommy and his fam'ly? If those crooks 'ad come and gone, leavin' the van, Tommy would've phoned the police, and the van wouldn't be there any more. The police would've taken it away as evidence. I don't like the fact that it's still there.'

'Freddy, we've got to go to the police,' said Cassie.

247

'I know where I'm goin' first,' said Freddy.

'Where?'

'To see Boots,' said Freddy. 'He's the one, Cassie.'

'But, Freddy, the police have got to be told, you know that.'

'Boots isn't far away,' said Freddy, 'let's tell him first. One of those crooks owns a gun, Cassie. I reckon he might use it if the police turn up. It might be different with Boots. Boots has always got ways and means. Come on, Cassie.' From out of his concern appeared an encouraging little grin. 'Come on, beloved.'

The police sergeant on duty at the Walworth station, after noting down the caller's particulars, listened in keen receptive interest as Bill Chambers explained why he was there. The sergeant thought the gent might only be a milk roundsman, but he could string words together, and was very convincing. His lady companion kept looking at him with a smile.

'Right, sir,' said the sergeant at the end of Bill's informative discourse, 'if you and your lady wife would like to take a seat, I'll phone the Yard.'

'Unfortunately, the lady's not my wife,' said Bill.

'Ah,' said the sergeant, reaching for the phone, 'unfortunate, is it, sir?'

'I've missed out on the happy-ever-after stakes,' said Bill, and sat down with the amused Lilian.

'You'll miss out on other things if you don't watch what your tongue gets up to,' she whispered.

'Was it my fault he thought you were my wife?' murmured Bill.

'I should say it was mine?'

The sergeant got through to the Yard, to a Chief Inspector Carson, in charge now of the case concerning the bank robbery, and gave him details of the information just laid by a Walworth resident, Mr Chambers. When he put the phone down he said to Bill, 'There'll be two officers from the Yard here quick as a flash, sir, to interview you.'

'Exactly how quick is quick as a flash, Sergeant?' asked Lilian.

'Pretty lively, miss,' said the sergeant.

'It's Mrs Hyams,' said Lilian. 'I'm a widow.'

'Ah,' said the sergeant.

'Don't mention it,' said Lilian, not precisely sure now why she was here, unless it was simply a little exciting to feel involved. The bank robbers were obviously still at large, but Bill's information could probably help the police identify one of them.

A uniformed constable came in, leading a scruff of a lad by his ear.

'Hello, what've we got here, Constable Parry?' asked the sergeant.

'Name of Willy Dobson, alias Tiddler, of Brandon Street,' said the constable.

'What, again?' said the sergeant.

'Seen breakin' a neighbour's window,' said constable.

'What, again?' said the sergeant.

'Happened this afternoon,' said the constable, 'and I've only just caught up with him.'

'It's a bleedin' lie,' said Tiddler Dobson, 'and if you don't leggo me ear, I'll tell me dad.'

'Denying the charge, are we?' said the constable.

'Yus, I am,' said Tiddler, one of the terrors of Brandon Street.

'He was seen by the complainant, Mrs Hardwick,' said the constable.

249

'Course I wasn't,' said Tiddler. 'Leggo me ear, will yer?'

The constable released it, and Tiddler rubbed it.

'Remind me, how old are you, young Dobson?' asked the sergeant.

'None of yer business,' said Tiddler, eleven and skinny. 'Anyway, old Mrs 'Ardwick couldn't even see an elephant even if it was sittin' on 'er doorstep, so she couldn't 'ave seen me. It's a bleedin' false arrest, and wait till me dad finds out.'

'He's going to find out, so's your mum,' said the sergeant, 'we'll be talking to them tomorrow. Why'd you break the old lady's window?'

'Me?' said Tiddler. 'Corblimey, I ain't stayin' 'ere listening to you coppers. Me mum'll sue yer for damages, and for twistin' me ear as well. Why don't yer go and arrest old Mrs 'Ardwick for chuckin' a bucketful of pertater peelings over me 'ead, like she did yesterday? I dunno I ever been more aggravated, and it's a crime, that is, chuckin' pertater peelings in washin'-up water over anyone's 'ead. Can I go now?'

'When I've taken some particulars,' said the sergeant. 'Let's see, Willy Dobson of fourteen Brandon Street, I think, witnessed in the act of breaking a neighbour's window. What did you use, Tiddler, a brick?'

'Crikey, you're comin' it, you are,' said Tiddler. 'I told yer, I ain't guilty, nor of unsound mind, neiver.'

'Didn't you break some other neighbour's window with a brick about two months ago?' said the sergeant.

'That was different,' said Tiddler, 'me 'and slipped. Tell yer what, mister, you let me go 'ome now and I won't say nuffink to me mum an' dad about bein' false arrested. That's fair, ain't it?'

'But is it fair to Mrs Hardwick?' asked the constable.

'What, that old biddy what can't see straight?' said Tiddler.

'She saw you, me son,' said the constable.

'I ain't standin' for this no more,' said Tiddler. 'Can I see a slister?'

'Solicitor?' said the sergeant gravely.

'Yus, can I?'

'We'll have a word with your mum and dad first,' said the sergeant.

'Cor, you ain't 'alf bleedin' 'ard on an innercent party,' said Tiddler.

The dialogue continued. Bill was amused, Lilian fascinated.


'Polly, you're crazy,' said Rosie. They were in the first-floor living-room, used by Boots and his family when they weren't spending time with Chinese Lady and Mr Finch downstairs.

'Just a suggestion, Rosie old thing,' said Polly. Her idea, put to Boots over cups of tea in Lyons, was to contact Rosie's natural mother, believed to be Mrs Milly Rainbould, and to find out if it was possible for the woman to declare she couldn't recognize Major Armitage as the man who fathered Rosie. A little gift, say in ready cash, might help to foster that lack of recognition, in which case any civil action by Major Armitage to have the adoption set aside would barely stand up in court. Polly was willing to visit Mr Tooley and to persuade him to let her know where his daughter, Milly Rainbould, could be found. Polly would then arrange for the woman to be brought face to face with Major Armitage, who was bound to have changed to some extent over a period of nearly twenty-one years. 'I'm very much on your side, ducky,' said Polly, 'and, of course, it would only be a precautionary measure taken to discourage Major Armitage from ever breaking his promise to you.'

'Charles Armitage is a gentleman,' said Rosie.

'Dear girl, I've known a score of gentlemen all capable of putting self-interest first,' said Polly.

'The idea's still crazy,' said Rosie, 'and questionable as well.'

'Questionable?' said Polly. In a tan-coloured dress of uncrushable velvet she looked extremely fetching considering she was in her thirty-ninth year. But somehow Polly kept the ageing process from taking any real liberties with her. Her natural vitality helped. Her bobbed hair and the piquancy of her features still made her look like a flapper whenever her brittle gaiety was ascendant. 'Good grief, we're not going to play by the rules, are we?'

'Boots was against your idea in the first place,' said Rosie, 'and wouldn't give it house room now.'

'Saints alive, what's turned him into a Boy Scout?' asked Polly. 'All that play up and play the game stuff, for God's sake.'

'Is that what he told you to do, play up and play the game?' smiled Rosie.

'Not literally,' said Polly. 'What he did say was that he was touched by my concern, but didn't approve of Major Armitage being victimized by any hanky-panky, and that it wasn't what he expected of a Girl Guide. I said I'd never been a Girl Guide, and he said it wasn't too late for me to join. I said that with his kind of principles he'd make a better Boy Scout than I would a Girl Guide. This was all in Lyons, of course.'

'And what happened then?'

'He laughed,' said Polly, 'and if I hadn't drunk my tea, old thing, I'd have emptied it into his lap. I mean to say, don't you know, with Major Armitage hovering darkly over the family, who wants to be a Girl Guide?'

'Well, try,' said Rosie, 'because there's no need for any further action, Polly. In any case, no-one, not even the gods of thunder and lightning, can split this family. And I really don't want anyone to contact Mrs Milly Rainbould, particularly as it's quite unnecessary now.'

Polly looked at her. Rosie's mention of her natural mother hadn't been spoken with any hint of bitterness or regret. In fact, there was a little smile on her face, and Polly knew she felt neither bitterness nor regret. From the age of reason until now, her life had been spent with Boots and Emily, and Polly suspected if there was any regret at all, it was for the fact that she hadn't been born of them. She probably felt, however, that it was entirely natural for her to belong to them. Polly had never heard her speak one word about the woman who had conceived her. This was the first time she had mentioned her in Polly's hearing.

'Are you positive, Rosie, that you really can trust Major Armitage not to have second thoughts? You see, sweetie, you're a very special kind of person, and if the man has no sons or daughters except you, I can easily imagine how much he'd like to have you in his life.'

'He's given me his word,' said Rosie, 'and we parted as friends – hello, another caller?'

The front door bell was ringing.

Tim answered it, and found Freddy and Cassie on the step.

'Oh, watcher, Cassie, hello, Freddy,' he said.

'Aren't you growin'?' said Cassie.

'Is your dad in?' asked Freddy.

'Everyone's in,' said Tim.

'Just your dad, if 'e can spare a couple of minutes,' said Freddy.

'Come in,' said Tim, and they entered the hall. He closed the door and said, 'Crikey, you two look married already.'

'What makes you say that?' asked Cassie.

'You're both sort of flushed,' grinned Tim.

'We've been bike-ridin' up and down Denmark Hill,' said Freddy, 'but I didn't know it was goin' to make us look married. Could you get your dad, Tim?'

'Go in the front room and I'll get him,' said Tim.

Boots arrived with a smile, said hello to them, and asked if they'd dropped in with a query about their wedding. Cassie said they didn't have any queries about that unless Freddy got himself disorganized. What they did have, she said, was some worrying news. Freddy took over then and gave Boots a pretty exact account of the day's happenings, and how he and Cassie had finally caught up with the bank robbers' van.

'It's standing at the back of someone's house?' said Boots.

'That's a fact it is,' said Freddy, 'and—'

'Boots,' said Cassie painfully, 'it's your brother Tommy's house, "The Manor".'

'Tommy's?' said Boots, and thought of Tommy's family and two short and peculiar phone conversations. 'Jesus Christ,' he said.

'Me and Freddy have an awful feeling the men are still there,' said Cassie, 'and in the house. Boots, d'you think they could be? Only if they weren't, if they'd gone, Tommy would've done something about the van, about tellin' the police, wouldn't he?'

'Cassie,' said Boots, 'they are still there, and in the house.' He knew now the reason for Tommy's odd remarks over the phone, remarks that he'd been turning over in his mind since he'd put the receiver down only five minutes ago. Among other things, Tommy had said he'd got visitors. 'I've been on the phone twice to Tommy this evening, and each time he hasn't made sense. Freddy, you were the bloke knocked out at the bank? You saw the gun?'

'One of the ruddy crooks hit me with it,' said Freddy.

'We've a serious crisis,' said Boots, 'and that's putting it mildly.'

'We'll just have to tell the police,' said Cassie, 'we can't stand here talkin', can we? I keep thinkin' about what might be happening to Tommy and his fam'ly.'

'It's not going to be easy, Cassie, trying to lay hands on a pair of armed desperadoes who won't think twice about using the family as a bargaining factor,' said Boots. 'The Home Office might call the Army out. It's the way the Government sometimes deals with armed criminals who are holed up. Let me think.'

'Freddy's relying on you to do just that,' said Cassie, 'but we both hope you won't take too long.'

'At least, there's one way of getting into the house without breaking down the front or back door,' said Boots.

'What way?' asked Freddy.

'Down into the coal-hole at the side of the house, and then up some steps to the inside door next to the kitchen,' said Boots.

'I like that,' said Freddy.

'But if the police do that,' said Cassie, 'they could still get shot as soon as they showed themselves in the house.'

'Well, we need a distraction, don't we, Cassie?' said Boots.

'And we need to be quick,' said Cassie.

'We need to get Tommy and his family out of harm's way, and that's a fact,' said Boots. 'Have you asked each other why the two men are still there, which I think they are? Why haven't they taken Tommy's car and made a run for it?'

'Perhaps because they think the police are still lookin' for them,' said Freddy, 'which could mean they're waitin' till they think the coast is clear. They probably think they're as safe as ruddy houses stayin' where they are. I mean, who's goin' to look for them there?'

'First-class point, Freddy,' said Boots.

'Boots, I can't think why you're not doin' something,' said Cassie, every nerve fidgeting.

'We need to be sure of exactly what we can do and the best way of doing it,' said Boots. 'My guess as to what they're going to do themselves is that they'll probably make their move sometime after midnight, when police activity will have quietened down.'

In the ground floor living-room, Emily was asking Tim what Cassie and Freddy had wanted Boots for. Tim replied that they didn't say, but that they looked very keen to talk to his dad.

'Just your dad?' said Chinese Lady.

'Yes, just him, Grandma,' said Tim.

'Then I don't suppose it's about any aspect of their wedding,' said Mr Finch, a grey tint in his hair adding its own touch to his distinguished looks.

'Shall I go and ask Papa what it's about?' suggested Eloise.

'No, I don't think so,' said Emily. 'Stay here, Eloise.'

Rosie, coming downstairs with Polly, heard voices in the room now known, in Chinese Lady's terms, as the parlour. The door was open and she looked in.

'Well, my goodness, see who's here, Polly,' she said, as the two of them entered the room. They said hello to Cassie and Freddy.

'There's something up,' said Polly

'Is there?' said Boots.

'It's written all over you,' said Polly.

'So it is,' said Rosie. 'You tell, Freddy.'

'All right, tell them, Freddy,' said Boots, 'while I have a word with my stepfather before I phone the police.'

## Chapter Sixteen

It was while Freddy and Cassie were conducting their search in Denmark Hill that Chief Inspector Carson of Scotland Yard, along with a detective-sergeant, arrived at the Walworth police station to talk to Bill Chambers. Only a few minutes later, the Scotland Yard men were on their way with Bill and Lilian to the house in which a suspect had lodged.

'This the place, Mr Chambers?' said the Inspector as Bill and Lilian came to a halt in Stead Street.

'That's the house,' said Bill.

'And you saw the van parked here?'

'Right outside the door,' said Bill.

'And the name of the lodger who moved out this morning was Barnes, you said?'

'That's the name in my customers' book,' said Bill.

'Well, you've given a pretty fair description of him,' said Inspector Carson. 'Let's see what the landlady can tell us.'

'Only what she told me, that he's gone,' said Bill.

'Landladies can usually tell a lot more than that about their lodgers,' said Lilian, who had recently come to think there was a lot more to Bill than bottles of milk and offers of new-laid eggs. 'I was a lodger myself for several years after the war, when I only had a war widow's pension to live on.'

The landlady, Mrs Wetherby, became a flustered

woman when she found four people on her doorstep, two of whom were policemen from Scotland Yard. But she didn't lose her manners, she invited them into her parlour, and her flustered state changed to excited curiosity the moment Inspector Carson began to ask her questions about Mr Barnes, her departed lodger.

No, she didn't know his Christian name, his rent book just said J Barnes. He'd been lodging with her about three months and kept himself to himself. No, he didn't have many visitors, not as far as she knew, but he did have one or two call on him. No, she hadn't actually seen them, only heard him go down and let in whoever it was who'd knocked. She'd never been a nosy woman, she didn't come out of her kitchen to see who it was he took upstairs. No, he hadn't left any forwarding address. What did the police want to see him about?

'Oh, just for formal enquiries,' said Inspector Carson. 'When he left this morning, what did he take with him?'

'Only 'is suitcase,' said Mrs Wetherby. 'Bless us,' she said, putting a hand to her fluttering bosom, 'he ain't a criminal, is he? Only he never said much and always looked as if he 'ad something to hide, like.'

'What was his job?' asked the Inspector.

'I don't know he 'ad any job,' said Mrs Wetherby.

'Didn't he drive a baker's van?'

'Not as I know of,' said Mrs Wetherby.

'Wasn't there one outside sometimes?'

'Not as I ever saw.'

Inspector Carson glanced at Bill.

'There was one outside last Monday week,' said Bill.

'Not as I noticed,' said Mrs Wetherby, 'but of

course I can't see what's in the street when I'm in me kitchen, like I mostly am if I ain't out shoppin'. 'Ere, just a minute, ain't I recognizin' you now, ain't you our new milkman?'

'That's me, Mrs Wetherby,' said Bill.

'Well, if you say you saw a baker's van outside me home sometime last week, I believe yer,' said the landlady.

'Why d'you believe him?' asked Lilian.

'He's got an honest look, and doesn't 'ave eyes like marbles like Mr Barnes did,' said Mrs Wetherby. 'Mind, I ain't sayin' Mr Barnes wasn't honest, only that he didn't say much, and his eyes looked most times as if he 'ad something to hide, like I said before. Of course, if he did 'ave, it wasn't my business.'

Inspector Carson asked if he could look around the vacated room. Mrs Wetherby said yes, she hadn't touched it yet. The Inspector and his sergeant carried out an inspection and search, but found nothing. Down in the parlour again, he asked Bill if he'd like to accompany him to Scotland Yard and take a look at photographs of known criminals, with a view to finding out if he recognized Barnes among them. Bill said certainly, and Lilian asked if she could go too. The CID men had no objections.

In the back of the police car on the way to Scotland Yard, Bill said, 'Nice to have your company, Mrs Hyams, I'm pleasured.'

'Myself, I'm daft,' said Lilian, 'I've got a hundred things to do at home.'

'I'll drop in tomorrow evening and help you with them,' said Bill.

'If you do, you'll find yourself having to iron my smalls,' whispered Lilian.

'No problem, seeing I iron me own,' said Bill.

Tommy and his family, locked in the attic, had made up their minds that the stony-faced bank robbers were going to make a run for it any moment. The attic was full of family junk, such as old suitcases, an ancient trunk, pieces of rolled-up carpet, and discarded kitchen chairs. They were at least able to sit down, on the trunk and the chairs. An electric bulb ensured they were not without light. Tommy had suggested they all remained quiet for the time being, so that they would be able to hear the sound of the car's engine firing. When it did, and when the car was on its way, they could then use chairs to smash the door open. Vi said she could hardly wait to hear the sound of the car.

They sat in silence, Tommy thinking the children were bearing up like the King's troopers. Actually, poor old Kingy wasn't very well, but his troopers were young and healthy, and would help him celebrate his Silver Jubilee next month. I'll take the family to see that, thought Tommy, they'll enjoy a bit of pageantry and flag-waving. Be a lot more lively and healthy than what they're putting up with now, bless 'em. As for Vi, if I didn't know before what she was worth to me and the kids, I know now.

Vi thought if this is a nightmare, I'll be glad when I wake up. Still, there's one thing I'm sure of, and that's that I'd have gone off my head if Tommy hadn't been here. The way he talked to those rotten crooks, calm as you like, which helped to keep the children from panicking. Not even Boots could have been calmer considering I know Tommy was furious underneath. Well, if things don't get any worse than this, we can still enjoy the double wedding on Saturday, and take the children to Brighton on Sunday. That'll do us all good, a trip to Brighton. Oh, Lord, when's that car going to start?

I'd like to kick those men, thought David.

I'd like to give mum and dad a kiss, thought Alice.

Paul was simply relieved those men weren't with them any more.

Outside, at the end of the landing, Ginger Carstairs was using kitchen scissors to cut lengths of cord from the large ball.

'Better keep that for later,' said Miller, 'no point in tying these weak-kneed middle-class cockneys up just yet.'

'I can't stand their kind,' said Carstairs.

'Nor any kind,' said Miller.

'Most people are bloody idiots, the rest are a pain in my elbow,' said Carstairs. 'Okay, we'll truss this family up a few minutes before we go, and before we've changed our clothes.'

'It'll keep them from informing on us until it's too late,' said Miller. 'I think I'll have that second Scotch now, I need something that'll help me keep awake all night.'

'Whisky won't help,' said Carstairs.

'It'll help me,' said Miller.

'You're a bloody weakling, then,' said Carstairs. 'See if there's any coffee. Middle class cockneys might drink coffee and kid themselves they've got real class.'

Boots had spoken to Mr Finch, who agreed with his suggested plan of action. Boots thereupon phoned the local police, gave his name and address, then advised the sergeant on duty that a friend, one

Freddy Brown, had located the bank robbers' van. He detailed where it was, behind the house of his brother Tommy Adams, and that the police could reasonably assume the wanted men were in the house, particularly as two phone conversations with his brother had indicated something out of the ordinary was happening. He recounted the gist of the conversations, including the fact that his brother had said they'd got visitors.

The local police sergeant said a colleague would put a phone call through to Scotland Yard at once, on another line, and Boots heard him urgently instructing the man.

The sergeant then said, 'Carry on, Mr Adams.'

Boots pointed out there was a way of getting into the house without alerting the wanted men until the police were in. This was to drop down into the cellar through the outside coal-hole, and up the cellar steps to a door adjacent the kitchen. The police would understand it was necessary, however, not to take the risk of rushing into the house without knowing where the wanted men were holding the family. That might cause havoc. Once the police were up the cellar steps and at the door, they should wait for a distraction, that of the phone ringing and being answered. Obviously, the phone would have to be answered, and it would ring until it was. Boots said he'd see to that. His brother would probably be the one who'd be allowed to answer it, but not without one of the wanted men accompanying him, leaving the other to keep an eye on the rest of the family. That would split the swines, and the one with Tommy could be taken first. The policemen waiting at the cellar door would know when to make their entry, for they'd be able to hear the phone ringing in the hall and to act the moment it stopped. That would be when Tommy lifted the receiver, and the cellar door wasn't far from the hall.

'Are you with me so far, Sergeant?'

'I'm with you, Mr Adams. But they're armed, those wanted men. At least, one of them is.'

'He'll be the one who accompanies my brother to the phone,' said Boots. 'I'd bet on that. I hope it'll be Tommy who answers. He's a formidable physical specimen. But there's a chance it may be his wife, of course.'

'But who at your house will know when to make the call to your brother's house, sir?'

'I'll arrange that,' said Boots.

'Well, you're a cool one, Mr Adams, I'll say that.'

'Believe me, Sergeant, at the moment I'm livid,' said Boots. 'I'll meet your men and the men from Scotland Yard in Denmark Hill, a little way from my brother's house, and be there in ten minutes or so.'

'Hold on a bit, Mr Adams.' The police sergeant went absent from the phone for a few minutes, then returned to say, 'Chief Inspector Carson of the Yard is on the other line, and wants you to know you're not to take any action by yourself until he sees you, and then, sir, it'll all be done by the police.'

'I'll still make certain arrangements,' said Boots.

'That's as maybe, Mr Adams. At the same time, don't think we're not appreciative of all this information and suggested action. We'll get men there quick, and they'll then wait for Chief Inspector Carson and his men. He'll be leaving the Yard any moment.'

'Ask him not to hang about,' said Boots, and put the phone down.

Then he spoke to Rosie, Polly and Mr Finch.

Five minutes later, Polly was all nervous tension. She was even experiencing the kind of apprehension she hadn't known since the war years, when she and other ambulance drivers knew there was another big push coming.

She was on her way to Tommy's house in her sports car, Boots beside her. They'd left Cassie and Freddy behind, although Freddy had wanted to come. He still owed those geezers, he said. But Boots said no, he had his wedding to think of. And Cassie had put her foot down, in any case. You're not going down any coal-hole, she said, or you'll arrive at the church looking like a chimney sweep, and I'm not making my vows to a chimney sweep. Freddy asked what it was that was holding him back. Me, I'm holding you back, by your trousers, said Cassie, to make sure they stay here, with you inside them.

Mr Finch and Rosie were close to the phone, the phone Boots had used to call up the local police station and to speak his piece. Since then, Scotland Yard had been alerted by the station, two night-duty constables ordered to stand by, and two CID officers contacted in their homes. From the Yard, Inspector Carson was rushing to Denmark Hill. The call had come at a moment when Bill Chambers, looking through a file of photographs, had picked out a man whom he recognized as Barnes, but whose real name was Miller.

Inspector Carson had asked the local police if it was definitely known that the wanted men were in the house in question. No, it's not definite, according to the information given by Mr Adams of Red Post Hill, but it's almost certain because of the attendant circumstances. Inform your men to do nothing until I get there, said the Inspector, who had also asked for Boots to do nothing off his own bat.

Polly, travelling behind a bus on Denmark Hill, slowed down and pulled up thirty yards from Tommy's house. She switched off the engine. Street lamps illuminated the hill at intervals, the night traffic desultory. The sky was completely clear of clouds now, the half-moon brilliant. Polly touched Boots's knee with a gloved hand.

'Now what do we do, old scout?' she asked.

'We wait for the police,' said Boots.

'But I'm game to investigate if you are,' said Polly.

'Haven't you heard about fools rushing in, Polly?'

'I'd rather play the fool with you, old love, than hang back with the angels,' said Polly. 'Got a fag?'

Boots produced his packet of Players, Polly helped herself and Boots took one. He struck a match, Polly leaned close and he applied the flame to the tip of her cigarette. Boots lit his own. Polly suggested he wasn't quite himself.

'Does it show?' he asked.

'Usually when you're up to something out of the ordinary, you suck your pipe,' said Polly.

'Forgot it,' said Boots.

'Forgivable on this occasion,' murmured Polly. 'It's Tommy and his family, isn't it? I'd feel the same in your shoes. I feel the same now. In fact, old darling, I'm bloody pent-up. What a ghastly pair of lousy crooks, if they're really in Tommy's house and frightening the life out of

266

Vi and the children. The thought's killing me, and I know it must be killing you. It's been one damn thing on top of another for you lately.'

'You're damned right it has,' said Boots, but he wasn't thinking of Major Armitage, he was thinking that not so long ago his stepfather, Edwin Finch, had been held hostage by a couple of pro-Hitler Germans. He and his brothers had pulled Mr Finch out of that situation, without any blood being spilt and without any publicity. It wasn't going to be so easy to deal with armed bank robbers. Back home, he'd left Emily, Tim, Eloise and Chinese Lady ignorant of present events, having told them he had to go out on behalf of Freddy and Cassie. Emily asked if Polly was still with Rosie. Not now, he'd said. Polly at that particular moment had been waiting for him in her car. Chinese Lady asked him what her husband was doing. Talking to Rosie, he said.

He thought now of Alice, David and Paul, Vi's cherished trio. He'd have given much to know exactly what was happening to them at this moment, while hoping it was nothing that would scar their young minds. Tommy had been cryptic on the phone, but not desperate, which might have indicated that he and his family were helpless but in no real danger. Real danger, however, might rear its ugly head if the police made a mess of things. Boots had in mind a pistol being pointed at Vi's head, and a threat of murder being issued unless the police allowed free exit for the two thugs.

'It's a swine, Boots, sitting and waiting,' said Polly.

'It's not what I like doing,' said Boots.

'I know,' said Polly. 'I don't want to sound flippant, but how about a little loving, would that help? There's

267

no-one about, and even if there were, well, you know me. I'd be the last one to scream for help if your redhot passion made you force yourself on me.'

'I'd be tempted if—'

'If you weren't such a family man,' said Polly, blowing smoke. 'I've a colleague at school who's convinced that acceptance of the family as a basis for an orderly society is rhubarb and rubbish. Families suffocate society, she says. She's one of a large family herself, and assures me that at every reunion it's a wonder murder doesn't take place.'

'I daresay there are times when most family relationships amount to hard going,' said Boots, 'but murder's not my idea of a solution. Too messy, and you can't undo it.' He regarded the lights and shadows of the hill.

'Well, dearly beloved, I've wanted to murder you more than once,' said Polly, 'but if I did and I couldn't undo it, I'd shoot myself. Oh, hell, what's the point, anyway, of trying to get you to seduce me here and now? You're totally with Tommy and his family, aren't you? Come to that, old sport, so am I, and I'm gassing on about nothing very much to hide my screaming nerves. Hello, who's that?'

A couple, walking up the hill, emerged from shadow into lamplight. Arm in arm, they strolled past Tommy's house, came up with the parked car and gave its occupants an intrigued glance.

'Waiting for Christmas?' said the young man.

'No, we've had Christmas,' said Boots.

'It's Easter we're after now,' said Polly.

'Easter's nice for weddings,' said the young lady, and the couple went on.

Polly's hand touched Boots's thigh and gently pressed.

'I'd like a wedding, old love, if you'd like a divorce,' she said.

'Can you make do with a chocolate Easter egg?' said Boots.

'Yes, if you'll bring it in person at bedtime,' said Polly. 'Don't knock. Come in through the back door.'

A police car, travelling down the hill, pulled up behind them. A plainclothes man alighted and came up. He spoke quietly to Boots.

'You Mr Adams, sir, of Red Post Hill?'

'Yes,' said Boots.

'I'm Detective-Sergeant Halliday, sir. There's a colleague of mine somewhere around, watching the house, and I've got two uniformed men in the car. We're to wait, along with you, for Inspector Carson of the Yard. Who's the lady, sir?'

'A friend of mine,' said Boots.

'I don't think Inspector Carson will go for having a lady around, Mr Adams.'

'I'm not that kind of a lady,' said Polly. 'I'm made of stern and grim stuff.'

'Miss Simms will play her part,' said Boots. 'You know the house?'

'Yes, "The Manor", sir,' said the CID man. 'Just down there.'

'We haven't seen your colleague,' said Boots.

'Well, that's good, he's got orders not to be seen. Not much traffic about, or people, that's good too. We don't want the operation turned into a circus. Hello, I think this could be the Yard car.'

A car, headlamps off, side lights on, was travelling at speed up the hill. With nothing coming the other way, it crossed the road, the driver switching off the engine to coast a few yards in neutral until the car stopped with its bonnet six feet from Polly's spirited roadster. Two men got out, one tall and burly, the other as lean as a whippet. They closed the car doors with the merest click of sound.

'Chief Inspector Carson?' said Detective-Sergeant Halliday.

'Yes, and this is Detective-Constable Fellowes. You're—?'

'Detective-Sergeant Halliday, sir.'

The Inspector conducted a quiet conversation with him, which helped to formulate an accurate picture of the circumstances and the situation. Boots was introduced as the man who had laid certain information with the police station, and who would show the Inspector how to get into the house. The Inspector said he understood it was by way of the coal cellar.

'It's the only way without breaking doors,' said Boots.

'Well, I'm damned if I could squeeze myself down through the hole,' said the Inspector, 'but Detective-Constable Fellowes can, and so, I hope, can your men, Sergeant.'

'They're stripped, sir, to their shirts and trousers.'

'Who's the woman?' asked the Inspector abruptly.

'The owner of this car,' said Boots, 'and she'll use it to get back to my home at speed.'

'H'm,' said the Inspector.

'I'm a hundred per cent reliable,' said Polly, showing no evidence of strung nerves.

'It might've been advisable for you to have taken on that responsibility, Mr Adams,' said the Inspector.

'It might, yes,' said Boots, 'except it's my brother's house and I intend to be around when your men go in.'

'I see,' said the Inspector. 'Very well. The place is under surveillance, Sergeant?'

'It is,' said Sergeant Halliday.

'And there's been no movement, as far as you know, no signs that the wanted men are there?'

'None, sir. We've had no signals from our man.'

'I hope we're not going to make fools of ourselves,' said the Inspector. 'Mr Adams, what exactly did your brother say over the phone?'

'That I wasn't to come over, that he'd got visitors,' said Boots.

'And you weren't due to go over, anyway?'

'No,' said Boots. 'That, and the fact that the van's parked at the back of the house, according to the young lad I mentioned, made up my mind for me.'

'Well, it's made up my mind too,' said the Inspector. 'Right, let's start moving. Sergeant, get your men out.'

A few moments later, the two constables were out of the local police car, and two others had emerged from the back of the Yard car. The responsibility of the latter men was to divert the attention or curiosity of any passers-by. There was a lack of people out-of-doors at this time of night, but always a possibility that some would appear.

'Ready, sir,' said Detective-Sergeant Halliday, his uniformed men in shirts and trousers, helmets off.

'Mr Adams, would you care to lead the way?' asked the Inspector, bowler-hatted.

A gloved hand touched Boots's arm as he moved out of the passenger seat of Polly's car. A whisper followed.

'Take care, darling.'

'Don't you think it was a bit ungrateful, Scotland Yard leaving us to come home on a bus?' said Lilian, as she and Bill arrived at the door of her house.

'It looked like there was a sudden emergency,' said Bill. 'Well, you're back safe and sound, anyway, so I'll push off.'

'My life,' said Lilian, 'are you going to be ungrateful too?'

'In what way, might I ask, Mrs Hyams?'

'By pushing off and leaving me alone,' said Lilian, opening her front door.

'Well, as it's late and you've got your reputation to think about—'

'I didn't know I had a reputation,' said Lilian, 'but if I have, it can look after itself. Well, don't just stand there, come on in and I'll make us a pot of tea.'

'Mrs Hyams, that's handsome of you,' said Bill, and stepped in.

Lilian smiled and closed the door. Tomorrow, she thought, I'm going to have to tell Tommy I invited the milkman in late at night. I'm getting ideas about the man. Can I help it if I want to see him with his shirt off? It's the first time I've had a weakness about a milk roundsman's chest. I'm going daft. But I admire a weakness like that. It shows I'm still a woman. Not that I expect to get his shirt off tonight. In due course, say, and without letting Rabbi Solomon know.

'How long before Polly gets back, I wonder?' said Rosie to Mr Finch. They were in his study, the hall phone not far away, and Cassie and Freddy were

272

outside the house, at the gate, waiting. 'Not too long, I hope.'

'I think the police will be very deliberate in their actions,' said Mr Finch.

'You mean it'll be some time before we're required to make the phone call,' said Rosie. 'Freddy and Cassie won't go until the whole thing is over, and Eloise will be looking in any moment to demand to know what's going on, I shouldn't wonder.'

'And Emily's curiosity will also get the better of her,' said Mr Finch.

'Well, Grandpa, if either of them come asking questions,' said Rosie, 'I'll leave you to answer them. You're like Daddy, you're so good at giving disarming answers. I'm much more like George Washington myself.'

'I think you can hold your own when awkward questions are flying about,' smiled Mr Finch. 'I think Major Armitage found he'd met his match.'

'That gentleman isn't relevant at the moment,' said Rosie. 'We're only concerned with Uncle Tommy and his family, and frankly, Grandpa, I'm frightened to death. Only the Lord knows how I'm managing to sit here waiting, especially as we both know that neither of us can trust Daddy to keep his head out of the way. But first and foremost, I'm praying for Uncle Tommy, Aunt Vi and their children. Is there a hope that we've drawn the wrong conclusions, that those wanted men aren't really there?'

'It's a hope, a wish and a prayer, Rosie,' said Mr Finch, and Rosie reflected on his apparent calmness. There was always more to him than met the eye, she thought. He and Boots were very close friends, and much alike in the way they disarmed the curious.

Boots never showed alarm or panic in any crisis, he just gave his mind in very controlled fashion to the problem and its solution. It was no wonder that in any family crisis, his brothers Tommy and Sammy accepted his leadership. She knew why he hadn't contacted Sammy and Aunt Susie about this really alarming crisis. Aunt Susie was expecting her fourth child next month. Boots was the last man who'd land her with a shock at this stage of her condition.

Rosie thought it wasn't unusual for Polly to be in on this emergency. Somehow, she always seemed to be around whenever there was any kind of family trouble. It would have to be Polly, of course, who was with Boots now. When she returned, then at last the phone call could be made.

'Grandpa, what work do you actually perform for the Government?'

Mr Finch mused on the question.

'I suppose you could say I'm a civil servant,' he said.

'You might suppose that,' said Rosie, 'I don't.'

'Well, you're a very intelligent young lady,' said Mr Finch.

'That's no answer,' said Rosie. 'Grandpa, you're deep.'

'Am I, Rosie? What makes you say that?'

'My intelligence,' said Rosie. 'Listen, I think someone should go out and talk to Cassie and Freddy. Having to put up with this unwelcome business when their wedding's taking place on Saturday can't be doing them much good. Will you stay here while I do that? As soon as Polly comes in sight, I'll fly back to you.'

'Very well, Rosie,' said Mr Finch.

Cassie and Freddy, waiting on tenterhooks, were happy to have Rosie join them at the gate.

At this moment, Lilian and Bill were sitting together on her small settee listening to the wireless and waiting for the next news broadcast. Bill was chatting in his usual way, and it occurred to Lilian that he had the virtue of not being a boring man. He hadn't mentioned new-laid eggs once. He kept that for his rounds. My life, thought Lilian, I'm bothered if I'm not beginning to like him quite a bit.

And I don't feel at all daft about it.

I think I'll give him an order for six eggs tomorrow.

Now, come on, wireless news, let's hear if Bill has helped Scotland Yard to lay their lawful hands on the villains of the piece.

Apparently not, according to the measured tones of the newscaster.

'Hard luck,' said Lilian.

'Give 'em time,' said Bill. 'By the way, you ought to come round to my place one day and look at the piano. See if it'll fit against your wall there.'

Lilian laughed.


Chinese Lady, Emily and Eloise were now in a decidedly fidgety and curious state about what was going on. Tim said not to worry, his dad was sorting it all out on behalf of Cassie and Freddy. He added, irrelevantly, that he'd just remembered he'd promised to take Nick's sister Fanny to the pictures one day.

'If you made a promise, you ought to keep it,' said Emily.

'She's got a nice little nose,' said Tim.

'You funny boy,' said Eloise.

# Chapter Seventeen

The approach to 'The Manor' was made silently, and without any resident or pedestrian in sight. Boots walked at the front of the little file of men, Inspector Carson immediately behind him. One of the constables was carrying a length of coiled rope. Boots had a torch and so did Detective-Sergeant Halliday. The high front hedge of the house was on their left as the men advanced to the open gate. An additional man materialized and joined them, the man who had had the place under surveillance.

From her car, Polly watched, gloved hands a little clenched, mouth set. Bank robbers armed with a gun, exactly what kind of men were they? Thugs to begin with. Freddy could have suffered a fractured skull. With his perky gift for repartee, he and that imaginative girl Cassie were an engaging young couple, cockneys both, and making no bones about it. Freddy, who worked in Sammy's brewery, ought to have the kind of job that would enable him to keep Cassie in style when they were married. Cassie had the kind of looks and character that entitled her to some of the good things of life. Well, thought Polly, I've known every Adams family member long enough to ask Sammy to give Freddy a job with genuine prospects. A brewery, for God's sake, what sort of future did that hold for him? The keeper of the vats? Not good enough, Sammy. I'm going to do some work on you.

Ye gods, she thought, what am I now, some kind of floating fairy godmother?

Except for the two men responsible for ensuring members of the public were kept away, the slow-moving line of policemen, turning into the drive of Tommy's house, disappeared from her vision, and she began to hold her breath. She jumped as a man on a bike cycled past the cars, going downhill at a lick.

Boots stopped when he reached Tommy's car in the drive. Here and there the house showed lights behind drawn curtains. Inspector Carson moved noiselessly on to pass the side of the house and to vanish. Boots and the rest of the men waited. Back came the Inspector. He nodded, an indication that he had seen the parked van. Boots crossed the forecourt to the other side of the house, and everyone else followed like flitting ghosts on rubber-soled footwear. In the lee of the house, Boots switched on his torch, and the beam picked out the iron lid of the coal cellar. The men formed a circle around it. Boots illuminated coal dust around the lid.

'Recent delivery,' he whispered.

'There's a heap of coal down there?' breathed Detective-Sergeant Halliday.

'Someone could break a leg,' said Boots.

'Lift the lid,' whispered the Inspector.

One man took a grip of the handle, flush with the lid, and cautiously heaved. Up came the lid to reveal a gaping black hole. Carefully and gently, the lid was set down at a distance. Boots pointed his torch and its beam shone downwards into the cellar. Blue-black chunks of coal glinted. The man as lean as a whippet took off his hat and jacket and laid them down. The rope was handed to him and he tied it around his waist. From the house there was no sound, and if it had not been for the lights at some windows, one could have said it was sleeping.

The roped man sat on the rim of the gaping hole and let his feet and legs drop in. Colleagues took hold of the rope and steadied themselves. The detective-constable from the Yard slid in, the rope taut, his hands gripping it. He was lowered slowly and cautiously into the cellar. His feet touched the top of a large stack of coal. The summit collapsed beneath his feet, but the taut rope held him. The beam of the torch shone into the cellar. There were little sharp sounds as pieces of coal fell away.

'Steady, man,' hissed the Inspector.

The rope held firm, and was slowly played out as Fellowes manoeuvred himself downwards over the small mountain of fuel. His feet found the dusty floor of the cellar. He unwound the rope, gave it a tug, and it was drawn upwards. He lifted one hand high, and Detective-Sergeant Halliday, on his knees, used the light of Boots's torch to reach down through the hole, his own torch in his hand. Fellowes took it from him, switched it on and looked around. He saw stone steps leading upwards to a door. He knew what he was to do. He went up the steps and very cautiously indeed he tried the handle of the door. It was not locked. He came down the steps, pointed his beam at the round open circle above him, and switched it on and off twice.

'Door's not locked, Inspector,' whispered Sergeant Halliday.

'Right, get your two constables down there,' whispered the Inspector.

One after the other, the two local constables were lowered. The time taken because of the necessity to ensure silence had its effect on everyone's nerves, and there was one moment of excessive tension when a large lump of coal dislodged itself and fell noisily to the floor.

'I'll break somebody's leg myself,' hissed the Inspector.

From below the torch flashed three times, which meant all three men were in position.

'They know where they'll be when they open the door, do they?' whispered Boots. 'The kitchen will be on their left, a passage leading to the hall on their right.'

'They know, Mr Adams,' said Sergeant Halliday. 'Our men were briefed following your phone call.'

'Perhaps I'd better get down there myself,' said Boots.

'No, you won't, Mr Adams,' breathed Inspector Carson. 'This is as far as your help goes. From now on it's exclusively a police matter.' He whispered orders to the remaining men and as they moved into position, Boots made his way back to the gate. From there he signalled to Polly with his torch. Polly, who had had her engine idling over for a few minutes, swung out from between the two police cars, did a swift U-turn and went racing along to Red Post Hill.

In the cellar the three men were on the stone steps, the leading man up against the door.

In the house, Miller said, 'Time to tie them up, Ginger.'

'You're in a hurry now?' said Carstairs.

'No, I'm thinking of what they might be getting up to,' said Miller.

'That's the trouble with some professionals, they're always looking over their shoulders,' said Carstairs.

'The point is I don't trust the husband,' said Miller. 'He's got too much to say, and I can't see him sitting up there doing nothing. There's that skylight. I wouldn't put it past him to get it open and to start chucking some of that junk out to attract attention.'

'Reasonable, I suppose,' said Carstairs. 'At the moment, we hold the aces. No-one knows we're here. Let's keep it that way. So all right, we'll truss the chickens, and when we've done that you can get the clothes and suitcases from the van and we'll change. And instead of waiting until midnight, we'll leave in thirty minutes, say. Further, instead of heading away from London, we'll drive to a mews in Knightsbridge in this family's car, and tuck ourselves away with it, then head out of town in the morning by train. I've a feeling that that move will fox every copper in Scotland Yard.'

'And there won't be much chance of the chickens being able to squawk until someone gets into the house and starts looking for them,' said Miller. 'That could be a hell of a while.'

'It bothers you?' said Carstairs.

'Not me,' said Miller, 'I hate jumped-up middle class cockneys.'

'I suppose you would, as the son of a Kent coalminer,' said Carstairs. 'Me, I hate everybody. Well, come on, let's go up and start trussing.'

They began to climb the stairs.

Rosie was still at the gate with Cassie and Freddy when she saw the approaching lights of a speeding car. Freddy drew a breath.

'That's her, bet a quid,' he said.

'Hope so,' said Cassie, 'my nerves are all wearin' out.'

Polly careered, braked, made a fast turn into the drive, and let herself be heard when she saw Rosie.

'Make the call, Rosie!'

Rosie flew back into the house, Polly backed the car out into the road, slewed round and was away again, heading back to Denmark Hill.

'Ruddy holy Joe,' breathed Freddy, 'was that a flash of lightning?'

'No, just that lady, Polly Simms, movin' a bit fast,' said Cassie. 'Oh, lor', my nerves really are bad, Freddy.'

'Hold my hand, Cassie, mine are up the spout too,' said Freddy.

Inside the house, Mr Finch, with Rosie beside him, and Eloise looking on in a puzzled frame of mind, dialled Tommy's phone number.

On the stone steps of the coal cellar, the torch switched on, the three policemen waited, tensed to spring. The two local constables had their boots off and were in their socked feet.

Meanwhile, Carstairs and Miller had reached the top landing, on which lay lengths of the strong cord.

The phone rang.

'Bugger it!' hissed Miller. 'Is it that bloody nosy brother?'

'It's got to be answered,' said Carstairs. 'This time

281

get the woman. She's not as tricky as the man. Be quick.'

Miller unlocked the attic door, and Carstairs had the revolver out. In went Miller fast. The phone bell was a ringing disturbance, and the policemen at the cellar door could hear it.

'You,' Miller said to Vi, 'come and answer that phone. Now. Out, out.'

'I'll answer it,' said Tommy, but Miller pulled Vi to her feet and Carstairs had the revolver aimed at Tommy's legs.

'There's no need to drag me,' said Vi, 'I'll come down.'

Out she went, leaving Tommy and the children to the ordeal of waiting for her to be brought back. Miller closed the door and locked it again, and it was Carstairs who accompanied Vi down to the hall, hustling her. Vi disliked this silent fiend even more than the loud-mouthed character.

Mr Finch was letting the phone ring.

'Someone's got to answer,' said Rosie.

'What is 'appening, please?' asked Eloise. 'And where is Papa?'

'Oh, it's one of those evenings,' said Rosie.

Emily came into the hall and demanded to know what was going on. Rosie said it was a private matter concerning Cassie and Freddy. Boots had left strict instructions for nothing to be said that would alarm the rest of the family.

At Tommy's house, the policemen in the cellar were at their most tense, straining their ears. When the phone stopped ringing, that would be the signal to make their rush. They knew it would continue to ring until it was answered. The man at the door opened it a fraction, and the ringing came more clearly to the ear then.

Outside, Boots was at the front door, and he too could hear the phone, if faintly.

Vi reached the hall. Impatiently, Carstairs gave her a push.

'There's no need for that,' said Vi, and picked up the phone, Carstairs close beside her, ugly of countenance and expression. 'Hello?'

'Hello, Vi, Rosie's grandpa here,' said Mr Finch, 'what kept you?'

'Oh, I was upstairs with the children,' said Vi, throat dryer than ever, nerves screamingly taut. 'Is that—' She stopped as three men effected a rushing interruption. Carstairs whirled about. The leading man, seeing a revolver with a silencer attached, simply hurled himself at the bowler-hatted, grey-suited figure wearing horn-rimmed spectacles. Carstairs met the full force of a hard impactive body, and crashed to the floor beneath the man. The second man leapt, and a socked foot slammed down hard on the hand that held the revolver. Carstairs kicked and swore and struggled. The bowler hat fell off, and with it a black wig. A wealth of fiery auburn hair leapt to Vi's eye. The third man was there, bending low to wrench the revolver from the pinned hand. He stared as a colleague, clued up by the fallen wig, peeled off the swearing prisoner's moustache.

'Christ, it's a woman,' he breathed.

'There's a man upstairs,' gasped Vi.

Miller, alerted by the noise, was already on his way down, taking the stairs two at a time.

'Sod you all!' yelled the raging Ginger Carstairs, daughter of a dissolute artist, and the sound of her

283

voice precipitated Miller fast into a bedroom on the first floor. Up went the two local constables, while the CID man, astride the raging auburn-haired woman, turned her onto her face and reached for his handcuffs.

'Vi? Vi?' said Mr Finch over the phone. 'Vi, are you there?'

'Oh, wait a bit, wait a bit,' gasped Vi.

Miller had the bedroom window open when the two constables rushed in. The room was dark, but they saw him framed by the open window. They rushed. Miller hissed an imprecation and charged at them. Together, they made bruising contact with him, and all three men hit the floor.

At the house in Red Post Hill, Emily, her blood up, said, 'I'm not standin' for this, Dad. Why're you on the phone to Vi if it's a private matter just concerning Cassie and Freddy? And where's Boots?'

'Yes, where is Papa? I want to know,' said Eloise, given at this stage of her life to nuances of speech that implied she had the largest share in the ownership of Boots.

Mr Finch, the phone at his ear, lifted a hand to ask for quiet. Vi spoke again then, a tremor in her voice.

'We've had a bit of trouble here, Dad, but I think it's all been settled now, and I'll get Tommy to ring you back.'

'Wait, is it all settled, Vi? We know the extent of the trouble. You'll find Boots around somewhere.'

'Yes, it's all settled,' said Vi, and Mr Finch quite clearly heard her draw noisy breath. Then she said with a slightly hysterical little laugh, 'Trust Boots to always be somewhere around. Oh, I must go now, I must see to the children. Everyone's all right, though, truly.' She rang off then, and Mr Finch put the phone down.

'Well, Dad?' said Emily, whose own auburn hair was of a dark hue that had escaped ever having been called ginger.

'Yes, I think I can explain now,' said Mr Finch.

'The siege was successful, Grandpa?' said Rosie.

'So I gathered from Vi,' said Mr Finch.

'If someone doesn't tell me exactly what's been goin' on,' said Emily, 'there'll be ructions that'll take the roof off this house, d'you 'ear me, Dad?'

Chinese Lady appeared then, with Tim, and there was a general examination of those in the know, Rosie and Mr Finch, by those who'd been kept in the dark. Chinese Lady, Emily, Eloise and Tim all asked questions, and mostly at the same time, thereby creating confusion, which Mr Finch dealt with by taking them into the living-room and asking if he might start at the beginning.

The phone rang then, and Rosie answered it. Boots was on the line from Tommy's house. He advised Rosie that everything really was all right, the wanted persons had been arrested, one of whom had turned out to be a woman who'd disguised herself as a male bloke with a moustache and a City look. Rosie said what a terrible blow to her sex. Boots said her sex were generally indispensable as far as he was concerned, and that Rosie could now put the others in the picture regarding all that had happened.

'Grandpa's already doing that,' said Rosie.

'Well, you can add your piece of comfort to his,' said Boots, 'it'll help soothe any injured feelings. Otherwise I might have to stay out all night.'

'Oh, between us, Grandpa and I will save you from death by rolling-pins,' said Rosie, 'but tell me, are Uncle Tommy, Aunt Vi and the children suffering at all? I mean, it must have been utterly traumatic for them.'

'I don't doubt it,' said Boots. 'They're shaken, Rosie, but recovering fast. I'll tell you more when I get home.'

'Bless you, Daddy old soldier,' said Rosie, 'you always come up trumps, don't you?'

'So do you,' said Boots.

'Love you,' said Rosie, and rang off.

She let the others know that Boots had confirmed that the ordeal for Tommy and his family was over, then went out to talk to Cassie and Freddy. They were still at the gate, and having a cuddle to ease the strain of waiting. Neither of them wanted to go until they knew how things had turned out. Rosie told them the crisis was over. Aunt Vi had said so, and Boots had just confirmed it.

'D'you mean the police 'ave copped the pair?' asked Freddy.

'Yes,' said Rosie. 'I think the phone call worked wonders as a distraction, as Daddy hoped it would.'

'Oh, me shakin' legs,' said Cassie.

'Don't worry, I'll see to 'em,' said Freddy. 'Well,' he went on in cheerful relief, 'I've always been admirin' of your dad, Rosie. He was born, y'know, to sort out trouble and knock it on the head.'

'D'you think so, Freddy?' smiled Rosie.

'All the way,' said Freddy. 'When I'm married, which I will be on Saturday to Cassie, if her shakes have improved, I might have some trouble of me own occasionally.'

'Yes, and you will if you come home one day with your head knocked off for bein' a hero again,' said Cassie.

'That's when I'll need your dad, Rosie,' said Freddy. 'Now I think we'd better get back, Cassie. We can stop at Tommy's house on the way just to see for ourselves that everything's all right.'

'Oh, by the way,' said Rosie, 'one of the bandits was a woman.'

'Beg pardon?' said Freddy.

'A woman,' said Rosie.

'I don't believe it!' said Cassie.

'Yes, what a rotten blow to our sex, Cassie,' said Rosie, 'we're all supposed to be sweetness and light compared to men.'

'Well, I am, compared to anybody,' said Cassie. 'Freddy, didn't you know one was a woman?'

'No I didn't,' said Freddy, 'I only know they both wore bowlers and suits, and both 'ad moustaches.'

'False, I expect,' said Rosie.

'Well, I don't know,' said Freddy, 'what's the world comin' to with a woman puttin' on a false moustache and robbin' a bank?'

'Was she the one who knocked you out?' asked Rosie.

'I hope not,' said Freddy, 'it's against me self-respect to be knocked out by a female.'

'Never mind, Freddy love, I expect your lump's gone down quite a bit by now,' said Cassie.

They said goodbye to Rosie then, and Rosie said she'd see them on Saturday, at the double wedding, and for a knees-up later in St John's Institute.

'And thank goodness you called in and told Daddy about that van,' she said.

'Oh, Freddy does show a bit of sense sometimes, Rosie,' said Cassie, 'and we've all got to be grateful for that.'

Rosie laughed, and away went Cassie and Freddy then, on their bikes. They stopped at Tommy's house and there they found Boots and Polly talking with the whole family. Alice, David and Paul were still up and still a little shaken, but visibly happy that the nightmare was all over. Vi was glowing with relief, and greeted Cassie and Freddy with hugs and kisses. Boots had recounted their part in the events, and Tommy shook Freddy's hand vigorously and gave Cassie a grateful smacker.

Miller, overpowered after a titanic struggle, had been taken away by the police along with his partner, Dorothy Amelia Carstairs, who'd been known as Ginger all her life, and had come to a point where she hated the penniless aspect of her life with her feckless parents. With the help of Miller, a known criminal, she had planned the bank robbery, even though she despised him. But she despised the whole human race, and would have been much happier if she'd been born a tigress.

Inspector Carson had thanked Boots and Polly for their help before departing with the rest of the police and their prisoners. He had also asked Boots to thank the young man, Mr Brown, for having discovered the whereabouts of the van.

Cassie and Freddy left to cycle home at last.

Boots asked Tommy and Vi if they'd suspected one of the crooks was a woman, and Vi said well, she had begun to have suspicions after an hour or so. There was something odd about that one's movements, and the look of her waistcoat, and about the fact that she wore very small shoes for a man. Also, she never said anything, the man did all the talking. Yes, there was something funny about her. Nothing funny at all about a female like that, said Tommy. Vi said she meant funny peculiar, and that if nobody minded, what she'd like as soon as she'd got the children to bed was a pot of hot tea. Would Polly and Boots like to share it with her and Tommy?

'Thanks, but not for me, Vi,' said Boots, 'it's time I went back home.'

'Time that I did too, old things,' said Polly, 'time for you and your family to have your home to yourselves again. Shall I drop you off, Boots?'

'I'd appreciate that,' said Boots.

'Thanks ever so much, and you too, Polly,' said Vi.

'Spoken with feelin' for both of us,' said Tommy. 'Pop in anytime you like, Polly, we keep open house for all our best friends.'

'Polly, you're a lovely person,' said Vi.

Polly, quite touched, said, 'I'll tell some of my pupils that, those who think I'm a dragon.'

'Goodnight,' said Boots, and left with Polly.

'Well, old sport?' she said on the drive back to his home.

'I'm thinking what a help it was, Tommy and Vi and their family keeping their heads, and Cassie and Freddy calling in,' said Boots.

'I imagine Vi died a thousand deaths,' said Polly, unusually sober. The night was very fresh now, her coat collar turned up. 'I hope she doesn't suffer delayed shock tomorrow. By the way, I thought I helped a little myself.'

'I haven't forgotten that, Polly,' said Boots.

'Bless the man, he's remembered to give me a mention,' murmured Polly, coasting down Red Post Hill, headlamps on.

'Not only for tonight, but for other occasions,' said Boots.

'My word,' said Polly, coming to a stop outside his house, 'you've known a crisis or two in your time, haven't you?'

'One or two,' said Boots.

'I suppose you realize I like sharing them with you?'

'We're old friends now, Polly,' said Boots.

'Don't I know it,' said Polly. 'D'you think it's worth a celebration?'

'What kind of celebration?' asked Boots.

'Need you ask?' said Polly. 'Let's drive into town and stay at the Savoy for the night. We could start with champagne and then do what comes naturally. Well, for God's sake, we don't want our friendship to grow so old that we'll need a book of instructions on how to do what comes naturally, do we?'

'If we do,' said Boots, 'get one with illustrations.'

'I'll order it for my eightieth birthday,' said Polly. 'Do you still make love to Emily?'

'Ask me another,' said Boots.

Polly smiled wryly.

'The next time I get any change out of you will be the first,' she said, and Boots got out of the car.

'Goodnight, Polly, and many thanks,' he said.

'Ye gods,' said Polly, 'after an evening like this, and all my palpitations, don't I even get a kiss, you stinker?'

'You deserve one from all of us,' said Boots.

'I don't want one from all of you, I want one from

you,' said Polly, face turned up. Boots bent his head and kissed her. Much to her pleasure, it wasn't a peck. It was a full-blooded kiss. 'Thanks,' she said when it was over. With another wry smile, she said, 'Do you sometimes wish I'd disappear?'

'Never,' said Boots.

'How sweet,' she said a little mockingly, 'because I don't intend to.' She slipped into gear and drove away.

Emily was in the hall when Boots entered the house.

'That woman,' she said.

'Polly?' said Boots.

'Well, who else?' said Emily, green eyes snapping. 'I'm goin' to tell her one day to stop tryin' to make you her prize possession. And what d'you mean by running about all over the place with her and leavin' me and Chinese Lady in the dark? We're not children, I'll 'ave you know, you should've told us what a dreadful time Tommy and his fam'ly were havin'. Are they really all right? Lord, imagine it, those two disgustin' people keepin' them prisoners in their own house. It must've been a nightmare for Vi, thinkin' what might 'appen to Alice, David and young Paul.'

'It was a nightmare for all of them, Em, but Vi and the children stood up to it like the King's troopers, according to Tommy,' said Boots.

Eloise appeared then. She ran at Boots and hugged him.

'Papa, 'ow good, you're back at last,' she said.

'Not without gettin' an earful,' said Emily.

'Earful?' said Eloise.

'Yes, and he's goin' to get another one from his mother,' said Emily.

Which Boots did. Well, Chinese Lady wouldn't have been herself if she hadn't delivered a few matriarchal admonishments into his hearing apparatus. Eloise noted, however, that he took them all without looking in the least discomfited. He was very distinctive in his way, her English father, even if he wasn't a nobleman like Rosie's father.

Their long evening lengthened more for Cassie and Freddy by reason of having to acquaint the Browns with the sequence of events, and then Cassie's dad. Mr Brown, Mrs Brown and Sally could hardly take it all in, and Mrs Brown said that if she'd known what was going on she'd have had a chronic fit in her own kitchen, and her husband would have had to tidy her up. She didn't like to think, she said, that something quite wicked had been happening with the weddings only a few days away. She hoped Freddy and Cassie wouldn't get their names in the paper, because if they did the whole of Walworth would turn up at the wedding, and young children could get trampled.

'Yes, that's just what could come from Freddy being a hero,' said Cassie, 'but I'll make sure it doesn't happen again, Mrs Brown. Now I'd better get home to me dad. Thanks ever so much for the loan of your bike, Sally. Freddy and me both hope you have a lovely weddin', same as ours.'

'Bless you, Cassie,' said Sally.

'Oh, a pleasure, I'm sure,' said Cassie.

'I'll take you home,' said Freddy.

'Oh, thanks, Freddy beloved,' said Cassie, 'sometimes you're really nice.'

'Well, I'd like to tell your dad all the news meself,'

said Freddy, 'he might get a story like Ali Baba and the Forty Thieves from you.'

In bed eventually, Vi whispered, 'Give me a cuddle, Tommy.'

'Give you six and a bit more, Vi,' said Tommy, and took her into his arms. He had a feeling his Vi was going to have a good cry at last, but she didn't.

'Oh, I feel safe now,' she breathed, her warm body pushing close.

'Girl in a million, you are, Vi,' said Tommy. 'I'm not unadmirin' of Em'ly and Susie, or of me sister Lizzy, but you're the best, and I'm that proud of you I could decorate you.'

'What, hang medals on my jumper?' said Vi.

'Sev'ral,' said Tommy.

'Oh, I don't want any medals,' said Vi, 'I don't need any, I've got you and the children.' She thought for a moment, back to the nightmare when she'd been praying for Tommy and the children and had realized how much she cherished her everyday life with them. 'Still, there is something I'd like.'

'Name it,' said Tommy, 'and you can have it twice over.'

'Tommy, I don't want to be greedy, once will be enough,' murmured Vi.

'What once?' asked Tommy.

'Just you and me,' said Vi.

'Vi, you sure, after all you've been through?' said Tommy.

'Well, I'm wide awake,' said Vi, 'and we ought to do something nice to pass the time.'

'That's my girl,' said Tommy.

Vi sounded just like her old self a few minutes later

when she said, 'Oh, my nightie, where's it gone?'

'D'you mind if we don't look for it right now?' said Tommy, and Vi, of course, didn't mind at all.

In bed with Boots, Emily said, 'I'm goin' to stick pins in that woman.'

'What woman?' asked Boots.

'As if you didn't know,' said Emily.

'Polly, you mean?'

'Of course I mean her,' said Emily.

'Seems a pity to do that to a family friend,' said Boots.

'Fam'ly friend?' said Emily. 'Don't make me laugh. I could divorce you just from the way you let her look at you.'

'What way is that, Em?' asked Boots, switching off the bedside light.

'I never saw any woman eat a man more with her eyes like she does you,' said Emily. 'It's disgustin'.'

'Chinese Lady would probably say it's unlegal as well, Em.'

'She'd be right,' said Emily. 'If it 'adn't been such a shockin' evening for the fam'ly, I'd have told that woman not to cross our doorstep again. I can't think why Chinese Lady likes her – 'ere, what's going on? Oh, no, you don't – oh, me gawd, the sauce you've got when I'm feelin' like I want to spit.'

'Did you know you've been acquiring a couple of pumpkins these last months, Em?' said Boots.

'Oh, you common beast,' breathed Emily, 'you're not first thing decent.'

Boots laughed.

Emily cuddled up. It was one thing to want to spit, it was another to be made a fuss of, even if it wasn't first thing decent. It made her feel she was still exclusive.

In their own beds, Lizzy and Ned, and Susie and Sammy, slept in blissful ignorance of the dramatic events.

## Chapter Eighteen

Young Paul woke up crying the next morning, but Tommy and Vi performed a miracle of parental reassurance, and Alice treated him to a generous dose of sisterly affection, and even gave him sixpence out of her savings for his money-box. Since Paul, even at only four, seemed to be taking after his Uncle Sammy in his fondness for his money-box and what was in it, parental reassurance and sisterly generosity brought him out of his bed with a smile on his face.

Vi, having made a strong effort last night, with Tommy's help, to put the nightmare out of her mind, was about to begin preparing breakfast when the phone rang. She had just entered the kitchen. Tommy was already there. They looked at each other.

'Tommy, who could that be?' she asked.

'I'll go,' said Tommy.

Boots was on the line.

'Seen your morning paper, Tommy?' he said.

'Oh, Jesus, it's not all over the front page, is it?' said Tommy. 'We 'adn't thought about the papers, and I don't think anyone's picked ours off the mat yet. We've been sortin' out headaches.'

'Well, there's a hell of a lot about you and your family in our daily,' said Boots. 'The next thing you know, you'll have reporters on your doorstep, and photographers as well. Chinese Lady is against all that.'

'So am I,' said Tommy.

'Take the day off, then, all of you,' said Boots. 'It's Good Friday tomorrow, anyway, and the schools break up today, don't they? Go somewhere far away in the car, and don't come back till it's dark. The police have released all details to the Press, and you're on the wireless as well. And don't hang about, chum, get out of the house as soon as you can. Just tell the kids it's a treat for them. Freddy's got a mention too.'

'What about you?' asked Tommy.

'Unfortunately, self as well, and Polly,' said Boots. 'So I'm giving my tribe a run down to Cuckmere Haven for the day in the car. They're all running about getting ready. You start running about yourselves.'

'We 'aven't had breakfast yet,' said Tommy.

'Well, hurry it up,' said Boots.

'I think I'll take your advice, Boots.'

'Exactly how are Vi and the kids?' asked Boots.

'Nearly as good as new,' said Tommy 'See you and your lot at Cuckmere Haven, eh?'

'You're welcome, Tommy, and the weather looks fair,' said Boots. 'Edwin's off to work and taking Chinese Lady with him. She'll spend the day shopping in the West End.' Boots rang off.

'Sammy? Sammy, come down here this minute.' It was a demanding call from Susie. Sammy, who'd just finished dressing, came out of the marital bedroom. Daniel, from his own bedroom, let his treble voice be heard.

'Crikey, what you done now, Dad?'

'I'm innocent,' said Sammy. Down he went to the

kitchen. Susie, apron on, had the morning paper in her hand.

'You won't believe this,' she said, and showed him the front page story. Sammy took it in like a man whose business had grown suicidal legs and jumped off Beachy Head.

'I don't believe it,' he breathed.

'I said you wouldn't, but it's there, Sammy, in black and white.'

'Ruddy O'Reilly,' said Sammy, 'am I dreamin'? Those two crooks, one of them a peculiar female woman, parked themselves with their lousy gun on Tommy and his fam'ly?'

'I'm glad I didn't know,' said Susie, 'I'm glad that when I did, five minutes ago, it was all over. I'm goin' round to see Vi as soon as I've got Daniel and Bess off to school. I'll take little Jimmy with me. Heavens, what Vi and Tommy must've gone through, thinking about their children. And, Sammy, look at all the names mentioned. Boots, Vi, Tommy, Polly Simms and Freddy. Freddy was actually the young man who got in the way of the thieves just as they were leavin' the bank, and the one who found where the van was. Sammy, why weren't you there?'

'At the bank?' said Sammy, reading the report a second time.

'No, with Boots and Polly Simms, helpin' to guide the police to Tommy's coal cellar.'

'I happened at the time to be dead ignorant of what was goin' on,' said Sammy.

'Well, phone Boots and ask him why he didn't let you know,' said Susie.

'Susie, you've just said you're glad you didn't know.'

298

'He could've told you,' said Susie. 'Tell him that for the first time ever I'm cross with him. Phone him now.'

Sammy rang Boots. Boots said that under no circumstances would he have let Sammy and Susie know what was going on. Sammy said he was much obliged, that he understood why, but that all the same Susie was going to dot him one in his mince pie when she next saw him. Boots said he'd take it as manfully as he could, and would like to leave it at that. He was in a hurry, he said, to get everyone out of the house before any reporters arrived, and that Tommy and his family were also going to vanish.

'Well, I can understand that,' said Sammy, 'but—'

The phone went dead. Boots had rung off. That's what I get, thought Sammy, for trying to talk to the family's Lord-I-Am when he's in a hurry. One day I'll have to make it clear to him I'm not the office boy.

Informing Susie of what Boots had said, he pointed out that it meant it was no good her going to see Vi as she'd draw a blank. Susie said she'd go tomorrow, in that case, she wanted Vi's own version of the horrible happening.

Lizzy and Ned had also seen the report in their morning paper, and had read it in utter amazement. Lizzy then immediately rang Boots, but couldn't get through. The line was engaged, or something. It was 'or something'. Boots had taken the phone off its hook in case any newspaper reporters thought of ringing him. So Lizzy then rang Tommy, although she felt he and Vi were probably still in too much of a state to want to talk to anybody. Vi answered the phone, let Lizzy know everyone was much better, thanks, but that she couldn't talk because they were

299

all going down to Cuckmere Haven to join Boots and his family there. Lizzy wanted to know what for. So we can dodge newspaper reporters, said Vi.

'Oh, yes, you've got to, Vi, or Mum will have fifty fits,' said Lizzy.

'I know,' said Vi, 'so excuse me, Lizzy.' She rang off. Not long after she and her family were away in the car. The van, of course, had been removed by the police last night.

Boots and his family were on the road too, heading south, with Eloise thinking life had never been more dramatic or exciting, Rosie thinking the atmosphere of university not quite like that of home, and Tim thinking his dad wasn't just a good cricketer.

By departing in haste, both families escaped the hordes of reporters and photographers who arrived at their respective homes before Big Ben had struck nine o'clock. The eager gentlemen of the Press failed to understand why the birds had flown, for it never occurred to them there were people who actually didn't want to be featured in newspapers. Of course, the source of this reluctance was Chinese Lady. As far as she was concerned, nearly every person whose name appeared in any lurid or sensational newspaper story suffered incurable damage to their respectability, particularly if the *News of the World* took an interest.

Wise were the birds to fly the coop, for Chinese Lady would have plucked more than a few feathers if they hadn't. She herself had left the house with Mr Finch well before nine.

In Walworth, plump and placid Mrs Brown's objections to Freddy being in the newspapers related mainly to the effect this could have on the double wedding. When she opened her front door at a little after nine, a dozen strange men were clustered on her step. She had seen her daily paper, so had Mr Brown, Sally and Freddy, and they'd all read every line of the report with breathless interest. Mrs Brown had said well, it's done now, there'll be a mob of people at the church. But a mob of strange men at her door, men who turned out to be reporters and photographers, was something else. Still, it took a lot to fluster Freddy's mother, and since the story was out, anyway, she invited the men in and made a large pot of tea while answering their questions about her younger son. Yes, she said, it was Freddy who'd been felled by one of the robbers, but had managed to help the police in a chase of the escaping pair, and been responsible later for locating the van. In answer to one question, she said yes, she had to admit that Freddy had been both heroic and clever. She modestly put it down to him taking after his dad, who'd been a soldier in the war and had medals. She wasn't brave or clever herself, she said, just a wife and mother, but didn't have any complaints about it. As the reporters were all very nice to her, she told them where Freddy worked, and then gave Cassie such a memorable mention that it sent some of the reporters to a certain florist's shop in Kennington while the rest made tracks for Sammy's Southwark brewery.

At the florist's shop, the reporters asked if a young lady name of Miss Cassie Ford could be interviewed and photographed. Cassie, with the permission of the owner of the shop, allowed herself to be photographed holding a bridal bouquet after letting it be known she was to marry Freddy on Saturday. She also allowed herself to give a very imaginative description of her beloved fiancé and his heroic endeavours. It was the kind of description that more or less invited the reporters to believe Freddy had something in common with King Arthur of Camelot. Of course, said Cassie, that was due to the way she had brought him up.

'Brought him up, Miss Ford?'

'Well, not exactly like his mum has,' said Cassie, 'more like givin' him needful advice on how to be alert, brave and chivalrous so that he'd make the kind of husband I deserve. I'm not someone ord'nary, you know.'

'Perish the thought, Miss Ford,' said a reporter. 'I'd say you were both out of the ordinary.'

'Oh, what we did last night anyone else would 'ave done,' said Cassie modestly. 'Anyone else out of ord'nary, I mean,' she added. 'Are you goin' to take photographs of Freddy as well as me?'

'There'll be reporters at the brewery doing that.'

'I don't know I want him photographed in his leather apron,' said Cassie with a slight frown. 'He won't look very heroic in that.'

'It'll probably be head and shoulders only, Miss Ford.'

'Oh, I won't mind that, Freddy's got lovely shoulders,' said Cassie, 'and I daresay the lump on his head has gone down a bit since yesterday. Well, I've got to get back to my work now.'

'Thanks for talking to us.'

'Oh, my pleasure, I'm sure,' said Cassie.

'Good luck for your wedding, Miss Ford.'

'Yes, we'll both be there, Freddy and me,' said Cassie.

As for Freddy, the brewery manager did his best

for him by announcing to clamouring reporters that young Mr Brown wasn't at work today. Unfortunately for Freddy's modesty, some of the cunning swines entered the brewery by way of its loading bay, and with the assistance of a grinning employee they cornered and surrounded Freddy.

'Mr Freddy Brown, we presume?'

'Beg pardon?' said Freddy.

'We understand that's you.'

'No, I'm Charlie Cook,' said Freddy.

'So's my Aunt Daisy,' said the grinning fellow-worker. 'It's a fair cop, Freddy, speak yer piece.'

So Freddy was interviewed and photographed, his dad coming to listen. While Cassie had let her imagination run riot during her interview, Freddy kept his answers and comments simple, but the reporters liked him, all the same. When he was asked who downed him by hitting him with the revolver, the man or the woman, Freddy said much to his regret he reckoned it was the woman, seeing the one who did it was a thin character. The other crook was too big and burly to be the female.

That over, Freddy resigned himself to being in the evening papers, and at midday on the advice of his dad, he gave up his dinner break to go to the bank again with the cheques. Recognized, he was given a welcome by the cashiers and the chief clerk, then taken to see the manager, a well-dressed upright bloke with a manly handshake and a sense of appreciation. He congratulated Freddy on being primarily responsible for the recovery of the stolen money.

'Kind of you,' said Freddy, 'and can I open me

account with you now? I've brought two cheques for fifty pounds apiece.'

'A pleasure, Mr Brown,' said the manager. 'You're depositing a hundred pounds?'

'For saving,' said Freddy.

'Then, Mr Brown,' smiled the manager, 'the bank will be delighted to add a further hundred to the deposit.'

'Pardon?' said Freddy.

'A reward in a case like this is the usual thing, Mr Brown.'

'A hundred quid?' said Freddy.

'In token of you locating the van, Mr Brown, which led to the recovery of the money.'

'Well, bless my soul,' said Freddy, 'you mean me and my fiancée, Miss Cassie Ford, will 'ave two hundred pounds in your bank to start our married life with?'

'In your name, Mr Brown.'

'In that case,' said Freddy, 'someone can hit me over the head again, and I'll 'ardly notice.'

'I hope that won't happen,' said the bank manager.

'To be honest, so do I,' said Freddy. 'At least, not until after the 'oneymoon.'

'Freddy, oh, I can't believe it,' cried Cassie in transports of delight that evening. 'Two hundred pounds! Oh, ain't you glad you always wanted to marry me?'

'Did I?' said Freddy. 'What for?'

'What d'you mean, what for? If I hadn't let you get engaged to me you wouldn't have had two cheques to take to the bank, nor have got that lump on your head that made you go lookin' for the van and the rotten beasts that did it. Freddy, two hundred pounds, oh, you love.'

'All ours, Cassie,' said Freddy, 'and I daresay the bank manager will let us spend a bit on some summer outfits for you, and leave the rest as savings. I've got a cheque book.'

Not for the first time lately, Cassie's brown eyes went all misty. With her low wage, she'd never had a lot to spend on herself, and if her dad hadn't treated her frequently she wouldn't have had much of a wardrobe.

'Oh, you're sweet really, Freddy,' she said.

'Good on yer, Freddy,' smiled the Gaffer, 'you're a bloke after me own heart, and you're doin' Cassie really proud, blowed if you ain't.'

'Yes, we'll go round to our house in a bit,' said Cassie, 'and you can do me more proud there, Freddy, by helping me finish the parlour wallpapering.'

'Who'll be up the ladder?' asked Freddy.

'Me,' said Cassie, 'in me dad's boiler suit.'

'Blow that for a lark,' said Freddy.

Reporters had also appeared in Dulwich that day. General Sir Henry Simms, having seen *The Times* and the *Daily Telegraph* first thing, had made tracks for the War Office immediately after breakfast. Lady Simms, after some quizzical exchanges with Polly about the slightly Bohemian nature of her stepdaughter's friendship with Boots, departed in haste to one of her orphanages, while Polly disappeared at speed in her sports car for her last day at West Square School before the Easter holidays began.

Thus did these other reporters find one more

bird had flown, together with her parents. They considered the flight unfriendly, for an interview with the daughter of a well-known general of the Great War wasn't something to be sneezed at. Polly wasn't having any of it, however. She knew the reporters might find it irresistible to link her too intimately with Boots, which would make Emily fume.

As it was, the reports in the evening papers covered only interviews with Mrs Brown, Freddy and Cassie. The reporters representing morning papers waited around all day outside Tommy's house and Boots's home in the hope of catching them, but when darkness fell, neither of the families had appeared. Boots and Tommy, fully aware of the attitude of Chinese Lady, kept themselves and their families well out of the way until late, by which time the reporters had given up. Chinese Lady felt enough damage had already been done by what had appeared in this morning's papers. Anything in addition to that would, in her opinion, give her the feeling that the end of her ordered world was nigh. She and Mr Finch did not go home when he had finished his office stint. They met by arrangement in Whitehall, dined in town and went to a theatre.

Mrs Lilian Hyams had seen the report in her morning paper, and she too was staggered. Tommy and his family at the mercy of crooks all last evening? Tommy, the factory manager, and as nice a bloke as one could meet? My life, I can't wait to see him and get the full story out of him.

But Tommy failed to put in an appearance, so she rang Sammy at his office. He told her why Tommy was absent. Lilian asked if the family had come through the ordeal unscathed mentally. Sammy said yes, they had, according to Boots. Lilian then informed him about the part played by her milkman, who had taken note of the van one day, and informed the police yesterday evening. She'd gone with him to Scotland Yard.

'Did you say your milkman?' said Sammy.

'He's after me,' said Lilian.

'Your milkman?'

'Yes, my milkman,' said Lilian.

'What's he after you for?' asked Sammy

'Not my gramophone records,' said Lilian.

'Is he synagogue?' asked Sammy.

'No, but he's still after me. God knows what Rabbi Solomon's going to say if he gets me.'

'Are you talkin' about your milkman treating himself to a little bit of what he fancies?' asked Sammy.

'I've got hopes,' said Lilian.

'Lilian, did you just say what I think you did?'

'Yes, but I'm not myself lately,' said Lilian, 'I've just done a quick preparatory sketch for an evening gown and it's come out looking like me being carried off in a milkman's float, with the milkman whipping the horse into a gallop.'

'Lilian, I'm suffering a bit meself today on account of what happened last night to Tommy and his fam'ly,' said Sammy, 'but I don't think I feel like you do. Go home early and lie down with an Aspro.'

'My life, be caught lying down by my milkman?' said Lilian. 'I should ask for it?'

'He's visitin' you today?' enquired Sammy.

'This evening, and I'm bolting my door,' said Lilian.

'Some milkman,' said Sammy.

'You can say that again, Sammy.'

Lilian, however, didn't bolt her door, and when she opened it, Bill was able to step in. Lilian made a pot of tea and over it they had a long chat about the events of last night, especially in relation to Tommy Adams and his family. Lilian let it be known that Tommy ran the garments factory in Shoreditch, where she worked as a designer for Adams Fashions.

'That's a good job, is it?' said Bill.

'I could afford to live in Maida Vale,' said Lilian, 'but I like it here. I like the people. And you like being a milkman, do you?'

'Well, what I earn on my round and what I get from my annuity helps me to live comfortably.'

'Well, I'll say this much, you do wear good suits,' said Lilian. 'What annuity, by the way?'

'One arranged by my favourite aunt, payable to me from the time she passed on, poor old lady,' said Bill.

'My life, that's different,' said Lilian.

'What's different?' asked Bill.

'Have some more tea and a slice of Madeira cake,' said Lilian.

'Madeira?' said Bill.

'Yes, I always offer it to my best friends,' said Lilian. 'Oh, and you can take your jacket and waistcoat off, if you like. The fire's making the place warm.'

That done, Lilian thought that in his shirt he looked to have a splendid chest.

At the Harrisons' home in Browning Street, Walworth, Fanny answered a knock on the front door. She found Tim on the step.

'Hello,' said Tim.

'Oh, crikey,' breathed Fanny.

'Want to come to the pictures next Wednesday?' offered Tim.

'Me?' gulped Fanny, going wobbly.

'I did promise,' said Tim.

'Oh, I'll ask Ma and Pa,' said Fanny. 'D'you want to come in and meet them?'

'Might as well now I'm here,' said Tim.

Fanny fainted with bliss. Well, almost.

## Chapter Nineteen

They were in evidence again the next morning, the reporters, and not at all tranquillized by the holy atmosphere of Good Friday. They were as extrovert a bunch as ever, pencils sharpened, notebooks at the ready, and experienced noses sniffing in search of the quarry at Tommy's house, Boots's house and the Simms's mansion in Dulwich.

But they drew another three blanks. Tommy and family were all in hiding at Sammy's house, having gone there to eat breakfast with them and to stay for the day. Boots and family were with Lizzy and Ned. And as for Polly and her father and stepmother, although they were in residence, their servants were a bar to any intrusion. Further, Sir Henry's Alsatian hound was on the prowl in the grounds, and not muzzled, either. Having seen what yesterday's evening papers had made of interviews with Freddy, Cassie and Mrs Brown, all quarry laid low again.

In Walworth, Rabbi Solomon met Lilian in Browning Street.

'Ah, good morning, Mrs Hyams, a pleasant day.'

'I hope it's just as pleasant tomorrow, there's a double wedding at St John's Church involving friends of mine,' said Lilian, done up very fetchingly in a spring coat and an Easter bonnet.

'May I ask, Mrs Hyams, if there's friendship in the

making between you and Mr Chambers?' asked the paternalistic rabbi.

'In the making?' said Lilian.

'One hears things, Mrs Hyams,' said the rabbi gravely.

'Oh, it's gone past in the making,' said Lilian blithely, 'I'm on my way to his house now, in Rockingham Street. He doesn't have to work after his morning round on Good Fridays, and so he's invited me to lunch.'

'Mrs Hyams, I sorrow to hear this.'

'Sorrowing upsets the digestion,' said Lilian. 'Well, it upset mine when I was sorrowing for my late husband Jacob. But I'm long over that now, and can look forward to the lunch. A man who can cook could be an asset to a woman, don't you think so?'

Rabbi Solomon lifted his hands in shock.

'I am hearing such words from you about Mr Chambers?' he said.

'Such an entertaining man,' said Lilian. 'I'm to look at a piano in his house, to see if I'd like to have it in mine.'

'A piano, Mrs Hyams?'

'It's surplus to his requirements,' said Lilian, 'he doesn't play himself and I do. Should I upset a friend by not considering his offer of a piano? By the way, I think his intentions are honourable.'

'Mrs Hyams,' said Rabbi Solomon in new shock, 'are we talking about marriage?'

'Well, I am,' said Lilian, 'and I've an idea Mr Chambers has something similar on his mind. Of course, there are one or two little difficulties.'

'Mrs Hyams, there are a hundred.'

'My life, are there really?' said Lilian. 'Never mind, Rabbi, with your help I'm sure we can get over them.'

'What has Mr Chambers said about them?'

'About the little difficulties?' said Lilian. 'Not a word, actually. Well, he doesn't know, you see.'

'Doesn't know what, Mrs Hyams?'

'That I'm willing to consider a proposal of marriage as well as the offer of a piano,' said Lilian.

'Mrs Hyams, I'm sad and distressed.'

'You want I should be his mistress?' said Lilian.

'God forbid,' said Rabbi Solomon.

'There, you're a good man, Rabbi,' smiled Lilian. 'Marriage is the thing, isn't it? Now I must be on my way, and perhaps come and have a talk with you later on.'

She resumed her walk, wondering what Sammy, Boots and Tommy would say if she told them she was thinking of compromising herself with her milkman unless he came right out with a proposal of marriage. Well, he was a fine-looking bloke with a dairy round and an annuity of two-pounds-two-shillings a week, and the kind of man who'd offer to make an honest woman of her. Of course, one of them would have to convert. She didn't mind which one.

Sally said she hoped the ordeal suffered by Tommy and Vi wouldn't stop them coming to the wedding. Horace said he'd understand if they didn't appear. Jim and Rebecca Cooper said they'd understand too, but Ethel said she didn't want any guests to miss seeing her as a bridesmaid. Horace said that if Tommy Adams and his wife Vi didn't turn up, he'd ask other guests to look twice at her to make up for it. Ethel said you ought to stop having funny turns, Orrice, now you're nearly married. Sally said she'd got quite fond of his funny turns, but that he wasn't to have any at the wedding. Rebecca said that she and Jim would do everything possible to ensure Horace went through the day in a sane and sound frame of mind.

'From start to finish, Mum?' said Ethel. 'Orrice? Some hopes,'

'Horace, who's goin' to the stag party?' asked Sally.

'Me,' said Horace.

'I know that, silly. Who else?'

'Freddy, Nick, Percy, Danny, Johnny Richards, a few others and Dad,' said Horace.

'Dad, you're goin'?' said Ethel.

'I must,' smiled Jim, 'someone's got to make sure that Horace and Freddy find their way home.'

*     *     *

Easter Saturday dawned with April in a frisky mood. The service at St John's was to begin at twelve-thirty, and by twelve-ten the church was packed and there were crowds outside. The local paper, the *South London Press*, had sent a reporter and photographer.

Every guest who should be there was there, including Tommy and Vi. Members of the Adams and Somers families were present in force, and so were special guests like Lilian and Polly, and also Mrs Rachel Goodman, whom Sally knew well. As a director of Adams Fashions, Rachel had kept a warm and friendly eye on Sally, an Adams shop-assistant.

At twelve-eleven precisely one bride, Cassie, was ready. She and her dad and her eldest sister Annie were now alone in the house, her bridesmaids having departed for the church. Down the stairs she came, floating in her wedding finery, Annie following.

'Dad? Dad? You ready?'

The Gaffer, all done up in a new dark grey suit and grey tie, came out of the kitchen. He looked up at his descending youngest daughter. Her gown was pure white silk, designed by Lilian and paid for happily by the Gaffer, her shoes silvery, her veil up over a little circlet of artificial pink tea roses, made by the wife of the owner of the florist's shop. Her bridal bouquet, also created at the shop at no charge, was of hothouse pink roses with lilies of the valley. Her brown eyes were swimming with light and excitement, and the Gaffer's soft heart was well and truly touched.

'Cassie, me pet, blowed if you don't look a princess,' he said. 'Don't she just, Annie?'

Annie, who had helped to perfect Cassie's appearance, smiled.

'Wait till Freddy sees her, Dad,' she said. 'Good luck, Cassie dear, you look lovely.' She kissed her sister fondly. 'I'm off now to go with Will and the children to the church.' Will and the boys were waiting outside, at the gate. 'Shouldn't the car be here by now?'

'It's only a couple of minutes to the church, it'll be here on time,' said the Gaffer. 'Afterwards, of course, it's Mr Greenberg's pony and cart that'll be takin' the brides and bridegrooms to the Institute.'

'You mean horse and carriage, Dad,' said Cassie, as Annie slipped out to join her family, who'd been told they weren't going to see the bride until she came down the aisle. Annie's departure left the Gaffer and Cassie waiting for the ordered car to turn up. 'Yes, you do mean horse and carriage, Dad,' admonished Cassie.

'Well, so I do, Cassie, so I do,' said the Gaffer. 'Bless yer, me love, you always were one for dreamin' about 'orse and carriages. And I'm glad yer fond of Freddy, he's right for you, y'know.'

'Dad, there's never been anyone else except Freddy,' said Cassie, and the Gaffer thought about the fact that from the moment she'd met Freddy as a young girl she'd never looked at another boy. Made for each other, those two were.

There was a knock on the door. The Gaffer opened it. Mr Greenberg, a beaming smile on his face, doffed a shining top-hat.

'My pleasure, I presume, Mr Ford?' he said.

The Gaffer stared. Not only was Mr Greenberg sporting a top-hat, he was dressed to the nines in black tails and striped grey and black trousers. His beaming smile seemed to touch his beard with benevolence.

'Well, I'm blessed,' said the Gaffer, 'you're done up a treat, Mr Greenberg.'

Cassie appeared then, looking surprised, her veil still up.

'But, Mr Greenberg, we're goin' to the church by car,' she said. 'It's the reception you're takin' me and Sally to, with Freddy and Horace.'

Mr Greenberg's beam spread and widened as he beheld Freddy's irresistible soulmate in virgin white.

'Veil, vell,' he said, 'vhat a bride, ain't she, Mr Ford? Vhat a picture, ain't she? Vhy, Cassie, ain't it my special pleasure to drive you and Sally to the church and then the reception as vell? Vasn't I so commanded by Boots vith the permission of Freddy

315

and young Mr Cooper? Vhy, so I vas, and here I am, all of us havin' said a prayer that it vouldn't rain.'

'Boots and Freddy and Horace told you to—' Cassie stopped and drew a breath. Street kids were outside, and no wonder. They were gawping at a carriage, a real carriage, an elegant four-seater canoe-landau, its twin hoods down. And there were two horses of such pure grey that they were white to Cassie. A carriage and two white horses? For her wedding, and Sally's? 'Oh, Mr Greenberg, you darling.' Mr Greenberg blushed a little. 'Are the carriage and the horses from Buckingham Palace?'

'Vell, not exactly, Cassie,' said Mr Greenberg. 'Borrowed, you might say, borrowed.' He meant hired from a Kensington establishment that specialized in the provision of such vehicles. The idea had emanated with Boots, who had a very soft spot for imaginative Cassie and a great liking for Sally. Sammy had backed the idea, and Freddy and Horace had given it unreserved support, while leaving the brides thinking an ordered car would pick them up for the short journey to the church.

'And Boots and Freddy and Horace arranged it with you?' said the enraptured Cassie.

'For you and Sally, Cassie, and ain't it my happiest pleasure?' smiled Mr Greenberg, with the Gaffer still blinking at the impressive sight of the standing carriage and pair. 'Now, vill you lower your veil, and take your place vith your respected father, and then let us drive to pick up Sally? Vhile time ain't money today, it von't stand still.'

The street kids gawped some more as the Gaffer and Cassie left the house, and neighbours came

316

off their doorsteps to witness the picturesque scene in the April sunshine.

'Cor, Cassie, don't yer look swell?' said a round-eyed boy.

Cassie boarded the landau, the hem of her bright shimmering gown dancing to her movements. The Gaffer followed on, seating himself beside her. Mr Greenberg, up on the high driving seat, took hold of the reins, drew the whip, gently flicked it, and away the carriage went to the resounding cheers of the kids. Cassie thought she was dreaming as the elegant vehicle proceeded on its way to Sally's home, with people staring in admiration and delight. Good luck wishes followed her throughout the gentle ride, and Cassie was so touched with emotion that the misty look was back in her eyes. The Gaffer patted her hand.

'It's right for yer, me pet, it's right for any princess,' he said.

'But I still can't believe it,' she breathed.

'Well, Cassie love,' said the proud Gaffer, 'it strikes me that there's people around that's specially fond of you and Sally. I reckon Sally ain't goin' to believe what's comin' her way, either.'

Sally indeed lost her breath when the dazzling carriage and pair arrived outside her home. She looked quite superb as she came out accompanied by her dad, her gown as pure white as Cassie's. She lifted her veil in order to convince herself that what stood waiting was not a car but a horse-drawn landau of perfect Victorian elegance. Like the Gaffer had, Mr Brown blinked in disbelief.

'Well, bust me new braces,' he said.

'Cassie!' exclaimed Sally, with street kids gawping as much as others had outside Cassie's home.

317

'Bit of a turn-up for the book, eh, old-timer?' said Mr Brown to the Gaffer.

'I ain't complainin',' smiled the Gaffer, 'nor is Cassie.'

'This is really for us, Cassie?' breathed Sally.

'Vhy, that it is,' said Mr Greenberg, down from his seat and top-hat doffed, 'and vhat a handsome cart and nags, ain't it?'

'Carriage and pair, Mr Greenberg, if you please,' said Cassie, 'and all arranged by Boots and Freddy and Horace, Sally.'

'Oh, I could kiss them all for ever,' said Sally.

Mr Greenberg, somewhat overcome by the radiance of both brides, dug for his handkerchief and blew his nose. Sally seemed to float up into the landau in her gown. She took her seat opposite the Gaffer, and Mr Brown, following, sat opposite Cassie.

A crowd of fascinated onlookers had gathered by the time the landau moved off. Sally was still breathless, Cassie in sheer delight. Mr Greenberg drove to Browning Street, heading for the Walworth Road and the turn into Larcom Street.

In the Walworth Road, they stopped the traffic and were cheered to the echo. Cassie fluttered her hand in royal acknowledgement of public acclaim, and Sally, coming to, waved at an entranced tram conductor. The Gaffer and Mr Brown exchanged smiles. On the landau went in regal style, carrying the brides to the church, where Freddy and Horace awaited them.

'Vhat a happy occasion, ain't it, my beauties?' said Mr Greenberg to the carriage horses.

The graceful pair nodded, and the carriage turned into Larcom Street, the site of the church and its vicarage. Within the church and among the people who had ceremonial duties to perform, only one was suffering worries. That was Horace's best man, Percy Ricketts.

Percy was still not sure if he ought to include a saucy story in his speech.


**THE END**

# A SELECTED LIST OF FINE NOVELS
# AVAILABLE FROM CORGI BOOKS

| | | | |
|---|---|---|---|
| 14229 8 | CEDAR STREET | Aileen Armitage | £4 99 |
| 13313 2 | CATCH THE WIND | Frances Donnelly | £5.99 |
| 14095 3 | ARIAN | Iris Gower | £4 99 |
| 14140 2 | THE CROOKED MILE | Ruth Hamilton | £4.99 |
| 14297 2 | ROSY SMITH | Janet Haslam | £4.99 |
| 14220 4 | CAPEL BELLS | Joan Hessayon | £4.99 |
| 14262 X | MARIANA | Susanna Kearsley | £4.99 |
| 14331 6 | THE SECRET YEARS | Judith Lennox | £4.99 |
| 13910 6 | BLUEBIRDS | Margaret Mayhew | £5.99 |
| 10375 6 | CSARDAS | Diane Pearson | £5.99 |
| 14123 2 | THE LONDONERS | Margaret Pemberton | £4 99 |
| 14057 0 | THE BRIGHT ONE | Elvi Rhodes | £4.99 |
| 14318 9 | WATER UNDER THE BRIDGE | Susan Sallis | £4.99 |
| 13951 3 | SERGEANT JOE | Mary Jane Staples | £3 99 |
| 13845 2 | RISING SUMMER | Mary Jane Staples | £3.99 |
| 13299 3 | DOWN LAMBETH WAY | Mary Jane Staples | £4.99 |
| 13573 9 | KING OF CAMBERWELL | Mary Jane Staples | £4.99 |
| 13730 8 | THE LODGER | Mary Jane Staples | £4 99 |
| 13444 9 | OUR EMILY | Mary Jane Staples | £4.99 |
| 13635 2 | TWO FOR THREE FARTHINGS | Mary Jane Staples | £4.99 |
| 13856 8 | THE PEARLY QUEEN | Mary Jane Staples | £3 99 |
| 13975 0 | ON MOTHER BROWN'S DOORSTEP | Mary Jane Staples | £3 99 |
| 14106 2 | THE TRAP | Mary Jane Staples | £4.99 |
| 14154 2 | A FAMILY AFFAIR | Mary Jane Staples | £4.99 |
| 14230 1 | MISSING PERSON | Mary Jane Staples | £4 99 |
| 14291 3 | PRIDE OF WALWORTH | Mary Jane Staples | £4.99 |
| 14375 8 | ECHOES OF YESTERDAY | Mary Jane Staples | £4 99 |
| 14418 5 | THE YOUNG ONES | Mary Jane Staples | £4.99 |
| 14296 4 | THE LAND OF NIGHTINGALES | Sally Stewart | £4.99 |
| 14263 8 | ANNIE | Valerie Wood | £4.99 |